PRAISE FOR BETHANY TURNER

"Pitch-perfect comedic timing, a relatable heroine, and a refreshing sweetness elevate this novel above the sea of modern rom-coms. The rare author who can make me laugh out loud, *The Do-Over* is Bethany Turner at her best."

—LAUREN LAYNE, *NEW YORK TIMES* BESTSELLING AUTHOR

"For anyone who's ever questioned the path they've chosen, Bethany Turner's *The Do-Over* offers a heart-warming look at what happens when life goes off-script. She takes that old saying 'People plan and God laughs' and runs with it in the most entertaining and endearing fashion. A sweet and satisfying read."

—MELONIE JOHNSON, *USA TODAY* BESTSELLING AUTHOR

"A charming and delightful story of what-if's, second chances, and discovering what you really want. *The Do-Over* pulled me right in from the get-go and had me grinning all the way to happily ever after."

—KATE BROMLEY, AUTHOR OF *TALK BOOKISH TO ME*

"Bethany Turner has crafted a delightful, witty story with zippy dialogue, warmly relatable characters, and hilariously apt pop culture references. I found myself sneaking off to read just one more chapter. I'm still smiling thinking about this book. Reading *The Do-Over* felt like eating a big bowl of Lucky Charms mixed with Fruity Pebbles. A colorful explosion of happy. ;)"

—RACHEL LINDEN, BESTSELLING AUTHOR OF
THE ENLIGHTENMENT OF BEES

"Turner crafts an entertaining rom-com that spans ten years and keeps the reader guessing who will claim the heroine's heart . . . As the slow-burn romantic mystery of who Olivia will end up with builds to an amusing and satisfying conclusion, Olivia's witty narration will hold readers' attention. This is a treat."

—*PUBLISHERS WEEKLY*, FOR *PLOT TWIST*

"Turner's humorous latest has an enjoyable New Adult vibe . . . There is a happily ever after, but not the one most readers will be expecting."

—*LIBRARY JOURNAL*, FOR *PLOT TWIST*

"*Plot Twist* gave my rom-com loving heart everything it could hope for: pop-culture references, frequent laugh-out-loud lines, an enduring friendship, a determined heroine to root for, and (of course) a love story with plenty of twists and turns. A sweet, funny read about the many kinds of love in our lives, perfect for anyone who loves love or dreams about meeting George Clooney."

—KERRY WINFREY, AUTHOR OF *WAITING FOR TOM HANKS*

"With a decade-long span of pop-culture fun, playful romantic possibilities, and the soul-deep friendships that push us to be real, *Plot Twist* is everything a reader has come to adore from Bethany Turner . . . plus so much more!"

—NICOLE DEESE, AWARD-WINNING AUTHOR OF *BEFORE I CALLED YOU MINE*

"Funny, clever, and sweet, *Plot Twist* reminds us that sometimes love doesn't look just like the movies—and that it can be so, so much better than we ever dreamed."

—MELISSA FERGUSON, BESTSELLING AUTHOR OF *THE CUL-DE-SAC WAR*

"Bethany Turner just keeps getting better! *Plot Twist* is like experiencing the best parts of all my favorite rom-coms, tied together with Turner's pitch-perfect comedic timing, an achingly sweet 'will they or won't they?' romance, and the BFF relationship most girls dream of. Add in some Gen-X nostalgia, and you have a book you'll want to wrap yourself up in and never leave."

—CARLA LAUREANO, RITA AWARD–WINNING AUTHOR
OF *THE SATURDAY NIGHT SUPPER CLUB* AND *PROVENANCE*

"With a sassy Hallmark-on-speed hook and a winning leading lady, Turner loans her fresh, inimitable voice to her strongest offering yet: a treatise on how love (and the hope for love) paints across a canvas of fate and happen-stance, and how life undercuts our expectations only to give us the biggest romantic adventures."

—RACHEL MCMILLAN, AUTHOR OF *THE LONDON RESTORATION*

THE DO-OVER

Also by Bethany Turner

THE DO-OVER

BETHANY TURNER

THOMAS NELSON

Since 1798

Dedicated to Henry Blumenthal,
whom I'm not quite ready to acknowledge isn't real.

The Do-Over

Copyright © 2022 Bethany Turner

Published in Nashville, Tennessee, by Thomas Nelson. Thomas Nelson is a registered trademark of HarperCollins Christian Publishing, Inc.

Published in association with the literary agency of Kirkland Media Management, LLC, P.O. Box 1539, Liberty, TX 77575.

Thomas Nelson titles may be purchased in bulk for educational, business, fundraising, or sales promotional use. For information, please e-mail SpecialMarkets@ ThomasNelson.com.

Library of Congress Cataloging-in-Publication Data

Names: Turner, Bethany, 1979- author.
Title: The do-over / Bethany Turner.
Description: Nashville, Tennessee : Thomas Nelson, [2022] | Summary: "McKenna Keaton is perfectly content with her single life-until a work scandal, a family curse, and the reappearance of Henry Blumenthal make her question a life's worth of good choices"-- Provided by publisher.
Identifiers: LCCN 2021045256 (print) | LCCN 2021045257 (ebook) | ISBN 9780785244974 (paperback) | ISBN 9780785244981 (epub) | ISBN 9780785245094
Classification: LCC PS3620.U76 D6 2022 (print) | LCC PS3620.U76 (ebook) | DDC 813/.6--dc23
LC record available at https://lccn.loc.gov/2021045256
LC ebook record available at https://lccn.loc.gov/2021045257

Printed in the United States of America

22 23 24 25 26 LSC 5 4 3 2 1

Prologue

My name is McKenna Keaton, and I am the daughter of Scott and Diane. Yes, my mother's name is Diane Keaton. It probably goes without saying that my mother is not *the* Diane Keaton, but that hasn't stopped my dad from affectionately calling her Annie for more than forty years. As in Annie Hall. And my mom loves it, to the point that only those closest to her know that Annie Keaton is not actually her name.

My parents got married by a justice of the peace during their two-hour break after a full day of classes at the University of California, Berkeley, where my dad was studying to be a history professor and my mom was pursuing a degree in theater. They were pronounced Mr. and Mrs. Keaton, Scott kissed his bride, and then they ran off to their respective night jobs as a bartender and a telephone operator. On their wedding night, my mom had to pull a double shift at the phone company, so my dad hung out at the club where he was working long enough to catch Herbie Hancock's entire set before driving his VW Bug—the same one that had transported him from Indiana to California—to pick up some fried chicken to take to my mom. At three in the morning, once the calls had died down, he laid out a blanket on the floor by the switchboard, popped open a bottle of sparkling cider (so his new bride wouldn't get in trouble for drinking on the job), and treated her to a newlywed picnic. When her shift ended at 5:00 a.m., he drove her to Indian Rock Park, and they climbed up to the lookout, laid out that same blanket, and watched the rising sun from the east reflect off the Golden Gate Bridge to the west. Then they got back in the Bug, drove to campus, and each went their separate ways for another full day.

Or so the story goes.

That was 1978. In 1982, Erica was born. I followed in 1984. And then in 1995, our baby sister, Taylor, surprised us all by joining the family long after our parents began taking for granted that their diaper-changing days were behind them. We had just moved to New York City so my dad could take a job at Columbia. At least that was the official reason—and it was a big one. That was certainly the reason that was going to pay the bills for a while. But really, I always thought it was about giving my mom a chance to follow her dreams of being on Broadway.

She was a pretty big deal in Durham, North Carolina, where we'd all settled while my dad got his master's from North Carolina State, and then up until 1994, while he was an adjunct at the University of North Carolina at Chapel Hill. She basically defined the Durham theater scene for the better part of a decade, oversaw the renovation of a historic theater, and taught night classes for free—just because she loved sharing her passion for performing with people who otherwise might never get the chance to step onto a stage.

When my dad was working, Erica and I would tag along and watch my mom in her element, leading an enthralled group of aspiring performers through acting exercises and monologue readings. Once in a while she would pull us on stage, and we'd try to keep a straight face while getting yelled at by Maggie the Cat or while Claudio from *Measure for Measure* attempted to pour his heart out to two little girls who couldn't stop giggling. Looking back, it was reasonable to have assumed then that I would never be happier than I was in those moments, seeing a side of my mother that wasn't tied down to making sure those two little giggling girls brushed their teeth before bed and had a peanut butter and jelly sandwich packed and ready to go for school the next morning.

But then my dad got the job at Columbia, and Erica and I traded in our days of playing Uno in Felix Unger and Oscar Madison's spacious apartment with no fourth wall for a tiny two-bedroom in Morningside Heights. The air-conditioning was out more often than not, and since my dad didn't believe in wasting an educational opportunity, he would take us up on the roof and enlighten us to the history all around while we escaped the stifling heat. From there we could see across the Harlem River to the Bronx and across the Hudson River to New Jersey. He'd tell us about Hamilton and Burr crossing the Hudson to duel at Weehawken and the Bronx bootleggers of the 1920s.

But it was what we were able to see when we walked at street level that made me fall in love with New York. At nine years old, I would have happily passed on a trip to Disney World or the gift of a Game Boy in exchange for hours spent walking up and down Amsterdam Avenue. Dad would tell us about the rich history of our neighborhood—from the sermon Martin Luther King Jr. preached at the Cathedral of St. John the Divine and the music Duke Ellington and Leonard Bernstein made there to the books that had been written at the tables of the Hungarian Pastry Shop and the significance of those delicious hamantasch cookies within the Jewish faith.

Most Saturdays, the four of us would sit and eat apricot linzer tarts (except for my mother, who always chose the dense chocolate Sacher torte) at one of the metal tables on the sidewalk and then burn up our sugar intake with a walk or bike ride through Morningside Park. I didn't know that the crime rates were high or that my dad probably had to pick up extra shifts tutoring in order to pay for all those tarts and tortes. I only knew life was perfect, and the previous happiness in North Carolina had just been the warm-up to the joy of life in Manhattan.

And that side of my mother that Erica and I had loved to catch glimpses of on the stage in Durham was, in New York, unleashed. She would make sure Erica and I had breakfast, then my dad would walk us to our school, which was just down 110th Street from his office. Then, most days, Mom would change into her audition clothes, take the train from the 116th Street Station to Times Square, and spend the day dancing, singing, and acting her heart out at cattle-call auditions. She took classes in all those things, too, despite the fact that she was more qualified to teach them than almost any of her teachers. "The only people who don't know anything are the people who think they know it all," my parents loved to say. So she kept learning.

I didn't know then that she'd given herself one year to devote to auditioning, and that if nothing came of it, she'd have to take whatever sort of paying job she could get. I only knew that I rarely saw her without a smile on her face.

I'll never forget the day, after we'd been in New York eleven months, that I saw her cry for the first time—at least the first time I remembered. She picked Erica and me up from school, which wasn't the routine but happened sometimes, and took us home to change out of our school clothes into our best dresses. Dad was already home, dressed in a shirt and tie, though he didn't know why. But there was nothing to worry about. How could there be when Mom had that smile on her face?

We took the train to 66th Street–Lincoln Center, walked together into Central Park, and had dinner at Tavern on the Green. After dinner we took the train to Forty-Second Street and walked up to Forty-Fifth and the Imperial Theatre. Mom sat between Erica and me so she could quietly explain little things about *Les Misérables* that went over our heads. In the first act, after Fantine sang "I Dreamed a Dream," my mom whispered to us, "There are all sorts of dreams, girls. And sometimes they come true." That was when I noticed the tears streaming down her face, and I knew that my perfect life had somehow gotten even better.

We left the Imperial and walked to East Sixtieth for frozen hot chocolates at Serendipity, and that's where she finally told us all the big news. She had been offered the role of Mrs. Potts's understudy in the Broadway cast of *Beauty and the Beast*. Her dream had become a reality.

That reality lasted exactly four days, and then she found out she was pregnant with Taylor.

Erica tried to explain to me that there was a lot of dancing in the show, and that they made the costumes to fit a certain size—even when the costume was a teapot—and that there were all sorts of reasons a pregnant woman couldn't star in a Broadway show. And she said Mom wasn't a big enough star yet to ask them to work around her or wait until after she had the baby.

I didn't know then that I was going to be forced to say goodbye to Amsterdam Avenue. I only knew that everything was going in the right direction, then it stopped.

Within a few months, we were back in North Carolina and my dad was teaching at Duke. Mom was always there to tell us to brush our teeth. Peanut butter and jelly sandwiches were always prepared. Then Taylor was born and our house was always loud—but at least we had a house. That's what my parents said whenever I complained about not being able to hear my friends when I was talking to them on the phone, or when I had to go to my room and watch *Boy Meets World* on the little portable television Erica and I shared. That's what they said when I complained about being back in Durham. At least we had a house.

So, great. We had a house. A house where I never once got up on the roof—and even if I had, there would have been nothing to see apart from other houses. But it *was* nice that Erica and I each had our own bedroom. Of course, that only lasted until Taylor turned one and Mom and Dad tried to move her from their bedroom to mine. No way. I was twelve years old. There was no way I was going to share my room with someone who didn't even have all her teeth yet. I begged Erica to let me move into her room—and swore a binding oath to help her with her chores for two whole years. And so my big sister became my roommate until she moved out to go to college when I was sixteen. She went to Duke, but she wanted the dorm experience. At that point Taylor was in preschool and was the most annoying human being on the planet. I couldn't wait until it was my turn to get out of there. Ignoring my dad's advice that Duke was one of the best schools in the country and would make the most economical sense for my undergraduate studies, I didn't think twice when I got accepted to Princeton. I was living in New Jersey, more than four hundred miles from everyone I knew—most notably my little sister—a full month before the fall semester began. I got my degree in political science and then went to law school at NYU.

Finally, I was home, and I didn't have any intention of ever leaving again.

A couple years later Erica married Jared Pierson, and three years later my niece, April, was born. Then came Cooper and Charlie. They're all living in Raleigh with some dogs and a white picket fence and beautifully straight teeth everywhere you look. (Jared is an orthodontist.) Erica inherited my parents' love of learning and teaching and teaches US history at a private high school.

Meanwhile, Taylor forged her own path, branching out (slightly). She also went to Duke but landed a visual arts degree and was quickly making a name for herself as a successful interior designer in Durham.

I stayed in New York after law school and began climbing the ladder. I didn't make it back to Durham very often, but I FaceTimed with my parents most weeks. Erica had remained my best friend in the world, and my niece and nephews loved me. I looked forward to having them spend some time with me in the city once things leveled out at work. And once they were all old enough not to wet the bed or choke if I didn't cut their food into small enough pieces. (Erica said they were already well past those stages, but I thought we should wait a while longer, just to be safe.)

And I just kept chasing the dream. The plan was always to be promoted to senior partner before I turned forty and become a name partner by the age of fifty. I had my own apartment in a brownstone on the Upper West Side, an eclectic group of people to socialize with, my dry cleaner sent me a Christmas card every year, and I was well on my way to the corner office.

There are all sorts of dreams, and sometimes they come true. As far as I was concerned, mine coming true wasn't optional.

Chapter 1

It's shocking what children don't know about our country," Erica was saying to me on the speakerphone blaring out into my office. "Keep in mind these are advanced students, supposedly, and yet yesterday a boy called Benjamin Franklin 'the one with syphilis.'"

I grinned as I slammed the palm of my hand down onto my stapler. "He's not wrong."

"I know he's not wrong, and maybe I would have been impressed that he knew that if he hadn't gone on to say, 'And polio, right? Wasn't he the one who misled the country by never being seen on TV in his wheelchair while he was president?'"

Okay. Children were stupid.

"I don't know how you do it," I muttered. Sorting my packets as I stood from my chair, I looked across my desk, satisfied I had everything ready for my board presentation.

"I don't know how *you* do it. At least high schoolers are, in a lot of cases, teachable. But working day in and day out with *lawyers*—"

"At least lawyers, generally speaking, know that Ben Franklin and FDR were not the same person."

The stapled papers in my hand began to scuff against each

other as the annoying tremble returned to my fingers. *Stop it, McKenna. You're ready. You were born for this moment.* I exhaled.

"Well, enough about the failings of our education system," my sister asserted. "You feeling ready? How long do you think it will take? Do you think you'll have a chance to call me after? I bet Mom and Dad are just nervous wrecks. Has Mom been texting you all the Amy Poehler 'You got this!' GIFs? What I wouldn't do some days to be able to turn back the clock to that magical time before Tay taught our mother about GIFs . . ."

I cleared my throat and combined my thirteen neat little piles into one neat big pile. "I didn't tell Mom and Dad."

"You *what*? McKenna! They're going to kill you!"

"No, they won't. I'll call them after the board makes their decision, and they'll never know there was anything I wasn't telling them. It's better this way." Better for all of us. They wouldn't have to stress, and I wouldn't have to *be* stressed by endless GIFs of Nick from *New Girl* telling me to "Do your thing, girl."

"Did you tell Taylor?"

I scoffed. "No, of course I didn't tell Taylor. When, in the past three months, has Taylor ever shut up long enough to listen to anything anyone else has to say?"

My little sister had an annoying way of removing what little enthusiasm I was hanging on to about anything. She always asked so many questions—and they were the wrong questions. If I told her about a great meal I'd had at a legendary restaurant in SoHo, she asked how many carbs I thought I'd consumed. If I told her about a life-changing leadership book I had just finished reading, she asked if I'd heard about the plagiarism accusations against the author. And it wasn't that I believed myself impervious to carbohydrates or that I wanted to endorse the stolen writings of a criminal. But once—just *once*—I wanted to allow my balloon of good news to run out of air and sink lower and lower to the ground over time, all on its own, rather than see its life taken from it far too soon, courtesy of a ready-and-waiting Taylor needle.

But, like I said, since she and Jackson had gotten engaged three months prior on New Year's Eve, there had been very little opportunity within family conversations to discuss anything else.

"Are you coming home for the dress fitting?" Erica asked.

"What dress fitting?"

"*The* dress fitting. Taylor's dress. And our bridesmaid dresses—"

"Not you too." I stifled a groan. "No, *Mother*, I cannot make it back to Durham to try on a dress. Have we forgotten the reality of my life? Not to mention the reality my life is about to become after the meeting I'm walking into in just a few minutes. I'll just send my measurements or something."

"But the engagement party . . ."

Admittedly, I'd have a more difficult time fulfilling my duty as a big sister and a bridesmaid via registered courier.

"Of course I'll try to make it out for that if I can. I'll just have to see what—"

"McKenna." She growled my name in a way that made me feel like Mom and Dad had docked her allowance after she took the blame for my bed not being made. "It's the same day. Remember?"

Irritation grew inside of me. "Well, that's stupid. Why would she do it on the same day?"

"Call me crazy, but I think she was actually trying to make it easier for people. I think the idea was that you could get fitted for your dress because you'd be here anyway." She exhaled into the phone. "You're busy. I get it. We *all* get it, McKenna. But this is a huge deal to her. She coordinated it with Jackson's family flying in from . . . well, from all over the place, from the sound of it. And she wants everyone to meet and all of that. It's going to break her heart if you're not there." I bristled slightly at the huffiness in her voice. "It's not like it's Christmas or someone's birthday or Mom and Dad's anniversary or any of those less important engagements we just throw at you to try to distract you from all those *meaningful* things you have going on in your life."

The groan I had previously stifled broke free. "Erica, I don't have time for your guilt trip right now. They're going to call me in there any minute and—"

"I know." She took a deep breath and then another. "I know. Sorry. Not the right time." She morphed out of Mom mode and back into awesome-big-sister mode. "So how many did you say will be in there?"

"Usually, the entire board shows up for these things, so that should be thirteen."

"Wow. And that includes the name partners?"

"Yes." I pulled a compact out of my desk drawer and touched up my lipstick as I spoke. "I saw the chairman in the hall earlier, so he must have flown in from Miami." I said it all so calmly, but my heart was preparing for takeoff right up the runway of my esophagus.

"I'm so proud of you. My little sister—the youngest partner at Wallis, Monroe and Burkhead."

"The youngest *senior* partner," I corrected. Jeremiah Burkhead had been promoted to senior partner at thirty-seven—and to name partner three years later—but he was five years older than me. I would take his place as the youngest. "But let's not count our chickens before they hatch."

Who was I trying to kid? Those chicks had already been lined up and inventoried.

"Whatever you say. Just be sure to call me the first second you can. Oh, and I meant to tell you . . . Jared has some frequent-flyer miles saved up. He and I were thinking that maybe after the engagement party, I could fly back with you for a couple days—"

Tap. Tap. Tap.

My sister's words faded into oblivion as I looked up in response to the fingers against my glass door. Mrs. Lewisham, the senior executive assistant, had been sent to summon me.

"Erica, I have to go. It's time."

"Okay, you've got this! Call me—"

I hit the button on my phone to end the call, cleared my throat, straightened my blazer, and smiled warmly at Mrs. Lewisham. She'd be my executive assistant soon, too, after all. I wanted to get off on the right foot. I nodded once at her, and she turned away to return to the boardroom. I indulged in a quick look around the junior-partner office that had served me so well, picked up my packets, and then brushed away nostalgia in favor of ambition.

❀

"Ms. Keaton. Please have a seat."

Wowsers. I'd been in that boardroom more times than I could count—to work through depositions, to prepare witnesses, to sip champagne as slowly as possible so that I could simultaneously avoid the "You need to loosen up, Keaton! Live a little!" comments and the "Whoa . . . Someone had a good day . . ." remarks that accompanied anything other than the perfectly moderated sip. But I'd never been alone with all three name partners before. Well, the three partners and Mrs. Lewisham. I'd been expecting the entire board, but the sight of only the three members who really mattered sent an even bigger rush of adrenaline through my body. All three of them sat stone-faced in their business suits, staring at me with indifference. Most of the chairs had been moved against the walls of windows, with views of Midtown that were meant to impress and intimidate. Only one empty seat remained at the table.

Thanks for saving my seat, boys.

The empty chair was positioned about twenty feet of the finest cherry wood away from Jeremiah Burkhead. He had quickly become the most powerful attorney in the entire firm with one of the most impressive litigation records in Manhattan. He was the guy who actually did the work, while Ralph Wallis entertained his mistress in Miami, and Ty Monroe took only the most glamorous clients with the most scandalous cases and then proceeded to pile all the work onto the junior partners if the day didn't include a press conference or a photo op.

But Jeremiah worked. He handled the less glamorous cases that actually mattered. The first time I second-chaired for him was in a big class-action lawsuit against a pharmaceutical company. And when he handed me my bonus check with a note that said, "Good work, Erin Brockovich," I'd known with absolute certainty I would be the next senior partner. He was my hero. My mentor. The attorney whose career I aspired to replicate.

I also strongly suspected we were going to get married someday.

"Ms. Keaton?" He tilted his head and quirked his eyebrow.

"Oh, yes." I pulled out the empty seat and lowered myself into it, setting my, in hindsight, far-too-plentiful packets on the table in front of me. "Thank you."

It's not that I was the romantic type who made a habit of falling for her boss. I wasn't. And I didn't. In fact, I never really fell for anybody. I didn't have a crush on him or imagine that he'd asked me to second-chair on *Morinskey v. Alventa Pharmaceuticals, Inc.* because he hoped to get me alone late at night after everyone else had left the office. No, he asked me to second-chair because I had proven myself to be the best at the firm when it came to researching precedent. And he'd probably called me Erin Brockovich because it was a charming way to cover that he couldn't remember my name at the time. We'd never shared a stolen glance, and our fingers had never brushed against each other as we both reached for the same file folder.

But the fact was the man was perfect for me. He had a dry sense of humor that he expertly utilized to put everyone in a room at ease—and more often than not, I was the only one in that room who neither sucked up by laughing too hard nor was too nervous to acknowledge the humor at all. On most nights, he and I were the last two people to leave the thirty-second floor of the Seagram Building, apart from the night janitors, and that meant we shared the same driving work ethic. I knew for a fact that he rode the subway from his apartment most workdays, and that meant he wasn't pretentious like the other name partners who got driven around in Lincoln Town Cars by chauffeurs—and the fact that he lived in Greenwich Village meant he was an actual New Yorker, unlike Wallis and Monroe, who kept Central Park West condos but actually lived in New Canaan, Connecticut. And Jeremiah Burkhead had a four-year-old daughter he sometimes brought to the office when she was with him in the summer and near holidays.

Not that I wanted to be a mother; that wasn't something that had ever appealed to me. But if I had to dive into those waters at all, I knew the best situation I could hope for was partial custody of little Marta Burkhead. Marta? Was that right? Or was it Gretl? It was *one* of the von Trapps.

"I want to thank you for taking the time to see me today," I began. I felt my nerves flit away as I began shifting into gear. The anticipation had been the worst. For days—months, years—I'd survived on Pepto-Bismol and Diet Coke as every waking moment (and the sleeping ones too) was devoted to making sure I was prepared. But now that the moment had arrived, *of course* I was prepared. I'd spent my entire adult life preparing for this opportunity, and there was little left to do apart from the formality of seizing the moment and claiming what was rightfully mine. "Mrs. Lewisham, if you would be so kind, would you please pass these to the gentlemen?"

"Pass what?" Ralph Wallis asked. It took me a moment to recognize that he had been the one to speak. I'd hardly heard his voice before, apart from the annual speech to the staff at the year-end party.

"Mr. Wallis, I've prepared a presentation of my—"

"You've got to be kidding me," Ty Monroe interjected.

I cleared my throat. *Don't let him get to you, McKenna. He just doesn't want to miss an opportunity to convince everyone there's a brain underneath those hair implants.*

"The presentation will be concise. I assure you, Mr. Monroe. I've only included a brief highlight of my case history—"

"Honey, what do you think this is?" Mr. Wallis asked. The chairman—who could have seemed grandfatherly with his white hair and twinkling eyes if not for a few characteristics (most notably the mistress)—leaned forward onto his forearms, which were resting on the table in front of him. "We're not here to listen to your book report."

"Ralph, please." Jeremiah looked disapprovingly at the older man and then back to me with those kind brown eyes. "My apologies, Ms. Keaton, but there does seem to be a misunderstanding. While I have no doubt that you have contributed a great deal to the firm, I'm afraid we're not here to celebrate your accomplishments. As I'm sure you're aware, internal audits take place frequently, conducted by an independent accounting commission."

There was silence, and all eyes were on me. But he hadn't asked me a question, *had* he? I opened my mouth to ask for clarification, but in an instant understanding washed over me. Well, that's not true. There was no understanding whatsoever. But it became difficult to swallow, and I felt my temples pulsating. At the very least, I understood I wasn't moving to a corner office today.

"Yes, sir," I finally croaked.

Seemingly satisfied with my answer to the unasked question, he continued. "I'm afraid to report there were some irregularities in several of your reports, along with those of a few other junior partners."

"'Irregularities'?"

The lump in my throat began to dissolve, and my vision began to clear. *Irregularities*. Okay, I still had no idea what was happening, but whatever it was, it was a mistake I could easily clear up. *Irregularities*. I had no doubt any report centered around me and my work might have potentially exposed all sorts of irregularities. It sure wasn't *regular* how I wrote cryptic reminders to myself about clients' personal details on the dry-erase board in my office before meetings with them so I could look like I remembered everything about them and they would never know I was cheating. It probably wasn't *regular* that I kept bowls of M&M's in my office for the sole purpose of observing how clients and peers picked which ones to eat—by the handful, one at a time, by color, randomly—to gain insight into their personalities. I'd developed some pretty irregular mnemonic devices in law school to help me remember various statutes.

And I wouldn't exactly call it *regular* how I got the job done twice as well in half the time of any of my coworkers.

Bring it on.

"What sort of irregularities, Mr. Burkhead? I'll be happy to help clear up any confusion." *And then I'll present my book report, Mr. Wallis.*

"Well, the fact is, Ms. Keaton," my future husband began, "over the course of the past eleven months, more than three hundred thousand dollars seems to have been misdirected through a complex accounting scheme centered around your retainer fees and your expense account." He pushed himself back from the table and crossed his legs so his left ankle was resting on his right knee. "So, yes. If you could clear that up for us, I think we'd all be extremely grateful."

It felt like all of the blood in the top half of my body drained to my ankles, and suddenly I was wearing bloody concrete shoes. Actually, I felt like one of those punching bags kids play with. I think we had a Mr. T one. Mr. T's face was drawn on the side of the four-foot-tall vinyl bag, and when you punched him in the face, you knocked him over. The weighted sand at the bottom always kept him coming back for more though.

Yeah, I felt like that.

Apart from the certainty that I'd bounce back.

"Wh-wh-what are you talking about?" I stuttered. "I'm sorry, Mr. Burkhead, but I genuinely have no idea what—"

"You genuinely have no idea how more than a quarter million dollars got misappropriated?" Mr. Monroe asked with a level of emotion I'd never before heard in that normally cool and collected room.

I had never been a crier. In fact, I couldn't remember the last time I'd cried, and I certainly had never allowed any of my coworkers—or anyone in *any* professional setting—to see me in tears. I wasn't ready to break my streak, but it took biting the inside of my cheek until I tasted a little bit of blood to keep it from happening.

I knew there had to be an explanation. It was indisputable that there had been a misunderstanding, but claiming that would do nothing to defend me. It was the explanation that was needed, not some emotionally flabbergasted victim. We were attorneys. Every last attorney in that room was trained to look at and interpret the evidence, and apparently the evidence pointed toward my having misappropriated three hundred grand. I needed to figure out the explanation. I needed to examine the evidence and determine the margin of error and . . .

Misappropriated.

"You think I embezzled from the firm?" It wasn't that I hadn't understood what they were saying from the beginning, but in an instant the gravity of their accusation registered in my brain. Confusion was brushed away, and clarity took hold.

Clarity. I'd always valued clarity prior to that moment. Until that moment, as my stomach began churning and my heart began beating so wildly I was sure even Mr. Wallis could hear it with the help of his infamously screechy hearing aid, I had always counted clarity as a trusted friend.

"We're not here to make unfounded accusations, Ms. Keaton," Mr. Burkhead replied.

I scoffed. "Is that so? It sure sounds like—"

"And we'll thank you kindly to keep your tone in check," Mr. Monroe scolded me as if I were a pedantic child.

"Ty . . ." Jeremiah Burkhead looked at Ty Monroe, seated on his left. In a soft tone of warning, laced with frustration, he added, "Let me handle this."

Mr. Monroe crossed his arms in a huff and leaned back in his leather chair.

"Ms. Keaton," Mr. Burkhead resumed. "This . . . Well . . . I must confess this has come as a shock to all of us. Me, especially."

I cleared my throat and swallowed down the pain. *You're defending someone else, McKenna. There's no time for personal feelings right now. Deal with the facts. Remain cool. Don't let them see you sweat.* "With all due respect, Mr. Burkhead, I can't imagine that you are half as shocked as I am."

He studied me across the table, and I didn't allow my eyes to flinch away from his. No matter how hurt I was. No matter how angry I was. No matter how much I thought I sensed compassion in them. I knew there was a decent chance compassion would rob me of the ability to deal with the facts and remain cool.

We stared at each other like that for several seconds until the corners of his lips rose slightly in what seemed to be a sad, resigned smile, then he pulled his eyes away first. He cleared his throat softly and looked down at the file folder in front of him for a moment. He opened it up and scanned the pages inside and then looked back up at me—and he was all business once again.

"We have no choice but to place you on unpaid administrative leave until the investigation concludes."

"'The investigation'?"

"Yes," Mr. Burkhead replied, now devoid of compassion. "Human resources will inform you of the rest of the details, but you can most likely expect to hear from us in six to eight weeks."

"At which time . . . ?"

"At which time," Mr. Monroe stepped in, "we'll deal with the results of the investigation accordingly."

Mr. Burkhead scowled at him again. "Yes. That's correct." Subtext: the details are correct, but the menacing inference should have been avoided.

"And when the mistake is discovered?" I asked. "Will *those* results be dealt with accordingly?"

Another flicker of humanity overtook Mr. Burkhead's eyes. "Yes. Obviously, that's the outcome we all hope for, and if mistakes have been made in the auditing process to this point, that will be wholly and completely acknowledged and made right." He softly added, "I do truly hope that's the case."

Stay cool. Deep breaths. No emotion. Let due process run its course, and the truth will be revealed.

"Is there something I need to sign?" I asked, maybe a little too coolly in my attempt to avoid feeling emotion.

Mr. Wallis responded. "Mrs. Lewisham, would you please escort Ms. Keaton to human resources? Thank you for your time, Ms. Keaton. That will be all."

Mrs. Lewisham was standing by my chair again, impatiently waiting for me to stand up. There was no glimmer of compassion in her eyes. No indication of motherly concern. I stood and picked up my undistributed packets—packets that demonstrated why I deserved to be sitting on the other side of the table with the three men who had just accused me of a white-collar crime—and heeded her gesture to go first. When I reached the door, I turned and glanced around the room one more time, inexplicably needing to cement in my mind the setting of my lowest moment. If there was ever a time for a powerful, passionate Erin Brockovich speech about justice and integrity, this was it. But there was too much pain blocking the path and keeping determination from rising to the surface. And it was in those most painful of seconds—when my life seemed to be flashing before my eyes and I saw a lifetime of hard work and dedication grow blurrier and less defined . . . irrelevant—that my eyes locked with Jeremiah Burkhead's once again.

"We'll be in touch," he said. "Hang in there, McKenna."

Well, what do you know? He *did* know my name.

Chapter 2

I couldn't remember the exact time I was last in North Carolina, and I wasn't thrilled to be there now. But my sister was a sneaky one.

I'd been escorted by Mrs. Lewisham straight to HR, where I was asked to sign papers saying I understood how everything was going to play out. As if I understood anything. But according to the paperwork, if the investigation cleared me, my job would be waiting for me and I would be paid retroactively for the forced administrative leave. If, however, the investigation concluded—as at least Wallis and Monroe seemed certain it would, even if Burkhead wasn't entirely convinced—that I was indeed a master thief, suspension would morph immediately into termination. And by the end of spring, I'd probably be sent to the same prison where Martha Stewart had crocheted her jail poncho. (The paperwork made no mention of any specific punishment, but if I were to survive the next six to eight weeks, I would have to picture myself in a minimum-security place with air-conditioning and a tennis court rather than behind the slamming metal doors of a cell in which my toilet doubled as my breakfast nook.)

Documents signed, I'd been escorted to my office to gather my personal effects while my coworkers looked on with the sort of rapt attention usually reserved for moments that began with the words "We, the jury, find the defendant . . ." My keys and entry badge were stripped from me, then I was followed by security guards until I stood alone on Park Avenue with a small box containing a framed photo of all of us at Erica and Jared's wedding, my long-dead Kindle that I had taken with me to work at the beginning of the year as part of a resolution to read during breaks (which, as it turned out, I never took), and a few boxes of Junior Mints I'd kept stashed away in case the break room ever ran out of ways to fuel the midafternoon energy lags. I'd chosen comfort over economy and taken a cab back to my apartment on West Fifty-Seventh—then spent the entire ride in supreme discomfort, watching the meter tick on and imagining my checking account draining at the same pace.

No matter how I tried to comfort myself with visions of a penitentiary stint that would finally allow me time for a pedicure, the reasonable side of me knew the mistake in the audit would be found during the investigation. I knew my name would be cleared. I'd receive my owed back pay and my path to senior partner (and to becoming little Liesl Burkhead's stepmother) would be fast tracked. Her father did know my first name, after all. It would be good. We would bond over this. It would become the hilarious story we told at parties for years to come.

But it wasn't funny yet, and I was about to not get paid for several weeks.

I was going to need to walk a lot more.

It was about the time my extravagant car ride came to an end that my cell phone rang. *Erica.* How in the world could I take that call?

Obviously, I couldn't right then. I had that tiny box of personal items to carry up the six steps of my building's landing. And then I had doors to unlock. A box to set down. Dozens of Junior Mints to eat. An unfair accusation to grapple with. A career to mourn.

But as the day went on, and there were no Junior Mints left, and I acknowledged that the grappling wasn't going to be wrapped up in time for dinner, and the mourning settled into my heart in spite of how optimistic my brain knew it should be, I accepted that I couldn't avoid my big sister forever. Besides, her calls every thirty minutes had transitioned into calls every twenty minutes, and I knew she wouldn't stop until I answered.

"How did it go?" she asked as soon as I answered the phone. "Have all the chickens hatched? How many are there?"

❀

Four days later I was standing at the red front door of my parents' white colonial home in Durham. There was still a trace of snow on the ground, but the noonday sun overhead and the 78-percent humidity combined to welcome me back in spectacularly sweaty fashion under my down bubble coat that had been warranted in Manhattan that morning. Erica had convinced me to sublet my apartment a month at a time, and she had used Jared's frequent flyer miles to get me home. I'd only agreed under the condition that she was to tell no one the real reason I was there. Except for Jared. The two of them had annoyingly adopted our parents' number one rule of marriage: keep no secrets from each other unless necessary to pull off a pleasant surprise.

I hadn't quite been able to come up with a way to repackage my situation according to those terms.

I texted Erica from the front stoop. She had promised she would be there to help me establish motive.

I'm here. Are you going to come smuggle me in or what?
Just ring the doorbell. Yay! So excited to see you!

Just ring the doorbell. I took a deep breath and did as I was instructed, after first making sure there was a smile on my face that would come across as genuine and might even give the impression I was happy to be there.

I heard my dad's voice call out, "No, I've got it," then footsteps approached. Then they stopped. I knew he was looking through the peephole. I contemplated ducking and sneaking behind the bushes—or maybe if I ran fast enough I could catch up with my Uber driver. Instead, I bared my teeth and smiled at my undoubtedly shocked dad, who I knew was on the other side of the wood trying to make sense of the strangely magnified view of his middle daughter's face. There was a sudden flurry of sound and movement, then the door was open wide. Nearly as wide as my dad's arms.

I'd never felt homesick. At least not for people. After we moved back to North Carolina, I spent years feeling homesick for New York. But when I missed people, I called them—and for nearly twenty years, I'd had Manhattan *and* gotten to talk to the people I loved whenever I wanted to. Homesickness never entered the picture. But in that moment, I wouldn't have traded the expression on my dad's face for anything. It was as if he'd been homesick for *me*.

"Oh, my goodness. McKenna." His voice was a whisper as he pulled me into his arms and wrapped them around me. "This is— How in the world— It is just so good . . ." He put his hands on my arms and pushed me back so he could look at me. "What are you doing here?"

The tears glistening in his eyes made me uncertain I could keep up my prebuilt defenses, so I embraced him once again. It did feel awfully good to be in his protective arms.

"Are you surprised, Dad?" I asked, though there was no need.

"*'Surprised'*?" He chuckled and rested his cheek on the top of my frizzy, untamed humidity curls. "One of the best surprises I've ever gotten."

"Good." I sighed and let everything that wasn't my dad slip away for a moment.

Until he pushed me away again and studied my face. "Who knew you were coming?" His voice was quiet as he confronted the exciting possibility that he was now a coconspirator. "Does your mother know?"

I shook my head. "Just Erica."

He threw his head back and slapped himself on the forehead. "*That's* why she said we should do Saturday family lunch instead of Sunday dinner this week. Don't tell her this, but your mother and I suspected she was going to announce she was pregnant again."

I laughed softly. "Can you imagine? I think we'd have to lock Jared up in a padded room if he found out they were going to start over just when Charlie finally got over his fear of staying the night at friends' houses."

"Are you kidding? Jared's been the one with baby fever. I figure if they're not expecting soon, he might just walk into a maternity ward and help himself to one."

"Scott?" My mom's voice rang out from upstairs, then I heard her footsteps approaching, muffled by the chevron-patterned carpet runner in the center of the wood staircase. "Who was at the door?"

My dad giggled to himself and winked at me. "Annie, did you mean to have *all* the wedding flowers delivered? I thought you and Taylor just wanted some samples sent over from the florist."

He could barely contain his laughter. Golly, he was proud of himself for that masterful deception.

"Oh no!" my mom cried out, and the pace of her footsteps increased. "Taylor! You'd better get down here!"

Taylor was here too? I could barely contain my grumble. *Thanks, Erica.* Although, I quickly reasoned, maybe that was for the best. That would leave very little chance that the focus would remain on me for any extended period of time throughout the day. *Thanks, Erica!*

"McKenna!" My mom rushed toward me as soon as she entered

the foyer. She wrapped her arms around me as my dad had, and it felt every bit as safe and secure.

"Hey, Mom."

"Look at you! I feel like I haven't seen you since you were a little girl."

"We FaceTimed last week."

She scoffed. "Oh, I know that. It's just not the same. And yes, before you say it, I know that the last time I saw you in person you were already a fully grown woman, but . . . Well . . ." My dad reached out and rubbed her back. "I just missed you. That's all."

I grinned at her, finally glad that Erica had insisted I spend some time in Durham. The joy radiating from my parents' faces was a pretty good indication that the visit was past due, and at that moment I couldn't imagine any other place on earth where I could be made to feel like I mattered. Where I could pretend—for just a little while—that I wasn't under investigation for a crime I hadn't committed. A crime that, were I to be indicted for it—or, in fact, anything apart from exonerated of all wrongdoing and offered a reputation-restoring apology and compensation for it—would signal the end of my career and everything I had spent my entire life working toward. I wouldn't just be fired and go to jail. I would be disbarred. I would be disgraced. I would have to leave New York and learn a new skill—like welding or calligraphy or something that didn't involve the law or money or children or anything that required people to have any sort of personal stake in my integrity.

My shoulders and jaw tightened, and I felt my breath growing shallow as the possibilities swam through my brain. *You have nice penmanship. You could do a whole lot worse than that calligraphy gig.* I abruptly gasped for air, and all four of my parents' eyes focused on me with concern.

"You okay, kid?" my dad asked, stepping closer.

"McKenna, honey? What is it?" My mom ran her hands up and

down my arms and used her gentle but commanding mom strength to guide me to the bench against the staircase. "Scott, grab a paper bag from the kitchen."

I guess I was hyperventilating. That whole sequence—from Mom instructing my dad to grab a paper bag to me breathing into said paper bag and my head being forced down between my knees while my mother rubbed rhythmic circles on my back—seemed to progress in a blurry instant. Although I do have a faint memory of my dad calling out, "How about the full-sized ones from the butcher? Would that work?" and my mom replying, "No, the ones in the drawer next to the refrigerator! Good grief, Scott, we're not covering up her head and filming a hostage video here."

However long it actually took, my mom soon brought calm to the chaos, and I was able to breathe again. The soothing patterns on my back continued. Her deliberate and paced breathing influenced mine. She hummed a lovely but unrecognizable tune under her breath. It all took me back to every time she had tried to comfort me through the years—through childhood disappointments and teenage panic attacks, all of which seemed so utterly insignificant now. Not only because the heartbreaks of then were small compared to what I was currently dealing with, but also because I wished I could go back and warn that little girl that even then she was setting herself up with goals and dreams that were one day going to be squashed by three men who didn't even know her. An entire lifetime of work, and it would all be taken away in a matter of seconds by a philandering octogenarian; a pretty face with fake teeth, a fake tan, and a grand total of sixteen brain cells; and the man I had thought represented my best chance at someday having what the world considered "it all."

"Thanks, Mom. I'm okay now."

She smiled at me even as concern mingled with examination and analysis in her eyes. "What's going on, sweetie? Did something happen?" She tilted her head and examined me further, then seemed to astutely land at the conclusion that the only thing that would cause this severe of a reaction in me had to be work related. "Something to do with a case you're working on?"

I shook my head and tried to access an unprepared file of excuses in my mind. I hadn't expected to need an excuse. Not for being upset anyway. My catalogue of excuses for why I was in Durham had been checked, double-checked, alphabetized, and backed up in the cloud. But what was my reason for being upset? I hadn't intended to be upset and therefore hadn't prepared an excuse.

My dad sat down on the bench on the other side of my mom, and they both gave me all of their attention. Loving concern was evident in my dad's twitchy fingers and the way he bit his lip as he watched me. He was desperate to find out who or what had hurt his little girl so he could figure out how to make it all better. My mom exuded patience and understanding through her comforting grin and focused eyes, and I sensed that we would be in the kitchen soon, baking snickerdoodles together just as we had every time my adolescent heart had been troubled.

"You know you can tell us anything, kiddo," my dad said, and I believed it. I *knew* it. Down deep to my very being, I knew it was true.

I filled my lungs with air and dug my fingernails into my knees, which were protected by a pair of jeans I'd bought more than a year ago and was wearing for the first time. Wallis, Monroe and Burkhead did not believe in casual Fridays. And even if they did, who was I kidding? McKenna Keaton did not believe in casual Fridays.

"Well, the truth is . . . ," I began. But before I could squeak out another word, my attempt at a confession that would have humiliated me, regardless of my innocence, got caught up in the Taylor tornado. It was as familiar to me as an approaching nor'easter to a ragged old fisherman who had spent his life pursuing an elusive catch on the sea. She came bounding down the stairs with the same recognizable cadence she'd had practically since she began walking.

Taylor didn't walk so much as she bounced and glided in equal measure.

"Mom? Did I hear you call my name a few minutes ago? I was on the phone with—" Her face morphed before my eyes into a mushy mess of emotion. In an instant mascara was streaming down her face, and her cheeks had turned the color of cotton candy. The pink kind. Not the blue. "I *told* them you'd come!"

I don't know exactly how I got to my feet. My dad may have pushed me up. Or maybe Taylor's magnetic energy pulled me in like that Wooly Willy toy we'd played with as kids. The thing where you move the iron shavings around with a magnet to form Willy's hair and beard. *Here, kids. Some little pieces of metal to play with!* Is it any wonder I became an attorney? Even as a child I recognized the liability risks. Regardless, I was on my feet and being cried on before you could say "settle out of court."

"Hey, Tay." I hugged her back. She was annoying, but I loved the brat. I think I'd even missed her—not that I'd realized it before right then. "What's wrong?"

"'What's wrong?'" she repeated. "How could anything be wrong?" She pulled away until her face was about six inches from mine and whispered, "This is the happiest day of my life."

She was a little too in my space. Even as representative of another one-third of the six X chromosomes Scott and Annie Keaton had put out into the world, she and I didn't know each other well enough for her to be standing so close.

"Well," I muttered as I attempted to pull away. "That can't possibly be true."

"No, it *is* true! Mom said you couldn't come, and I thought she was being ridiculous. But then Jackson started telling me I needed to prepare myself in case you actually couldn't come. And he was telling me I needed to be more understanding because you have an important job and everything. But I still knew you were coming.

Then when Erica said you really, *really* weren't coming, I figured it had to be true. If anyone would know if you were coming, it would be Erica. But even *she* didn't—" Her eyes widened, and a grin as broad as sunrise overtook her face. "That little punk! Erica!" She yelled toward the back door and took off running. "I can't believe you tricked me!"

I felt dizzy, and not just in a commotion-all-around-me way. I felt sort of like that cow that Helen Hunt and Bill Paxton watched fly through the air in *Twister.*

My dad's arms, suddenly wrapped back around me, provided stabilization. "You're a good kid, McKenna. I'm sure it wasn't easy for you to get away, with all you've got going on. But thanks for being here for her."

Thanks for being here for her? Surely not even the *Twister* cow was as confused as I was.

"Oh, sweetie," my mom chimed in with a sigh as she stood from the bench and placed her hand on my arm. "Why didn't you tell us the panic attacks had started again?"

"They haven't, Mom. Really."

"I'm sorry that taking time off work is creating so much stress for you." I stared blankly at her, and she continued. "I mean, that *is* what's causing the stress, right? Or is there something else—"

"Nope," I asserted. "There's nothing else." Whatever vulnerability I'd been feeling had to be halfway to Oz by now.

My dad kissed the top of my head before he pulled away. He grabbed my suitcases from the front stoop and brought them into the foyer. "If you need to talk, you know we're always—"

"Aunt McKenna!"

Just in time to distract from a conversation I didn't have the energy for, three voices and six feet came running at me with a herd-of-buffalo quality I knew would have resulted in a "No running in the house!" back in my day. Erica's too. Maybe the way our parents had spoiled Taylor prepared them for grandparenthood.

"Hey, guys!" I called out as I planted my feet and prepared to be tackled. Ten-year-old April and seven-year-old Cooper were nearly as tall as I was, and at four years old, Charlie looked on track to outgrow us all. I wrapped my arms around them as they reached me. "I've missed you!"

"We've missed you too," April said, tilting her head up slightly to look at me. "Are you here for Aunt Taylor's party?"

Oh, of course.

Well, that was fortuitous. Erica said no one would even question my being there. I hadn't been too sure about that, so I'd crafted stories of use-it-or-lose-it paid time off and situations in which my bosses had said things to me like, "You work so hard! You need to get away for a while and recharge." My little sister's engagement party would work in a pinch, I supposed.

"I sure am," I replied.

"Alright, that's enough." Erica's voice presided over the chaos like the superteacher and supermom that she was as she entered from the back of the house. "Let's at least let Aunt McKenna get her coat off."

The kids scattered, my dad started carrying luggage upstairs, and my mom disappeared after mumbling something about her Instant Pot.

"Hi," I whispered to Erica as she walked toward me. "I'm really happy to see you." I grabbed her hand as soon as I could reach her and wrapped puffy coat-ensconced arms around her shoulders.

She clung to my waist. "It's been too long, McKenna."

"Not you too. It hasn't been *that* long—"

"It's been three years."

Had it?

"Oh. Well, that *is* too long, I guess. But I don't need you to make me feel guilty—"

"I'm not trying to make you feel guilty." She leaned her head back and looked at me. And it was okay that *she* was in my space. "I just missed you. That's all."

"I missed you too." I sighed and pulled away and finally began stripping off my coat.

Erica took it from me. The moment it was in her hands she said, "You're drenched."

I shrugged and attempted to appear as nonchalant as I could. "It was a lot colder in New York—"

"McKenna . . ." She was surveying me with concern, but there was warning in her voice—as if I'd better not dare to be anything less than completely truthful with her.

Being human is not a weakness, McKenna. I exhaled as I remembered the words Dr. Krabbe, my first therapist, had said to me at the age of eleven.

"Everything got chaotic a few minutes ago and I'm tired. Plus, I was thinking about everything going on . . . and I had a minor panic attack. First one in years." Erica studied me and refused to flinch until I raised my hands in front of me and added, "I promise."

She pulled my sweaty body to her and embraced me firmly. "It's going to be okay."

"I know." I rested my head on her shoulder for a moment and then pulled away after a quick squeeze. "So remind me . . . When's this engagement party?"

She flung my coat over her shoulder. "Next weekend."

I nodded and picked up my carry-on. *Okay. Next weekend.* With any luck, Wallis, Monroe and Burkhead's investigation would unearth the egregious error well before then, and I'd be on a plane by the following Monday.

Chapter 3

That's not at all what happened!" I exploded with laughter. Everyone else at the table had already lost it through the course of Erica's journey down memory lane.

Her jaw dropped, and she stared at me in disbelief. "Are you kidding me? That's *exactly* what happened!"

I shook my head with vehemence, but the grin didn't shake loose. Though I had no precise recollection of the memory she was sharing with our family, I couldn't deny it sounded like something I would do.

"You're a nut job," I insisted nonetheless, finding too much fun in the teasing.

"Mom, Dad, back me up on this," Erica pleaded. Of course, my parents were useless—my dad because he was laughing too hard, my mom because she was busy serving up French silk pie for dessert. "She walked in from school one day and asked us all to gather around a flip-chart presentation that she had made, and she spent the next hour laying out the course of her life."

Taylor was laughing hardest of all. "At seven?"

Erica nodded. "Yep. And I'm not just talking 'I want to be a lawyer' and 'I'm going to marry George Glass.'"

I nearly spit out my coffee at the mention of George Glass.

"Ooh! Who's George Glass?" Taylor asked. "I've never heard about *any* of the guys Kenna dated!"

I looked at Erica and rolled my eyes. A perfectly executed spit take on my part had been wasted on the young.

"George Glass was Jan Brady's imaginary boyfriend from *The Brady Bunch*," Jared interjected, probably in an attempt to keep his wife and senior sister-in-law from choking his junior sister-in-law, who had just made the other two feel approximately one hundred and twelve years old.

"It was the cutest thing!" Erica continued. "She drew a timeline, starting with the summer-school programs she wanted to enroll in for extra credit, that went all the way up through passing the bar and becoming senior partner in a law firm."

The proud and amused grin fell from Erica's face as our eyes met. Tears pooled in hers as mine began to sting, and I knew that we were sharing the same depressing brain wave. She'd just accidentally presented a long-forgotten memory as evidential proof that I really was in the midst of losing everything I had worked toward my entire life.

I saw Jared's hand slip to his wife's knee. He offered a compassionate smile in my direction and then replaced the gravity on his face with a carefree, good-natured smile.

"Hey, now," he began. "Just because George Glass wasn't involved doesn't mean we shouldn't talk about some of the real, non-imaginary boyfriends McKenna had. Because we definitely should."

Erica looked at him like he was her knight in shining armor. I, meanwhile, pointed across the table from my eyes to his in the international symbol for "I'm watching you, Pierson," which caused his smile to widen. I was grateful that he had stepped in, and he knew it.

I loved Jared. I'd always loved Jared.

We were heading into a discussion that, I suspected, was about to draw attention to the fact that I had never been boy crazy. But Erica had been. She had been one of the most popular girls in school, all throughout our childhood, and she'd always had her pick of any boy she wanted to date. Football captains, basketball stars, student-council presidents . . . They'd all gone out with Erica. So when she'd taken a liking to Jared Pierson her sophomore year at Duke, even though Jared was a high-school senior, like me, I hadn't understood what was happening. He had actually been my friend first, and she'd interacted with him through the years at various school events. He'd even been over to our house a few times when he and I were part of the same study group. Things like that. He was great.

He just wasn't the type of great that Erica had ever found to be great.

There had been three of us battling it out for valedictorian throughout most of high school. Jared, me, and Henry Blumenthal. Henry moved to Oregon just after Christmas senior year, leaving Pierson and me to duke it out. I'd ultimately triumphed, but I'd always suspected he had slacked off in AP European History and accepted a plain old A instead of an A-plus because he was too shy to give a speech at graduation. He'd heartily congratulated me on my victory, fulfilled his role as salutatorian like a champ, and then gotten over his timidity enough to ask out my big sister before graduation night was through. Apart from a few months after she graduated from college, in which Jared had tried to convince her she could do better than him, they'd been together ever since. Although I wasn't too sure he had ever gotten over his belief she could do better—even after fourteen years of marriage and three kids. He still looked at her like he thought he might wake up from his dream one of these days.

"Now we're talking!" Taylor exclaimed. She leaned over to Jackson and said, "I missed out on all the good stuff."

I shook my head. "No, you didn't." I smiled up at my mom, who had just placed pie in front of me. "There is no good stuff. At least not for me. Now, Erica, on the other hand . . ."

Erica wrapped her arms around Jared. "Erica didn't get to the good stuff until this one came along."

I grimaced at her, and she winked, properly interpreting my disgust at her schmaltz and not backing down for a moment.

"I just don't remember you ever having any boyfriends, Kenna," Taylor said. Her fork hovered in the air as she stared into space. After a long while she shrugged and sighed. "Nope. Nothing."

"I was too focused on my studies." I directed a sickly sweet and innocent grin at my dad.

"That's my girl."

"Oh, whatever!" I think it was Erica who said that. It was difficult to tell over my brother-in-law's riotous laughter.

I feigned shock. "What? Do you question my laborious dedication to my studies?"

My mother jumped to my defense. "No one ever could."

Erica swallowed down a piece of pie. "That's right. No one ever could. And that laborious dedication kept you from going on dates with your boyfriends, but it didn't keep you from having them."

Jackson laughed. "What does that mean?"

I couldn't help but look at him in surprise. He *did* have a voice! Well, that wasn't fair. He had greeted me very nicely when we were introduced before dinner. But ever since the entire family had been seated at the dining-room table—with my niece and nephews eating at the small table in the kitchen—I hadn't heard him utter a word. Taylor hadn't given him a chance. Or maybe he liked it that way.

I took a deep breath. "Well, I always liked the idea of having a boyfriend. Mainly so I didn't have to suffer through the whole upheaval of having to find a date for prom or wonder if anyone was going to ask me to dance at homecoming. It was easier to find a boyfriend during the social-calendar off-season, before everyone got desperate."

My family laughed at me as I explained my high-school dating philosophy. I was neither offended nor surprised by their chortling.

I was used to it. They had always loved me and accepted me. But understanding me? That was another matter entirely.

"You can laugh," I told them, still feeling good-natured about it all. "But that was the only way I could have pulled off the grades I did and still make it to all of the school events. It worked pretty well, thank you very much!"

Jared scoffed. "It worked for *you*! Meanwhile, you had these poor guys committed to you for months at a time and then being dragged along just to be your escort."

My hand flitted through the air, brushing off his concern for the "poor guys." It wasn't that I hadn't cared about the feelings of any of the boys I dated. Even without a strong outpouring of romantic inklings or much appreciation for the so-called joys of being in a relationship, I had never been the type to play with boys' emotions. I had carefully chosen each and every boyfriend. They had been second- or third-tier friends, mostly. People I could stand being around and who didn't seem to hate spending time with me, but they had to be low maintenance. That meant they had to have something else that kept them busy—be it sports or a job or video games or whatever—so that I had time to study. They had to like being around me but not want me around all the time. And they had to be guys whom other girls didn't seem to be fighting over, since I never would have been so cruel as to keep them from more affectionately predisposed girlfriends.

I was able to brush off Jared's concern for the "poor guys" because they had always known what they were signing up for. I hadn't misled a single one of them. A couple of them may have liked me as something more than a friend, but I'd told them honestly from the beginning that I was too busy to fall in love with them. Most of them were just glad to have a girl to hang out with at pep rallies or the occasional dance.

The skeptical look on Jared's face seemed to indicate he wasn't completely convinced.

"What?" I asked him with a mouthful of pie.

"You were the biggest heartbreaker in the whole senior class!" he exclaimed, his wide eyes staring at me from across the table.

In response to his impassioned declaration, Taylor maneuvered up onto her knees on the dining room chair and looked as if she might just bounce away into the air, unable to control her giddy excitement.

"McKenna Keaton was the biggest heartbreaker of the senior class?" she questioned in surprise and euphoria. "You have to tell me *everything*. I'm serious, Jared. Everything!"

My dad spoke up for the first time in a while. "Well, now, I'm not sure we need to hear *everything*."

I chuckled. "Don't worry, Dad. There's nothing to hear." I turned to Taylor next to me and repeated, "There's nothing to hear." And then my attention was back on Jared. "Seriously. I don't know what you're talking about. I was never a heartbreaker. None of those guys ever cared. We were friends who went out. That was all."

"Your version is boring," Taylor said to me, and the entire table dissolved into hilarity. Myself included. "Jared, tell us your version."

"So many guys were in love with her," he indulged, leaning across the table and pointing his fork at Taylor once he was able to maintain his straight face again. "And each one of them thought they were going to be the one to tame her."

"'*Tame*' me!" I chortled. "What sort of Shakespearean trope were *you* living in high school, Pierson?"

"It's true! Guys who went out with you were the living personifications of all sorts of cliches, actually. A little bit Shakespeare, a little bit John Hughes . . ." He had Taylor's rapt attention and was playing it up for full effect.

"I had no idea," Taylor breathed. I was suddenly sitting next to the heart-eyes emoji. "Tell me everything."

"Seriously, Tay, there's nothing to tell. I have no idea what Jared is talking about."

"But didn't anything ever come of any of those relationships? Something must have."

I rolled my eyes directly at my little sister. "Yes. Didn't I tell you? I'm actually married to five different guys right now. I spread them out across the New York City boroughs just to avoid awkward run-ins and confusion as to whom I'm supposed to meet where on date nights."

"Hardy-har-har." She sat up on the edge of her chair. "I just want to know how you broke their hearts."

"I didn't break anyone's heart!" My voice elevated a bit more than I had intended, so I quickly cleared my throat and manufactured a smile again. "Now, as fun as this is, I daresay we've discussed my past enough for one evening."

Taylor nodded once with sharp affirmation. "Agreed. Let's talk about your present."

Jared stood from his chair with an exasperated sigh. "Well, that's not fair. I have to go." He pointed at Taylor and sternly ordered, "There is to be no discussion of McKenna's current romantic escapades until I get back." He smiled smugly at me as he stepped behind Erica and placed his hands on her shoulders.

"There is to be no discussion of McKenna's current romantic escapades . . . period." I stuck my tongue out at my brother-in-law as his smug expression expanded—bolstered by Taylor's rapturous enthusiasm for the subject.

"You live this glamorous life and have this glamorous job, and I hardly know anything about any of it! You live on the Upper West Side, McKenna! Do you know who else lives on the Upper West Side?"

"Jerry Seinfeld?"

"No, not Jerry Seinfeld!"

"No, he does. I used to see his kids riding their bikes all the time. Of course, they're all grown up now—"

"Kathleen Kelly. Joe Fox. Harry. Sally. Carrie Bradshaw."

"Don't the Ghostbusters work there?" Erica interjected.

I shook my head. "Tribeca."

Taylor was undeterred. "The Upper West Side is the romance capital of the world, McKenna!"

"No, Paris is the romance capital of the world. The Upper West Side is the capital of specialty bagel shops."

Erica laughed. "Might as well give it up, Tay."

"Just tell me one thing." Taylor pleaded, very much *not* giving it up.

"One thing?" I asked, and she nodded. "One thing about my exciting, glamorous life on the Upper West Side?" Her eyes grew wider as she went full-on bobblehead. "Okay, sure. In January, I spent an entire week working from my apartment, processing briefs that amounted to four and a half million in fees for the firm. And during that week, I ordered so many Swiss-and-tomato-on-pumpernickel sandwiches from Barney Greengrass that whenever I called, they started referring to the sandwich as the McKenna." I shrugged. "That was pretty cool."

She could have asked if they were going to put it on the menu that way at Barney Greengrass. If I dared to dream big dreams, my little sister even could have asked how it felt to handle such big cases and if the partners had appreciated all my hard work and dedication. But this was Taylor.

"Just tomato and Swiss? No turkey or anything?"

Frustration and relief brushed over me in unison. Taylor had asked the wrong question . . . again. Of course. But how long could I count on her being so concerned about romance and condiments that the conversation got effortlessly steered away from my reality? How long would it be until someone asked the questions that actually made sense—about cases I was working on now or how many billable hours I was currently processing? Surely any minute my dad would make some supportive comment about how I was overdue for a promotion.

Tightness began overtaking my airways, and I had to place my hand on my knee to keep it from shaking.

Being human is not a weakness, McKenna.

I cleared my throat and stood from my chair. "Jared, where are you going? Can I tag along?"

"He's going to a soiree," Erica replied on his behalf.

Jared adjusted the wire frames on the bridge of his nose and pushed in his chair. "I hate these sorts of things so much."

"'These sorts of things.'" Erica mimicked him in a low, masculine voice made to sound posh enough for *Downton Abbey*. "Apparently, he goes to more soirees than I knew."

Jared sighed. "I just mean . . . social things. Things where you have to talk to people and . . . Well, that's it. Things where you have to talk to people."

With a ragged chuckle as I felt my pulse return to normal, I begged, "Will someone please tell me more details about this thing other than it's a soiree where Jared will have to talk to people?"

"It's nothing. It's just a premiere—or a premiere party or something—for this guy I went to high school—" He shook his head slightly as things clicked into place in his mind. "Oh, duh. You know Henry."

"Henry who?"

"Blumenthal."

My eyebrows rose. "Oh! Sure, I know Henry. What's he up to these days? What sort of soiree could Henry Blumenthal be having? As I recall, he was even less fond of being social and talking with people than you."

"Yeah, I bet he hates it. But I can't imagine he has much choice." Jared shrugged. "I haven't actually talked to him in years, but we stay connected on Facebook. We send each other Christmas cards. That sort of thing."

"I'm sorry," Erica interjected. "*Who* sends Christmas cards?"

He stepped behind her again and kissed the top of her head. "Oh, come on. Everyone knows you're the one who keeps us enrolled as members of the civilized world. It goes without saying." She craned her neck to look up at him, unrelenting, and finally with a sigh—but also a besotted twinkle in his eye—he turned to me and gave her the credit she deserved. "Henry sends me Christmas cards, and Erica sends Henry Christmas cards on my behalf. And obviously we've all followed his career."

"I'm sure he's followed yours, too, sweetie," Erica encouraged with a yawn.

Jared cackled. "Oh, yes. I believe I've inspired his next project, in fact. He's covered everything from the Emancipation Proclamation to 9/11, from the Crash of '29 to the *Chariots of Fire* guy—"

"Eric Liddell," my dad assisted.

"But it's all just been building up to his latest masterpiece: Orthodontia in the 21st Century."

I shook my head and smiled at their silliness. I was amused, but I didn't have a clue what they were talking about. "Is he a modern-art guy or something?"

In one fluid, energized moment, Taylor found the motivation to move past the anticlimax of Barney Greengrass. "You're kidding, right? Do you really not know who he is?"

I was thoroughly confused . . . until I suddenly wasn't. The clues they had laid out before me appeared in my mind as sepia titles, accompanied by original, nondescript orchestrations that were generic enough not to get caught in your head but recognizable enough to become the soundtrack of an entire brand.

I gasped. "You're saying Henry Blumenthal is *Hank Blume*? Our Henry? From Model UN and chess club? As in the worst Mercutio in the history of *Romeo and Juliet*? Hank Blume is *Henry*?"

I didn't have a lot of time for television, but I was pretty sure I had never missed a Blume documentary. My DVR was pretty much exclusively reserved for them, in fact. (Well, Blume documentaries and *Outlander*, if I'm being honest.) It was difficult to believe I had never made the connection, but the truth was I'd never thought much about the filmmaker, only the films. The subjects of the films. I always thought that was part of the beauty of them, actually—though perhaps I'd never thought of it in those terms.

You know how the really good actors make you forget they're acting? Well, a Blume documentary made me forget I was watching a documentary. They somehow evoked the emotion of a brilliantly scripted drama while simultaneously making you feel that you weren't watching entertainment at all but were rather a fly on the wall as surreal historical realities played out before you.

I never would have guessed that I'd once split a corndog with the genius who made me feel that way.

"I can't believe you didn't know that!"

Jared's bewildered exclamation carried to the kitchen.

"Didn't know what?" my mom asked as she stood in the doorway, returning with the coffeepot.

"Can you believe that your typically astute middle daughter had no idea about our local-boy-makes-good?" Erica asked.

Mom looked at me quizzically. "You mean Henry? You know Henry, don't you? You went to school with him."

"I know!" Golly, I felt dumb. "I just didn't realize that's who he was."

So subtly it was nearly indiscernible, the conversation erupted in a rapid-fire roundtable of jokes and witticisms, all centered around the theme of how my cluelessness about Henry Blumenthal was proof positive I had been away from home too long. It was harmless teasing, but I'd only been back in Durham for approximately seven hours, and I needed to get away.

As the razzing continued, I hurried around the table and grabbed Jared's arm. "Take me with you," I whispered emphatically. "Please.

43

I'm begging you. If you care about me at all— No, wait. If you care about anyone in this house at all and don't want them to be witness to a nuclear meltdown while you're at a soiree, please . . . take me with you. Do it for your wife. Do it for your children."

He chuckled softly. "Go get dressed. Business casual."

Chapter 4

The Durham Armory had gotten all dolled up for Hank Blume. In fact, it appeared that all of Durham had rolled out the red carpet for, perhaps, its most famous son—with the obvious exceptions of a comedian known as Pigmeat Markham and Christopher Martin, a rapper who was one-half of Kid 'n Play.

I could never remember if he was Kid or Play.

To look around the open ballroom of the Armory, packed with hundreds of buzzing locals and even a few representatives from national media outlets, you had to think that the guy who'd taken three hours to beat me at chess—despite the fact that he was supposedly a master and I had just joined chess club to impress my senior advisor—had surpassed even those Durham legends in renown.

"Would you look at this place?" I muttered to Jared as we made our way across the ballroom and each took a flute of champagne from a tray as it was offered to us. "I really can't believe I never put it together that it was Henry. He never went by Hank when we were growing up, did he?"

Jared took a sip and shook his head. "Not to my knowledge. But still, McKenna."

I sighed. "I know. But I don't really follow entertainment news or anything like that. It just never occurred to me to even wonder."

We smiled at people as we passed by all sorts of attendees. You could be pretty sure what type they were just by looking at what they were doing with their eyes or what they were doing with their hands.

If eyes were focused on whomever the person was speaking to and hands were casually holding champagne glasses or resting at their side, I figured they were the socialites. The Durham elite who were there because that's just what they did on Saturday evenings. In fact, that was probably what they did most evenings. See and be seen. They weren't worried about whether they'd get a chance to visit with the guest of honor because either (a) they didn't care and weren't even entirely sure as to the purpose of the party or (b) they knew Henry wouldn't dare end the evening without groveling before them.

I found those people to be largely uninteresting. But I was increasingly intrigued by those whose eyes darted around the room as if they were about to be discovered and evicted. Their fingers drummed on their flutes or on the cocktail table in front of them, and if they were carrying on any sort of conversation at all, it was usually with someone who looked every bit as nervous as they did.

Did shy, nerdy Henry Blumenthal have groupies?

Jared and I settled against a banister along the far wall and began sipping our champagne. For a moment I was self-conscious of both my eyes and my hands, but I quickly determined my brother-in-law and I belonged to a third demographic. That of old friend. We were there because Henry wanted us there. Well, Henry wanted Jared there. And I didn't have any reason to suspect he would be displeased that I had tagged along.

"I guess it's just a little surprising," Jared began between sips, "that no one ever discussed him with you. He's in the local news about things all the time."

"About his films and such?"

"Yeah, but also because he does a lot for Durham. He's paid to renovate theaters, and he gives lots of money to the schools and hospitals. Stuff like that. And, of course, the fact that Full Frame takes place in Durham."

"'Full Frame takes place in Durham'?" I echoed. "What's Full Frame?"

He groaned and laughed simultaneously. "Seriously, Keaton, have you *been* to Durham?" He pointed at the door we had entered through and the huge banner that hung over it that proclaimed, "Full Frame Documentary Film Festival Honors Hank Blume."

I read the sign and felt vindicated. Copying his pompously chiding tone, I said, "Seriously, Pierson, why on earth should I know anything about some local documentary film festival?"

He leaned in closer to me and spoke softly. "Because it's not 'some local documentary film festival.' It's one of the top documentary film festivals in the United States. Probably in the world. It's a qualifying festival for the Academy Awards. It's probably sort of like Sundance or Cannes or something for documentaries. And as you can perhaps imagine, the fact that the biggest thing in documentaries since Ken Burns is actually from here basically makes him the patron saint of the festival."

I smiled at him. "Are you speaking quietly because you're ashamed of me for not knowing all of that?"

He nodded and whispered, "Yes. Exactly. Very much so."

I guess it wasn't fair to say that Henry was nerdy. It wasn't like he wore a pocket protector or hung out at *Star Trek* conventions or anything like that. It was more like his brilliance made him awkward. Whereas I had always embraced my workaholic mentality and gleefully sacrificed any attempt at true acceptance, and Jared had somehow managed to succeed at all things academic while still maintaining a social life and not getting lumped in with any smart-kid cliques, Henry had never quite figured out what approach he wanted to take. Truth be told, he was smarter than me and worked harder than Jared, and if he hadn't moved away, he would have most likely won our battle for top of the class.

But he didn't fit into that smart-kid clique that Jared had avoided and that I would have been a part of, if I'd been part of any clique at all. When he walked into a room, it was like he did all he could to become invisible—even amongst his similarly intelligent and awkward peers who should have been his people. But that never stopped him from walking into the room. Thinking back on the years I had known him—from sixth grade until he left for Oregon—it was easy to see now that he had been a silent observer. A studier of human nature. Perhaps even a documentarian in the making.

"So, what do you know about him?" I asked Jared.

"You mean apart from the Emmy Awards and the Peabody Award and—"

"Yes. Apart from that. Where's he living now?"

"I don't know."

"Is he married? Does he have a family?"

He scrunched up his face, thinking hard. "Um . . . I don't think so? I don't really know."

"What's his new documentary about?"

"America, maybe?"

I slapped him on the arm. "You're useless."

With a shrug he said, "Look, I liked the guy in high school. I guess we were friends. And when he moved away, we stayed in touch. Then he became a big deal, and now I'm one of his seventy-five-gazillion Facebook friends. He shot me a thing on Messenger inviting me to this. I said I'd be here, and here I am. With my sister-in-law—a disgraced Durhamite who tagged along just to get out of the house. That's all I know."

I didn't know that my emotions were being communicated on my face until I saw the smile leave Jared's lips. "What's wrong?"

Suddenly my mouth felt dry, and I couldn't see him through the haze clouding my eyeballs.

He put his hand on my arm. "McKenna, what's wrong? Did I say something? I was just teasing. I'm glad you tagged along."

"'Disgraced Durhamite'?" I croaked.

Horror was instantly etched on his face. "Oh no! I just meant . . . I mean, I wasn't talking about your work stuff or anything, if that's what you're thinking. I just meant because you're from Durham and you're clueless about Henry. That's all I—" He squeezed my arm gently. "I'm sorry. Is that what you thought I—" He shook his head and cleared his throat. "I'm so sorry. I would never say that, and I would never even *think* that. I know you and I haven't talked about any of the stuff you're going through, but I know you know Erica told me, and you have to know that neither she nor I would ever believe you were capable of anything they're accusing you of. We know who you are, and we're on your side. Always. And I wouldn't even make a joke—"

I threw my arms around him just long enough to say, "I know. I'm sorry," before I pulled away and released an uncomfortable and embarrassed chuckle. "I don't know where that came from. So sorry."

"You don't have anything to apologize for. I can't even imagine what's going on in your mind through all of this." He chewed on his lip for a second before saying, "You know, if you ever want to talk . . ."

I counted Jared as my brother in every single way, and there was no one else on earth I ever could have thought was deserving of Erica—my absolute favorite person. But we'd never had that sort of relationship. The "if you ever want to talk" relationship. The brief hug we'd just shared was, to my recollection, maybe the third time we'd ever hugged in the twenty-five years or so we'd been in each other's lives, if you didn't count the brief requisite arrival and departure embraces at the beginnings and endings of trips.

"No, it's okay. Thanks."

"It might actually be good for you to talk—"

"I talked to Erica," I interjected.

He nodded. "I know. And I'm not saying you have to talk to me. I just want to make sure you know we all love you, and the entire family would be—"

"The entire family would be *what*? Understanding? No, they wouldn't." I took a giant swig of champagne but refused to cough when the intensity of the bubbles took me by surprise. I just carried on—watering eyes, burning nose, and all. "They'd be supportive, I'm sure—"

"Of course they would."

"But they wouldn't be understanding. They'd tell me I was too good for that place. They would tell me it was all for the best." I placed my empty glass on a passing waiter's tray and committed to looking for my next opportunity to grab another round. "They would tell me that the best was still ahead of me."

Jared stuffed his hands into his pockets and shrugged. "And that all sounds like exactly what they *should* say."

"To be supportive, yes. But not to be understanding." I lifted my index finger into the air, and a young man in a white tux swung by and gave me more champagne. "To be understanding would be to say, 'McKenna . . . that sucks. That really, really sucks. Everything you've been working toward your entire life has been taken from you.'" I felt my voice elevating, and Jared certainly detected it. He was too good a friend to shush me, but I did catch him looking around to see if anyone else was within earshot. Another gulp of champagne made me realize I really didn't care if they were or not. "And do you know what else an understanding family would say? They'd say, 'You're going to have to work harder than ever to get your life back on track, if you even can.'"

"If you even can work harder, or if you even can get your life back on track?"

"Either. Both. To understand would be to know that I can't possibly work harder than I have, but that I'm going to have to try."

He considered this for a moment as he sipped slowly on his first beverage. "Well, I don't think you give everyone enough credit." I opened my mouth to argue, but he stopped me. "Hear me out. I actually think Erica and I are supportive *and* understanding—"

"Well, sure. You and Erica are. But—"

"And we're the only ones you've given an opportunity to be," he countered.

"I know, but . . ." I exhaled with great deliberation.

The brief silence between the two of us was all it took for us both to detect that the crowd noise was increasing all around us. We looked around at all of the people making their way from the cocktail tables along the periphery to the rows of wooden chairs in the center of the room, and then back to each other. With silent consensus, we decided to avoid the aggressive push for the best seats that we were witnessing and instead stayed right where we were, standing at our table, off to the side in the shadows. We looked toward the stage in front of the giant projection screen at the front of the room in response to that instinctive buzz that fills the air when an event is about to begin.

"For the record," Jared said, leaning against my shoulder as we turned to face front and stand side by side. "To Erica and me, being understanding means acknowledging that you're in a really crappy situation. But don't you dare think for a minute, McKenna Keaton, that we're not going to support you with everything we've got. And that means refusing to believe for even a second that you aren't going to find a way out of this mess that will leave you better off than you ever were before."

I nudged him with my elbow and whispered, "Thanks, Pierson."

"Good evening." A posh British voice boomed and echoed throughout the vast space, but there was no one on the stage. I looked around for the speaker for a moment until Jared tapped my arm and pointed to the screen, which was still being brought into focus. "Catherine and I wish we could be there in person with you tonight, but we certainly weren't going to allow the slight inconvenience of impossibility to stand in the way of helping to honor our friend, Mr. Blume." The crowd began to cheer but in real time seemed to remember they were watching a recorded message and didn't know if the person speaking had factored in pauses for audience reactions. The crowd noise ceased in awkward fashion just about the time the man began speaking again.

"'Impossibility,'" a low voice muttered to us from just behind Jared, causing us both to jump slightly. "Sure, because *of course* the future king of England can't find a babysitter last minute."

We turned to face the source of the voice, and my breath caught in my throat as I glanced up and recognized him as Hank Blume. Not my old nerdy friend, Henry. I hadn't gotten to the point of that unlikely connection making sense yet. Not when Henry had been so lanky and awkward, with braces and bad skin, just like the rest of us, and the man before me suffered from none of those things. Maybe if he'd been drinking a Fruitopia and talking on his Nokia cell phone while bragging about all the music he'd downloaded on Napster and telling me I had to get the latest version of Encarta, I would have had the sensory clues I needed to fully understand that I'd eaten pizza rolls baked by the mother of one of America's foremost documentarians.

"People will say anything to avoid having to change out of their sweats," Jared replied in a hushed tone. A smile overtook his face—and Henry's, I think I detected in the dimmed light—and Jared put out his hand. "Good to see you, man."

"You too," Henry replied as they shook. "I'm glad you could make it." He faced me. "And it's good to see you, Erica. It's been a long time."

Jared was left to clear up the understanding, because I hadn't regained the ability to speak just yet.

"No, Erica couldn't make it. I'm sure you remember Mc—"

He was completely drowned out as the crowd erupted into cheers and applause. The video message ended, and the lights in the room got brighter. All eyes moved to the guest of honor, who had been spied by the anxious, keyed-up crowd.

"That's my cue!" Henry threw over his shoulder toward Jared as he hurried up to the stage. "Catch you in a bit?"

"We'll be here," he replied.

Henry stood in front of the screen and faced the welcoming crowd. "Wow, Durham! You never cease to amaze me!" A staffer handed him a microphone so he no longer had to shout. "Thank you for that kind and generous welcome. Thank you, Durham, thank you, Full Frame, and thank you, of course, to the duke and duchess. It means the world to me that they went to all that trouble to record a greeting." He winked in our direction, and I stifled a laugh.

And then Jared and I stared at each other—wide-eyed and impressed—as all that information sank further in. *That really was William and Kate in the video . . . honoring the guy who got excused from ever having to participate in PE class not because of asthma, or anything respectable like that, but because he had such a bad sweating problem that it came with a doctor's note.*

"As you'll see when we screen the film in a few minutes," he continued as I snapped back into focus, "their generosity carried over into the level of access they gave. I hope you enjoy your time with the royal family as much as I did, and I look forward to meeting you back here after."

Applause filled the room again, and Henry returned to where we stood. "You guys want to go grab a bite to eat?" he asked us, seemingly unaffected by the fact that every eye was still on him as the man who had handed him the mic stepped up to issue specific instructions about the screening portion of the evening.

Jared laughed. "Isn't your time sort of spoken for?"

"Nah. I've seen the film. I just have to be back for the Q and A afterward. I have an hour and fifty-three minutes. There's this great ramen place around the corner. Do you like ramen?"

The lights were progressively dimming again, but it didn't matter that I couldn't really even see him. I still couldn't stop staring at him. If I'd passed him on the street, I wouldn't have known I'd ever met him. If I'd watched a six-hour Hank Blume documentary *about* Hank Blume, no number of letters from the field or artistically zoomed-in shots would have made me think I'd ever seen the man in person. There I was, staring straight at him . . . and I still barely had a clue it was my old classmate. And Prince William had just told me it was.

"I'm not Erica," I stated very awkwardly. I don't know how else I could have cleared up the confusion, but there had to have been a better way than the one I chose. I mean, he was walking away from me, and we were all squeezing past a few hundred of his nearest and dearest who were preparing to be enraptured by his unprecedented glimpse into the house of Windsor. So, yeah, I probably could have waited for ramen.

"Sorry, what?" he whispered over his shoulder as a strangely Americanized but undeniably noble "Rule, Britannia" performed on guitar and banjo began bouncing around in the cavernous space.

I cleared my throat and tried again as we reached an alcove that led to an exit. "I'm not Erica."

It was a small space, and we were walking single file, with Henry leading the way and me bringing up the rear, so when he turned his head, I could tell that he could see Jared, but he couldn't see me.

"I'm so sorry about that," Henry said as we reached the door and he pushed the bar to open it. "I guess I'm not as up-to-date on things—"

"No!" Jared and I protested in unison.

"She's my sister-in-law," Jared continued. And then he seemed to feel the need to make very sure everyone was on the same page. "Erica's sister. I'm still married to Erica. This is—"

"McKenna?" Henry asked as I became the last person to step out onto the sidewalk, the door shut behind me, and our eyes began adjusting to the darkness of the Durham night.

"Hey, Henry. Nice to see you."

We could still hear the bass of the documentary's soundtrack through the closed metal door, and something about the scene— something about standing on a street in downtown Durham with Jared Pierson and Henry Blumenthal, I suppose—took me back to high school. Homecoming, junior year, had been at the Armory. Our football team was number one in North Carolina that year, and that apparently justified the additional expense of renting a venue rather than gussying up the gymnasium. My date had been Jimmy Clark Jr., my boyfriend at the time. He had danced with every other girl in our class, all night long, and I had spent most of the evening sitting in my formal gown on the very sidewalk on which we now stood. It had been a night of eating corn nuts and playing I Spy with Jared, Henry, and a couple of Jared's friends, and it was probably the most fun I ever had at a high-school dance.

"Wow," Henry muttered, snapping me out of my nostalgic reverie. "McKenna Keaton. That's a name I haven't heard in a while."

He was giving no indication whether the unexpected was welcome or not. I didn't have any reason to think it wouldn't be. As far as I knew, Henry and I had been friendly competitors who had tended to bring out the best in each other. Jared was driven and focused on succeeding, too, but he was such a nice guy, even back then, that you couldn't ever really look at him as your rival. Even in head-to-head competition, you couldn't help but find yourself rooting for Jared— even as you did all you could to squash him like a bug. But Henry?

Henry was fun to beat. Henry was a good sport when he lost, but you also knew that you were going to have a much more difficult time beating him twice in a row. Be it class elections, chess, Model UN, roles in school plays . . . Henry didn't like losing any more than I did. And that just meant I had to work harder to win.

"Before tonight, I have to say that 'Henry Blumenthal' wasn't a name I had heard in a while either. Now, 'Hank Blume' is a name I hear all the time, of course."

"She didn't know it was you," Jared interjected with a little too much glee and enthusiasm. His glance at me just screamed #sorrynotsorry, and I couldn't help but smile as he made the most out of his opportunity to make me look a little bit ridiculous. "She's a big fan of your work, and yet she never put it together that she went to school with you."

I shrugged and smiled, my embarrassment minimal and certainly secondary to the revelations I was trying to take in as my eyes and senses continued to adjust to standing face-to-face with Henry underneath a dim streetlight. "If it's any consolation, I was nearly thirty before I realized the voice of Darth Vader is also the voice of Mufasa. I'm not too bright about this stuff."

And if James Earl Jones himself had told me, "McKenna, I am your father, and by the way, Henry Blumenthal has grown into a ruggedly handsome adventurer sort of man who no longer wears oversize T-shirts and loose denim shorts, and who looks like he's had his nose broken repeatedly," I would have asked him to repeat what he'd said about Henry, and we'd come back to that paternity revelation later, after we sorted out the details that *really* didn't make sense.

Henry kept staring at me, and the smile began to slip from my lips. Maybe my embarrassment should have been less minimal. Had I offended him? If I had . . . I was mortified. But also, how vain was he? And let's not forget, it was all Jared's fault, regardless.

"I'm starving, and I'm down to an hour and forty-seven minutes."

He didn't glance at his watch or even pretend to listen at the door to determine how far into his film they had gotten. He just stated the fact and then turned on his heel and threw a friendly arm around Jared to pull him along with him—leaving me to trail after them for a block and a half.

Chapter 5

Fifty-five minutes later, Henry was slurping down ramen and catfish kamaboko (a true North Carolina take on sushi if ever there was one) like a pro, while I stuck to comparatively safe and boring things like edamame and every kind of sprout. In addition to still being pretty full from my mother's Instant Pot creation, I hadn't yet been able to shift into "It's just Henry!" mode. When he and Jared talked about old times, he sort of *sounded* like "just Henry." But then he would say things like, "Will and Kate are the most down-to-earth people you'll ever meet" or "The last time I was at the White House . . ." or "The Dalai Lama actually just spends a lot of his time doing jigsaw puzzles." And since I couldn't think of him as "just Henry," there was no way I was comfortable enough to eat the messiest of all trendy foods in front of him.

Not that he was paying any attention to me. Seriously, I didn't even know why I was there. From time to time Jared tried to pull me into the conversation, but I never could find my grounding, so I was just left to eat my bean sprouts and watch him—and while I watched, I wondered what I had done to offend him.

He was super nice to Jared. He had been super nice to me for the few seconds he thought I was Erica. It was clearly personal, but I just couldn't imagine what he had against me. The more I thought about it, the more I realized it couldn't even be because I hadn't known who he was. His entire demeanor had changed when *he* discovered who *I* was, not when he discovered that I hadn't known who *he* was.

I took advantage of a brief pause in the men of Jordan High chat fest. "So do you go by Henry in your everyday life, or is it Hank?"

"Henry is fine," he replied as soon as he had slurped in a noodle. Clearly he had the confidence I did not to consume ramen in mixed company.

I waited for a little more. Something. Anything. But he just kept eating. I locked eyes with Jared and gave a small, wide-eyed shrug. He returned the gesture as he adjusted his slipping glasses.

I refused to let Henry ice me out for no good reason. He was perfectly entitled to ice me out if he had a reason, but I hadn't made a career of *not* pursuing, demanding, and defending facts. "How did 'Hank Blume' become the brand? I don't remember you ever going by Hank in school."

He shook his head and turned his body toward me for the first time. Wow. Was it possible that my invisibility potion had worn off and I had finally appeared at the table?

"I didn't. Not here. Hank started in Oregon. And then when I started making films, it only took me one festival, maybe two, to realize everyone envisioned 'Henry Blumenthal' as an eighty-year-old tailor or deli owner from Brooklyn."

It wasn't much, but it was something. At least he'd given me *something* to work with.

"So, what's next, Henry?" Jared asked. "After *At Home with My Friends, Will and Kate*, I mean."

Henry chuckled. "It's called *She Dreams of America*."

"Great title." I couldn't keep the awe from working its way into my voice. Just as I'd begun making progress in my mind, reconciling my memories of Henry Blumenthal with the cool, confident man in front of me, I'd been transported back into Hank Blume fangirl mode. I cleared my throat and studied my sprouts. "What's it about?"

Just making conversation. Totally *not jumping up and down inside at the anticipation of an inside scoop.*

Henry shuffled forward in his seat. "I wanted to focus on the women in history who risked everything to come to America. The first person ever processed through Ellis Island was a thirteen-year-old Irish girl named Annie Moore, and yet apart from a statue here and there, we never talk about her." He shrugged. "There are a lot of women who helped craft the pursuit of the American dream and who shaped all of the families and stories to come. Most of them never got a statue."

Jared swallowed and wiped at his mouth with his napkin. "Your dad will love that. Won't he, McKenna?" He seemed to be unaware that the world was currently shifting on its axis, and I was only slightly aware that he'd said my name. Heck, I was only slightly aware that that *was* my name.

"Hmm?"

Bless Jared and his nescience.

"My father-in-law is majorly into genealogy. Has been for as long as I've known him. He loves unearthing the little nuggets that no one else takes note of."

"I think I remember that, actually." Henry tilted his head as his brow furrowed in concentration. "Didn't he talk at an assembly sophomore year?"

Jared shook his head. "Junior. Mr. Stenson's history class."

Henry snapped his fingers and then pointed emphatically. "That's right! Jordan High Heritage Day. He presented the Keaton family tree."

Jared laughed. "That was just the beginning. The tree has grown into a mighty oak since then."

I leaned in from my side of the booth, across the table to the side where Henry sat with Jared. "You know, that's something I thought about a lot. You moving to Oregon, I mean." I knew I was not demonstrating my brilliant conversational skills in that moment, but I had to grab on to whatever I could. And right then, what I could grab was the brief interlude from earlier. The one that had fallen between "Why doesn't Henry like me?" and "Why can't I feel my legs?"

His eyebrows raised and the smile on his face was replaced with confusion. "Really? That's something you thought about a lot?"

Yes, I had. Mostly about how his move—combined with Jared's fear of public speaking—had cleared my path toward valedictorian, but still. I spoke the truth. "That must have been hard. Starting over across the country just a few months before graduation."

"It wasn't my favorite thing."

"Am I remembering correctly? You moved because your mom remarried, right?"

He nodded. "It ended up being exactly what I needed. Dennis—that's my stepdad—is great. And it was a move home for him, so at least I inherited some aunts and uncles and cousins, whereas here it was always just my mom and me."

I had an unexpectedly vivid memory flit through my brain of Mrs. Penelli, our eighth-grade counselor, instructing us to be extra kind to Henry when he returned to school after his father's funeral. I'd made him a copy of my algebra notes and slipped them through the slats of his locker.

"And I loved Oregon. Ultimately, it was a chance to reinvent myself, I guess." He took a bite of something from his plate that I knew was raw fish, but it was so bubblegum pink it was difficult to imagine it tasted like anything other than cotton candy. "And in both the original and reinvented versions of myself, one thing remained the same." A wry chuckle caused his teal eyes to twinkle beneath his dark lashes, and for just a moment, my breath caught in my throat.

That's one way to say it. "My breath caught in my throat" sounds so much better than "I unexpectedly took an involuntary breath that, in a really bad stroke of luck, allowed a whiff of wasabi to shoot up my nose, caused my eyes to react as if I were Erica watching Nicole Kidman die in *Moulin Rouge*, and made me cough like I *was* Nicole Kidman dying in *Moulin Rouge*."

"You okay?" Jared asked. Henry didn't appear too concerned. His attention was once again devoted to his Hubba Bubba sushi.

I gave Jared a thumbs-up as I downed my glass of water. I felt like my Henry insight window was closing, and I needed to act quickly.

"What?" I choked out.

"What *what*?" Jared sought clarification, but of course I wasn't talking to him.

"What remained the same?" I dabbed at my eyes with my napkin—pausing quickly before I did to make sure there wasn't any wasabi on the cloth. "Old version versus new version?"

The teal eyes were on me again, but this time I wasn't taken off guard. His full lips twitching at one corner, as if he were contemplating whether or not a joke was worth telling, was slightly more unexpected, but I was able to put all my courtroom experience to good use and maintain my stoicism.

"Neither version is a fan of talking about himself."

"I'm with you there, man," Jared responded, seemingly unaware that Henry and I had been sharing a moment. And by sharing a moment, of course, I mean we may have been somewhat on the verge of his official acknowledgment of my existence. "McKenna's always been much more comfortable with that, so if you ask me, that's the perfect segue into her getting you caught up on the last twenty years of *her* life."

The earlier #sorrynotsorry had been replaced by a smug #yourewelcome. Bless him. My clueless brother-in-law actually believed he had just masterfully circumnavigated the awkwardness at the table and provided the perfect opportunity to break through a tension that I was certain Jared understood even less than I did.

Henry inhaled another noodle and pierced the soft-boiled egg yolk over his dish as he said, "Of course. I'm sorry. I never even asked. What's life like for you these days, McKenna? Married? Any kids?" There was weight in his tone and in his expression, but I didn't have a lot of time to try to figure out why before he continued. "I don't know why I started there. That was . . . well . . ." He shifted in his seat. "I don't know what that was. Forgive me."

Huh?

I scrunched up my nose and shrugged. "I think they were just questions, right? Is there some reason I should view the questions as inappropriate, or—"

"Not inappropriate, no. I certainly hope not." He tilted away from Jared and crossed his ankle over to rest on his knee. "They just weren't the right questions."

"I think they were pretty standard questions. I don't see—"

"She's a big-time lawyer in New York," Jared declared, no doubt trying to diffuse what he interpreted as conflict—and causing me to hold my breath as I waited to see if this was the moment when I had to reveal that my title of "big-time lawyer" currently had an ominous, big-time asterisk by it.

Ain't no party like a McKenna Keaton party, because a McKenna Keaton party is uncomfortable.

Henry pointed his finger toward Jared but didn't take his eyes off of me. "And that's all I meant. I should have started there. I've made a career out of unearthing the story behind the facts, but for some reason I just sought out new details that have nothing to do with the foundation of your story."

Our eyes remained locked for a few seconds, and I could sense Jared in my periphery bouncing his eyes back and forth between us, as if he were watching a match at Wimbledon. I leaned in as a waiter took away my half-eaten bowl of edamame that I'd pushed to the edge of the table and asked if we needed anything else.

"Just the check," Henry replied with a polite smile, and then his eyes followed the young man until he began speaking to another table.

"And what is the foundation of my story?"

Those dazzling eyes twinkled with delight as he scratched at the five o'clock shadow on his jawline. "Do you remember Melanie Chapman?"

I probably would have had a difficult time placing the name if it had been thrown at me in any context, but thrown at me out of the blue, when I was expecting something very different—even if I wasn't sure what that something different could have been—he might as well have said, "Do you remember Gobbledygook McGillicuddy?"

"Oh, sure," Jared answered. "Come on, McKenna. You remember Melanie." I shrugged and he continued. "Prom queen—"

"*Everything* queen," Henry contributed.

"—cheerleader, dated . . . oh, what was his name? Captain of the football team."

"Marcus Grant."

Jared slapped his booth-mate on the arm. "Yes. Marcus Grant."

It was my turn to be at Wimbledon, as they threw out casual memories about two people who clearly had never been awarded space in my brain. "Okay, what about her?"

Henry leaned in and rested his elbows on the table. "Well, Melanie was smart—"

"Was she?" Jared asked.

"Yeah. She was legitimately smart. I'd been in at least some class or other with her ever since kindergarten, and she'd always been smart. We were never friends, of course . . ." He trailed off and thought for a second, then corrected himself. "That's not true. In elementary school, I'd say we were friends. Maybe even a little bit into middle school. But then, you know . . . We didn't exactly run in the same circles, and my circles were decidedly less cool than Melanie's. I mean, I only ran around with people Melanie considered losers."

"Thank you for that," Jared enthused good-naturedly as he smiled and raised his glass.

"No problem, man." Henry remained straight-faced as he raised his own glass and clinked it against Jared's. "But sophomore year I noticed that her name was on the list of kids invited to join the National Honor Society, but she didn't join. And that bugged me. *Really* bugged me. Much more than it should have. And I felt like it was my duty to make it right. So even though we weren't friends anymore, and even though I knew she wouldn't even want to be seen talking to me, I marched up to her after chemistry one day and confronted her about it."

That was difficult for me to imagine. It was difficult for me to imagine teenaged Henry marching up to anyone about anything.

"What did you say?" Jared asked, nearly bouncing in his seat. To sweet, friends-with-everyone, glass-half-full, there's-no-reason-we-shouldn't-all-get-along Jared, this juicy gossip probably carried with it all the weight of other friend groups' revelations that the leader of their pack had been carted off to juvie.

Henry settled into the narrative but didn't relax his posture. He did begin turning his head as he spoke to include Jared in story time, for which I was grateful. It wasn't easy to pull away from eyes that focused entirely on you.

"I told her she was throwing her life away. I told her that she didn't understand how much things like National Honor Society made a difference on college applications, and that I knew how smart she was." The waiter returned to the table with the bill, and Henry handed him his credit card. "If she just applied herself a little more, she could end up at the top of the class." He must have somehow detected my silent, judgmental inner scoff, because with a smirk he added, "Not the very top, of course."

"And how did she reply to that?" I asked, even as I began envisioning the many humiliating ways it might have played out for the nerd who'd had the guts to confront the most popular girl at school.

"She told me she was only going to college to meet her future husband. Her dream was to marry a rich man and be a perfect wife." He shrugged as he grinned at the memory. "Of course, I instantly attacked Melanie's dream like the heartless cynic I was. I told her that she should demand better for herself and that we lived in a patriarchal society in which she'd been made to believe her best play was to stand by her man, but she had so much to offer the world . . ." He trailed off and rolled his eyes as he flipped his hand through the air. "On and on." Henry took one last sip of his drink, nodding as he drank, and simultaneously raising his wrist to check the time. I looked at my own watch in response and realized he was due back to his soiree in ten minutes.

"Good for you," I said, trying to picture it. But I just couldn't. Again, not the Henry I had known. "I get so frustrated when women think they have to settle—"

"See, that's the thing, McKenna." It was the first time he had said my name, apart from the first moment when he realized who I was, and it was somewhat jarring. His eyes were locked with mine again, and even as he told of his memories that seemed out of sync with my own, it was as if the walls of being strangers had finally been knocked down. "She wasn't settling. She wasn't settling *at all*. She knew exactly what she wanted, and every decision she made was carefully chosen based on a path she had lined out for herself. She had a plan."

He signed his credit card receipt, and then he and Jared gathered their things to leave. It all felt so abrupt. I'd been expecting him to say more about Melanie's plan. I still felt unbalanced from his utterance of my name, and when he pulled his eyes away, it was as if I'd lost the railing I'd been holding on to for support. But when Henry slid out of the booth and Jared followed, I had no choice but to put my shaky equilibrium to the test and slide out after them.

"Have a good night," Henry said to the hostess as we reached the exit. He held the door open for us, and Jared stepped aside to allow me to pass through first before following me out onto the sidewalk. Henry got caught holding the door for two ladies in their fifties or sixties—both of whom seemed to take a great deal of pleasure in passing through the door slowly and at the same time so at least one of them was forced to brush up against Henry at any given moment.

Once he was done with his duty, seemingly unfazed by all the flirting and ogling, he joined us in a makeshift circle in front of the door. Jared and I stared at him, waiting for him to finish his story, but he was in his own little world. He glanced down at his watch and then stared off into space so intently that Jared turned around to see what Henry was focusing on. But there was nothing apart from a parking garage and the intersection of North Mangum and East Chapel Hill Streets.

"Are you okay on time?" I asked.

"What?" He snapped back to reality and faced me. "Oh, yeah. We should get back just in time for Charles to tell us it's a new, modern day, et cetera, et cetera."

He really was a handsome guy. Henry, that is. Prince Charles wasn't exactly my cup of tea. Of course, I could never confess to anyone that I found Henry attractive. Well, I could say it to Erica if it ever came up. If I said it to Taylor, she would equate my finding him attractive to my being attracted to him. As if the ability of my brain to appreciate someone's square chin and strong jawline was inextricably linked to the heart's desire for love and the biological clock's desire not to wind down to inanimate silence like Cogsworth when the last rose petal fell in *Beauty and the Beast*. But the only ticking I heard was from the pedestrian signal at the crosswalk and the time bomb in my brain as I waited for him to get to the point.

"So . . . Melanie," I said. There was a passing moment of silence during which I wondered if he was just a bit of an airhead. If he had brought up Melanie—what was her name? Clarkson? Clampett?—for no good reason whatsoever, and now he'd completely forgotten we had actually been talking about me. The unmarried, childless, big-time lawyer from New York.

I should have known better than to ever suspect Henry Blumenthal was an airhead.

"Melanie." He muttered her name softly—nearly indecipherably—as he jammed his hands into his pockets and began walking back toward the Armory. Once again, he and Jared walked side by side, and I trailed slightly behind, but he spoke over his shoulder so as not to exclude me. That was progress.

He shrugged and exhaled. "I guess my point is that knowing all of that about Melanie—her hopes, her dreams, what she was working toward, what mattered to her, how determined she was to make it happen—I never would have gone up to her, if I saw her for the first time in twenty-whatever years, and asked, 'Have you started your own law firm yet?'" He shrugged again and then stopped so suddenly that I nearly bumped into him, and Jared got about six steps ahead before he realized we weren't with him. Before he could even make it back to us, Henry turned to face me, and I looked up into his eyes, and he whispered, "It's been a long time, McKenna, but I remember your hopes and dreams and what you were working toward. I remember what mattered to you, and I remember how determined you were to make it happen. I should have started with the foundation of *your* story, not Melanie's."

Equilibrium? What equilibrium?

Chapter 6

And that is why I believe the *monarchy is uniquely equipped to progress into the world as we know it today. It is, indeed, a new, modern day."*

"Wow! You're good," Jared enthused in a hushed tone as we opened the door to the Armory just in time for Prince Charles's words. "I don't think I know any movie that well. Not even *The Matrix.*"

Henry smiled. "If you'd spent months of your life in the editing room with *The Matrix*, you would."

He held the door and ushered us into a more discreet part of the venue than where we had been previously. This time Jared went through the door first, and I became the sixty-year-old lady lingering just a little longer than I should have as I passed by Henry. I'm going to say he smelled like teakwood. Mind you, I didn't actually have any idea what teakwood smelled like, but it sounded like a scent that was masculine and unpretentious and equally at home on safari or at the Palace of Versailles. It seemed right.

"Thank you," I said as I passed by him more closely than should have been comfortable.

"Sure thing," he responded.

Truth be told, "comfortable" wasn't how I would describe what I was feeling.

I was transfixed. Positively transfixed. *What in the world is happening?* I tried to scream inside my brain to jolt myself into action—because I was still standing there like a doofus, looking up at him, only about one foot of distance between us—but I didn't even recognize the scream. Even my internal call to action was floating around in jelly, just like all of my internal organs.

"Um . . . I've got about forty-five seconds to get in there."

Oh, crap. "Yeah!" I cleared my throat and tapped on my forehead. "Shoot. Yeah . . . I was going to say something, and for the life of me . . ." I lifted my shoulders up near my ears as I scratched the sides of my head in a motion that I thought, at first, would convey I was getting old and losing my mind but which I quickly realized communicated something more along the lines of the equally sexy, "I probably have head lice." "I'll think of it," I declared, still so close to him. "Sorry to hold you up." And then I thrust my hand in front of me.

He blinked about five times in a row and looked down at my hand and then back up to my eyes before putting his hand out and shaking mine.

"Please welcome our guest of honor, Peabody, Producers Guild, and two-time Emmy Award-winner—Durham's own—Hank Blume!"

I hadn't let go of his hand.

"I should—"

"For sure." It was sort of like when you're trying to straighten out plastic wrap and it keeps folding over and sticking to itself, but I did finally manage to let go. "Go, team!" I called out with enthusiasm as he squeezed past me—with one more confused and perhaps frightened glance my way.

It's fine, McKenna. I attempted to console myself. *You'll never see him again, so you don't have to worry about any of that. In fact, you'll never see any of these people ever again. They'll never come visit you in your igloo in Greenland. Yes. That's the best place for you now.*

"What in the world was that?" Jared asked me quietly as Henry took the stage on the other side of the room.

"I don't know," I muttered.

"Did you just say, 'Go, team!'?"

I buried my face in my hands and let out the frustrated groan of a hungry brown bear that has forgotten the combination to the locker where all the food is being kept. "We have to go." I pulled my hands away from my face and grabbed his bicep. "Come on."

He crossed his arms, planted his feet, and refused to budge. "Why would we go? Henry's just starting to speak—"

I glanced behind Jared up toward the stage where Henry was, in fact, being handed a microphone and speaking into it—though it was impossible to hear a word he was saying over the enthusiastic crowd. But his eyes were on me and the tug-of-war match I was losing against my brother-in-law. He tilted his head and smiled at me as he stopped speaking—again, who knows if he was actually saying anything anyway, but his mouth stopped moving—and he settled onto the stool that had been set on the stage for his question-and-answer session.

"Jared, we have to go," I implored, speaking through my teeth.

He smirked at me. "Does the unflappable McKenna Keaton have a crush on a boy?"

I could feel the heat rising up my neck, all the way to the tops of my ears. "You're insane. I'm just . . ." Time was running out. Any second, the crowd noise was going to die down, and anything I said in the ballroom would bounce off the walls. Any second, I wasn't going to be able to help myself, and I was going to look up at the stage again and probably see that Henry was still looking at me, and any second everyone else in the room would realize he was looking at me too. And then *they* would be looking at me. Any second, he was going to start speaking into the microphone, and his voice would actually be able to be heard, and I was pretty sure my gelatinous insides weren't going to be fortified in the face of that development.

Desperate times call for desperate measures.

"I need to deal with female issues, Jared."

I had never used that excuse in my entire life. I'd never called into work or said it was my reason for being late to a meeting—not that I had ever been late to a meeting, obviously—and never once had I gotten out of an awkward situation in which I had snapped at someone by mentioning anything about female issues. What in the world was happening to me? Quicker than you could say "teakwood," I had become an unacceptable caricature of who I had always sworn I would never be.

Having said that, it worked. The teasing, determined smirk on his face vanished, and he reached into his pocket and handed me his keys. "I'll get an Uber."

I snatched the key ring from his fingers and made it through the door just as Henry said, "Once again, Durham, you're too kind."

I didn't stop to think or breathe or process, and I certainly didn't stop long enough to wonder what he could possibly have said that was so funny I could still hear the laughter as I exited the Armory. I didn't stop at all until I was sitting in the driver's seat of the Piersons' Honda Pilot, adjusting everything so I could reach the pedals.

The past four days had been the worst of my life. I'd felt betrayed by a company I loved working for, dismissed by coworkers I believed should have known better, and my values system that kept me focused on the hard work and determination to succeed had been rocked to its very core. But in the face of all of that, my beloved brother-in-law had been the one to deliver perhaps the harshest blow of all.

The truth.

The unflappable McKenna Keaton had a major, *major* crush on a boy.

"I blame *Up Close & Personal*," Erica said to me thirty minutes later as we sat on Mom and Dad's couch.

Charlie's always-messy hair was splayed across Erica's lap, and she was combing her fingers through it in an attempt to get her rambunctious youngest child relaxed to the point that his eyes would betray him and close for a few minutes. A few minutes that, with any luck, wouldn't end until sunrise. He wiggled in resistance between us, so without a word I grabbed his stinky, socked boy feet and wrangled them up on to my lap. I applied just enough pressure that he couldn't bounce around as easily, and he shot me an expression of betrayal in response.

"The Robert Redford movie?" I asked. "I haven't thought about that movie in a million years."

"Well, think about it now. Actually, do you want to watch it now? I bet it's streaming somewhere."

I laughed. "No, I really don't. But I do want you to tell me what some depressing love story from the nineties has to do with my depressing evening out."

"Well, just think about it for a minute. Close your eyes." I raised my eyebrow at her, but she remained unrelenting. "Seriously, close your eyes."

I sighed and shook my head but did as I was told.

"Okay, picture the scene where Robert Redford goes back into the field—"

"Erica, I haven't seen that movie since high school."

"It doesn't matter. Picture it. I know it's there, in the deep recesses of your mind." She began talking in a softer, more monotone way that I figured probably meant my nephew was nearly asleep and she was sealing the deal. But I also wasn't completely sure she wasn't trying to hypnotize me into an *Up Close & Personal* trance.

I sighed again. "Okay. Let's see . . . I remember Michelle Pfeiffer got super successful, and Robert Redford's masculinity was threatened, so he had to remind the world that he was the man, with the manly job—"

"Good grief, McKenna." She laughed but still continued to talk in that weird, hypnotic way. Mom skills. Nothin' like 'em. "Can you put feminism on hold for just a minute and focus on the all-that-is-good-and-wonderful-in-this-world beauty of Robert Redford?"

"I'll try. But remind me why we're doing—"

"You're worse than my kids!" she exclaimed, and I felt Charlie's feet jerk around on my lap. I added a little extra pressure as she returned to monotone and guided his slumber with skills Joseph Gordon-Levitt could have put to use in *Inception*. "It's okay, baby. Mommy and Aunt McKenna didn't mean to be so loud. Go back to sleep."

And through it all, I kept my eyes closed because my big sister had told me to. I may have been as obstinate as her kids, but I defied any of them to be as much of a rule follower as I was.

"Now, where were we?" she asked, and I yawned. I couldn't help it. She had a gift.

"We were thinking about Robert Redford and setting women's rights back a generation or two."

"Ah. That's right. So Robert Redford wanted to go back to work as a reporter—*not*, in my opinion, because he was insecure in his masculinity but because his partner had inspired him to be the best version of himself—and so he left to go chase a story—"

"Is that when Celine Dion started singing?"

She just ignored me that time. "And then do you remember when Michelle Pfeiffer talked with him on the video feed when he was on assignment and she was in the studio?"

Sadly, I did. I hated to admit it, but I was able to picture it all very clearly. "I think I might have a vague recollection of that, yes."

I could hear the smile in her voice as she said. "Head-to-toe khaki. A little bit dirty even though we're used to seeing him in a suit. His hair is ruffled and just *so very Redford*. And of course—"

"The boots."

"Yeah. The boots."

The rest of the Keatons had always been movie people, and when I was forced to join them in the family room for movie night, I usually had something to read and a book light tucked beneath my legs at the ready. But, yeah . . . *Up Close & Personal*. That hadn't been a family movie. It had been an Erica-and-me movie. I had been, in retrospect, putting too much pressure on myself as I prepared for the SATs, and I'd begun having panic attacks. Not for the first time in my life, and not for the last, but that bout may have been the most severe. Up until then, the attacks had always been few and far between, brought on by things in my life that made me feel as if I didn't have any control, or made me fear I couldn't measure up.

High school, college, and law school presented endless possibilities for me to fear losing control and letting everyone down.

Erica took a week away from college, and Mom and Dad pulled me out of school for a couple days—which at first did nothing to lessen the panic, I assure you, but in the end helped a great deal. Erica's sole focus was to help me relax. Help me put some things into perspective. To help me remember to breathe. She dragged me to this kitschy retro movie theater in town that featured a different year in movies during the middle of the week. It may have been January 2002, but that week Erica and I spent most of our time in 1996. We watched everything they had showing, from *The Birdcage* to *All Dogs Go to Heaven 2* to *Down Periscope*. Remember *Down Periscope*? If not, count yourself lucky.

But it was *Up Close & Personal* that finally, at least for a couple hours, got my mind off of the expectations and stress that I always strapped onto myself like a Babybjörn filled with dumbbells. Erica and I spent an entire day with Pfeiffer and Redford, sitting through every showtime the theater had on that Tuesday, and each viewing—in which we were more often than not the only people in the theater—got more ridiculous as we quoted every line and sang along with Michelle's "The Impossible Dream" performance and tried to say things to each other in Stockard Channing's snarky tone.

So, yes, I could still see the khaki and the ruffled hair and the boots in my mind. I didn't have to try very hard at all to hear "Because You Loved Me" as I pictured the montage of Warren Justice and Tally Atwater flouncing around in the ocean and driving across the bridge in the morning. Pretty much every sense was engaged in the memory. Thinking about that popcorn made me salivate a bit as my taste buds recalled the mental association of nothing but popcorn, Pixy Stix, and warm Betty Buds for lunch and dinner. The scent was a little bit popcorn and a little bit CK One, which was the only perfume Erica ever wore in those days. (A unisex fragrance that smelled good on a man *and* a woman? It defied the laws of science!) I chuckled at the memory of the two of us debating what perfume Tally would wear. We had agreed she definitely wasn't hip enough to wear CK One. She would want to smell like the type of woman she was trying to be, so probably Passion or White Diamonds, or maybe something that came in the trial packages you got with purchases over a certain amount at the Elizabeth Arden counter. Warren was a different story, of course. He was a *man*. A mature adult. He knew who he was and had earned his stripes, and probably wore something like Givenchy Gentleman. Or maybe that wasn't rustic enough. He probably smelled like—

My eyes fluttered open and were greeted by the sight of her staring at me with an amused and satisfied expression on her face, and Charlie sound asleep between us.

"Teakwood," I whispered.

The satisfaction faded for a moment. "What?"

"I was just thinking about how Robert Redford smells—"

"A totally normal thing to do."

"—and the word that came to mind was *teakwood*."

Her eyes wandered off to the side as she thought about that.

"Yeah, I can see that. I'm not exactly sure what teakwood smells like, but it sounds super sexy."

"And earlier, I smelled Henry." Who was I kidding? I could *still* smell Henry, and it was mentally intoxicating enough to overpower even my nephew's feet. "I don't know what teakwood smells like, either, but Henry smells clean and woodsy and like a *man*. You know? Sort of like how we said Warren probably smelled in *Up Close & Personal* . . ." My voice trailed off, as did my thoughts. But then everything jolted back with a vengeance. "Hey! Is that what you meant? When you said you blamed *Up Close & Personal*? But I didn't even tell you about teakwood."

She gently lifted Charlie's head off of her lap and held it with one hand while she slipped one of the pillows from the couch underneath it with the other. Again, mom skills. I began to lift his feet and he stirred instantly, even though he hadn't even twitched during the repositioning of his head. I looked at Erica with panic in my eyes, and she took his feet while I slid out from underneath them and then returned them gently to the couch. He let out a sleepy, contented groan and fell back into his rhythmic breathing.

As she stretched her arms over her head and yawned, she said, "I just meant you have a type. And you've proven it here tonight."

I scoffed. "I don't have a type."

And I meant that. Not because I had a wide variety of tastes when it came to men, but because I hadn't just been trying to fool myself or anyone else with all of the declarations I had made through the years. Sure, there were men whom I found attractive for various reasons— because they were smart or funny or had beautiful eyes or smelled good—but crushes and infatuations weren't things I dealt with. I didn't have time. I didn't have the energy.

"You *do* have a type," she countered. She headed out of the living room, and I followed her. She leaned her ear toward Dad's study and listened for a moment.

"Are they still in there?" I whispered.

She nodded and rolled her eyes, and I followed her into the kitchen. "Dad's hit the jackpot with that little history nerd of mine. Cooper loves that genealogy stuff."

I reached into the fridge and grabbed us each a bottle of water. "I don't have a type, Erica. So maybe Robert Redford and Henry Blumenthal both have ruffled blond hair and skin tones that will look good in khaki and smell like what I imagine to be teakwood, but—"

She shook her head as she gulped down her water. "It's not that. Although . . . yeah. It's that. But like you said, you didn't tell me about teakwood. I just know you better than you know yourself, McKenna Keaton, and you have a type. Every so often you come across what you perceive to be the unattainable." I opened my mouth to protest—or maybe just ask her what in the world she was talking about—but she held up a finger and silenced me. "Not just any guy you can't have, of course. That used to be Taylor's type, not yours. Your type has to check all the boxes. He has to be brilliant. He has to be successful. He has to have a good personality and have his head screwed on right. He has to be fiercely independent and accept that *you* are fiercely independent. Not just accept it—he needs to celebrate that fact. And, yeah, he has to look like he fell out of *GQ*'s tribute to the Audubon Society or something. He has to, at least metaphorically, smell like teakwood. Of course, all any of that does is draw you in. That simply forms attraction, and you are far too sensible to be swayed by attraction. But when he checks all the boxes *and* he doesn't like you. Or he checks all the boxes *and* he's a loner. He checks all the boxes *and* he travels around the world and doesn't have time for a relationship . . . Well, then he's irresistible. Because you like knowing from the very beginning that it will never work. That way you don't even have to waste any time convincing yourself you don't care one way or another."

Once again, I opened my mouth to protest, and this time she didn't stop me. But nothing came out. I sensed I should be offended by what she had said, and I knew that if anyone besides Erica had said it, I would have been. But even then, I was torn between a feeling of *How dare you say those things about me?* and *So? What's wrong with that?* More than anything, I was finding myself stuck in *Is that true? Is that really how I think?* I shook my head, even though no one had heard my silent question. No. That much I could be sure of. I didn't *think* that way. I just wasn't sure if that ruled out that I *was* that way.

"I'm going to need examples."

"You mean *besides* Warren Justice and Henry Blumenthal?"

I nodded. "Yes."

"Okay, well, first of all . . . guy from work. Your boss."

If she had ever had the fortune to be exposed to the absurdity and very un-teakwoodness of Ralph Wallis or Ty Monroe, I would have made a joke, but it would have been lost.

"And yet with Jeremiah, I've never looked at him as unattainable."

She waved her hands in front of her and tilted her head back and forth as if to say, "Maybe, maybe not." "But that's only because you've engaged the long-term planning part of your brain. He's been an option on the table long enough to where you've been able to sort through it all, but you were only able to get to that point because he fit into the original attraction model."

"He doesn't wear khaki."

"But you said he rides the subway and takes off his jacket and tie after hours. That's the attorney equivalent of khaki."

The beam of headlights bouncing off the garage shone through the window over the kitchen sink as a car pulled into the driveway, and I felt a flood of emotions. Relief coursed through my veins, knowing that Jared was back and Erica and the kids would be leaving, and I wouldn't have to talk about any of this anymore. I could finally go to bed. I had been back in Durham for about eleven hours, and I'd somehow managed to survive it without a single cup of cappuccino-fudge coffee from Zabar's. Enough was enough already.

But I was also filled with dread, certain that Jared would bring news of how great the rest of the evening had been, and maybe even an anecdote or two about how Henry joked with the crowd about his crazy former classmate who had run out of the ballroom like a madwoman. A madwoman who—if you threw in Jared's explanation of events—was suffering from cramps.

"Hey." Erica placed her hand on top of mine on the kitchen table. "How long is Henry in town?"

I snapped out of my consternation. "I don't have any idea. Why?"

A smile crept across her face as she shrugged and feigned innocence. "Oh, I don't know. I mean . . . you're here . . . he's here . . . A man has to eat, and let's face it, you're probably going to be dying to get out of this house every so often . . ."

My eyes opened wide. "You think I should ask him out?"

She patted my hand and then stood with her water bottle and crossed to the other side of the kitchen to drop it into Mom and Dad's recycling bin. "All I'm saying is I understand why you don't have time to date—"

"It's not just that I don't have time," I interjected. "Though I *really* don't have time."

She held up her hand. "I know. I'm saying I understand. You don't have time. You don't have any desire. You have a million more important things going on. You don't want the distraction. Usually. I get it. I'm not judging you for that or doubting your convictions. I'm just saying that you are in town for a little while, you aren't allowed to work, your family is already driving you nuts, and there just so happens to be a handsome, brilliant, world-renowned documentarian who smells like teakwood and who has managed to capture just a little bit of your interest. Why not take the opportunity to do something different, just for a change of pace? For once, wouldn't a touch of distraction be a welcome thing?"

A date? I couldn't remember the last time I had been on a date. I mean, a real date. Anything more than asking some guy from my gym to accompany me to banquets and ceremonies or agreeing to be set up on blind double dates by colleagues whose help I needed on cases— and who were probably just seeking ways to get me to stop discussing legal strategy with them for a little while. (That never worked, by the way. Blind dates were a great opportunity to get a stranger's perspective. It was like sharing fondue with a jury.) But a real date?

There had been one time that I thought Jeremiah Burkhead asked me out, but when I walked into Balthazar in SoHo and he leaned over and whispered to me, "Okay, Brockovich, if you think you can handle taking on Wollensky, now's the time to prove it," I realized he had invited me to something so much better than a date. He'd invited me to a power lunch with Wallis, Monroe and Burkhead's fiercest rival, Anita Wollensky of Wollensky and Powers, who intimidated the snot out of all three of the big boys at W, M and B. (For the record, though it may not have been a date in the traditional sense, that was the most romantic thing that had ever happened to me, and if I'd had a girlfriend to chat with after I more than proved myself as a worthy opponent to Anita in front of Jeremiah, that's when I would have predicted, "I'm going to marry that man someday.")

"Besides," Erica added. "He's an old friend. If a date seems like too much, just ask an old friend to dinner."

"I'm not sure he views me as an old friend at all. I told you, he clearly does not remember me with the same fond nostalgia with which he remembers Jared." My face contorted into a grimace. "I mean, I guess I really wasn't as likable as he was . . ."

Erica scoffed. "Are you kidding? Don't give him that much credit. It's all about the Christmas cards."

"Anybody still up?" Jared asked as he entered through the front door of the house.

Erica's eyes widened, and she rushed out of the kitchen, undoubtedly to shush him before he woke up their youngest child.

"'Anybody still up?'" I repeated to myself with a chuckle. It was ten forty-five. Apparently Jared wasn't accustomed to the sort of nightlife he had experienced tonight. I got up from my chair and grabbed a rag from underneath the sink, dampened it, and began wiping off the countertop. I didn't get very far, however, before Erica was back in the kitchen beside me, staring at me with much wider eyes than she had left with.

"What's wrong?" I asked. "Did he wake up Charlie?"

"Henry's here," she whispered.

It didn't register, so I just echoed her words, at full volume. "Henry's here?"

"Shh!" She placed her open palm over my mouth and spoke through her teeth as she glanced behind her. "He drove Jared home. Oh, heavenly days, McKenna. You weren't kidding. That is one beautiful man in there." I raised my eyebrow and she quickly added, "There are two beautiful men in there, of course. No one's more handsome than my Jared. One's just a little less *orthodontist* than the other. That's all I'm saying. You've got to ask him out."

I tried to talk but her hand was still firmly planted against my lips, so I did the only thing a self-respecting little sister *could* do. I stuck my tongue out.

"Gross!" she grumbled as she reached out and wiped the palm of her hand on my shirt rather than her own. "How old are you?"

"How old are *you*?"

Ah. There was that old, legendary, witty Keaton repartee.

"McKenna, you understand I'm saying he's in the living room right now, don't you?"

There it was. It all clicked into place, and the words, which should have been perfectly clear before, began to mean something. I matched her bewildered expression, though mine may have been slightly more manic, and nodded.

"Got it," I whispered. "Okay, I'll just stay in here, and you can let me know when he—"

"No way! Now's your chance. Go talk to him."

Talk to him. About what? I mean, sure, there was actually tons of stuff I would love to talk to Hank Blume about. I was willing to chat at length about the subject of *any* of his documentaries. Every day was a good day for an in-depth tête-à-tête about the Grand Tetons or methemoglobinemia—that genetic condition that made a whole inbred family in Kentucky turn blue. But could I carry on a rational conversation with him about any of that if I had to look at him or, heaven forbid, smell him?

I scoffed and rubbed my hands roughly across my face, and as I did I felt like my sanity came rushing back to me. *Get hold of yourself.* I slapped myself on the cheeks a couple times as I coached myself back toward handling myself like the rational adult I was.

You're a little lost right now. That's all it is—and that's totally understandable. You're grappling for something to hold on to because everything feels so uncertain. You haven't lost your mind though. You haven't gone off the deep end. You don't "have a crush on a boy." There is a sexy, successful, sophisticated man whom you find attractive. Nothing wrong with that. But you'll be going back to New York soon, McKenna, and when you get back you'll be named senior partner. You won't have time to date. You certainly won't have time for a long-distance relationship. Where does he live again? I shook my head. *Nope. Doesn't matter.*

"You okay?" Erica asked, concern in her eyes.

I nodded once and pulled down on the stretched elastic waistline of my orange Princeton sweatshirt. That was when I sort of remembered what I was wearing but also couldn't quite recall, so I had to look down. The sweatshirt was fine. Old and tattered and not usually suitable for anyone without the last name Keaton or Pierson—or Boyd, I supposed, now that Jackson was part of the family. But Henry had shown up late at night—ten forty-five, that is—unannounced. It was okay that I was dressed for comfort. I wasn't trying to impress him, I reminded myself. No, my gray joggers weren't flattering, but that was for the best. Looking like an Ivy League hobo would keep me grounded in reality.

"I'm fine," I replied. And I meant it. I'd once walked out of a gusty hailstorm, in which I'd gotten a run in my pantyhose and a bit of tree branch stuck in my hair, and straight into an elevator with Ruth Bader Ginsburg. This was nothing.

Chapter 7

I took one more deep breath and let it out slowly, then followed Erica into the living room. My eyes went first to Charlie, still sound asleep on the couch, and then to Jared, who had his back to me as he and Erica stepped aside to greet each other with a quick kiss and a hushed check-in. Henry was nowhere in sight.

"Did he leave?" I asked with complete and total indifference. Or so I thought. Erica's quirked eyebrow made me wonder if I hadn't nailed it quite as much as I'd thought.

"Bathroom," Jared replied. He planted another kiss on Erica and then leaned up against the banister. "Where are April and Coop?"

"April and Mom are upstairs watching a movie, and Cooper's in with Sodie." *Sodie.* One of those ridiculous grandparent names that sticks because a kid can't pronounce a word properly. In my dad's case, it had been one-year-old April who had never quite latched on to "Pops," the name he had chosen for himself to go along with my mother's early-adopted "Nana." In an attempt to ingrain it in her little head, he had tried everything from singing "Lollipop" and "Pop Goes the Weasel" to reading Dr. Seuss's *Hop on Pop* ad nauseam. It was his experiment of making soda pop fizz and explode to April's amusement and delight that finally led to his grandfather name christening. He'd hated being called Sodie for about a minute, but all these years and two more grandkids later, I was pretty sure he would have had his birth certificate changed to say Sodie Keaton—which my mom always said sounded like an old-time baseball player—if he could have.

"Oh, that's perfect!" Jared declared with enthusiasm, though his volume remained at child-sleeping levels. "Your dad's working on ancestry stuff, I assume?"

"Always," Erica confirmed.

"Good. Henry's interested."

I cleared my throat. "Sorry, but what are you talking about? Henry's interested in . . . *what*, exactly?"

"The great and mighty Keaton oak tree."

Laughter burst from me, but Erica's scowl caused me to quickly lower the volume. "Sorry," I whispered. "But why in the world would he be interested in our dad's hobby?"

"You heard him," Jared responded. "He's knee-deep into all of this stuff right now for his next film."

"Yeah, I know. But the Keatons aren't exactly the Vanderbilts or the Rockefellers. There's nobody in our family tree anyone's even heard of . . ." My voice trailed off, and not just because I had a vague recollection of my dad once telling us we were about seven or eight times removed cousins of Clara Peller, aka the "Where's the beef?" lady. My eyes flashed up and met Erica's. "So, if he's not here to survey the mighty Keaton dogwood tree—"

"You *know* I said oak," Jared protested.

A knowing smile spread across my sister's face. "He's here to see you," she said almost silently, but between the distinct enunciation and the fact that we were on the exact same wavelength, I caught every word.

Jared, on the other hand, was surfing across a wavelength all his own. "Um . . . I don't think so actually. I mean, nothing personal. I don't think he'll be mad you're here or anything, but in the car I was telling him more about the family obsession, and he seemed genuinely interested."

I chortled at the thought. "Oh, *okay*. I'm sure the great Hank Blume—who, may I remind you, just got done premiering a film for which he apparently had admin access to the ancestry.com account of the house of Windsor—is *totally* interested in our ancestors, whose greatest claim to fame is as a pitchwoman for burgers in the eighties."

"Well, yes, actually," Henry said from behind me. "I am."

My heart began pounding in my chest, and I quickly assured myself that was just a result of my embarrassment at being caught talking about him. I turned to face him and felt my cheeks get warm at the sight. Again, simply because it was so embarrassing. It had absolutely nothing to do with the realization that I was seeing him in adequate lighting for the very first time. Nothing to do with noticing that his five o'clock shadow was mostly blond but had a surprising amount of gray mixed in there, considering every strand of that tousled, flaxen hair on his head looked like it belonged to a young cowboy who spent all his time in the sun.

I may have looked at him in silence for just a little too long. I wasn't entirely sure, but I thought that might have been what Erica was trying to communicate to me when she cleared her throat, crossed her arms, kicked her foot out in front of her, and looked as amused as I had ever seen her.

I wasn't singing "Because You Loved Me" in my head. You were!

"Is that alright?" Henry asked me with a tilt of his head. When I didn't answer in the very first second of silence, he added, "And for the record, the Windsors have to use ancestry.co.uk."

I was in trouble. I was in a whole lot of trouble.

"That's funny," I stated with a straight face, and the corner of his mouth tilted upward in response. "Will you excuse me for a moment?" I didn't wait for an answer but pulled Erica with me into the kitchen with an as-normal-as-I-could-make-myself-sound, "Can you help me with something?" Then I made the mistake of looking back at him to call out, "Won't be but a mo'!" and had only Erica's quick mom reflexes shoving me to the side to thank for keeping me from running into the wall.

"'A mo'?" She covered her mouth as the laughter began bubbling up in her and making its way out. "'Won't be but a mo'?"

I was not amused. I leaned my backside up against the kitchen counter, where my abandoned dishrag still lay, and grabbed on to the edge of the countertop with both hands. My pulse was racing, and the room was spinning, and—

"Good grief, why is it so hot in here?" I began fanning myself with one hand, but it didn't do any good. I reached across to the table and grabbed a place mat to give that a try, but it just flopped in my hands. I set it back down on the table and noticed I'd left behind a pool of moisture with it. I looked at my sweaty hands as if I were the girl in a movie who woke up covered in blood and had no idea why. I hurried over to the sink to wash them. "It's a thousand degrees! Aren't you dying?!"

"Hey, hey . . ." My sister's humor faded as she stood behind me and wrapped her arms around my shoulders. I kept running water over my hands, and she kept holding me. "It's okay, McKenna. You just need to take deep breaths."

Deep breaths, my booty! What I needed was an icebox to climb into.

"I'm not having a panic attack," I assured her. I didn't know what was happening, but it wasn't that. "It's just roughly the temperature of the surface of the sun in here." Without any thought as to how close she was standing behind me, I captured all the water my clasped hands could hold and splashed it onto my face.

Well, I splashed it onto *our* faces.

Okay, mostly hers. My aim had not been good.

"I'm so sorry!" I looked around for something to wipe her dripping face with and nearly reached for the cleaning cloth before I thought better of it. Instead, I grabbed a roll of paper towels, but it was a new roll that hadn't been started yet. My trembling fingers couldn't find the starting point. Frustrated, I just began dabbing her face with the roll.

"McKenna, stop!" she commanded, and I did as I was told. She took the roll of paper towels out of my hands and easily found the starting point—mom skills—and pulled off one rectangle. Once her face was mostly dry, with only a few beads still clinging to or dripping from her hairline, she set the paper towels back on the counter, reached over me to turn off the faucet, and then grabbed my shoulders. "What in the world is going on?"

I was ashamed to say the words aloud. It wasn't like earlier, when I first got home from the soiree and told her about the silly little ways I had been caught off guard by Henry and the way he made me feel. This time I thought I knew what I was getting myself into. This time I should have been prepared. This time I knew that control wasn't necessarily going to be the easiest thing to come by, but I really thought I had it nonetheless.

This time, no matter how ridiculous my actions, I didn't feel like a silly little girl with a silly little crush on a boy.

I took in all the air my lungs would hold and then released it as slowly and methodically as I could. *Just say it. You can say it to Erica. And then you can start dealing with it.*

"I think I really like him," I whispered quietly. Earnestly. It was as if I were exposing my deepest secrets and greatest flaws and begging for help, all in six words.

She stared at me. "Well, yeah. But what's going on?"

I gently shoved her away from me. "That *is* what's going on! I just revealed my soul to you—"

"By telling me something that's so obvious I could have already had the 'McKenna Loves Henry' T-shirts back from the screen-press place a half hour ago?"

I gasped and pointed my finger in her face. "I did *not* say 'love.'"

Who was I kidding? I shouldn't have even said "like." I didn't know if I liked him or not. I was charmed by him. Maybe even fascinated. If Erica wanted to make some shirts that said, "McKenna Is Intrigued by Henry," my protests would be without merit. But I needed to stop my thoughts from running away to anything more substantial or less irrefutable than that.

She wrapped my finger in her curled fist and brought it to her lips to kiss the tip of it. "I know. I didn't mean *love* love. I'm just saying you're attracted to this guy, McKenna. And trust me, it's not hard to see why. You *like* him. I think that's great."

"But I'm a blubbering idiot around him apparently. I don't *ever* get this way—"

"Well, of course you don't." She kissed my finger again and then released it. "What would be the fun of any of it if *every* guy made you feel this way?" She winked.

"But I can't even carry on a conversation with him."

"Oh, sure you can. It will be better now. Now you are acknowledging the situation, and you'll adjust accordingly."

That actually made sense. It was like that lunch with Jeremiah Burkhead and Anita Wollensky. Or the elevator with RBG. Sometimes in our lives things don't play out like we always envisioned they would. Sometimes we walk into situations—or elevators—that call everything we thought we knew about ourselves into question. In this case, I had just always assumed I wasn't capable of feeling those butterfly-type feelings that Taylor and an entire generation of Hallmark-movie addicts continually sought out and lived for. But the situation had changed—and, let's face it, it had only changed because I was experiencing a bit of an existential crisis. That was what it was. It was all temporary, but for the moment it was reality. As Erica said, I just needed to adjust accordingly.

I nodded and began breathing rhythmically without having to think about it so much. "You're right. You're absolutely right. There's a lot happening in my life right now, and I'm a little off-kilter. But like you said earlier, I typically wouldn't have even had time to give Henry or any guy as much thought as I have in the last few hours. *Normal* has new meaning right now." I leaned forward and kissed her on the cheek. "And I just need to adjust."

"Hey," Taylor said as she entered the kitchen, chomping on a handful of cashews. "Did you guys know Hank Blume is here?"

Erica winked at me again and then turned to Taylor. "Yes. He *claims* he's interested in Dad's genealogy project, but *really*—ouch!"

She looked at me in shock in response to the swift kick I had given her shin. It wasn't like I'd kicked hard enough to actually hurt her, so the *ouch* was a bit dramatic.

My brow furrowed and my lips tightened as I silently implored Erica not to open up that can of worms with Taylor. The last thing I needed as I attempted to adjust to my new and temporary reality— and as I considered possibly even giving in to all the ridiculous feelings of twitterpation I was experiencing—was my little sister's romanticism, enthusiasm, and general need for involvement.

Erica accepted my kick of warning and remained silent—though the daggers her eyes were shooting at me indicated we would have words later.

Taylor, meanwhile, picked up another cashew from the palm of her hand and popped it in her mouth. "Really *what*?" She looked from Erica to me and back again, but we said nothing. Taylor chewed on her cashews and shrugged. "I think you should go out with him, Kenna. He's super hot."

"I know!" Erica enthused. "I was telling McKenna he reminds me of Robert Redford in *Up Close & Personal*."

"I was getting more of a Tom Hardy in *Mad Max: Fury Road* vibe."

I think there's a Chinese proverb that says, "One generation plants a tree so the next can sit in the shade," or something like that. Sometimes it seemed like Taylor walked around with an ax and a bottle of sunscreen.

"I think we can all acknowledge he's a decent-looking guy." Erica showed great restraint by biting her lip and not unleashing the laughter that I'm sure she wanted to fling in my direction in response to my measured understatement. I ignored her and continued. "But he's not here looking for a date. He's just interested in genealogy stuff for a film he's doing, and—"

"Oh, *that's* why he's in there with Dad," Taylor said, again with a mouthful of cashews.

As has been well established by now, I never had the traditional dating life that many teenagers have. At no point when a boy picked me up for a date did I feel nervous about introducing him to my parents. I suppose you could say I wasn't concerned about whether or not they would approve, but that wasn't it, really. Although I really wasn't too concerned. After all, if at any point my parents had disapproved of one of my boyfriends, it would have been simple enough to move on. My only experiences introducing boys to parents had been simple and drama free.

I wasn't accustomed to the nervousness I was feeling knowing that Henry was in there making a first impression on my dad. And that my dad was in there making a first impression on Henry. And yes, it did occur to me that Henry and I had barely even had time to make a first impression on each other and that I had no idea whatsoever what his first impression of me had been. I mean, obviously, I was the crazy girl who'd said, "Go, team!" But that had, hopefully, fallen into the second-impression category.

"We've got to get in there," I stated calmly—because I was normal again, apart from the various kissing-in-the-rain and having-tea-with-William-and-Kate fantasies rushing through my mind. I took the first few steps toward Dad's study.

"Hang on," Taylor trilled as I passed. "Do you *like* him?"

I spun on my heel and glared at her with as much indifference as one could communicate with a glare. "What are you talking about?"

"You do!" she exclaimed in a high-pitched voice I was pretty sure dogs could hear.

"I seriously don't even know what you're—"

"You're blushing!"

Now *that* was just ridiculous. "I am *not* blushing. It's just warm in here."

I looked to Erica for assistance, but the traitor replied, "It's really not."

"Good for you," Taylor said. And then she grabbed my hands in hers and repeated, "Good for you." Her eyes widened. "Ooh! Kenna, you have to bring him to the party this weekend! That could be your way in, actually."

"My 'way in'?"

It was ridiculous. It was insane. It was comical and absurd and every other word I could think of that would communicate how much I felt like I was watching an episode of *Gilmore Girls* rather than experiencing a real thing in my real life. And I would have liked to have told them that. The only problem was that the engagement party that, to be perfectly honest, I kept forgetting about had just become so much more appealing in my mind. If Henry was there, maybe I could be freed from endless conversations with other people's friends and my distant relatives—most of whom I probably wouldn't recognize unless they were wearing name tags that also showed pictures of what they had looked like at the family reunion in 1999—in which they asked when I was finally going to settle down. Instead, I'd walk around with Henry and talk about the rainforest crisis and politics—from the fact-based perspectives of a documentarian and a lawyer, so it would never get heated—and the revitalization of Route 66. And since the party was still almost a week out, maybe we would have a couple of inside jokes by then.

He'd wink at me when my grandmother commented on my hair, because I would have told him, the first time he commented on how he loved the way my mostly chestnut locks revealed some completely black hues in certain light, that I had been born with a head full of black, wavy hair—and my dad's mom had been convinced they'd mixed up babies at the hospital.

He'd grab my hand protectively when my uncle Marshall made some remark about how it was up to Taylor and Jackson to give my parents more grandchildren, since Erica and Jared had already done their part and they'd given up hope of getting any out of me a long time ago.

I swallowed down the lump in my throat. It was a lump I didn't even understand. After all, I didn't need an advocate. I didn't need a protector. I certainly didn't *need* to have a man by my side in *any* situation—especially to appease my family.

"Yes, your way in," Taylor answered. "With Henry. Invite him to the party. Tell him you need a date—"

I threw my hands up in the air. "Oh, my gosh, Tay! No! Do you know me at *all*? There's no way I would ever lower myself to cozying up to a man because I don't want to go to a party alone. I'm *fine* with going to your party or *any* party alone. I do it all the time! And when I do, I'm not some loner or wallflower, waiting like—what's-her-face in *Emma* . . . Harriet what's-her-name—waiting for Mr. Knightley to take pity on me and ask me to dance. I'm alone when I want to be, *because* I want to be. And the fact that you think I would use some guy just so I didn't have to face the scorn of walking in alone is an insult—to him and to me. Seriously, you should know better."

Taylor's eyes were all glistening pupils—which sort of made her look like a beautiful anime drawing—and I instantly wished I could suck all of my impulsive words back in. Not that I didn't stand behind them. I did.

Well, I *did* until Erica cleared her throat, began gently rubbing Taylor's arm, and looked at me scornfully.

"That was all very uncalled for, McKenna."

I chewed on my lip and grumbled, "Sorry."

"I wasn't trying to say anything like that," Taylor whimpered. "I didn't mean it that way at all. I don't think you need a man. I just thought that maybe you and Henry—"

"Yeah . . . sorry."

"Hey, Tay," Erica said sweetly. "Why don't you go on in there? I want to talk to McKenna for a minute. We'll be right in."

I couldn't help but wonder how many times April, Cooper, and Charlie had each felt a shiver down their spine at their mother's declaration that she wanted to speak to them alone. I'd have to remember to tell them that the dread that accompanied the declaration would not diminish as they got older.

As soon as Taylor left the kitchen, I launched my defense. "Look, I'm sorry. You heard me tell her I'm sorry, and I will again. I just don't have any patience for that sort of thing, you know? You don't know what it's like being single at my age—and of course *she* doesn't even know what it's like to be my age at all. Or single. Has she ever gone *anywhere* alone? So, yes, I overreacted. But I stand behind what I said. I don't need a 'way in' to dupe some guy into going out with me just so I have a date for a party—"

"Except that's *always* been your MO, right?"

I scoffed. "What are you talking about?" But even as I asked the question, realization flooded through me, and I knew exactly what she was talking about. "That's different. That was high school. Sure, I wanted to have dates to high school dances. But not because I . . . I mean, it was *high school*! That's a very different scenario than being a thirty-eight-year-old woman who—"

"She was just trying to help. And the fact is I was just now telling you you should ask him out, and you didn't jump down *my* throat."

"I know." I sighed. "But you get me. You understand that I'm not looking for a love story, while Taylor seems to believe that's the only story worth telling. She doesn't know me, Erica."

"And whose fault is that?"

She and I stared at each other in uncomfortable silence—Erica refusing to back down from her assertion, me finally reaching a point in the impossibly long day where my brain couldn't process at full speed—until seven-year-old Cooper came running into the kitchen.

"Aunt McKenna!" The panic-stricken look on his face startled us both out of our showdown and even kept his mother from asking him to keep it down. He grabbed my hand and began pulling me toward Dad's study. "You have to come in here!"

"What is it, bud? Your brother's asleep in the living room, so—"

"You have to get married!" he exclaimed.

Oh, good grief, Taylor! Was she really so shameless as to draw our sweet nephew into her matchmaking machinations? I rolled my eyes in Erica's direction and then bent over a little (But not much. What were Jared and Erica feeding these kids?) so I could look him straight in the eyes as I said, "Hey, Coop, listen . . . Whatever Aunt Taylor told you—"

"It wasn't Aunt Taylor." He shook his head vehemently. "It was that man."

Presumably, he didn't refer to his father, his grandfather, or his future Uncle Jackson—was he here?—as "that man."

I cleared my throat, but that did nothing to negate the sensation that came from all of the blood fleeing my brain like cars cramming onto the Brooklyn Bridge for the mass exodus to the Hamptons every weekend. "Henry—" That came out very much sounding like a lawn-mower, and I instinctively reached out my hand. Erica—I'm guessing every bit as instinctively—placed my bottle of water in my palm. I gulped down as much as I could and then tried again. "Um . . . Mr. Blumenthal said I needed to get married?"

"Well, no, he didn't say that *you* have to . . ."

Seriously, kid? What kind of game are we playing here?

"He just said that if women don't get married and have kids before they're forty, bad things can happen—"

"Cooper . . ." There was a tone of warning in Erica's voice. "I don't know why you're saying all of this, but Aunt McKenna doesn't need to get married. No woman needs to get married or have kids unless she wants to. And Aunt McKenna doesn't want to."

"But, Mom . . ." His concern was palpable as his darting eyes looked from his mother to me and back again. Then he spoke in a voice just above a whisper and told Erica, "That man said—"

"Cooper, don't you worry, bud. I'll take care of 'that man.'" I could feel the support of generations of legendary unmarried women coursing through my veins as I attempted to straighten my unstraightenable sweatshirt. Women like Elizabeth I and Susan B. Anthony. Clara Barton and Louisa May Alcott. Mindy Kaling. What was it with people? First Taylor and now Henry? I expected it from my little sister, but *him*? After all that stuff about Melanie what's-her-face and *She Dreams of America*? After all of that, was he really just like everyone else?

I took one last swig of water and then set the bottle down with force and marched into my dad's study. All eyes were on me as I stormed into the room. Dad, Taylor, and Henry had all looked up at me with smiles on their faces, but Dad's and Taylor's had faded instantly.

Henry didn't know me well enough.

Right then, as I stood across my dad's drafting table from Henry and looked up into his surprised face, my attraction to him was not an issue. I wasn't thinking about going to parties with him or kissing him or even having intelligent conversations with him on a variety of fascinating subject matters. I was simply looking for answers. I actually felt like myself for the first time since I'd walked into the boardroom at Wallis, Monroe and Burkhead.

And if Henry had been on the witness stand, I would have known that my case was won.

Chapter 8

You told my nephew that women need to get married and have kids before they turn forty?"

"Um . . . no. No! Definitely not!" Henry's eyes darted around the room for assistance, but my dad and Taylor were finding all sorts of fascinating things to look at in books, on walls, on their fingernails . . . You name it. Erica and Cooper had followed me in and were standing by the door, Erica's arms wrapped lovingly around her concerned son from behind.

"Yes, you did!" Cooper protested. "You said that bad things happen if they don't."

Henry's face softened, and he released a breath. "Okay. I mean . . . Well, *yeah*, I guess I see, now that I think about it, how he may have gotten that from what I said. But that certainly wasn't—"

"Tell him," I instructed. "You can try to explain to me in a minute, but first would you please tell him that bad things are not going to happen, and his aunt does not, in fact, have an expiration date?"

His brows rose, and he nodded swiftly, then hurried over to Cooper. "Hey, pal, I'm so sorry if what I said freaked you out."

"It didn't freak me out," Cooper responded, desperately trying to prove he was grown up and didn't get freaked out over things,

I think. But even if I was a bit of an absentee aunt at times, the kid loved me. He'd always loved me, and I adored him. The thought of bad things happening to me did, actually, freak him out a little. And while I would never wish that concern on him, it was more than a little reassuring to know our bond still existed.

"Well, it would have freaked *me* out if I were you, I think, so you must not get freaked out as easily as I do."

Henry looked around the room, and now all previously avoiding eyes were on him. When his attention landed on me, one corner of his mouth rose slightly, and he shrugged. He lingered there just a little longer than was comfortable—probably waiting for me to return the grin—but I wasn't ready to smile at him. Not yet. He needed to finish making things right with Cooper, and then we'd see if he had a good enough explanation to make things right with me.

His focus snapped back to the seven-year-old in front of him. He gently punched him on the shoulder and said, "I make documentaries. Do you know what documentaries are?"

Cooper shrugged. "Like movies about real life?"

Henry's half smile spread across the rest of his face . . . all the way to his eyes. "That's good. Yeah, exactly. It's my job to find things in history that maybe no one else is really thinking about. We all know so much about Abraham Lincoln, for instance. Cooper, tell me three things you know about Abraham Lincoln."

Cooper looked up at his mom questioningly, and she smiled. Actually, I think she melted a little in the process. Or so I gathered by the twinkle in her eye as she quickly looked at me before returning her attention to her son. Her US history-teaching heart had been captured easily, and all thoughts of apparent predictions of her sister's impending doom seemed to be forgotten.

"Well, go ahead," she urged Cooper.

"He was shot in a theater."

Henry nodded. "Good. That's one."

"He helped end slavery."

"That's two. Do you have one more?"

"He was a lawyer like Aunt McKenna."

"Excellent!" Henry enthused. "Those are all great and really important facts about Abraham Lincoln. So if I were going to make a documentary about him, can you guess what I might focus on the most?"

Cooper shrugged. "Getting shot?"

Henry seemed to consider the suggestion for a moment, but then he shook his head. "Nah. That's so important and so interesting, but a lot of people already talk about that. I like to notice the things no one else really notices, and *that's* what I like to tell stories about."

"So what would you say?"

Cooper was rapt, completely caught up in all Henry was saying now. The entire room was. Myself included, though I was loath to admit it.

"I think I'd talk about what a good wrestler he was."

Cooper cackled in pure delight, like he'd opened a box on Christmas morning and found a puppy. "No, he wasn't!" he choked out through the giggles.

The whole room was giggling, actually. Well, I wasn't. I'd never been a giggler. But I couldn't deny that Cooper's chuckling made everything else matter a little bit less. At least for the moment.

Henry scoffed. "He was too." He held up three conjoined fingers and said, "Scout's honor. He wrestled something like three hundred matches in his life, and as far as anyone can tell, he only lost one of them. Ever. And I think that's fascinating, you know? We always picture him as unhealthy and kind of weak. Physically, I mean. At least I do."

"I do too," Cooper agreed. "He was super tall and skinny."

"Exactly! So, picturing him pinning 299 guys to the mat just blows my mind and makes me want to learn more. Those are the sorts of things I'm always looking for." His voice grew quieter as he leaned in a bit closer to Cooper, having expertly earned his trust, so he could say what he needed to say. "I saw something interesting in your grandfather's family tree—"

"It's my family tree too."

The smile reappeared on Henry's face. "You're right. It is. And there is some really fascinating stuff there. And that just makes me want to learn more. I was just looking for things in the family history that maybe other people wouldn't notice. But it's just that." He squeezed Cooper's shoulder. "History. Finding something interesting in your family's history doesn't determine your aunt McKenna's future any more than finding out Abraham Lincoln was a good wrestler changes the role he played in helping to end slavery. Okay? I'm sorry if I worried you into thinking anything different."

Jared walked into the room with his car keys in his hand. "Piersons, it's time to go." He looked around and seemed to sense the gravity in the room. "What's going on?"

"Oh, it's nothing," Erica answered as she kissed the top of Cooper's head. "Coop, go upstairs and tell April we're leaving."

"Did you know Abraham Lincoln was a wrestler?" Cooper asked his dad as he passed.

Henry stood from the slouched posture he had adopted to talk to Cooper on his level and smiled at Jared. "It's true." He turned and faced my dad, holding out his hand as he crossed the room. "I should be taking off too. Thanks again, Mr. Keaton."

"None of that, now." My dad shook Henry's hand. "Call me Scott. And you're welcome anytime. I'll be thrilled if you uncover anything interesting."

Henry held up a notebook in which he'd presumably been taking notes and then stuffed it into his back pocket. "I'll be thrilled too. I'll be in touch."

Taylor caught my eye—not sure whether it was the continual

"ahem" noises she was making or the "subtle" way she was waving at me just outside of Henry's peripheral line of sight—and once I looked at her, I knew she was encouraging me to stop him from leaving.

Ugh! Why did she have to do that? I hadn't gotten an adequate explanation from Henry yet, so of *course* I wasn't going to let him leave so easily. But my desire to keep Henry around a little longer was now going round for round with my desire not to give in to my meddling sister's matchmaking ploys. It was like a battle between John Cena and Abraham Lincoln, and it was anyone's guess as to who was going to win the three-count.

Henry offered me a small wave and apologetic smile and turned to follow Jared out, and then my words came flying out as if they'd been thrown from the ring by Honest Abe himself.

"I think you still owe me an explanation."

He stopped walking and looked over his shoulder. "You mean about all the horrible things that are going to happen to you if you don't get married in the next year or so?"

My dad stepped in in my defense. "Now, McKenna, that wasn't actually what he said."

Oh, my mistake. My dad stepped in in *Henry's* defense.

"Dad, let's go tell the kids bye." Taylor began pulling on him. "And you may need to wake Mom up so she can go to bed."

Then suddenly everyone was gone. Henry had been turned away from me, but the moment we were alone, he faced me again.

"So . . . lay it on me. How bad is it, Doctor?"

He chuckled. "Actually, your prognosis is excellent." His face fell. "I mean, because there's nothing to worry about and I don't know what I'm talking about. Not because I think you should get married or anything. I wasn't suggesting that was the way to save yourself."

"Glad to hear it. So, are you going to fill me in? How did we get from the Keaton family tree to an assault on women's rights?"

His eyes widened as his jaw dropped. "Hold on. *That's* what he thought I was saying? No! I didn't . . . I mean . . ." He slapped himself on the forehead. "Okay, I see it now. I see how Cooper could have gotten that out of what I said, but I never said women have to get married. I just said *Keaton* women have to get married." I watched his throat constrict as he swallowed incessantly. "No! Sorry, that's not what I mean. They—you—don't *have* to."

His uncomfortable rambling was slowly but surely making me feel so much better about the whole "Go, team!" debacle.

"Sorry." His face contorted. "I promise I didn't have my Ouija board out or anything. It really was just a trend I noticed in the gene-alogy." We stared at each other with anticipation bubbling between us until I realized he was waiting for permission to continue.

"Well, don't leave me in suspense."

And then he shifted into gear. The uncertainty crumbled into big chunks as he walked back around to the other side of my dad's table, where he had been standing when I first confronted him. "Your dad has done great work here. Really phenomenal. A lot of this stuff that he has found is better than the professionals can do on *Find Your Roots*."

Gorgeous, brilliant, fascinating, could pull off khaki, *and* he loved PBS. I couldn't miss the shift happening in my brain—from full-on attack to hoping he could explain his way out of all of this and we could move on. To what, I had no idea. But even if it was just having someone to watch *Antiques Roadshow* with, life could be on an upswing.

"He's never done anything halfway in his life. That's for sure." I ran my fingers across the printouts of immigration records stacked beside the notebook Henry was flipping through. "When we were kids, he used to tell us that research was the great American pastime. So you add it all together, and I guess you get *this*." I gestured to the stacks and stacks of documents and books.

He smiled. "So many Americans out there, wasting their time on baseball. I'm glad to see your dad knows what's what."

I smiled back at him. It was strange. Have you ever watched a movie in which an actor played a real-life celebrity you were really familiar with—like Jamie Foxx as Ray Charles or Tom Hanks as Mr. Rogers or Meryl Streep as Julia Child—and by the end of the film, it wasn't so much that you couldn't remember what the celebrity actually looked like as it was you were pretty sure they looked exactly like the actor who was portraying them? So much so that the next time you saw the real Mr. Rogers, you thought he looked weird and you weren't sure it was really him? That's how I was beginning to feel about Hank Blume's portrayal of Henry Blumenthal. The more I looked at him, the more I really couldn't even remember the way teenaged Henry had looked. All I could see was the ruggedly handsome, fascinating, well-dressed, confident-in-a-crowd man in front of me, and I couldn't help but be somewhat disappointed in myself for failing to recognize, when we were sitting next to each other in calculus, that he would someday turn into *this*.

"So, it started with Marilla," he said, returning his focus to the documents.

"Who's Marilla?"

He pointed to one of the branches on the tree. "Marilla Frances Keaton. Born 1781."

I shrugged. "Okay. And how did we get from Marilla's name on a line to me only having until I'm forty to get married or . . . what? I just lose all my chances?"

He raised his eyes to my face and began chewing on his bottom lip—in an attempt to prevent an ill-timed smile, I was pretty sure. "Well, you could say that."

He kept looking at me. And, if I wasn't mistaken, his eyes kept wandering to my lips. Not that I was watching his eyes all that much right then. I was sort of obsessed with *his* lips and the way they were being manipulated between his teeth. I cleared my throat. "Look, it's been a super long day . . ."

"Yeah, sorry." He shifted his body back toward the desk. "So . . . Marilla. She died when she was thirty-nine."

"Okay."

"Now look at this." He handed me the chart my dad had filled in over the course of who knows how many hours of research. Countless. Ending for now with April, Cooper, and Charlie and going all the way back to a George Keaton born in 1613. "Look at every generation, and see if you notice a pattern."

I did as I was instructed and began scanning the document. Some of the writing was so small that I had to squint, and at one point Henry pulled out his phone and shone the flashlight to assist me. But apart from my family's unfortunate fondness for naming Keaton men Beardsley, nothing really stood out.

"Maybe I don't know what I'm looking for."

"Okay, I'll give you a hint. Look at the branches that end where they are. No marriage and no kids. See if you detect a pattern there—"

"Or you could just tell me."

"I could. But what's the fun in that?"

"Well, maybe we have different definitions of fun."

He sighed. "Maybe we do. I've just always thought it was more fun to unearth for oneself the mysteries behind one's own doom." He elbowed me in the arm, and I laughed. I couldn't help it. "Do you really want me to tell you?"

Maybe there wasn't anything about the way the current, studly Henry conducted himself or looked that really reminded me of the nerdy Henry I had once known, but when it came to the moment of deciding whether or not to admit defeat to him, well . . . that was strangely familiar. And just like all those years ago, there was no way I was going to give in so easily.

"No," I answered, then began looking over the document again. "Give me another minute."

Focus, McKenna. He was in here with Dad and Taylor for all of five minutes, so it can't be that hard. Although, again, he was trained to seek out the great wrestlers in a field of Great Emancipators. *But you're no slouch in that department, either,* I reminded myself. How many cases had I won by unearthing the one detail no one else had thought of? He couldn't have been guilty of breaking and entering through a second-story window because he'd run out of refills for his vertigo medication. She couldn't have pulled *that* knife out of *that* drawer because she was left-handed.

I rubbed my eyes with my fist and then set about looking at my family tree with new eyes. Not the eyes of a skeptical family member but the eyes of a brilliant attorney.

Birth. Death. Marriage. Beardsley. Children. County registry. More Beardsley. More marriage. *Oh, wait.* He said I needed to look where there was no marriage. Marilla. Born 1781. Died 1820. No husband. No children. Same as Pippy. "Pippy?" I muttered aloud, and Henry chuckled. Pippy Lenora Keaton. No husband. No children. Born 1833. Died 1869. And then there was Wilda. Margaret. Beatrice. No husband for any of them. No children. Born in the late 1600s. Early 1700s. Mid 1900s. And died . . .

I snatched Henry's phone out of his hand and shone the light so I could see my dad's handwriting more clearly.

"Not a single one of them lived until they were forty."

"Yes!" Henry clapped once, much too loudly, much too close to my ear, and then apologized. His enthusiasm probably would have been contagious if I hadn't been envisioning my dad writing in the date of death under McKenna Rae Keaton's dead-end branch.

Well, no wonder Cooper had thought I needed to get married. Sure, it was ridiculous. Sure, it was just an anomaly. But the more I looked through the data for each generation, the more the facts had to be acknowledged. Five centuries were represented in my dad's work. And let me tell you, the Keatons were a fertile bunch from the looks of it. Generation after generation grew and expanded and spread throughout England, Scotland, Canada, the United States. New York, Ohio, Virginia, Louisiana, Delaware, North Carolina. And throughout that staggering history of one family, each and every generation boasted at least one female who died before the age of forty. Never the daughter who got married. Never the daughter who produced the next generation.

"Are you okay?" Henry asked. "You look . . . Well, your coloring doesn't look great right now. Do you need to sit down?" I nodded slowly, and he pulled up my dad's stool and placed it behind me and then assisted me onto it. "McKenna. You're not *worried* about this, are you? I meant what I told Cooper. It's interesting history. That's all. You know that." He leaned his face down and looked at me head-on. "You know that, right?"

Did I know that? That was the question he was asking, right? He was asking me if I knew that what had happened in the past had absolutely nothing to do with my future. Well, sure. There was a part of me that knew that. But *all* of me knew that Churchill or Kennedy or somebody had once said something about how if we ignored history, we were destined to repeat it. So where was the rational line between those two things? Of *course* there was no reason to think that something catastrophic was going to happen in the next twenty months simply because I was unmarried and childless. But . . .

"Do I have to do both?" I asked out of the blue.

"Do both what?"

"Be married *and* have kids?"

"McKenna, come on. You know you don't have to do either."

I nodded. "Sure, sure. I'm just asking, did any of the dead ones get married but not have kids, or vice versa?"

"Almost everyone on here is one of the dead ones now, so . . ."

I looked up at him, unamused, and the smile dropped from his face.

He shook his head. "No. The 'dead ones,' as we're so delicately referring to them, were never married *and* never had kids. It appears that many women who did one or the other went on to live long lives." He exhaled and ran his hand through his hair, and the clean, masculine scent of his shampoo wafting into the air beside me was *almost* enough to distract me from the Grim Reaper swiping through single ladies like he was on Tinder.

Henry looked around the room until he spotted another stool in the corner and then pulled it over and sat down beside me.

"You know this is ludicrous."

"Of course," I replied with a nod as I stared into space and began biting my nails for the first time since second grade. And that hadn't been an easy habit to break. My mom had ultimately used nail polish and glitter. (And I'm not talking about the nail polish we have now with glitter *in* it. No, this was sprinkling mountains of glitter from the craft store onto still-wet nails. Every time my fingers made it to my mouth, I ended up looking like I'd been eating an art project created by Drew Barrymore in *Ever After*.)

"No, I'm serious, McKenna," he insisted. He placed his hand on my knee in a way that I know was meant to be casual and support-ive. He didn't *intend* to set my skin on fire. "I never should have said anything. This is just . . . interesting. That's all it is. It's not like any of these women died *because* they weren't married or *because* they didn't have children." He patted my knee twice, and then his hand moved to my dad's desk in front of us. And I caught myself involuntarily looking down at my jogger pants to see if a hand-shaped hole had been burned through them. "For instance, tell me about your dad's sister. Your aunt . . ." He scanned the family tree and looked back at me. "Lindsey. Born 1957, died 1989. Do you remember her?"

"A little."

"And how did she die?"

For one twisted moment I really wanted to tell him that she had been poisoned by a spurned lover after turning down his proposal and telling him she had been barren from birth, but I thought better of it. Primarily because the little bit I remembered about my aunt Lindsey was how much my dad adored his little sister and how heartbroken he had been when he lost her.

"Car accident. She was hit head-on by a drunk driver."

Compassion overtook his eyes at the thought of the senseless death of a woman he had never met, gone for more than thirty years. "Horrible and tragic. But not, in any way, the result of her being single."

I knew he was right. I mean, *obviously* he was right. It was absurd, really. A strange, unexplainable coincidence that had nothing to do with me unless I allowed it to suck me in and make me neurotic. In which case, it would probably play out like some movie where I actually made a prediction come true by fighting against it. So why did I already feel like the battle had gotten the better of me?

"Yeah."

Compassion was still evident in his dazzling teal eyes—though, let's face it, one man's compassion is another man's pity—and I found myself wanting to confide in him. To tell him that I knew it was ludicrous and that despite what perhaps appeared to be the case, it wasn't really that I was taking any of it seriously at all. At least not any of the face-value stuff. Not the family tree and not the fact that I was thirty-eight and single. It was bigger than that. Heavier. And as someone who had known the path I wanted to take in life since the age when my peers weren't making plans any further out than crimping their hair and getting a new Caboodle to store all of their makeup in, I just wasn't prepared to handle the doubts running through my brain.

"It's just . . ." What could I say? How could I explain the way I was feeling when I didn't understand it myself? I shook my head, dismissing the thoughts. Or at least dismissing the notion of speaking them aloud. I sighed and smiled at him. "Never mind." I stood from my stool and pushed it underneath the table.

"What is it?"

I forced my smile to grow wider. "It's nothing. Really. I wasn't kidding about it being a long day." I yawned, right on cue.

His eyes locked with mine, and he tilted his head and looked at me as if he were examining an ancient artifact. To him I probably *was* an ancient artifact. A long-forgotten remnant from his past.

"History has a way of doing this, you know. Making us look through a different lens at the world all around us." With a deep breath he stood from his own stool and returned it to the corner. "And that, of course, is what makes it so extraordinary."

"I'm just not usually one to question. I'm usually pretty comfortable with my primary lens. And if it weren't for some other things going on in my life right now . . ."

My voice trailed off before I said things I wasn't prepared to say. Particularly not to Henry, who, though I had known him nearly as long as I had known my younger sister, was a stranger.

"There's a quote I love from Madeleine L'Engle. I think it's from *The Summer of the Great-Grandmother*. She said, 'One of the problems of being a storyteller is the cultivated ability to extrapolate; in every situation all the what-ifs come to me.' The first time I read that was when I knew I wanted to be a documentarian. Well, I may not have known what the actual job title would end up being, but I knew I wasn't really a historian. I was a storyteller." He leaned across the table. "I wasn't satisfied with just the facts. I couldn't stop myself from taking all the what-ifs into consideration."

I smiled. "But I *am* satisfied with the facts. I always have been."

His eyebrows shot up for a second, and then his eyes narrowed. "Really?"

"Yes, really. You said it yourself earlier. Just like Melanie, apparently, I always knew what my goals were, and I always knew what it would take to achieve them. And I never strayed from that—"

"And yet you always prepared for the what-if. You *always* did,

McKenna. You forget, I'm an eyewitness to your history. Whether it was studying everything about trigonometry that *wasn't* on the syllabus, just in case it slipped onto an exam, or making sure you had a date for homecoming, or—"

"Yeah, but those were contingencies. Contingencies come out of logic and preparedness, not through the whims of storytellers." A smirk crossed his face, and I realized that in my haste to segregate myself from those with flights of spontaneous fancy, I had classified the brilliant Hank Blume in a category he didn't belong in any more than I did. "I didn't mean—"

"It's fine," he assured me with a confidence I recognized as something I had carried around myself until very recently. "And it doesn't matter. Not really. I wasn't trying to say you are something you think you're not, or you're not something you think you are. All I was really trying to say is that it seems like there's just a little bit of extrapolation happening in your mind right now. Unless I'm wrong—and maybe I am—I think you're just wondering, a little bit, if the path you took was the right one. And I'm not saying it wasn't. But I don't think a little bit of 'what-if' here and there makes us weak or foolish. It just makes us storytellers."

My mouth opened, but no words came out. Instead, another yawn escaped, completely beyond my control.

He chuckled and stood from his leaning position. "I'm going to let you get some rest."

"Sorry," I attempted to articulate through yet another yawn. "I don't mean to run you off."

He followed me into the living room and seemed to instinctively lower his voice out of respect for the now-quiet household. "Not at all. It's been a pretty long day for me, too, truth be told. I just flew in from a film festival in Munich this afternoon, so—"

"Munich?" My eyes shot open with a temporary spurt of alertness. "And there I was feeling sorry for myself after my two-hour flight from New York this morning. I didn't even change time zones! How are you functioning?"

"I'm used to it." Henry smiled as we reached the door. "So how long are you in town?"

"My sister's engagement party is next weekend, so at least until then. You?"

He shrugged. "A while. I haven't quite decided yet."

A while. He was going to be in town a while. I knew that was good news, and I filed away the information for additional processing when exhaustion was less of a factor.

I reached for the doorknob. "Then maybe we'll see each other again before—"

"I had the biggest crush on you, McKenna Keaton."

I inhaled sharply, resulting in a coughing fit—this time without the benefit of wasabi as an excuse. "I'm sorry . . . *What*?" I sputtered.

"In school. I had the biggest crush on you. I think that's why I was so, I don't know . . . awkward. When I saw you tonight . . . It just . . . Well, it surprised me, I guess, and before I knew it I felt all of my old teenage defenses kicking in. I probably came across as rude, and I'm sorry." He smiled even as his feet shuffled somewhat uncomfortably. "Please don't tell your dad this—or Jared—but that was the real reason I wanted to come over here tonight. To apologize. The fact is, you and Jared were my only real friends in Durham for a big part of my life. I was a self-involved loner, and you guys hung out with me anyway. But now . . ." He sighed. "Well, since I've had some success, a lot more people want to be my friend. You know? I just . . . I just didn't want my poor handling of an unexpected—but actually very pleasant—surprise to mess up one of the more genuine friendships I've ever had. I hope you can forgive me."

I swallowed hard and tried to speak, but the Sahara Desert seemed to be taking an excursion through my mouth. I was suddenly very alert, but also very speechless.

"Of course," I finally managed to croak out.

He smiled. "Thanks. Well, get some rest. Good night." Henry stepped out onto the front stoop and hurried to his car after one last wave.

I managed to wave back and then shut the door and locked it before leaning against it and indulging in something I'd never been known to do. I wondered *what if*. What if I had been a little less focused on my studies in high school—maybe, just once or twice, accepting an A-minus instead of an A-plus—and had spent a little more time with Henry, actually getting to know him? Not just his brain, which I got to know pretty well, but *Henry*. Of course he still would have moved away, and I probably would have been heartbroken. Maybe I would have gone to the University of Oregon or somewhere in order to be close to him. I might have passed the bar exam there. Maybe I would have started my own law firm in Lake Oswego or something—surely people broke the law and sued businesses in Lake Oswego, right?—and we'd have gotten married and had a few beautiful kids with great hair and breathtaking eyes. And we would have brought our kids up to win and compete, because competing against each other would have been the root of how their dad and I fell in love. Family game night would go on for days, as each and every one of us fought to the death in Monopoly. But at the end of the day, we'd cuddle up around Henry, and he'd show us what he was working on and tell us stories about the Great Depression and the royal family and the *Chariots of Fire* guy.

No wonder I never indulged in *what if*. I had always enjoyed order and structure in my life, and *what if* brought nothing but chaos and confusion.

And yet somehow, in a matter of hours, Henry Blumenthal had turned me into a storyteller.

Chapter 9

By the time my eyes fluttered open—my arm shielding them from the sunlight bouncing against the bright-yellow walls of my old bedroom—I had a new outlook on life. Or at least I felt much better about my ability to maintain my sanity while the fate of my outlook was being determined. I guess the jury was still out in regard to the actual outlook. If Wallis, Monroe, and/or Burkhead were to call me and inform me that the true culprit or the missed zeros had been found, my outlook on life would be just fine, thank you very much.

Having gotten more sleep in one night than I'd gotten in many previous nights combined, I was able to see through the emotion and realize that, dependent upon the results of that impending call, this whole situation could be the best thing that ever happened to me. The name partners would be bowing and scraping to make amends, and I'd have a big, fat check to retroactively pay for more time off than I'd ever taken in my entire career.

I made a commitment to myself that from this morning on, I would treat the time as a gift. I would reconnect with my niece and nephews and get to know my soon-to-be brother-in-law. I'd find ways to help my parents around the house and do my best to be a supportive big sister at Taylor's engagement party. And, sure . . .

Maybe I'd get to know Henry better. I mean, why not? Minutes in his presence went quicker than I wanted them to—even when I was so tired I couldn't see straight. It would be foolish not to enjoy a few more conversations like that, since we both happened to be in town. And since there was a slight chance he might come to the house again. You know, to look through Dad's ancestry projects or visit with Jared. Or because he'd had such a massive crush on me in high school.

"Ridiculous," I muttered as I sat up in the bed. "That'll be enough of that."

It was one thing to enjoy spending time with him, but it was important that I stay sharp. For whatever reason, I knew that Henry Blumenthal had the capacity to get the better of me. I sensed it. I felt it in the way my nerve endings stood on edge every time I thought about him and the way I had lost the ability to focus every time he looked at me. And there was simply too much else happening in my life. Things that truly mattered. I couldn't allow myself to get carried away in one area just because I was feeling vulnerable in all the others.

Just like I had been vulnerable, just for a moment, to the notion that I was going to die soon if I didn't get married.

Henry had been right. He didn't even know my situation, but he was one of the more insightful individuals I'd come across in my life. He had been absolutely right when he guessed that I was questioning my path. Of course I was. How could I not? He'd figured that out without the knowledge that I was potentially on the verge of having my path diverted without my approval. I'd spent days wondering if everything I had worked toward was being taken away from me, and then we'd thrown a theoretical "If you're not going to hurry up and get married, you should at least decide who gets your 1853 first edition of *Bleak House* when you die" into the mix.

I sat up in Erica's old white metal-framed daybed and looked around. I hadn't changed much about the room when Erica moved out to go to college, apart from taking down her Ricky Martin and Destiny's Child posters and replacing them with the periodic table and other study aides. I'd moved her daybed to the wall near the window, loaded it up with pillows, and turned it into a reading nook. The location of the reading nook (and dual-purpose guest bed, of course) was all that remained of my interior-design attempts. Well, apart from my old beanbag chair in the corner. I'd probably spent more time on that pink beanbag than anywhere else in the house. For hours on end, I would sit there with headphones on and study.

With the now-yellow walls, the motif screamed "Easter-egg hunt" more than it had when everything had been painted the nice, subdued ecru I had always liked. But it all lent itself to a cheery atmosphere for my mom to read in, or for her to watch *Call the Midwife* in while she walked on the treadmill that stood where my desk had once been placed.

I hopped out of bed and darted toward the bathroom in the hallway, midway between what had been Taylor's room and what had been mine and Erica's. At least I'd have the bathroom to myself while I was in town. Another silver lining! The three of us, and then the two of us, had shared that one for years. Yes, Erica and I were teenagers, and Taylor was a little kid who used bubble bath that smelled like watermelon, but the battles we fought were enough to make you wonder if all the ugliness between Elizabeth I and her sister Bloody Mary could have been avoided if they'd had separate bathrooms growing up.

"Good morning, sleepyhead!" Taylor trilled as I rounded the corner into the bathroom and she popped out of it, scaring me half to death.

"What are you doing here?" I exclaimed as I leaned up against the wall in the hallway and tried to regulate my breathing and get my heart rate back to normal.

She tilted her head and smiled at me. "Are you kidding? I want to get as much time with you as I can. I'm staying in my old room while you're here."

No one had asked me how long I was planning to stay, but I figured it was safe to assume they thought I would be taking off after the engagement party. I was hopeful, of course, that Jeremiah Burkhead's assurance that Human Resources would be in touch would come to fruition much sooner than the forecasted six to eight weeks. I was hoping for something more along the lines of close of business Friday, at which point I would tell them I had committed to a family event, and I wouldn't be back in the office until midday on Monday. *That* would show them. (Of course, I'd actually be sure to take the early flight and be in before ten. Under-promise, over-deliver.)

I groaned and pushed past her into the bathroom. "You don't still use that watermelon bubble bath, do you?"

"What watermelon bubble bath?"

I pulled my hair down from its ponytail and quickly realized there was no hope for the tangled heap of frizzy curls without much more effort than I was willing to put in right then, so I promptly pulled it all back up to the top of my head—this time in a messy bun that gave off a cute and intentionally casual vibe.

God bless the messy bun.

"You know—that stuff that made the bottom of the bathtub all grainy and left that pink ring that Erica and I always had to scrub away."

She laughed. "Um, no. I don't use that anymore. And I promise, I won't make you clean up after me anymore." She wrapped her arms around me from behind and rested her chin on my shoulder, facing the mirror. "You know what else? I have these amazing seaweed facial masks. I was thinking we could get Erica over here one night and turn one of our rooms into a spa."

"I don't think Erica can just step away from her job and her family to come over for a sleepover. She's an adult. Aren't you?"

Her arms loosened around my shoulders, and her chin lifted, and, worst of all, her stung expression reflected back at me in the mirror. So much for making the most of the time I had with them. So much for looking at it all as a gift. But they all had lives, even if at that particular moment I didn't.

I sighed and turned to face her. Her deflated mood was no less evident than it had been in her mirror image. "Sorry, Tay. I didn't mean anything by it. It's just . . . I know *I'm* on vacation." I did all I could to resist the urge to sneer at the word. "But Erica still has school, right? And surely she doesn't want to be away from the kids overnight." That claim was probably ludicrous, but it was safe to assume Jared and the kids didn't want Erica to be away from them overnight. "And do you even have time? Mom and Dad have said your interior-design business is really starting to take off, so you must have clients fighting for your attention. Not to mention, you know, planning a big party for this weekend and a wedding coming up"—When was the wedding again? May, right? Best to be vague—"soon. So it's not that I don't want to have a spa day and a sleepover and eat cookie dough and all that jazz—"

One corner of her mouth rose in a sad half smile. "Yes, it is, McKenna. That's exactly what it is." She spoke so softly. Slowly. Differently than I had ever heard her speak before. She backed away from me and sat on the edge of the bathtub and began fidgeting with the corner of a towel that hung over the shower rod. "I get it. Really. I know that we've never been super close, and I don't know why I . . ." She quickly swiped at the corner of her eye, and the way her eyes darted away from me as she did—rather than toward me, to make sure I was watching, as she used to when she was little—took me off guard.

Looking at her sitting there, so much disappointment etched on her face, was a strange sensation. On one hand, she seemed as much like my baby sister as she had when she was four years old and came running to me to help her deal with the total heartbreak and devastation of the neighbor's beagle puppy chewing off the chin wattle of her Gobbles the Turkey Beanie Baby. But in another way, it was like I was seeing her as an adult for the very first time. She wasn't throwing a fit, she wasn't being dramatic, she wasn't pouting or pulling out the "baby of the family" card. She was just a grown woman who'd had plans and expectations, and her big sister who hadn't been home in three years had dashed every single one of them with one thoughtless comment.

"No, Tay, it's really not. I'm sorry if that's how it sounded. I just didn't want to impose on whatever you might have going on. Let's do it." She didn't say anything. Again, that was new. New to me anyway. I walked to the bathtub and squeezed in beside her on the edge. She scooted to make room for me. "I really am sorry. I . . ." I took a deep breath. "I'm sorry that I haven't been around."

"Are you kidding?" she whispered. "You don't have time to be around much. I know that. That's not something you need to apologize for."

"Well, I'm sorry anyway." And all of a sudden, I was. Sorry that I hadn't had the chance to get to know her as an adult. "I'm sorry we got off on the wrong foot this morning, and I'm really sorry about last night. I shouldn't have snapped at you like that."

She shrugged and remained unsettlingly silent.

I swallowed down the lump in my throat, and as I did, I wished I'd brushed my teeth before speaking with anyone. "You and I have just lived different lives, you know? That's not your fault or mine, I don't think, but eleven years is a big age gap. I mean, think about it. That's a Cooper and a Charlie combined. And . . . Well, I know I'm different."

"Different from me?"

I laughed. "Different from everyone. Everyone in this family anyway." Seriously, did my morning breath smell as awful as it tasted? How could she even stand being in the same room with me? "I'm happy for you and Jackson, and I'm happy for Erica and Jared. I'm even happy for our lovebird parents."

She groaned but then smiled—we both did—as she said, "They're pretty nauseating sometimes."

"But I've always wanted different things. So I guess I just get a little irritated when everyone hounds me about what they think my life should look like."

"I understand that, but I just hate the thought of you being lonely—"

I scoffed. "Who says I'm lonely?"

"Well, okay . . . *alone*."

Maybe I was fighting a losing battle, but the vulnerability in her eyes made me willing to try one more time to make her understand it from my perspective.

"That's sweet, Tay. Thanks for caring. But can I be honest?" She nodded, but her eyes were so big and guileless that I knew I needed to measure my honesty carefully so as not to damage her. "I think sometimes you project onto me what *you* want and need in order to be happy. And you love . . . well . . . *love*. But for me, a love life is just something that I don't have time, energy, or a desire for."

"Then what are we supposed to talk about?"

There it was. The wrong question.

I jumped up and crossed to the sink, wet the bristles of my toothbrush, and welcomed the much-needed minty relief.

"I don't know what to tell you," I muttered through the building foam in my mouth—almost entirely attributable to toothpaste, I assured myself, and not a result of my frustration with her manifesting as rabies-like symptoms.

"I get that you're independent and all that, but hasn't there ever been *someone*?" She jumped up from the edge of the tub and stood behind me again. "Some guy that you looked at and said"—she pointed at my reflection in the mirror, as earnest an expression as I had ever seen on her face—"'I'm going to marry that guy someday.'"

The slight acknowledgment of relevance that took place in my brain must have made its way to my eyes, because hers opened wide. "You have to tell me everything! What's his name?"

According to the US justice system, there are five elements of self-defense:

1. *Innocence.* In other words, it had to be established that the situation was of her doing.
2. *Avoidance.* I had to have tried to get out of the situation. If "I don't know what to tell you" wasn't given as legal precedence of avoidance in textbooks, I couldn't imagine what was.
3. *Imminence.* Clearly demonstrated by her arms once again wrapping around my shoulders and refusing to let me go, even as a bit of mint slobber ran down my chin.
4. *Proportionality.* Don't bring a knife to a pillow fight, and don't bite your sister's head off just because she's irritating.
5. *Reasonableness.* Because the laws that protect us in instances of self-defense don't require us to make perfect decisions—only sensible ones.

"Jeremiah," I muttered through my foam.

"Oh, Kenna," she sighed. *Kenna.* Her affectionate name for me ever since she learned to speak and the "Mc" was just a little more than she could handle. "I'm so sorry."

Her grip on me tightened. As if none of the pain she had been feeling on her own behalf had ever happened and my presumed pain was all that mattered. It was sweet and all, but it did make it difficult to spit without making a mess. I tilted my chin and did the best I could and then stretched out constricted arms and straining fingers and grabbed the towel to wipe the excess toothpaste and slobber from my lips. Through it all she never relented in her attempts to hug the misery right out of me.

"Do you want to talk about it?" she asked.

"Not really—"

"And before you answer, just know that I won't ask you to tell me anything you don't want to tell me."

"I'd really rather keep it to myself, if it's all the same—"

"I know how private you are. How private you've always been. So seriously, if you don't feel like talking about it, that's fine."

"Taylor, I really don't—"

"For the record, experts say that the longer you keep heartbreak inside of you, all bottled up, the more likely it is to grow and fester, and before long there's a pretty decent chance that you'll either suffer a complete mental and emotional breakdown—the kind that carries with it the high likelihood that you'll spend the rest of your life in a near-catatonic state—or that your heart will release so many toxins into your bloodstream—a result of, basically, emotional blood poisoning—that for all intents and purposes, your head will explode. I mean, your head won't *literally* explode, of course. It's more like your brain will explode *inside* your head. Some people say that's just a myth, but I say you can't be too careful with this stuff." Her reflection bounced back at me from the mirror, and a sly smile spread across her lips. "So, tell me, Kenna. What happened with Jeremiah?"

I chuckled. "You're a mess. You know that?"

Her smile widened, her arms released me, and her hands swept down to grab the towel from my hands and throw it on the counter. And then, before I could register what was happening, I was being pulled into her bedroom. With all the finesse of a magician whose hands were trying to convince me a woman had been sawed in half, she shut the door behind me, cleared off a space for me to sit on the edge of her bed, pulled her desk chair over and sat down in it knee to knee with me, and began holding my hands.

"When did you get a desk in here?" I asked as soon as I got my bearings enough to realize what was happening.

She looked behind her at the desk and then back at me with a bewildered expression. "Um . . . sometime around 2008, I think. Where else would I write term papers and cram for exams?"

The truth? The truth was I had never really pictured Taylor writing term papers or cramming for exams at all. But if I *had* envisioned those things, I probably would have imagined them taking place in her Barbie Dreamhouse, which used to sit where the desk now was.

"I guess I just haven't been in here in a while." It looked completely different than I remembered, but it was still a bedroom. Taylor was not relegated to a reading nook by the window to make room for an ironing board. I swallowed down the threatening flare-up of injured pride by reminding myself Taylor lived a few miles away and probably stayed over all the time, while I would soon be returning to the Stearns & Foster Reserve Hepburn mattress I had splurged on with my 2019 end-of-year bonus.

"So, tell me about this guy. Tell me about Jeremiah."

Referring to Jeremiah Burkhead as "this guy" felt to me about as absurd as every other aspect of the whole scenario. But as my mind raced and attempted to follow every potential conversational direction to its eventual destination, I realized that all I had to do was acknowledge some vague truth and Taylor's romance-addled brain would handle the rest. It was all about buying a little time until there was nothing to hide.

"He's an attorney."

She nodded compassionately, as if the utterance of his occupation had confirmed all of her suspicions as to the intense level of my heartbreak.

"And you thought you might marry him someday?"

I sighed and answered honestly. "Yeah. I guess I sort of thought I might. Maybe. Someday."

She squeezed my hands and looked into my eyes until I had no choice but to meet her compassionate gaze. "So . . . what happened?"

It was ludicrous. I knew I was pouring gasoline on a fire that I might never be able to put out. If I opened this door and allowed her to walk through, what chance would I have of ever getting her to understand that she and I didn't care about the same things? What chance would I have of ever getting her to acknowledge that not caring about the same things was okay? I knew all of that. But as her eyes began to glisten in response to whatever emotions she believed herself to be interpreting from my silence, I realized that, strange as it was, I understood how to put my reality in terms she would understand.

"He broke my heart." I paused, expecting her to ooh and aah and ask the wrong question and say the wrong thing, but she didn't. "I, um . . . I guess I thought we were heading a certain direction, but we weren't. Or, I mean . . . We still are. We just hit a snag."

I cleared my throat and attempted to clear my thoughts. This wasn't a good idea. My vague attempts at connection with my little sister had just gotten messy. How could I reconcile the heartbreak I was supposedly feeling with the determination that it was, in fact, just a snag? I *had* to keep believing the snag was temporary. I had to believe that phone call from HR was due any minute. Because if I didn't . . .

"How long had you been with him, Kenna?"

I forced myself to measure my breathing, in and out. *There's no reason to panic*, I assured myself. *It's all a stupid mistake. You know that, and Jeremiah Burkhead knows that. This investigation is your friend. Due process is your friend. The facts won't lie. The facts never lie.*

I took one more deep breath and was no longer able to feel my heart pounding in the base of my throat. "Off and on for about . . . well, about thirteen years, I guess."

"Thirteen years?!" Taylor's eyes were nearly the size of the inscribed gold plates hanging on her wall.

Hang on. Gold plates?

"Taylor, are those Jordan High Model UN trophies over there underneath your Justin Timberlake wall art?" It was a total toss-up as to which part of that sentence was most ridiculous, but it all combined to form a glorious distraction.

She glanced over her shoulder. "Yeah."

"How in the world did I not know that you did Model UN?"

"Silly." She chuckled, hopped up from her chair, and walked over to the wall. "They're not mine. They're yours." She beamed at me, then seemed to think better of her beaming. "I hope that's okay. I mean, they were just in a box after you went to college, and I thought they looked pretty cool. And then once I got into high school, I realized that you were kind of a legend around there. And I have Erica's debate team trophies too." She pointed to the shelf in the corner, where I had last remembered there being an entire village's worth of American Girl dolls. "I guess those things sort of made me feel like you were both still around."

I had founded Jordan High's Model UN club my freshman year, and when not even Erica would go to after-school practices with me, it looked like it might be dead in the water. But then, in a stroke of genius, I petitioned the school board to count Model UN as a half credit toward the honors diploma. At the very next club meeting, there were Jared Pierson and Henry Blumenthal. There was no way they were going to miss out on a half credit that I had in the bag. Before long, we were about twenty members strong, and by senior year we were sending a team to the National Model United Nations Conference in Washington, DC.

It probably overstated things a bit to call me a legend, but I did consider the Model UN club part of my legacy. A legacy I'd never known my little sister knew about, much less cared about.

"That's sweet, Tay. Thanks." Admittedly, that did make more sense, considering she was the same kid who had once asked me if Great Britain ever thought about downgrading their "Great" status after the Revolutionary War. "So, what were you part of in high school? Art club, right? Was Mrs. Holson-Brack still there when you were there?"

She was off, welcoming me into her world from a decade prior. A world I'd never asked to step into before. And thankfully, my heartbreak was momentarily forgotten.

Chapter 10

When the smell of bacon began wafting up the stairs, Taylor abandoned our conversation, and I was able to shower and get dressed. By the time I made it to the kitchen, the rest of the house was energetically greeting the day. And it seemed the world was still abuzz from the excitement of the visit from Durham's favorite son the evening before.

"I can't believe you missed it, Mom," Taylor was saying as I walked in. "He's so cute."

"Well, I've seen him on TV." Mom served scrambled eggs onto four plates and set the first two in front of Dad and Taylor. "But it would have been nice to see him in person."

"You've *seen* him in person," I said with a laugh.

"You have?" my dad asked her.

"Yes," I answered on her behalf, my tone drawn out and somewhat annoyed. "And so have you," I added in my dad's direction. "Before last night, I mean. I'm glad he's done well for himself, and trust me, I'm a fan of his work too. But don't forget this is ultimately just a guy I went to school with."

Taylor didn't do a very good job of hiding the smirk on her face even as she lowered her head and studied her eggs.

Mom placed a plate in front of me as I sat. "Thanks, but I don't usually eat breakfast."

"You *have* to eat breakfast," she insisted.

Being an adult who comes back home is all about picking your battles. "Yes, ma'am." Being an adult who comes back home is also why they invented Pilates.

Dad prayed a blessing over the food—while I silently put in a request with God to move that blessing over to our arteries. But even as my bowed head hovered over the plate, the scent of my mom's fresh buttermilk biscuit clouds, as we'd always called them—which were just barely visible beneath the bacon sawmill gravy with the perfect amount of black pepper, as always—was enough to make me add on the silent prayer amendment, *But if this is my last meal, you won't hear me complaining.*

"And you said he's going to be by again today?" Mom asked Dad as soon as he'd said amen.

I looked up from my plate—thick, crisp bacon practically melting on the inside of my mouth and dangling in a very uncouth fashion on the outside. It's possible I had jumped the gun on the amen.

"I'm sorry . . . What? Why? Henry? *Henry's* going to be by again today? By *here*, again, today? Why? *Henry?*"

Way to go, McKenna. That will get that smug, knowing smile off Taylor's face.

No big deal. I could dig myself out. "I mean, I just ask because . . . Well, he's a busy dude." *A busy dude? Really?* "I just don't think we should be nagging him about our little ancestry project—"

"He called this morning and said he had found something he wanted to show us," my dad replied with a shrug. "I don't really understand his interest, either, but who am I to discourage him?" Dad had mastered the appearance of blasé better than I had, but he'd checked his watch three times in the amount of time it took him to say that. So, yeah, I wasn't really buying it.

One thing I could say about Taylor: she had never been worried enough about what anyone would think of her to bother with faking blasé. She was practically bouncing in her seat, and she felt no shame.

"What if he wants to do a documentary on our family?"

I scoffed. "That's ridiculous."

Taylor and my mom exchanged amused glances over their coffee cups.

"What?" I asked.

"Oh, nothing." Taylor set her cup down and daintily dabbed at the corners of her mouth with her napkin. "I just said earlier that you'd say something like that."

"Because I have common sense."

"And I also said," she continued, "that he probably isn't coming over here for genealogy stuff at all. He's probably coming to see you."

What do you know? Bouncing in her seat and emphatically trilling the last word of every sentence *had* been Taylor's attempt at blasé. But all attempts were put aside as I looked up at her in dismay—or was it hope?—and she took my interest as permission to say all she wanted to say. At least I hoped so. It was very possible, I feared, that she was *still* holding back and there was about to be a Chernobyl-type situation on Morningside Drive when all of that energy released. Or if it didn't. I honestly didn't know which would be worse.

She turned in her chair to face me and scooted up until the fronts of her knees were saddled up against the sides of my leg. "You should have seen the way he was looking at you last night!"

I stuffed a bite into my mouth. "Presumably, I *did* see the way he was looking at me." My voice was muffled by fluffy egg and unamused. Even if my brain was engaging in battle again—wanting to implore her to stop, wanting to beg her to go on. Well, since she was bound and determined to go on whether I begged her or not, there didn't seem to be much reason not to just let it play out.

"See, I don't think so. I think you were too busy looking at *him* the way you were." She winked at me and then faced our mother. "The whole thing made me feel like I was watching *Beauty and the Beast*."

Laughter (and, unfortunately, a few little egg chunks) spewed from my mouth. "Henry may be a little bit of a rough-edged, independent, adventurer sort, but I would *hardly* compare him to the Beast."

"I wasn't, silly." Taylor giggled and rolled her eyes.

Hang on . . . Am I the Beast?!

She was talking to Mom again as she said, "You know when he saves her from the wolves and she nurses him back to health and he gives her the library—"

"I love when he gives her the library." Mom sighed.

"—and they both have to acknowledge to themselves that there's something between them? It was like that."

I will not let this get to me. I will not let this get to me. I will not let this get to me.

After all, I'd fallen asleep analyzing every glance and every incidental touch. There was nothing Taylor could point out that I hadn't already dissected. And in the end, no matter how much I acknowledged I was attracted to him and would love to spend more time with him—and no matter how much I replayed the confession of his high-school feelings for me—I knew that nothing would come of any of it. And that was fine. That was *better* than fine. Within six to eight weeks, I would be back at work. Busier than ever. Happier than ever. Eating more Swiss-and-tomato-on-pumpernickel sandwiches from Barney Greengrass than ever.

Okay, sure . . . Maybe I had a crush. Maybe Henry had made me feel things I didn't usually feel. But that was to be expected. The facts were, though I hated to admit it even to myself, I was in an extremely vulnerable state of mind. The facts were that Henry Blumenthal was no longer the dorky kid who never once seemed to find a barber who knew how to control his cowlick.

And the facts were that there was nothing more pathetic than unrequited love.

"Henry and I always got along really well in school," I said calmly as I spooned a dollop of butter into grits so creamy they made me wonder if my mom had found a recipe on Pinterest that combined cornmeal and unicorn dreams. "Do you remember, Mom, when he used to give me a ride home from school whenever my old Buick was in the shop?"

"When *wasn't* that Buick in the shop?" Dad groaned.

"I'm just saying, Kenna," Taylor resumed, turning back to me, "maybe Henry is just what the doctor ordered to get your mind off Jer—"

"I have to know. Am I the Beast in this scenario?" I interrupted as quickly as I could. Never again. Never. Again. And as soon as I was back at Wallis, Monroe and Burkhead, I would take great pleasure in making sure her knowledge of Jeremiah was sucked dry of all romantic intrigue.

She laughed. "No! Of course not. Although Henry is quite the beauty—"

The sound of the doorbell chiming cut her off, causing all four of us to momentarily freeze in place.

"I'll get it," Taylor said as she stood. "It *could* just be Jackson." She winked at me and then bounced out of the room.

Yes. It was probably Jackson. And it was totally normal that I quickly ran to the sink to wash the butter off of my hands and then ran my fingers through my hair, still damp from the shower, to make sure my waves had adequate volume. And of *course* I tried to use the front of the microwave as a mirror so I could check and make sure there wasn't bacon in my teeth. I mean, it's very important that one makes a good impression on one's future brother-in-law.

It was about the time I was examining my gut and sucking in—for Jackson's benefit, of course—the somehow immediate effect of my mother's home cooking that I noticed my parents looking at me with amused expressions on their faces.

"What?" I asked, and they both just smiled, shook their heads, and returned their attention to their plates in front of them.

"McKenna? Are you available?" Taylor called from the other room. "There's someone here to see you."

I swallowed down the lump that had risen in my throat, along with the saliva that my glands were suddenly and inexplicably producing like I was one of Pavlov's dogs hanging out with Quasimodo in the bell tower at Notre Dame. What were the odds that Jackson greeted his fiancée by asking to speak to her sister?

My dad tore apart another biscuit and spooned some gravy on top of it. "It's probably the mailman. He probably has a package for you. I mean, no one knows you're here but—"

"No, Scott," my mom interrupted, snapping her fingers as if she were trying to think. "You know who I bet it is? I bet it's Mrs. Connelly. Remember? The girls' old piano teacher? I bet she heard McKenna was in town and was itching to hear a little 'Canon in D' for old time's sake."

I rolled my eyes as they smiled at each other, very satisfied with themselves. "Hardy-har-har," I muttered, then brushed off my shirt one last time in case there were any lingering breakfast crumbs and went into the living room.

It was him. Of course it was him. No matter how my brain had tried to lie to me, my salivary glands had known the truth. He was back. In my parents' house. There to see *me*. Looking like he'd just climbed out of an Eddie Bauer catalog in his earth-toned green corduroys and his dark-gray field sweater with three buttons at the top—all of them unbuttoned. And his red flannel button-up peeking out from the open collar, unbuttoned just as low as the sweater and doing nothing to cover up his strong neck and defined Adam's apple and just a little bit of chest hair that wouldn't be tamed.

Good grief, McKenna. Since when do you notice or care about any of that stuff?

It was a valid point I was attempting to make to myself, and the only argument I had to present at that moment was, *I don't. But it's not his brain or his personality boasting a five o'clock shadow at eight thirty in the morning, distracting me beyond all get-out.*

"Hey there," he greeted me with a smile and investigative eyes. The way he studied me from head to toe and back again was enough to make me wonder if he was cramming hard for his upcoming McKenna exam. What was most surprising was that I didn't really mind. After all, despite all the time I had spent trying to convince myself otherwise, I appeared to be very much on the verge of switching my major to Henry.

"Good morning." I had braced myself before I said it, prepared to sound like a silly schoolgirl who couldn't speak around her crush, but my voice surprised me. This morning I seemed to be in control. I had no idea if I *was* in control, but at least I seemed to be. "Dad said you might be swinging by today."

He took a step farther in. A step closer to me.

"Yeah, I did some searches across a few of the sites I use and found something sort of interesting. I originally planned to come later in the day and not so early—"

"It's okay."

"—but the thing is . . ." His voice faded away, and his head turned slowly toward Taylor, who, since he had taken yet another step toward me, was now standing directly beside him, a little too close, staring at him with a look that can only be described as Hallmarkian. He returned her smile, though his was more . . . normal. I mean, dazzling. But normal.

"Hey, Tay?" I stepped forward and placed my hand on her arm, and she turned her focus to me. The goofy grin remained. "Would you mind giving us a minute?"

Her eyes sparkled in what I interpreted as delight. "Oh! Yeah, totally. Let me give the two of you some privacy."

I cleared my throat, and my eyes quickly flashed to Henry, and then even more quickly away when I discovered he was still cramming (and I don't just mean the Cliff's Notes method), and then back to Taylor. "It's not that we need *privacy*, just a little space to—"

"No, I get it. I get it. I've got to get ready for work anyway. I mean, it's Sunday. So not work. I just, um, have some work to do." She bit her lip as she lingered a little too long. In that time, I tried to speak to her with my eyes. *Be cool. Be cool.* But if the giggle that came out of her as she ran back to the kitchen was any indication, she didn't get the message.

Erica would have understood.

I chuckled self-consciously—or Taylor-consciously, to be more precise—and turned back to him. "Sorry about that."

"She makes me feel old."

A loud, abrupt laugh escaped from me at the unexpected declaration. "Me too."

"No, I mean it's hard not to still see her as a kid. Wasn't she in kindergarten or something when we were coming over here every week for study group?"

The air rushed out of my chest at the memory. I'd had so many memories of high school in the last twelve hours or so. So many memories of Henry. But they had all been sort of generic. Specific, but *generic*. Henry on a stage, massacring Mercutio's death scene by having an allergic reaction to something and sneezing on Tybalt not once, not twice, but three times. (It wasn't that Jonathan Elliot, who played Tybalt, didn't bother to move. It just all happened so fast.) Henry in a crowd. Henry across a room. Henry walking into Model UN with Jared, immediately claiming France because he had wanted to join French club instead, and then sitting in the back working on honors-diploma essays—never so much as balking at Chris Simon's pleas for financial support for Cambodia as part of the Economic Commission for Latin America and the Caribbean. (I mean, *what?*) But memories of Henry *in my house?*

"Something like that."

He clicked his tongue against his teeth. "Yeah, I remember she would ride through on her scooter when your parents weren't around. Presumably because she wasn't supposed to be riding the scooter in the house?"

"She wasn't supposed to be riding the scooter at all, actually. She had her own little one, but at every opportunity she'd grab Erica's from her room and ride the big-girl one instead."

"Ah. Yeah, that matches up with what I remember. There was definitely a desire to be seen as a big girl. What were we reading? *Catcher in the Rye?* And she just settled in for our discussion. I can't remember what we were talking about specifically at the time, but I remember us all looking at one another like, 'Is it okay for this kid to hear this?'" He was gazing off into the distance—the door to the kitchen, the door to 1999 . . . It was difficult to tell—and then a smile spread across his face at the exact same moment the memory became clear in my mind as well.

"*Lord of the Flies,*" we recalled in unison, and then I laughed while he continued to smile.

"That's right." He leaned against the banister and crossed his arms. "I think we were analyzing Piggy's death, and there's Keaton's little sister, hanging on to every word."

"She's always been a pest."

"Nah." He shrugged and rested the heel of his boot on the bottom step. "She just wanted to be wherever you were."

Good grief, McKenna. What has twenty years on the East Coast done to your manners?

136

"Hey, I'm so sorry, Henry. You don't have to just stand at the banister all morning. Come on in and have a seat."

"No worries. I actually just have a minute."

Well, that wouldn't do. "At least come sit for that minute." He followed me into the living room. "Can I get you some coffee or something to eat, maybe? My mother made enough breakfast to feed that entire *Lord of the Flies* study group. Maybe the actual boys on the island too."

He shook his head and sat down on the couch. "I'm good, thanks. I'm an early riser, so I ate already."

I stared at him as I sat down in the chair across from him and waited for him to say more, but he just stared back at me. I cleared my throat. "You said you planned to come later in the day and not so early, but . . ." Not that I was in a hurry to stop staring at him, mind you.

"Yes! I did say that, didn't I?" He scooted up onto the edge of the couch and leaned his elbows out onto his knees. "I have to go."

More opportunity to stare. "'Go'?"

He shook his head and chuckled. "Maybe I could use some coffee after all. My brain doesn't seem to be functioning very well."

I stood. "You bet. How do you like it?"

"Hmm?" He tilted his head and chewed on his bottom lip.

I wasn't sure what was causing the scatterbrained conversation, but I sure did like when his teeth and lips got going.

"Your coffee. How do you like it?"

"Oh!" He shook his head again. "Thanks, but I really have to get going." He bolted up from the couch. "I have to catch a flight to San Francisco. *That's* why I came so early."

"San Francisco? Wow. What's in San Francisco?" *Alcatraz, Ghirardelli Chocolate, the* Full House *house . . . Great question, McKenna.* "I mean, for you."

"This time all I have waiting for me is an annoyed board of

directors from the Golden Gate Bridge Highway and Transportation District." He rolled his eyes. "It's amazing the number of people who think 'unbiased and unfiltered access' means I'm creating a promotional video for their summer tourism campaign. And then I'm going to try and hop up to visit my mom and stepdad for a day or two while I'm on the Coast." He began walking toward the door, and I followed him. "Will you tell your dad I'll get back in touch with him soon?"

"You bet. But, um . . . Henry?"

"Hmm?"

"It's not that it's not nice to see you. It is. But if you don't mind my asking . . . um . . . Was there a particular reason you stopped by, or . . . ?"

"Oh! Didn't I give you the—" He patted the back pocket of his corduroys and then rolled his eyes as he pulled out an envelope. "Nope. I didn't. Sorry." He reached out and passed it to me. "I found something really interesting about Marilla."

I looked down at the plain white envelope in my hands and then back up at him. "I'm sorry, who?"

"Marilla Keaton. Born 1781, died 1820." When I responded with nothing apart from complete lack of recognition, he added, "Had a brother named Beardsley."

"Well, who didn't?"

He grinned. "Anyway, I'd love to talk to your dad about it when I get back in town." We both stopped when we got back to the banister. The banister it hadn't made sense for us to walk away from, as brief as the visit had turned out to be.

"And when will that be?" I asked, a little too eagerly.

"Definitely by the weekend." He looked down at his hiking boot-clad feet. "And maybe when I get back, if you have some time, you and I can . . ." His voice trailed off as he raised his head and his eyes met mine.

I placed my hand on his on the banister. Just for a second. I wasn't sure why I did that. It could have passed as nothing more than accidental contact, but that brief moment of feeling his long, firm fingers beneath mine was enough to make me so self-conscious about what I was about to say, but even more certain that nothing was going to stop me from saying it.

"I'd really like that."

If I'd required him to finish his sentence, maybe he would have suggested that he and I could have dinner . . . Maybe he would have suggested we cohost a Pampered Chef party. It didn't matter. I was going to see him again, and there was no longer any point in denying that I would really, *really* like that.

Chapter 11

The rest of Sunday was fairly relaxed and quiet, apart from Taylor occasionally leaning over to me with big, concerned puppy-dog eyes and saying things like, "Don't get me wrong, Kenna. I think Henry is great. Just be careful not to rush into anything if you're not ready. Henry's not the type of guy you use as a rebound." Of course, in the very next breath she was likely to say something about how Henry was perfect for me and I was a fool if I didn't give up everything to be with him.

I'd forgotten just how unpredictable life was when riding the waves of the Taylor Keaton coastline.

All day long I kept wishing the Human Resources lady had let me take my work laptop with me when I was booted out onto the street. Oh, sure . . . I knew there was no earthly way that ever would have been permitted, but it felt like such a waste to not use all of that free time to prepare for *Ducart v. Stanley Enterprises*. Yes, it was just a simple product-liability case, but Mrs. Ducart was a very important, very wealthy client, and the court *had* to find in her favor. If the W, M and B investigation stretched on very long, I wasn't going to have nearly the time I needed to—

"Stupid, McKenna," I muttered under my breath and buried my face in my hands.

"What's that, sweetie?" my mom asked from the other side of the living room where she sat in the wingback chair she'd had in that same spot, near the picture window, since we moved into the house. She placed her open book on her knee. "Is everything okay?"

Taylor looked up from the floor where she had been thumbing through a bridal magazine. "Mom, no offense, but I don't think Kenna's quite ready to talk about everything with the entire family just yet."

"'Everything'?" my mom asked, her curiosity piqued. "What's 'everything'?"

Oh, good grief.

I shifted on the couch so I was facing my mom and had my back to Taylor. That was the nicest way I knew to deal with her right then. "It's not a big deal. I'm just thinking about a big case I've got coming up at work." *Or, more accurately, I was thinking about the case and realizing it probably wasn't my case any longer.*

"No more work talk!" My dad was standing at the base of the stairs, pointing his finger at me in half-hearted scolding.

I smiled at him. "Yes, sir." I hopped up, grateful for the interference he had unknowingly run for me, and crossed over to the banister. I looked up at him on the bottom step where he stood. "What are you up to right now?"

Subtext: please give me something to do.

"I've just been looking at what Henry unearthed." His eyes began to sparkle as he looked into the living room, where both his wife and his youngest daughter had returned to their reading, then leaned in with a conniving elevation of his eyebrows. "Want to see?"

Subtext: everyone else in the family has to listen to me ramble on about genealogy stuff all the time, and they're presently avoiding eye contact so I don't try to suck them in.

Even understanding his subtext, my subtext won out.

"Yes, please."

I followed him around the landing of the stairs and through the dining room to his little study. While he shut the French doors behind us, I looked around. When I'd been in there the night before, I'd been distracted by Henry and my impending death at the hands of singlehood. But now, looking around, it felt like I'd stepped back into my childhood. The room was decorated exactly as it had always been. Maps and replicas of obscure historical documents decorated the walls; every nook and cranny sat filled with books. My eyes instinctively moved to the drafting table in the center of the room.

My dad had wafted in and out of various short-lived obsessions through the years—postage stamps and commemorative coins, designing and building Taylor's Barbie Dreamhouse—but his highest free-time priority, the Keaton family tree, could always be found on that drafting table. Getting to obsess over the family *and* history, all in one? It was like genealogy was made for Scott Keaton.

I lifted up books and notebooks in the piles and flipped through, not actually putting any effort into making out much on any of the pages. "I looked over some of this with Henry last night. It looks like you've made a lot more progress since last time we talked about it."

I wasn't entirely sure that was true. Most weeks during our FaceTime call, the subject of genealogy at least danced through the topic of conversation. My mom usually got us back on course before either she or I zoned out completely, but I was still certain there had been countless details that hadn't received my complete attention.

"It's fascinating!" He dug to the bottom of one of the stacks and pulled out a composition notebook filled to the brim with his hand-writing. "I've got a pretty complete picture now, all the way back to the mid-1600s. And I think I'm close to breaking through on a relative who served in the court of Edward III. That would take us back to the fourteenth century, so obviously, if I can unlock that information—"

"Is that what Henry found?"

He shook his head, set down the composition notebook, and

held up a trifold piece of paper he'd dug out from beneath a map. "Oh, you'll love this, McKenna. Henry discovered that your"—his eyes rolled up into his head, and his mouth moved silently—"great-great-great-great-aunt made several trips on a British passenger ship across the Atlantic to New York . . ." He scanned the page in front of him until he found what he was looking for. "And Boston once. But she never disembarked. Some of the Keatons had already come over, and it looks like a whole slew of them were trying to get here. Yet she came and went more times than any one person would ever dream of in those days, and never stepped on American soil. Isn't that *fascinating?*"

I hated to admit it, but yes. That was rather interesting. "Why was that? Was she not allowed?"

"We're not sure. Henry said this is all he has so far." He fluttered the paper and then handed it to me. "Here."

I took the sheet and studied it.

```
Marilla Frances Keaton. Born 1781, County of
Devon. Died 1820, At Sea.

Columns represent: Register Order, Name, Age,
Sex, Occupation, Port of Origin, Destination,
*Died on Voyage, Register Comment

  1 Marilla Keaton 37 F Spinster Liverpool New York Did Not Disembark
 42 Marilla Keaton 38 F Spinster Liverpool New York Did Not Disembark
  6 Marilla Keaton 38 F Spinster Liverpool Boston   Did Not Disembark
107 Marilla Keaton 38 F Spinster Liverpool New York Did Not Disembark
 31* Marilla Keaton 38 F Spinster Liverpool New York Cause: Cholera
```

Was that our curse? Not just to die before the age of forty but to be forevermore remembered in official documents as "spinster"? Well, no matter how close to home that one may have hit, at least my odds of having to deal with a cholera diagnosis seemed minimal, since I hadn't played *The Oregon Trail* in years.

I swallowed down the initial bitterness I felt on behalf of all of the Keaton women who, like Marilla, Pippy, Aunt Lindsey, and myself, never disembarked from the *HMS Old Maid*, and asked, "All that, and then she died at sea?"

"Fascinating, isn't it?"

"Even if she wasn't allowed to get off the ship for some reason," I pressed, "wouldn't you think she'd try to escape? I mean, if she was right there, and American soil was steps away . . ."

"I know. Obviously, she would have had things to deal with that we wouldn't understand today. Who knows what sort of servitude she was working under, or what sort of danger she could have been in."

"Danger?"

My dad shrugged. "Sure." A smile overtook his face as he settled onto the stool at the table. It went without saying that he wasn't smiling at the thought of his great-great-great-grandmother's sister in peril on the high seas, but he did love the mystery of it all. And, just like me, he loved when mysteries vanished in favor of answers. "I've created all sorts of scenarios in my head."

I took the other stool across from him. "Such as?"

"The obvious, of course. She could have just been scared."

I scoffed. "Scared?"

"Absolutely. A new world, all alone? Who wouldn't be terrified?"

"Well, sure," I consented. "But so scared that she decided to just stay put and make the trip all the way back to England? And say for a minute that was it. Say she did it because she was scared. By the *next* time they docked in New York, wouldn't she have built up her courage enough to get off the blasted boat?"

"That's certainly what makes sense . . . to us . . . in the twenty-first century." He winked, and I knew the professor in him was making an appeal to the student in me. For all the ways my family had never understood me, my dad and I had never had any problem connecting at a scholarly level. My thirst for knowledge was rivaled only by his passion and drive to teach. "But Marilla had to choose whether or not to disembark into an America that was still a century away from giving women the right to vote. Seventy years away from the relative safety and protection afforded by Ellis Island. Less than fifty years out from 'all men are created equal.' Honorable though I believe the intentions of most of our founding fathers to have been, I don't think they were putting all their collective genius and power into paving a road of comfort and prosperity for old-maid wenches from the old country."

Bitter laughter burst from me. Yes, the term had just been floating around in my brain, but that didn't make me any less offended to hear it said aloud by someone else. "'Old maid'? At thirty-seven?"

"Thirty-eight."

I laughed again, even as my eyes began to sting. "Oh well, in that case . . ."

He rested his elbows on the table and leaned forward. "Again, McKenna. We're looking at a different world here. Marilla wasn't married, she didn't have any money, she didn't have any family with her, and she certainly wasn't hoping to graduate at the top of her class from Princeton." His eyebrow raised, and I knew he was challenging me again. It was as if he were saying, "Come on. You can do better than this."

I sighed. "I know."

"By the time you factor in health conditions, sanitation, life expectancy, how difficult it would have been to make that trip even *once* . . . By thirty-eight, she was an old woman." His expression softened. "At the same age, you have nothing but possibility stretched out before you. But if you were in her shoes, are you really so certain you would have gotten off the ship?"

I bit my lip to keep it from trembling, and when that failed, I looked down at the piece of paper in my hands so at least the trembling wouldn't be visible.

I hated to admit it, even to myself, but I was suddenly picturing Kate Winslet's Rose DeWitt Bukater realizing the Heart of the Ocean was in her pocket as the Statue of Liberty came into view. *Nothing but possibility.* Sure, Marilla Keaton's story was probably slightly less glamorous—most likely without a Leo or a Celine Dion song in sight—but hadn't her life been nothing but possibility too? Just like Kate Winslet's? Just like mine? Surely she was on the verge of achieving everything she had worked for. Everything she had dreamed of. How could she just sit back and allow it to be stolen from her?

I shook my head and stood from my stool. "I don't know," I croaked. Surely my voice could make a better showing. I cleared my throat and pretended to be looking at the reproduction of Ptolemaeus's *Trapezoid Projection of the Caspian Sea* that had hung in our old house when we lived in Durham the first time and then made its way to Dad's office at Columbia when there was no room in our tiny Manhattan apartment. "I don't know." *Better.* "I get what you're saying. I do. But yeah. I think I would have gotten off the ship."

I had turned back to face him again, and he studied me intently. Maybe he was trying to figure out if I was okay. Maybe he was just trying to decide whether it was worth debating Marilla's decision. Either way, after looking into my eyes for a solid six seconds, he seemed to decide it was time to move on.

"Yes. I believe you would have."

❀

Minutes later I was feigning a headache—easy enough to blame on all that fresh Durham air and various plant life I wasn't used to—and excusing myself to my bedroom. I shut the door behind me and made my way over to my old stereo, which my mom had made her own—made evident by the stack of Simon & Garfunkel and James

Taylor CDs sitting beside it. I settled on a Joni Mitchell disc and pushed Play, the music that filled the space just loud enough to keep my voice from being distinct outside the room.

I sat on the edge of the daybed and flipped through my contacts until I found the number I was looking for, then took a deep breath and dialed. It rang once, and Carrie Keats from Accounting picked up.

"Hello?"

"Hi, Carrie. This is McKenna Keaton." The prolonged silence made me wonder if the call had dropped. "Hello? Carrie?"

"Yeah, I'm here." She cleared her throat. "So, um . . . how are you?"

Having friends at work had never been a priority for me. I was there to do a job, not socialize. Truthfully, there was little I hated more than when Ralph Wallis stood in front of the entire staff each year at the company Christmas party and called us a family. I *had* a family, and as nice as some of the people at W, M and B were, they weren't it. But there were some members of the staff whom I enjoyed more than others, and Carrie had always been near the top of the list. With our last names being so close, we'd had more mail mix-ups and phone extension misdials than I could count through the years, and it had always been fun to laugh about it with her.

"I'm great," I lied. "Really great." I cleared my throat. "I'm, um . . . I'm actually in North Carolina for my sister's engagement party. It's not until next weekend, but I thought I'd go ahead and take some time—"

"I'm glad you can be with your family during all of this."

Well, there you go. Any wondering I'd had as to the extent of Carrie's knowledge of the situation had been cleared.

I forced a chuckle and crossed one leg over the other. That was instantly uncomfortable, so I uncrossed and tried again going the other direction. "Isn't this just the craziest thing? I tell you, as soon as they figure out the mistake, we're going to have to make sure safeguards are put in place so this sort of thing never happens to anyone else. I guess that's the good that may come from it. Better systems and—"

"Look, McKenna, I really shouldn't be talking to you." Her voice was soft but controlled. "There's an ongoing investigation—"

"I know."

"—and you know as well as anyone that we just have to let due process run its course."

"I know," I repeated with a sigh. "But have you heard *anything*? I can't just sit around and . . ." I uncrossed my legs again and began rubbing my temples with the fingers of the hand not holding the phone. My headache no longer required feigning. "They're going to find the error. Right?"

Her soft voice became an even quieter whisper. "You're saying you really didn't do it?"

My head flew out of my hand. "Of course I didn't do it, Carrie! Hang on . . . Are you saying people actually think I did it?"

I heard her let out a full breath, and then she said, in a full and unwavering voice, "I really can't be talking to you, McKenna. I'm sorry."

The next thing I heard was a *click* as she ended the call, and then I was left to wonder if that was how Marilla had felt when she was sailing away from America. Maybe the very small difference between *nothing but possibility* and just plain *nothing* all came down to the direction you were sailing.

Chapter 12

By Friday evening I'd mostly come to believe in a philosophy of *Nothing but possibility* again, if for no other reason than I was a believer in *Nothing but the truth, the whole truth, so help me, God*. I may not have had access to any official W, M and B files, but I had complete access to my copies of my own records. Not of client information or case briefs, but every expense I had ever recorded and every hour I'd ever billed. And it was all there, in black and white. Present and accounted for down to the last meticulous penny. So, I would wait. Truth would win out.

When I wasn't sneaking away to my room to comb through all of my records that I had uploaded to the cloud, Marilla provided a nice distraction.

"You know what it was?" Taylor mused as we relaxed in the living room once there were no more arrangements to see to for the next day's festivities. "She was in love."

I rolled my eyes at her. I was going to have to stop doing that before the old adage our parents always told us finally came true and they got stuck that way.

"What makes you say that?" my dad asked, and I wanted to plead with him not to encourage her. But it was too late.

"Isn't it obvious?" As she talked, she feverishly carried on another conversation on her phone, all with the use of only one thumb. I had never felt older. I pictured my methodical two-thumbed technique, which, compared to hers, looked like Dad's index-finger-speeding-along-like-a-sloth technique compared to mine. "She was in love with one of the guys who shoveled coal or something."

My dad tilted his head and took her theory far too seriously. "Oh, you mean someone who worked on the ship?"

"Yep."

"Well, if that was the case, why didn't they just disembark together?" I asked.

She shrugged. "I don't know."

"Well, then, let's try to figure it out!" Dad practically squealed, his heart and head both threatening to combust in a joy explosion, I figured. His little hobby—long avoided by every other member of the family—had intrigued two of his daughters *and* he had an opportunity to teach and help us expand our minds? Yes, indeed. It was a good day for Scott Keaton.

Mom peeked around the corner, dish towel in hand. "Erica and the kids are going to be here soon. It wouldn't be the worst thing if someone set the table. Be sure to wash your hands."

I couldn't help but wonder how old we would all have to be before my mother had faith in our commitment to washing our hands before we touched everyone's silverware, even if she wasn't around to remind us.

"But by all means," she added, "I don't want to interrupt yet another conversation about Matilda."

I caught her eye, and she winked at me. Sometimes there was nothing she adored more than to lovingly antagonize her husband.

"It's Marilla!" Dad called out, but she had already turned back toward the kitchen and paid him no mind whatsoever. He kicked his feet from the ottoman and stood from his lounge chair, making his way toward the kitchen. He motioned for Taylor and me to follow him as he passed, and I resigned myself to the fact that I didn't have much choice but to acquiesce. No matter how much I would have rather asked my mom if there was some demanding manual labor she needed done in isolation instead.

Once we had all washed our hands and returned to the kitchen, Mom assigned each of us tasks, just as she had twenty-five years ago. Dad was responsible for shredding the roast for the BBQ pulled-pork sandwiches, Taylor had to put ice into each drinking glass, and I had to set the table with plates, utensils, and napkins.

And as we worked, Marilla's love story continued to grow to epic Kate-and-Leo proportions.

"Maybe they were working off his debt," Dad suggested. "Then they would be free to marry."

"Yes!" Taylor exclaimed as ice clanked against glass. "Would there have been any sort of servitude for someone in his position at that time? Like, do you think that maybe she was free but he wasn't, and she sacrificed her freedom until *he* was free, and then they were going to go to the colonies together?"

I guffawed. "'The colonies'? Tay, it was 1820. *Indiana* was a state by 1820."

They both ignored me. Understandable. Why would we want to inject a silly thing like reality into the conversation?

"Hey, hey!" my mom called out as we heard the front door open and her grandchildren made a beeline straight toward her. "About time you got here. How was school?"

She passed hugs and kisses around—as if she hadn't just seen them the day before—and gave them her full attention as Cooper insisted an incident that had occurred on the playground wasn't his fault.

I walked back to the living room just as Erica announced her fatigued presence with a drowsy, "Hey."

"I'm glad you're here." I wrapped my arms around her and really took a look at her while Mom continued her listening and Dad and Tay continued their dramatizing. "You look awful. Are you okay?"

"Yep. Just exhausted." She collapsed onto the couch. "Staff meeting before school, parking lot duty after school, and then one of Jared's patients broke a bracket, so I had to get the kids from their various after-school . . ." The words got cut off by a yawn, and she covered her mouth with one hand while the other gestured. "Yada yada, you know the drill. Same old, same old. I don't want to talk about this anymore."

Erica has very articulate hands.

"Is Jared still at work?"

She shook her head as she wrapped up her yawn. "He's on his way. How have things been going around here?" she asked once she'd gaped another time or two.

"Dad and Taylor are driving me nuts," I whispered.

"Dad is?"

I smirked. "I was trying to be nice."

"Marilla still?" She fluffed a pillow on the end of the couch and then reclined her head onto it.

"Yes!" I exclaimed. "Dad is playing it up for Taylor's benefit, and Taylor's just, well, Taylor. And now they've concocted this whole romantic epic starring our great-great-great-great-aunt and her able-bodied-seaman lover—"

A laugh exploded from her. "Ooh, I like that one!"

Jared opened the front door and came inside. He nodded at me where I was sitting on the arm of the chair across from the couch, and I nodded back.

"Hey, Pierson."

"Hey, Keaton. Did my wife make it into the house before falling asleep?"

"Just barely." I pointed at the couch, and she raised her hand into the air to wave at him.

He made his way to the couch, leaned over the back of it, and kissed her. "Why don't you go home? The kids and I'll stay for dinner, and then we'll be home."

Erica yawned something that sounded vaguely like, "I don't want to miss time with McKenna," and I blew a kiss at her.

Jared lifted her feet and sat down with them in his lap. He began removing her shoes and massaging her feet. "What's everybody been up to today?"

I sighed. "You know. The usual."

My mom's head poked around the doorframe again. "Come on, everybody. Dinner's on the table."

"Dad! I've got it!" Taylor exclaimed just as we entered the dining room. "What if some rich nobility guy was in love with her and wouldn't let her off the ship? It wasn't that she was in love. Someone was holding her captive!"

Dad seemed intrigued but skeptical. "And he was on the ship too?"

"Yes!"

"But that doesn't make any sense. Why would he be on the ship? Why would he keep sailing back and forth across the Atlantic? Why wouldn't he hold her captive on land?"

"Or maybe he was the captain or the first mate or something?" Taylor compromised.

I hadn't realized just how much Taylor looked like our father until I saw them both there, side by side, with the exact same crossed arms and the exact same challenged-but-enthralled expression on their faces.

"Maybe there was no way he could be with her on land," Erica chimed in, suddenly much more alert as she got engaged in the game. "Maybe it was more than a class thing. He may have had a wife and kids back home. So of *course* he had to keep sailing back and forth, from England to America and back again, in order to be with her."

I glanced at my watch and smiled. Only six more hours until the weekend. The weekend Henry had said he would definitely be home by. Then he and I . . .

I had no idea what he and I would do. But at the very least, I looked forward to the legendary Hank Blume bringing a little bit of objective sanity to the Keaton family.

❀

The next morning I was standing on a little round pedestal, wearing nothing but a bra from the waist up and nothing but my underwear and delicately pinned strips of chiffon on the bottom half—and being forced to confront that reality by the endless hall of mirrors that surrounded me—when my phone rang.

"Who is it?" I asked my mom, who was sitting on the settee in the center of the room, serving as the current custodian of the cell phones and handbags.

"Private number." She took a sip of her bridal boutique-provided champagne. "Do you want it?"

I couldn't imagine who would be calling me and figured it was probably a robocall. The seamstress had stepped out of the room, but I knew she would be back any minute—and if answering a spam number would get me out of listening to one more comment about how I had "mothering hips," I was willing to chat for a little while with someone informing me my Microsoft virus protection was out of date.

"Please."

She hurried it over to me, and I grinned as I answered with, "Whatever you're selling, I'm probably buying. All I ask is you take your time."

After a brief pause, a deep and familiar voice replied with, "That's the best greeting I've ever gotten from anyone."

Heat rose to my cheeks. "Henry?"

The chattering and giggling in the room on the part of my sisters; Taylor's best friend since college, Dana; Jackson's brother's wife, Anika; and flower girl, April, died down instantly—but that didn't stop Taylor from shushing everyone, just to be safe.

"Yeah. I hope you don't mind, I got your number from Jared."

"Not at all."

"How are you?"

I caught a glimpse of myself in the mirror and wanted nothing more than to step off the pedestal, put on some clothes, and take the call in private. But I had been ordered to stay put while more material was gathered for my hips—perfectly designed for childbirth, y'all!—and I knew that if I moved, I would undo a lot of hard work. I would also most likely begin bleeding from any number of precarious pin locales.

"I feel a bit like a Bridesmaid Barbie voodoo doll at the moment, actually. I'm currently being fitted for a bridesmaid dress. How are you?" Suddenly, a much more pressing thought entered my mind. "*Where* are you? Are you back in town?"

"No." He sighed. "I'm in Aberdeenshire, unfortunately."

I attempted to process the information. "Is that near Portland, or . . . ?"

"Not very near, no. Scotland. I'm actually about five minutes away from pulling up to Balmoral Castle."

My jaw dropped. "*The* Balmoral?" I could feel every eye in our private fitting gallery on me.

"Yes."

"Your cell signal is surprisingly good!"

He laughed. "The best of things seem to follow the queen around, I've noticed. The royal family requested a private viewing of the film. I didn't feel like I could very well say no. So, look . . . I know we didn't have any official plans or anything, but I thought I'd be back by now. Sorry."

I sighed. "It's fine, Blumenthal. I see where I rank." He laughed, and I carried on—equal parts disappointed and impressed. "No, seriously, that's very cool."

"Thanks. It will be fine, I'm sure." He was silent just long enough for me to wonder if he'd driven into an HRH dead zone, but then he was back. "I'm not going to miss seeing you, am I? I'll try to get the first flight out tomorrow."

Suddenly the fact that a roomful of women was staring at me on display in my skivvies didn't make me feel all that vulnerable or self-conscious. The thought that they could probably interpret every single bit of giddiness I was feeling, on the other hand . . .

"I'll be here. Yeah, just call me."

"I will. I hope everything goes well for your family today."

"And I hope everything goes well with the royal family today."

He chuckled. "I just hope I don't fall asleep in the back of the room as I'm forced to sit through this documentary for the twelve millionth time."

"You aren't responsible for your own marketing campaigns, are you? Please tell me you have people who do that for you."

"Yes, thankfully. Most of the time the best I'd come up with would be, 'I poured my heart, soul, blood, sweat, and tears into this, and you people just complain because it's on instead of reruns of *Downton Abbey*. Made possible by viewers like you.'"

Seconds later, he was approaching the castle and had to go, but before my mom was able to take my phone for me, he had texted.

Her Majesty's nice and all, but I really would rather be hanging out with you.

I was in so very much trouble.

Chapter 13

The engagement party actually ended up being a lot of fun—partially because my little sister was a phenomenal hostess who turned it into a warm and welcoming gathering at which everyone was made to feel like treasured members of the family and partially because Henry kept sending me texts with the queen's commentary of his film. It was like *Mystery Science Theater 3000: Royal Edition.*

During Sunday afternoon's regularly scheduled family dinner—at which several members of Jackson's family were crammed into the dining room with us—Taylor asked me for the first time when I had to head back to New York. Everyone was assuming, of course, that now the party had passed, my departure was imminent. I'd been prepared for the question, of course, and was ready to whip out my years without a vacation as justification for staying at my parents' rent free for a while longer, but she caught me at a good time. The combination of affection I was feeling for all of them, and the fact that Henry was returning to Durham with hopes of seeing me again, resulted in my unrehearsed answer:

"I don't know for sure, but I know I'm not quite ready to leave yet."

When I came downstairs for breakfast on Monday morning, confirmation that I'd made the right decision was waiting for me.

"Good morning," Henry greeted me from the armchair.

I nearly jumped out of my skin. Yes, he had startled me, but more than that, I was in a sudden panic, unable to remember what I was wearing or even if I was fully dressed. After quickly assessing the situation—Pants? Check. Shirt? Check—I smiled and made my way over to him.

"Good morning. I didn't know you were here."

"I wanted to follow up with your dad on some of his research, and he told me this would be a good time."

I glanced at my watch. Seven thirty-four. I released a puff of air and collapsed onto the couch. "Good grief. Do you ever sleep?"

"Not much, I guess. Especially when there's work to do." He was smiling, but then his brow furrowed. "Okay, to be honest, I may have used his research as an excuse to come over." I didn't even have time to process what I thought—what I *hoped*—he was saying before he continued. "Sorry. I hope that doesn't make it sound like I'm using your dad. I'm genuinely interested, and I think he's great. Seriously . . . I have entire teams of professional researchers working for me, and he makes them look like seventh graders writing a paper on stalactites and stalagmites."

"He takes it all pretty seriously."

"And I get the impression I poured gasoline on the fire with the introduction of Marilla."

"I have to admit, I haven't been as caught up in a lot of the elements of this as the rest of them, but I am intrigued by her."

He nodded. "Me too. Your dad and sister were telling me some of their theories—"

"Oh, gosh. Don't pay any attention to them on all of that. Taylor is like the MacGyver of romance. She could craft a love story out of a spool of thread, some barbed wire, and a potato."

That made him laugh—deep, free, nonconforming in its rhythm—and I felt acutely gratified by the achievement.

"Good to know. But pieced together with pipe cleaners or not, I strongly suspect she's onto something."

"What do you mean? You really think Marilla stayed on the ship for *love*?"

He settled deeper into the chair and crossed his arms. "You say that like it's a dirty word."

"Well, if it stands in the way of someone achieving their goals . . . yeah, it sort of is. I just can't wrap my mind around that, Henry. It's not like me hopping in the car and heading to Raleigh for dinner and then thinking better of it and deciding I'd rather stay in the car and swing through a drive-through. How long would it have taken to cross the Atlantic?"

"In 1820?" He thought for a moment. "Six to eight weeks, minimum. And that's if absolutely everything went right."

"And how often did absolutely everything go right?"

He grinned. "Not very often."

"So there you go. Probably eight to ten weeks. Maybe twelve. Double it for the round trip. And then again. And then again." I shook my head. "No way. No one would do that willingly. Even for *love*."

The grin remained on his lips, but it faded from his eyes.

"What?" I asked as he continued staring at me.

He chewed on his bottom lip, and the grin went away entirely. "Nothing. I'm just trying to remember if you've always been this cynical."

Laughter spilled out. "I'm not cynical! Having said that, if I am now, I think I always have been."

He adjusted on the cushion and leaned forward, toward me. Our eyes locked and remained that way for several seconds until he said, "I have a crazy idea, McKenna."

Crazy. Hmm. What would constitute crazy to Henry? Whatever it was, I refused to get my hopes up. Not that there was anything that would be worth getting my hopes up for, of course. Not that I was hoping for anything in particular. Or in general. No hopes at all. I had no hopes.

And if I had been hoping for anything, I probably would have forgotten what it was as I stared at him and examined the various healed-but-still-visible scars on his face. One on his chin, one under his left eye, one at the bridge of his nose—did he break it and get the scar at the same time?—and one above his right eyebrow. Teenaged Henry Blumenthal had probably never played a contact sport in his life—unless his stage-fencing as Mercutio counted (and take it from someone who was there: it shouldn't). But fully grown *man* Henry Blumenthal was another story entirely. His skin was weathered and tan—the kind of set-in tan that comes from so many years in the sun that you don't even burn anymore. The scars were surprising when I thought about them being obtained by the boy I had known, and something deep inside of me was desperate to know the story behind each one. Maybe because I would feel protective. Maybe because I would be impressed.

"I think you should help me research the film."

See, that's the thing about not having any hopes. You don't have to deal with ridiculous disappointment when a gorgeous man with whom you share memories from youth and whom you find intellectually stimulating and who makes you, inexplicably, want to read Hemingway and learn how to catch and descale a fish, has the most boring, least romantic, nerdiest, crazy idea ever.

"Oh. Um . . ."

"Hear me out." He hopped up from the chair and joined me on the other end of the couch. "I have a hunch—a big one—that there's something in your family's story that needs to be part of *She Dreams of America*. It might even need to be Marilla."

"You're kidding."

"Nope."

"You do realize Marilla didn't actually make it to the United States at all."

He leaned toward me and said softly, "There's a story there, McKenna. I know there is. I feel it in my gut. And I haven't gotten this far by not listening when my gut is screaming at me." He sat up straight again and exhaled and scooted a bit closer to me. I couldn't tell if it was his skin or his hair, but I caught a whiff of his scent. It was different from before, but it was just as good. It wasn't teakwood—or at least it wasn't the scent that I had associated with teakwood—but it was something equally manly and sort of generic. Mahogany? That was a thing, I was pretty sure. It was another wood. Or was mahogany a type of leather? Henry's hair didn't smell like leather. It smelled like wood so fresh that I could imagine he had cut down a tree on his way to my parents' house and slivers of bark had gotten lost in the blond tufts.

I inched myself backward just a little. Not so much he would notice but enough that our knees weren't so close to touching. If I didn't keep my guard up, I was afraid he would somehow convince me that research was sexy.

"Well, even if that's so, I don't understand why you would want *my* help. Like you just said, you have . . . people. Right? People who do that for you? And out of everyone in my family, I'm the one person who isn't all caught up in Marilla madness—"

"Exactly!" he exclaimed, and he reached out and tapped his knuckles against my knee at the same time. "I think that's why it has to be you. Well, that and the fact that I know what your mind is capable of."

"You knew what my mind was capable of as a teenager."

His chin lowered to his chest dramatically and his eyes peeked out at me from under the hair covering most of his forehead. "Give me a break. Wallis, Monroe and Burkhead isn't exactly known for hiring slouches who peaked in high school."

I did a double take. "I don't remember telling you where I work."

He raised his head and tilted it slightly as he surveyed me silently for a moment. "Do you mean to tell me you didn't google *me* at all in the last week?"

I shook my head, grateful I had only obsessed over him in my mind so that I could honestly tell him my obsession had not carried over to the internet. "I didn't. But considering I first saw you at an event declaring exactly what you do, and why you do it better than everyone else, and then you stood me up to spend time with the actual Queen of England, I feel like I could guess what the internet might say about you."

He sniggered and nodded. "Touché."

I got caught up for a moment in his reaction to my mention of his notoriety—mostly the fact that there wasn't much of a reaction at all, and it was clearly something he had come to terms with—but then a bigger, more important realization hit.

He'd googled me. After "Go, team!" and even after the discovery that I was destined to die an early, childless death because my heart—like the hearts of my foremothers before me—was an icy abyss, he'd walked away wanting to know more. Then, of course, I had to briefly consider what he may have found. That might have been worrisome if not for the fact that the ongoing investigation into my supposed misdeeds at W, M and B was, to this point, an internal affair. Until serving eighteen months to life at San Quentin for embezzlement or bribery or manipulating the stock market or stealing paper clips or whatever they mistakenly thought I did was added to my bio, I knew I was pretty darn impressive on paper.

"You're a well-respected attorney. You're the type of person to seek out the facts—the story behind the truth and the truth behind the story, not just the entertaining aspects—and you also have the irresistible family connection that I truly believe will provide all the entertaining aspects of telling this story that we could ever hope for." His knuckles were lightly touching my knee again, and

I had no control over the chills running through my body like a New York City subway map. "Wouldn't you love to find out? To find out why she never got off the ship? Sure, I have 'people,'" he said with air quotes, which required his hand to move and allowed my senses to relax, "but what's the fun in that?"

Okay, who was I trying to fool? I *did* think research was sexy. And Henry had somehow made it even sexier.

Thirty minutes later we were still sitting side by side on the couch—no longer close enough for any incidental knee contact—and we'd been joined by my parents and Taylor.

"Of course you can include our family in your documentary, Henry," my dad enthused, his eyes continually darting to my mom as if she were grounding him in reality and keeping him from having to pinch himself. "We're honored."

"Are you kidding me? *I'm* honored." Henry sat back and rested against the back pillows of the couch, the presentation portion of the morning complete. "Okay, so I'll have some documents for you to sign, and I'll sign some things that ensure I won't misrepresent—"

"That's not necessary, Henry," my mom insisted.

"Thank you for that, Mrs. Keaton. I appreciate the trust. But, unfortunately, it is necessary on my side. There are rules about what I can film and use as resources. Proprietary information. Stuff like that. But it will be easy and painless." He crossed his ankle up onto his knee and tapped me on my knee again as he did. And again, we were farther apart. It took actual effort for him to reach out and touch me that time. "That reminds me," he said to me as the casual tap gave way to a much more intimate—even if it was over before I realized it began—squeeze. "I'll have some things for you to sign too. Waivers and such. My lawyers will insist."

"They'd be horrible lawyers if they didn't."

"Hang on," Taylor interjected. "Why are there separate things for McKenna to sign?" She raised her eyebrows at me and chewed the inside of her cheek. She couldn't have possibly even suspected that I was going to be helping him with research, but her nerve endings were no doubt tingling at the slightest hint of there being an added layer between Henry and me.

He lowered his foot back onto the floor and leaned forward. "McKenna has agreed to help me some behind the scenes."

Taylor clapped her hands together and squealed, "Oh, goody!" I shot her a look of warning, and she tried to cover. "I mean, this is just all so exciting!"

I looked at Henry to make sure he wasn't weirded out by Taylor's awkward enthusiasm and discovered he didn't seem to be paying attention to Taylor at all. I caught him staring straight at me, and I smiled at him. And I have to say, I expected him to look away or pretend he had been studying the Tiffany lamp on the table behind me, but he was unabashed.

"So, um . . ." I wasn't having much luck pulling my eyes away from him, but I desperately needed him to pull his away from me. "When do we get started?"

That did it. He looked at my dad, and I felt relief course through my body. And disappointment.

"I'd love to just get in there and take some notes, Mr. Keaton."

"Of course. But I really must insist you call me Scott."

Henry laughed. "I'll try, but that's tricky for me since I've called you Mr. Keaton since I had braces."

"Fair enough." Dad stood from his chair. "Come on in and I'll—"

My mom placed her hand on his arm. "Hon, you have a lecture in less than an hour. Why don't you let McKenna show him, since she'll be working with him anyway."

Wow. She was much better at meddling than my "Oh, goody!" little sister.

"Do you mind?" Henry asked me.

Nope. Not even one little bit.

"No! I completely disagree. There is not a single justification that will *ever* make sense."

The past fifteen minutes had been new and fresh as Henry and I fell into a rhythm of working together. Yes . . . new and fresh. And fun. But as I continued to insist that I would never succumb to the romanticism that he, like Taylor and everyone else, was attempting to bring to Marilla's journey, it also felt familiar and nostalgic. And again, so much fun. I'd sort of forgotten that he and I had been on the debate team together beginning sophomore year, up until he moved to Oregon. But oh my, I remembered now. I mostly remembered that it was always the two of us left to duke it out when Mr. Graham hosted his monthly elimination bracket challenges during college basketball season. (College basketball is a big thing in North Carolina. Like Canada has hockey and Italy has pasta, we have March Madness.)

"Exactly!" His rebuttal was accompanied by laughter in those teal eyes, though his mouth was all business. "There is not a single justification that will ever make sense as to why she stayed on the ship—apart from the possibility that she wasn't *allowed* off the ship—"

"She could have found a way."

"—and you seem all too eager to forget that odds are she had zero legal rights, zero education, zero prospects on her own—"

"Then you die trying to make it work!" I protested. "You die trying to overcome those obstacles. You don't die at sea during your . . . what? Fourth? Fifth journey across the Atlantic?"

The smile finally made its way from his eyes to his lips. "McKenna, I'm saying I agree with you."

I rubbed the back of my neck as I thought through our debate. "No, you're not."

"I am."

I growled, and he snickered in response, which caused me to slug him on the arm. "No, you're not. All you've done since the minute we got in here is argue with me."

"Ah. See? There it is." He sat down on his stool and turned his attention back to the documents on the table.

"There *what* is?"

He spun his stool around in my direction and crossed his arms. "I don't know. Call it what you want. The difference between us. What makes you so infuriating." My mouth flew open, and he winked, and I forgot whatever it was I was going to say. "Also, it's what probably makes you a fantastic attorney. And definitely why *I* have honorary doctorates from Oxford and Brown and you don't."

My mouth didn't fly open that time so much as drop with a thud. "You do?"

"I do."

I crossed my arms and mirrored his stance. "Well . . . I could have *real* ones if I wanted."

"I don't doubt that one iota. All the same, I'm a doctor. You aren't." He kicked his feet off the floor and propelled the stool around 360 degrees once.

When he kicked off for another spin, I surprised him by grabbing on to the bars on each side of the back and stopping him from going anywhere. "An honorary doctor."

His face was only inches from mine. My thighs were brushing against his knees, and the awkward tension on my back muscles left me little choice but to respond to his instinctive invitation for me to step closer. He spread his knees and propped his heels up on the metal footrest on the stool, and I straightened myself out and released the bars that had been gripped in my ever-tighter, ever-shakier fists. I could barely see his eyes through his thick, dark lashes. I was looking down on his face, and he was looking up slightly, but his gaze wasn't making it as far as my eyes. He seemed to be distracted by my mouth, and even though he was looking straight at them, I had no choice but to chew on my lips in nervous anticipation of what I suspected was about to happen to them.

"Henry, I think you'll want to see this." My dad's voice shattered the taut, anticipatory silence.

Henry and I jumped away from each other with such a start that I honestly had no idea how we ended up in the positions we landed in. He was completely on the other side of the table, facing the door, and I was staring up at my dad's degree certificate from UC Berkeley, on the far wall, as if I were seeing it for the first time.

"Oh, hey there, Mr. Keaton," Henry greeted him as he walked into the office, and his voice actually cracked. He cleared his throat and then continued speaking in a voice much more befitting a nearly forty-year-old man. "You have something else to show me?"

"Yeah. I just got an email . . ." Dad's voice trailed off, and I turned around to see what had caused him to stop speaking. His eyes were darting from Henry to me and back again. "Am I interrupting something?"

Learning from Henry's mistakes, I cleared my throat *before* I opened my mouth. "No, not at all. We were just . . . looking at . . ."

"Manifests," Henry completed, rushing to my aid.

That was the moment we both realized that rather than questioning whether or not something romantic had been about to happen, my dad was probably just wondering what in the world we'd been looking at, and why. We both snapped to attention and headed back to the drafting table—and I even managed to stay standing upright when Henry briefly placed his hand on the small of my back to help usher me through the tight space between his body and the table and back over to the other side of him.

Seemingly satisfied with the explanation of all the unexplainable awkwardness there before him, my dad said, "Good. That's what I wanted to talk to you about, actually."

"You found a new manifest?" Henry asked.

Dad nodded and tapped on his phone, then rushed over to the printer behind us to grab the document as it shot out. Henry scooted a little bit out of the way, which caused his hip to brush against mine. He was so close that my senses were overpowered once again by all of those scents taken from nondescript nature. I wondered what would happen if I reached out and put my hand on his back, like he had on mine. Not to guide and assist him but for extremely selfish reasons. My mind wandered to what it would be like not just to reach out and touch him but to know it was my right to do so. To grab a belt loop on the back of his corduroys and pull him against me and wrap my arms around him. What would it feel like to be enveloped in his arms and just disappear for a little while?

"Is this what I think it is?" Henry asked, his voice dripping with giddiness. The change of tone grabbed my attention.

"Okay, so it *is* something?" My dad's excitement rose in correlation with Henry's. "I thought so, but you know what you're looking for a lot more than I do."

"What is it?" I got up on my tiptoes and peered over Henry's shoulder to try to see the paper between them.

What would it be like to feel comfortable enough to rest my chin on his shoulder? For him to throw his arm around me and pull me around to the other side of him? To kiss him as we transitioned?

As it was, he did the most chivalrous thing he *should* have done in front of my dad, considering we were still only a little more than a week into our first face-to-face interactions since an era when we both had acne.

"Here, look at this, McKenna." He handed me the paper and stepped back to make room for me, then began looking over my shoulder. With about five inches between his height and mine, it was obviously going to work much better that way. "This is the declaration from the captain of the ship to U.S. Customs agents of all souls aboard and all souls lost."

"Pretty neat, huh?"

I smiled at the pride on my dad's face. His family was going to be featured in a Hank Blume documentary—and Scott Keaton had apparently unearthed a gem to add to the mix. Yep. Pretty neat indeed.

"Mr. Keaton, this is fantastic. Where did you find this?"

"There's a visiting professor in the history department who used to be a curator at the Family History Library in Salt Lake."

"Of course. Brilliant. I hadn't even gotten around to *thinking* about—"

"I know. Neither had I. I was just talking to him last week, and he was intrigued by the fact that her register order was number one, so—"

"Hang on." Henry's eyes lit up as he reclaimed the manifest from me with urgency. "That's right! Marilla's register order was 'one' on her *first* voyage. Oh, Mr. Keaton, this is unbelievable."

"So here's what I was thinking, Henry. If we cross-reference the other names on the declaration, there will probably be some answers to be found. And if we can track down the other manifests . . . What if there's another name that's on the ship every time Marilla is?"

I'd never seen my dad as crestfallen as he was in the very next moment when my mother's voice rang out. "Scott, you're going to be late."

He swallowed his disappointment at having to leave and said, "If you need me, I could cancel class today . . ."

Henry pulled his eyes away from the paper and looked at my dad with surprise and compassionate tolerance. "Oh. Well, I mean, I'd hate for you to have to—"

"I'm here to represent the Keatons, remember?" I placed my hand on his arm and got up on my tiptoes again, this time to kiss my dad on the cheek. "I promise I'll do my best to make you proud and represent you well."

When I pulled away from the kiss, I noticed his cheeks were flushed and his eyes were misty, and panic washed over me. I hadn't meant to hurt his feelings. And I certainly hoped I hadn't embarrassed him in front of Henry. I knew that would be devastating to him. But I'm pretty sure I had interpreted all of the cues with very little accuracy.

"I'm *always* proud of you, kiddo. And as far as a representative for the family . . ." He scoffed. "There's nobody better."

I swallowed down the lump in my throat and croaked out, "Thanks, Daddy."

"Scott!"

He and I both chuckled at Mom's determination to keep him on schedule. It was a duty she had always taken seriously, and he knew as well as everyone else did that without her, he would be lost.

"Have fun, you two," he said as he headed out the door.

And then Henry and I were alone again. I wondered if there was any chance we were going to pick back up with the fun we'd been having before my dad interrupted us, but one look at the enthralled expression on his face made it abundantly clear we'd moved on to a different brand of fun.

Research didn't feel very sexy anymore.

"McKenna, look at this," he told me again, but his enthusiasm had grown from the time my dad gave him the manifest. "Do you know what this is?"

"You said it was the—"

"No, look." He kept telling me to look at it, but he wasn't giving me a chance to. He began pacing the room, the document in his hands. "Have you ever heard of the Steerage Act of 1819?"

"Of course."

He stopped pacing and looked at me in surprise. "It was basically one of the first immigration laws. It was passed by Congress to—"

"To improve travel conditions aboard ships bringing immigrants to the United States. I said I'd heard of it, Henry."

Seriously. What did he take me for?

"My apologies." A smirk broke free on his lips. "You take on a lot of litigation that requires you to be brushed up on half-hearted, largely ineffective, sorely disappointing acts of Congress from the nineteenth century, do you?"

"No. But I paid attention in US history junior year. As you should know good and well, since that was the year I beat you out for the David McCullough scholarship."

"Stephen Ambrose."

"What?"

He took a step toward me, and I witnessed that smirk on his face morph into an inviting smile. Truthfully, though, I wasn't sure what he was inviting me to. Was he daring me to challenge him or inquiring as to whether or not I was interested in finishing what we had started before my dad walked in?

Either way, I considered myself up to the task.

"The scholarship—which you didn't actually beat me out for since I never submitted my application—was named after Stephen Ambrose. Not David McCullough."

Oh. Shoot. Yeah, he was right about the name. And presumably he was right about the status of his application. So maybe challenge wasn't on the table after all.

Maybe I needed to RSVP to a different invitation.

"Hey, so do you think we should talk about—"

"You mean you're not going to argue with me?" He crossed his arms over his chest and leaned up against the table.

I sighed as dramatically as I knew how. "Unfortunately, no. Not this time. It appears this may have been one of the few occasions in which you were right and I was . . . somewhat less right."

"I believe the word you're looking for is *wrong*."

"Anyway . . ." The word was long and drawn out, causing him to laugh at me. He had a small dimple high on his cheek, under his left eye, which I'd never noticed before. Maybe I hadn't seen him laugh quite as freely as he was laughing just then, or maybe I had been paying attention to the wrong things. In high school it might have been covered up by the enormous glasses he wore.

"Can I get back to the Steerage Act now?" he asked, regaining focus but allowing the humor to remain through the sparkle in his eyes.

And while the Steerage Act wasn't *quite* the titillating subject I had hoped to discuss next, I had little choice but to say, "If you must."

"See, here's what's fascinating, McKenna. Look again at this declaration." This time he handed it to me and actually allowed me to do so. "Do you see the date?"

I scanned the paper until I spotted it. "January 7, 1820. So?"

Henry leaned over my shoulder and pointed to the top right corner. "Look here."

I read aloud. "A report to the United States Congress from the Collector of Customs at New York. Report dated January 7, 1820. Document volume . . ." I tilted my head up over my shoulder at him. "Volume one?"

He snatched it back out of my hands and studied it, and I turned my body toward him. I still didn't understand *why* he was so excited, but I sure did enjoy watching his eyes feverishly scan the page as he soaked in as much information as he could, and I didn't think I'd ever get tired of looking at his teeth chew on his bottom lip.

"McKenna, this is the first declaration under the Steerage Act. The very first. The mandates would have been effective at the start of the year, so this was probably the first ship into New York Harbor that was required to give the US a list of passengers. The first ship that ever legally had to confess that anyone had died during the journey."

"Okay, I understand why that's interesting. I guess I just don't really understand the significance."

His shoulders fell, and I worried for a moment that I had burst his bubble, but it didn't take long to see and understand that his bubble was still very much intact. "The significance is that it's discoveries like this that stand at the precipice between history and storytelling. We knew that Marilla was number one in the register order of her first voyage, but now we know she was number one on *voyage* number one. The Steerage Act really accomplished nothing—of course you already knew that as a recipient of the Doris Kearns Goodwin fellowship, or whatever." I rolled my eyes at him—but also couldn't have wiped the grin off my face if my life depended on it. "But for the first time, on this voyage . . . the United States government claimed that the life of every single passenger on board mattered. She could have been the very first immigrant to step foot on American soil to take her chances and put her trust in that claim. Instead, something possessed her to keep making that perilous journey until it killed her."

"Wow." I released the breath I had been holding. "So that's what you look for. The human-interest aspect?"

The left corner of his lips rose as he leaned in and whispered to me, "I look for the moment that makes the nothing-but-the-facts attorney hold her breath and say, 'Wow.'"

Wow.

"So, what now?" I asked him. I could feel my cheeks growing warm, and I caught myself tucking my hair behind my ears unnecessarily. It was a self-aware gesture I wasn't used to making, but his body was so close to mine that I was beginning to lean backward over my dad's drafting table. It wasn't that I wanted distance from him. Quite the opposite. But I certainly wasn't accustomed to sharing my personal space.

He reached past me to grab one of Dad's notebooks—his chest brushed against my upper arm—and then he pulled away, as if the world *weren't* on the verge of spontaneous combustion.

"Well," he replied with a sigh as he flipped open the notebook and sat himself down on the stool in the corner. "Now I head to New York."

It wasn't as if I'd never heard the name of my favorite city in the world mentioned, and of course I'd only been away from it for nine days. But hearing it mentioned by Henry's voice caused a response in me that I didn't quite recognize—but which was also the most familiar thing in the world. New York had a different rhythm than anywhere else. It was *my* rhythm. Being anywhere else was like trying to dance a waltz to a rhumba beat.

"You're going to New York? Why? For research or—"

"No, nothing quite as exciting as that, I'm afraid." He smiled up at me, and I kept staring, waiting for more. "Fundraising," he finally said. "One of the more tedious aspects of the job. Friday night is the first of"—he rolled his eyes upward and seemed to be calculating—"seven scheduled fundraisers for *She Dreams of America.*"

"What do you mean, fundraising? Meeting with producers or something?"

He shook his head. "I don't have producers. I have sponsors. That way no one gets any control apart from me."

"I'm sure people are lining up to give you money, right?"

He laughed. "Yes. Yes, they are. Until I tell them that whole 'No one gets any control apart from me' thing. But I always end up with enough to get the film made . . . eventually."

I couldn't help but think of it all from a legal perspective. His filmmaking process was interesting. Marilla was interesting. The

revelation that throughout my childhood I should have been pray-
ing, "If I should die before I mate, at least I reached age thirty-eight,"
was morbid and somewhat depressing . . . but interesting. But the idea
that American treasure Hank Blume had to pound the pavement to
get his films made? That was downright fascinating.

"So, are you a nonprofit?"

He pulled his phone out of his pocket in response to a ding, typed
for a few seconds with his thumbs, then said, "Yep."

"And you get paid by the nonprofit or—"

"I get a salary." He looked up from his phone and stuffed it back
into his pocket. "I'm sure you make significantly more money than I
do, in case you're wondering."

"I wasn't wondering that. Really, I wasn't. I guess I just never
thought about how this all works." I shrugged. "So, you have to go
raise money? You do that every time?"

Henry stood from the stool. "Every time."

"And the films . . . If you don't mind me asking—"

"They each cost about five million to make. Spread out over the
two to three years on average that it takes to complete a project. And
I usually have two or three films in various stages of production at
the same time."

My jaw dropped. "Wow."

Laughter burst from him. "See, that's not the 'wow' I'm seeking."

I shrugged again. "Call me a nerd, but this is fascinating to me."

He tilted his head and studied me, then brought his thumb up
to his mouth and began chewing on the tip of it lightly. I couldn't
imagine what could possibly merit so much thought. I had expected
him to call me a nerd and move on.

"Then come to New York with me," he said after several more
seconds of apparently intense deliberation. "Go to this fundraiser
with me. I'll introduce you to the high-stakes world of documentary
filmmaking."

"Oh. I don't know . . ."

Sure, McKenna. Now you gain enough humility to acknowledge to him that there is something you don't know.

New York itself was the only aspect of the idea of going to New York with Henry that was actually making any sense in my mind. I didn't typically just take off and go places. I certainly didn't typically take off and go places—like New York or, you know, dinner and a movie—with men I was attracted to.

Of course, when was the last time I had been attracted to a man? Oh, sure, Jeremiah Burkhead was pretty handsome. And he and I had once taken the Long Island Railroad from Penn Station to Massapequa together to meet with a client. But it was the day before Thanksgiving, and the train was so packed we weren't even able to sit in the same car.

I very nearly got derailed. In my mind. Not on the Long Island Railroad, thank goodness. Thoughts of Jeremiah and the way I had felt every time I was his pick for second chair sent bursts of exhilaration through my body. I could still remember that feeling of confidence and achievement—even though it felt, at the moment, like something from my distant past rather than January. Every moment I'd ever spent with Jeremiah had been purely professional. The more tantalizing moments had bordered on friendly, and of course there had been the ongoing aspirations toward one day being Brigitta's stepmother. When I worked with him, I was calmly self-assured and stressed out to within an inch of my life, all at once, and I wouldn't have had it any other way. I wouldn't have imagined there *was* any other way.

But being Henry's de facto number two on Project Marilla had created all sorts of new sensations.

He placed his hand on mine on top of the desk—putting a few of those new sensations to work—and said, "Please, McKenna. Come with me."

Wow.

Chapter 14

Early Friday afternoon I landed at JFK with an overnight bag, a jumbled-up stomach that was full of anticipation and uncertainty, and a little per diem cash from In Blume Productions. That was a jumble of emotions in and of itself for me. Henry'd had my parents and me sign all those agreements he'd told us were necessary, and as an official consultant on a project, it was legally and morally acceptable for him to pay my way to New York. After all, he'd assured me, he was going to put me to work. The only part about any of that that bothered me was knowing that if he *hadn't* offered to pay, I wouldn't have been able to afford to take the trip. I mean, I had money in my savings account, and I certainly had enough to live on for a while. I'd always been smart with money, and apart from my apartment—which was currently being sublet, of course—clothes for work, and food, I had never been one to spend much of my hard-earned income. But that applied doubly when nothing about my future was stable, so it was good that I was on the clock with Henry.

At least that was what the sensible side of me said, no matter how much it hurt my pride. The *less* sensible side of me hated the confusion exacerbated in my mind by knowing that we were working together and I was there for business purposes. That certainly went a long way toward reining in my fantasies about making out with him in a horse-drawn carriage.

Okay, no, it didn't. Those fantasies were pretty unbridled.

I was preparing to hop on the Jamaica AirTrain to Penn Station to meet Henry at Shake Shack for lunch as we had arranged when I got a text from him.

Did I catch you? Sending a car.

Well, thank goodness for that. I certainly wasn't above taking the train; in fact, it was my most familiar mode of transportation in the city. But I *hated* the AirTrain from JFK. For every one New Yorker like me who knew where they were going, kept their head down, listened to music on their earbuds, and packed sensibly, there were two or three families with parents who were trying to wrangle their kids while simultaneously attempting to read a Metro map and asking those of us with earbuds in if this was the train to Times Square. And rest assured, those families always had huge rolling suitcases that inevitably rolled all through the train and bumped into my shins repeatedly.

I wasn't fooling myself that what I felt for Henry up to that point was anything more than attraction, friendship, and sincere respect, but sending a car to pick me up at JFK would have inched me closer to love with even a hideous, mind-numbing ogre.

My Lyft driver, Antonia, was there to pick me up in a Hyundai Santa Fe just a few minutes later, and I dozed off before we hit the Brooklyn Queens Expressway. The next twenty-five minutes or so gave me, perhaps, the most satisfying sleep I had ever had as an adult. I don't know what it was. Maybe it was the feeling of being back home and being able to pretend, even just for a day or two, that everything was right with the world again. Except it was right in a way that cut down on my stress levels, at least in regard to deadlines and pressures at work.

Of course, those stresses were replaced by butterflies that felt every bit as invasive . . . and yet much more pleasant. But thinking about spending time with Henry certainly still gave my blood pressure a workout. It gave me an opportunity to experience the adrenaline rush of stress—the part I loved and lived for—without feeling that the entire world was riding on my shoulders. Specifically, between my rhomboid major and rhomboid minor, as Gerald, my massage therapist, would be all too happy to share with you while he was yelling at me that I needed a vacation. (Oh, yeah. I spend money on my apartment, clothes for work, food, and Gerald.)

I guess it's also possible that my amazing rest came as a result of Antonia listening to an audio reading of Ayn Rand's *The Fountainhead* at 75 percent speed.

I woke up from the best power nap ever—I'd have to make sure that fact made it into Antonia's review—to the familiar soundtrack of Central Park South. I don't know fully how to explain it, but it's an indisputable fact that the traffic and congregating around Columbus Circle and Bloomingdale's sounds different from, say, Herald Square and Macy's.

"Excuse me," I said to Antonia. "I think we're supposed to be going to the Shake Shack at One Penn Plaza."

She instructed Siri to pause her book—although I think we could have had a pretty in-depth conversation about the Cold War's effect on global economics and she would have only missed a paragraph or two.

From underneath her sunglasses I saw her eyes flash at me briefly in the rearview mirror. "No. The Plaza."

I sighed as she pulled up in front of the valet entrance of the Plaza Hotel. Yes, the word *plaza* was used in both cases, but this really wasn't a difficult distinction.

"I'm sorry, but you got your information wrong. This is the Plaza Hotel," I pointed out, very unnecessarily. From the back seat I pointed at the historic, flag-decorated entrance. And that's when I saw him. Henry Blumenthal under the awning of the Plaza Hotel, in a light-gray, tailor-fit suit and darker gray tie. Waving at me. Transitioning those fantasies I'd been having from a horse-drawn carriage to the Plaza's Palm Court. Maybe immediately following afternoon tea.

"I'm sorry. This is right. I didn't know the plan had changed." I thanked her and got out of the car, smiled at the bellhop as I passed, and braced myself for the added impact that Henry in a good suit was going to have on my nervous system.

"Hey there. Everything go okay?"

"Yeah. This is not Shake Shack."

He looked behind him in faux shock. "It's not? *That* explains why the lobby doesn't smell like onions." He laughed. "No, it's not. I just thought it made more sense to give you a little time to settle in first." He nodded at the doorman, holding the entrance open for us, and then once again did that shiver-inducing thing where he put his hand gently on the small of my back and ushered me through.

"'Settle in'? We're not staying here, are we?"

"I thought we might. Unless it doesn't meet your standards. There's a Y in Flushing that gets great reviews on Yelp, if you would prefer."

We walked through the opulent lobby with its cream walls and gold accents and crystal chandeliers overhead. I'd been there before, of course. For lunches. Meetings. Tea with clients from out of town who, no matter how rich they were or how extravagant their lifestyles, seemed so caught up in the old–New York mystique of the Plaza that they half expected Eloise to come sit and visit for a while. But I'd never stayed there. And knowing that a month of the lease on my Upper West Side apartment would only get me about three or four nights at the Plaza certainly raised some concerns.

"Trust me, I'd love to stay here." I followed him into an elevator and began speaking more softly, even though we were alone. "But we're here for a fundraiser, right? I guess I just didn't expect all those funds to go to the Plaza."

He chuckled as the elevator came to rest on the seventeenth floor. "Before I answer any questions that could incriminate me, I must know—and in fact, I think you're legally required to be forthcoming with the information—are you asking as a lawyer, or are you asking as the girl I'm trying to impress?"

My heart stopped beating. It just full-on stopped beating, right there in my chest.

It felt very much like the moment called for a little flirting, and I would have given anything to realize—*before* that moment—that I had no idea how to flirt. It would have been nice to ask Erica for some coaching. To go back and rewatch *Up Close & Personal* for the sole purpose of copying Tally's seduction tactics, because all that "I want you here in the morning" stuff had certainly worked on Warren. Something. I was a great student, and with a little cramming . . .

Stop it, McKenna. The lecture was not new, but the purpose of it was. I wasn't worrying about something that wasn't there. I only needed to . . . stop worrying. Because this was Henry. And even with him standing close to me in an elevator, with him saying things like that, with him *looking* like that, I felt comfortable. I mean, I was totally dead, of course, in light of the heart thing, but I was still . . . comfortable.

I cleared my throat. "Well, as an attorney, I feel it is imperative that I first ask if the answers will be different depending on the role I'm playing when I ask."

Without missing a beat, he nodded. "Without a doubt."

The elevator doors parted, and he placed his hand across the opening to ensure it stayed put as I stepped out. He had taken my overnight bag from my shoulder somewhere along the way. Had a couple weeks in North Carolina dulled my New York senses to the point that I didn't even notice when my bag was taken from me? Or was Henry responsible for the dulling of my senses?

See, that just didn't seem right. I was pretty sure that Henry was responsible for setting every last one of my senses on high alert. Regardless, he was now carrying my bag with his left hand as he pulled a room key from his pocket with his right.

"What would you tell me as an attorney then?"

"That the Plaza is a corporate sponsor of my production company, and that they provide complimentary rooms as needed whenever I'm in town working. And it works great for meetings and lunches and such because so many of my biggest donors are the same demographic that likes to walk into the Plaza and pretend they're in a Neil Simon play."

Ah. That made sense.

"Okay, then," I began, a small hitch in my voice combining with a breathlessness I couldn't quite seem to control. "What would you say to the girl you're trying to impress?"

I followed his lead and stopped in front of a door on our right, where he leaned past me—more like *over* me, to be precise—to unlock it, then pushed it open. He then stood inches from me in the doorway as he looked into my eyes and said, "I'd tell her she's worth it."

What's more dead than dead? Has there been any research done on the phenomenon? Whatever it is—that's what I was. I couldn't speak or breathe, but I wouldn't have wanted to anyway. Any of that might have gotten in the way of feeling his breath dance across my skin. Might have distracted me from watching the way his eyes were transfixed on my lips as if he just couldn't pull himself away.

Finally, he tilted his head toward the door. "This is us."

Us?

I didn't have to ask the question aloud. He must have seen the panic in my eyes. "It's a suite. You've got your own room." He pulled away from me slightly, and a sly grin swept across his face. "But I saved the address of the Y, just in case there's a problem."

My cheeks grew warm from embarrassment knowing that he'd interpreted my panicked expression as suspicion that he had other things in mind. They grew warmer still from embarrassment—and other things—knowing that those were the *exact* suspicions I'd rushed to. "Nope. No problem."

"Good."

He opened the door farther for me, and I stepped inside. "Wow," I breathed.

"I sure do like the way you say that word."

He opened the door to the bedroom on the left of the foyer, walked in, and set my bag down at the foot of the bed. The huge, luxurious bed. The bed so magnificent that I suspected that if it was even half as comfortable as it looked, it would give me a night of sleep that might put even Antonia's Santa Fe to shame.

I rushed over to the picture window, glimpses of green assuring me of the view I would have waiting for me.

"Oh, Henry. It's gorgeous."

I stood there, looking out at Central Park in all its grandeur while he leaned against the wall beside the window and, if I'm not mistaken, looked at me.

"How long have you lived here? In Manhattan, I mean."

"Since I started law school. So . . ." A brief moment of self-consciousness threatened to take over as I prepared to reveal my age—until I remembered that my age would not come as a surprise to the guy who'd bragged about getting his driver's license first when he turned sixteen two months before Jared and five months before me. "Nearly seventeen years, I guess."

He chuckled. "And yet you're standing here looking out this window like you had no idea there was a big park in the middle of all the buildings."

I sighed and stepped closer to the window, then rested my forearm against it and leaned my head against my arm so I could look down at Fifty-Ninth Street. That strange, fantastic thoroughfare where you seemingly step through a portal and the hustle and bustle of shopping and taxis and New Yorkers always in a hurry transforms into street musicians and carriage rides and a touch of relaxation, right before your eyes.

"I love this city, Henry. It's my first love, and as stupid as it may sound, sometimes I sort of feel like it's my soul mate."

"That doesn't sound stupid at all," he replied gently.

I found the Lake—not that you could miss it—and then quickly got my bearings. That was my section of Central Park. It only took about fifteen minutes to walk down Seventy-Fourth from my apartment and then turn one way or the other on Central Park West, depending on the mood I was in. If I was seeking solitude and peace, I'd turn left, enter the park, and go walk among the blooms in the Shakespeare Garden. It was, in my opinion, the most underappreciated handful of acres in all of Manhattan. (My frustration on that point always gave way to my hope that it stayed that way, so it didn't lose the tranquility I was always able to find there.)

More often, I'd turn right, swing past the Dakota, and enter the park at Strawberry Fields. I wasn't a Beatles fan. I mean, not especially. I'd always had a healthy appreciation for them—Scott and Annie Keaton were latent hippies who'd brought their children up on John Lennon as much as *Sesame Street*—but if I'd been alive in the sixties, I wouldn't have been one of those girls screaming her head off every time Ringo lifted his stick in the air or anything. But Strawberry Fields was magical. You could sit on a bench for hours at a time and see hundreds of people pass by, and you could watch them change. Right before your eyes. You could watch the worries of the world outside Central Park slip away. People of every nationality and every language would join in impromptu Beatles sing-alongs, and at least for a few minutes certain aspects of what John Lennon had dared to imagine seemed to come true.

I continued facing the window, but I closed my eyes. I could still see the park just as clearly.

"Someone once said, 'Central Park is the great unifier of humanity. The tragedy, of course, is that its power and beauty lie in it being an exception rather than a rule.' I love that. It's so heartbreakingly, exhilaratingly accurate." My eyes began fluttering open at the sound of his shuffling feet. I looked up at his face, which I could really only see in the reflection in the window. "What are you thinking?" I asked in response to the pensive expression on his face.

He loosened the knot of his tie and allowed his neck a little more space. "Truthfully, I'm trying to determine the line between carrying on with that whole 'trying to impress the girl' thing and sounding like an egotistical heel." He turned his head back to face me, shoved his hands in the pockets of his slacks, and smiled. "That was me."

"What was you?"

"You said, 'Someone once said.' Well . . . I'm the someone. You just quoted a line from my 2015 *New York* film."

My mouth fell open. "No . . . surely not. That was . . ." I muttered, but even as I protested, I saw aerial shots unfold beneath the words that had meant so much to me, spoken by . . . "Emilio Estevez?"

Henry glared at me with incredulity. "No, I'm serious. I wrote that line. I know because . . . Well, *because I wrote it.*"

I laughed so hard at the realization that he thought I was trying to attribute his beautiful quote to Emilio Estevez. "No," I choked out and placed my hand on his upper arm. "I was just trying to remember who the voice actor was."

"Oh." His shoulders relaxed, and he laughed with me. "Kiefer Sutherland."

"Yes!" I squeezed his bicep and giggled. Maybe at mistaking Kiefer for Emilio. Maybe at the unexpected muscle beneath his suit.

"That's right. Kiefer Sutherland. I can't believe I forgot that." Social norms probably dictated that I should have removed my hand by then, but I had not. I was too fascinated by the tense twitching beneath my fingers. "I think I've watched it every time it's ever aired on PBS." My hand fell away suddenly as the magnitude of the situation finally registered. That treasured love letter to *my* city was from *Henry*.

Without thinking—because if I had been thinking, I never would have done it—I stood on my tiptoes and planted a quick kiss on his lips. He didn't make any move to stop me, but his hands stayed in his pockets, and his eyes closed. In fact, they didn't just close. They scrunched up so tight I figured he had to be trying to repress the image of me kissing him before it made its way to his memory, where he would be stuck with it forever. And obviously all of that was enough to make me start thinking. It had been so much nicer when that wasn't happening.

"Henry, I'm sorry. I didn't mean to . . . I mean, I think I just got caught up in . . . I mean, it's Central Park—"

That was as far as I got in what I'm certain would have been a very heartfelt and eloquent apology. In an instant his eyes were open, and his arms were so very available. A gasp escaped me as he clenched one arm around my waist and pulled my body tight against his.

"I think it's more than just Central Park," he whispered before lowering his lips to mine and committing fully to an idea I had only tested.

If my mind was taken by surprise, my body didn't seem to know it. I met his lips pulse for pulse in intensity and threw my arms around his neck and tried to pull him even closer to me—and he was more than accommodating. He rested the hand that was not around my waist on the picture window and then pressed my body up against it, his body against mine. His left arm—fingertips to elbow—stayed pressed against the giant picture window, seventeen stories above Fifty-Ninth Street, but his right hand was on the move. It made its way from my waist to my upper back, the gentle, deliberate pressure causing me to arch farther into him. And then the next thing I knew, his fingers were brushing the hair away from my skin so his lips had a clear path from my mouth, across my jawline, along a brief detour at my earlobe, before finally arriving at my neck, where his soft trail of kisses made me contemplate throwing our suite's ice bucket through the window just so I could get a little cool air. Even in my state of charged, out-of-control senses, though, I still had enough reason to know I didn't want to be responsible for the death-by-ice-bucket of a hot dog vendor or two. So I'd just have to deal with the heat.

As his lips left a trail across my collarbone, I managed to rasp out, "In high school, I would not have imagined that you kissed like this."

"In high school I *didn't* kiss like this," he muttered against my throat, and then I felt his lips morph into a smile against me. He pulled back a few inches and matched his eyes evenly with mine, and I was able to see up close that what I had been referring to as teal actually included as many shades of blue and green as the Mediterranean from dawn to dusk. "In high school, I didn't really kiss much at all."

I shook my head. "Me neither."

He raised his body, and though his weight was no longer pressed against me, I instinctively went with him away from the window, like a magnet. His fingers returned to my hair and tucked it behind my ears on both sides. "But, for the record, I did spend a lot of time in high school imagining how *you* kissed."

My eyes grew wide. "You did?"

"Oh, yeah." He kept playing with my hair, twisting my unruly waves around his fingers and watching with keen interest as each curl broke itself free. "I told you. Massive crush."

"Why didn't you ever tell me? At the time, I mean."

He tilted his head and smiled at me. "Would that have made any difference?"

I wanted to say yes, but the reality was plain as day. "No." I let out a deep breath and continued to grow more comfortable in the proximity of his body. The proximity of his eyes. I raised my hands up to rest on his chest. "It just seems a shame to not have known."

He brushed a finger down my cheek and then his fingertip gently across my bottom lip. "If it makes you feel any better, I have a pretty massive crush on you now too."

My lips parted slightly beneath his exploration, and the shudder in his breath that resulted was enough to fill my courage meter to capacity. "Only 'massive,' huh? I'm pretty sure my crush on you has your piddly little crush on me beat."

I grabbed the lapel of his jacket—making a mental note of where the nearest one-hour dry cleaner I knew of was, just in case I wrinkled him—and pulled him toward me. Once again, there was laughter in those teal eyes, but once again, his mouth was all business.

Chapter 15

Apparently you didn't follow up making out with Henry Blumenthal for the better part of an hour on a couch in the Ellington Park Suite at the Plaza Hotel with lunch at Shake Shack. He wouldn't hear of it, despite my protests that if he didn't understand the uncomplicated perfection of Shake Shack, he didn't understand New York the way I thought he did. He told me that argument might have worked when Shake Shack was a uniquely NYC thing, operating out of a hot-dog stand in Madison Square Park, but once they opened their Mall of America location, I lost all credibility.

That was going to be an ongoing challenge with Henry. He just knew too much.

We pulled ourselves apart long enough to go to our separate bedrooms to change—me into something a bit nicer, him into something a little less nice—and then stepped out onto Central Park South and into the park. I didn't know where we were heading, but I didn't care. Food was the last thing on my mind as we shared information and introspection about everything around us.

I felt like a schoolgirl. I mean, not like *myself* as a schoolgirl, of course. Like a *normal* schoolgirl. I just couldn't help it. Everything he said was brilliant and funny, and he looked cute saying it. Central Park was even more magical with him in it.

"What's your favorite part of the park?" I asked him after I finished sharing my fondness for Strawberry Fields. "If you have one, that is. I know for me it depends on my mood—"

"Sheep Meadow," he responded without hesitation just as we arrived at it.

Hmm. Well, that was an interesting choice.

"Are you just saying that because you saw it on the sign?"

He laughed quietly. In fact, his voice got softer as he took hold of my hand—the intertwined fingers, boyfriend/girlfriend way, not the palm-to-palm way you hold hands with your mom to cross the street when you're a kid—and stepped into the open space. "No. I genuinely love it."

I looked around and tried to see what he saw. Don't get me wrong. It was beautiful, of course. The lush green grass, uninterrupted by trees or flowers, seemed to stretch on forever, and it was a great place for a picnic or just to sit and get some sun. Although I'd never used it for any of those things. It was usually crowded, and I actually appreciated it more in the winter months when it was closed to visitors. We happened to be there during its first open weekend of the year.

"You're going to have to tell me why."

"Sure. In fact, I'll give you three reasons why it's the best spot in all of New York."

I raised my eyebrows. "I was just looking for one reason you think it's the best spot in the park. Don't you think you're shooting a little high there, stud?"

Stud? Did I actually just call him *stud?*

He didn't seem to mind. He twirled me until I was holding on to his hand at my shoulder, and he was standing behind me with his arm wrapped around me. My arm across my chest, his enveloping me at my collarbone. From behind me, he lowered his chin onto my shoulder and said, "Number one: the view."

It was difficult to argue with that one. From the center of the meadow where we stood, the city looked like a pop-up book all around us. "Well, sure."

"Number two . . ." He twirled me back around to face him. "This used to be an actual meadow for sheep. Until, I don't know . . . All the sheep started inbreeding and it got messy, I guess." I snickered, and he smiled in response. "But in a city—let's face it, in a *country*—where there is nothing more powerful than the almighty dollar, in the confines of these fifteen acres, the health of the grass comes first. The city turns down millions of dollars each year by refusing to allow events that could damage the grass. How countercultural is that? For this little meadow in the center of the city that never sleeps, rest comes first."

I should have known better than to think he wouldn't be able to rise to the challenge of selling me on his favorite spot.

I cleared my throat. "And number three?"

The corners of his mouth twitched but refused to break into a grin. "Number three is obvious." He twirled me again and kept twirling me slowly as he spoke. "There are noise ordinances and no sports allowed. No dogs. No glass bottles. But do you know what *is* permitted?" His left hand above my head helped me complete one last rotation, and then his right arm captured me around the waist and pulled me to him. "Dancing." His body began swaying, and I was powerless to do anything but go along for the ride with him. And for the life of me, I couldn't think of a single reason why I would ever consider doing anything else.

A few minutes later, shortly after my stomach started growling while slow dancing with Henry—which, thanks to Sheep Meadow's noise ordinances, he was able to hear and laugh at me about—I decided I actually cared about lunch very much indeed. We walked the short distance to Tavern on the Green and got seated right away, which I'd never known to happen.

"Is Tavern on the Green a corporate sponsor too?" I asked.

"No. Why?"

"I've always had to make reservations."

He glanced at his watch. "It's three thirty."

Ah. That explained it.

We sat in relative silence until after we had each ordered—the Tavern Cobb Salad for me and the Shaved Sirloin Steak Sandwich for him—and then we sat in *complete* silence. And for the first time in quite a while, I was incredibly aware of . . . everything. Caught up in our romantic frenzy, I'd been too carried away to overthink the transition we were making from friends to more, and what any of it meant. But suddenly we were sitting together in public with a table between us and a bunch of people present, and all sorts of societal rules to keep us from brushing the dishes and breadsticks from the table and meeting each other in the middle of it for a little more of my new favorite recreational pastime. But I also didn't know how to act like none of it had happened. I didn't *want* to act like none of it had happened.

"What are you thinking?" he asked, snapping my attention back to reality. Not that reality was much more than a blurry figment at that point.

"I guess I'm just not exactly sure what we're supposed to talk about right now."

He adjusted in his chair and leaned in. "What do you *want* to talk about?"

"Everything. Nothing."

"Let's start with everything." Henry's smile grew wide. "And . . . go!"

With a laugh I insisted, "You first!"

"Sure. Okay, let's start with this: I love my job."

"And you're very good at it," I understated.

He smirked. "I'm okay. But here's the little bit of 'everything' I want to tell you about that. I love my job. I do. But sometimes I've been known to love it too much. You know? The truth is I'm a workaholic by choice." I chuckled and prepared to confess that I could relate, but then he added, "When my dad died, I stopped sleeping. Something in my brain shifted gears, and from that point on, I never felt like I had any time to waste. I just needed to keep moving. I still don't sleep a lot, but I've adjusted. That part's not a choice anymore so much as a habit, I guess. But I'm always restless. I'm always thinking about what's next. Sometimes that's exhausting." I tilted my head and took in that information and the acceptance with which he communicated it, and he shrugged. "So, what about you? From one workaholic to another, how many hours of sleep do you need each night?"

"Let's see . . . A normal night is probably six."

He held up the five fingers on his right hand and said, "Be jealous."

I chuckled and then found myself looking away as voluntary vulnerability—not something I had experience with—overtook me. "For me it's all about the impossible standards I set for myself, I think. I *know* they're impossible, but it's like knowing they're impossible just turns them into a challenge. And I refuse to back down from a challenge."

"And I bet you face plenty of them at Wallis, Monroe and Burkhead. How long have you been there?"

Okay. I was mistaken before. It wasn't until he mentioned W, M and B that I truly found myself grappling with reality again. That little bit of reality that I hadn't been able to forget but that hadn't been at the forefront of my mind, my concerns, or my priorities for the first time in as long as I could remember.

I attempted to ignore the clammy sensation and answer the straightforward question as I would have a few weeks prior. "They hired me straight out of law school. Before I even passed the bar, I was clerking, and then as soon as I passed, I became an associate. And I just kept moving up from there, I guess."

"What are you now?"

"Junior partner." I swallowed down the lump in my throat. "I'm hoping that senior partner is just around the corner."

He whistled softly through his teeth. "I'm impressed. I've worked indirectly with them at various times through the years. It seems to be a great firm."

I nodded and bit my lip. It was a great firm, and I had always carried immense pride at being part of that greatness. But how could I tell him that I was now suspected of stealing from that great firm?

"How long are you going to stay away? I'm sure they're desperate to get you back."

"The truth is . . ." I took a sip of my iced tea and set it down, and then I picked it up again and gulped down half the glass. "The truth is, I had to take a leave of absence."

This was it. The moment of truth. The moment when Henry found out what I was accused of and he had to disassociate from me. *He'll have to disassociate from me!* I felt like a total fool as I realized the position I had put him in. He was including me in his production. He had paid for my trip. Until my name was cleared, why *wouldn't* he believe it was true? And it wasn't exactly good for the reputations of nonprofits when they provided suites at the Plaza and lunch at Tavern on the Green to white-collar criminals.

He sat back in his chair as he took in that information and then leaned in again to speak quietly. "'A leave of absence'? Is everything . . . I mean . . . *why?*"

I couldn't tell him. I simply couldn't tell him. My name would be cleared soon enough. I had to believe that. I *did* believe that. And once the whole unfortunate misunderstanding was behind me, I could tell him the truth. We'd lie in the grass at Sheep Meadow and look up at the sun glistening off the skyscrapers, and he'd listen as I talked through it all. I might even cry some, but that would be okay. He wouldn't think I was weak. He'd understand. And he'd understand why I hadn't been able to tell him the truth. We'd slow dance again—in fact, slow dancing without music in public places would maybe become our special thing—and he'd reassure me that he didn't blame me for thinking I had to keep the truth from him. I was just trying to protect his business integrity, after all. But he'd also tell me that from that moment forward, there was nothing I couldn't tell him. Nothing. And I'd believe him. Like I almost wanted to believe it now, even on day one of whatever we were building beyond friendship.

I chuckled dryly and implored my eyes to remain every bit as dry. "I, um . . . thought I was going to marry . . . well, someone I work with. Someone with seniority over me."

His face remained expressionless as he sat back in his chair. "I see."

"What does 'I see' mean?"

He shook his head and shrugged. "It just means . . . I don't know. I guess it means, 'I see.'"

I didn't know what he thought he saw, and I didn't even know what I *wanted* him to think he saw. But I could see straight through 'I see,' and I didn't like what I saw.

"If you're thinking I went off the deep end or something—"

"I didn't say that."

"I assure you it wasn't anything like that, Henry."

"I wasn't assuming that it was." He took a deep breath and then opened his mouth to continue, but food was placed in front of us, so he waited. Once our waiter was gone he said, "There's just a lot we don't know about each other." He leaned in again, and for the life of me I could not interpret what was happening behind those eyes. It was nightfall at the Mediterranean. "McKenna, if you just canceled a wedding—"

"Oh!" Relief and frustration flooded simultaneously through every inch of me. "No. It's not that." I couldn't win. There was absolutely no way to win in this scenario. "I just thought . . . but there was never really anything . . ."

What was I doing? It had been bad enough allowing Taylor to believe what she was going to believe anyway about Jeremiah. But in that case I'd never actually lied to her. *Objection, Your Honor. Leading the witness.* Yeah . . . sure. But sometimes you had to lead the witness just a little bit, even when you knew an objection was imminent. It's all about setting the tone. Controlling the emotions. Priming the pump.

With Henry, I was committing perjury and was very much in danger of being held in contempt of court.

I forced myself to sit up straight rather than slip under the table and hide from his questioning eyes, as I would have given just about anything to be able to do. I put my hand on the table, palm up, and looked from it to his eyes. He looked down and then placed his hand in mine. "Can I ask you to trust me?"

"Of course I trust you—"

"No, Henry, can you just . . ." I squeezed my eyes shut. The horrible nightmare would be over soon. It would. It had to be. "There are things I can't talk about right now. And I agree, there's so much we don't know about each other. And this whole leave-of-absence thing is something I'll be able to tell you all about. I just can't quite yet. And it probably would have been better if I hadn't even said what I said. It's just—"

"Of course. Take all the time you need." He squeezed my hand gently and then brushed his thumb across my knuckles. When he smiled at me, I wanted to believe all was well, but it felt forced, and I didn't understand why. He squeezed one more time before he released my hand and picked up his fork. "I guess we should get to eating. We don't have a ton of time."

I didn't move. I just kept looking at him. "Henry . . ."

He smiled again, and it seemed as if daylight had returned to his sandy beaches. "I'm sorry I reacted the way I did. I was just surprised. But to the best of my knowledge, you haven't done anything to intentionally hurt me since you assigned me Turkmenistan in Model UN. I trust you."

Chapter 16

I knew the fundraiser that evening was black tie, and I had come prepared. In my trusty overnight bag, I had a very lovely black evening gown that had serviced me well at multiple galas and retirement parties and upscale weddings through the years. But as Henry and I finished lunch and began walking back toward the Plaza, I was suddenly assaulted by another round of *what-if* thinking. This time was different, though, and my initial analysis of the situation made it appear as if open-ended wonderings about what *could* happen were much more pleasant than second-guessing the past.

"Hey, so remind me what time this thing starts tonight."

"Eight."

I glanced at my watch. It would be tight, but I could make it work. "And it's at the Paley Center?"

"Yeah."

I placed my hand on his arm as we prepared to circumnavigate Sheep Meadow and head back to Fifty-Ninth, and he stopped walking and faced me. "Do you have plans for me between now and then?"

A mischievous twinkle overtook his eyes and, frankly, I was relieved to see it. We had moved past the awkwardness over lunch, and we'd had some great conversation—about everything from high-school memories to how he got each of his scars. (He had, in fact, gotten the scar on the bridge of his nose and broken it at the same time. In Pamplona in 2012. He assured me the shots he'd gotten of the running of the bulls had been well worth the inconvenience and lifelong changes to his face.) But it had felt like he'd shifted out of trying-to-impress-the-girl mode, and that only bothered me because I feared he no longer considered me worth impressing. But the mischievous twinkle seemed to take us back to pre-leave-of-absence-revelation-awkwardness levels of flirting and romance.

He placed his hands on my shoulders and then rubbed up and down my arms for a moment before pulling me in closer to him. "I can think of one or two ways we could pass the time." He placed his hand under my chin and gently tilted my face toward his, and I melted into him. Our passionate make-out session had been filled with urgency and fun as we'd giggled our way through something new and exciting. (Okay . . . I'd giggled. Henry was not exactly a giggler. Come to think of it, I hadn't thought I was much of a giggler either.) We really were like what I imagined two teenagers would be, steaming up the windows of a car parked at Makeout Point. (I don't know—is Makeout Point an actual thing outside of *Happy Days*? I really missed so much by being an academically driven nerd in high school.)

But this . . .

His lips were exploring mine like they had all the time in the world and nowhere else they'd rather be. His hand left my chin, and his arm wrapped around me and pulled me in even closer. My neck was in the nook of his arm, and I instinctively wrapped my arms around his waist as he dipped me slightly and made up for lost time— the awkward time over lunch, yes, but also the last twenty years, it felt like.

I was still being supported by his arm when he pulled his lips away and muttered against my jaw, "Why? Do you have somewhere else to be?"

Nope. Let's just keep doing this for the rest of the day. Thanks so much for asking.

I sighed. "Well, you're making it difficult for me to remember anything else I could possibly need to do, but yeah. I have a couple of errands I'd like to run."

It was his turn to sigh as he brought me back upright. "*Errands.* Such an unsexy word." He kissed me gently—almost casually, which in and of itself was exciting, knowing that we were at the "casual kissing" stage—and then let his arms fall away.

"You said you have people you should meet with before the fundraiser anyway," I reminded him.

"Wow. Thanks, Keaton. Who needs cold showers when they have you around?" He winked, and I laughed.

"So, I'll see you there?"

"You're leaving from here?"

I pointed back behind me. "I'm going to head out to Central Park West and grab a cab. Will you be okay on your own? Did you remember to bring your Mace?"

He smirked at me. "I'll call you if I need rescuing."

"So not just an, 'Oops, that shouldn't have happened. I got caught up in the moment' sort of kiss, but like full-on?" Erica's voice was so enthusiastic and elevated I knew my taxi driver was probably at least picking up tones if not words.

"Yep." I put in as much effort as I could to keep both my volume and tone a little more muted than my sister's. "Full-on. We were at the window for . . . I genuinely don't know how long. And then we went and sat on the couch, and I thought that might be the end of it, but . . ." Whew, buddy, that had *not* been the end of it. "But I'm not even sure that was the best part." Though it was a very, *very* good part. "When we were walking to lunch, he held my hand, and he told me what he loves about the park, and we danced—"

"You danced?"

"Yes. Right there in the middle of a meadow in Central Park, surrounded by hundreds of people and Henry's favorite view of Manhattan." My cab stopped in front of Bloomingdale's, and I paid and stepped out onto Third Avenue. "It was really the most romantic thing I've ever . . ." I was about to say it was the most romantic thing I'd ever experienced, but that almost went without saying. And it just seemed so inadequate. "It was the most romantic thing ever."

I heard her take a deep breath, and then when she spoke again, her voice was much softer in volume and tone. "McKenna . . . He's the one, you know."

I stepped aside from the doorway and stood in front of one of the display windows. I couldn't stand it when people walked through a crowded department store talking at full volume on their cell phone. I was definitely a modern girl dependent upon her technology, but I could still remember the days when we used to be able to wait until we got home from shopping to have personal conversations in the privacy of our living rooms.

"The one *what?*" I asked, causing my sister to chuckle.

"*The one.* He's who you've been waiting for."

Everything in me wanted to revolt at the comment—including my digestive system that, for just a few seconds, grew so tumultuous I made sure I was within lunging distance of the nearest trash can just in case. My face grew clammy, and I attempted to keep gulping in enough air to make sure I didn't pass out on Third Avenue. Once I was sure I could at least keep breathing, I leaned back against the Bloomingdale's window display, featuring a mannequin dressed up in the high-collared, straitlaced wardrobe of Mary Poppins—apart from a pink boa and six-inch stilettos—as I prepared to verbally launch all of the protests building up in my mind.

There was no one—probably not for anyone, certainly not for me.

The only one I needed was myself.

I wasn't waiting *for anyone.*

But then, in spite of myself, my own words gave way to hearing Erica's in my mind again. *He's who you've been waiting for.* Was it possible that everything I believed was true—I didn't need a man, I didn't have time for a man, and I was perfectly fine on my own—but that it was just as true that the entire point of spending my adult life making sure I was fine on my own was so I would be ready for Henry?

"I know," I finally whispered.

Silence permeated the air—even as eighty school-aged children from PS 354 passed in front of me in their navy-and-white uniforms.

"Did you say, 'I know'?" Erica asked breathlessly.

I stared into space and nodded.

"McKenna?"

I shook off the stupor in response to hearing my name through my phone. "Um, yeah. I . . . well . . . yeah. I did. I said, 'I know.'"

Erica squealed in a high-pitched tone that I swear made her sound just like Taylor, and I pulled my phone away from my ear to avoid my eardrums bursting. I stretched out my face while quickly massaging the point of impact, and then once I was satisfied all the dogs in Raleigh had been summoned to Erica's side by her special signal only they could hear, I returned the phone to my ear.

"Good grief, Erica. What in the world—"

"I just knew it." She sniffed. "I knew you were going to fall in love with some great guy someday—"

"Whoa, whoa, whoa!" I shouted that a bit more loudly than I had intended, and a few children walking by in single file slowed down on the sidewalk in front of me. Their eyes were on me, as if I was about to warn them they were going to step into a manhole.

"Sorry. Not you!" As one of their chaperones ushered them on and looked at me warily, I added, "You're doing great! Thank you for your service."

"Are you in the middle of a veterans' parade or something?" Erica asked.

"No. Field trip." I stepped away from the processional before I was forced to by a passing security officer or something and stood at the corner of Third and Sixtieth. "Listen, don't get ahead of yourself. I'm not *in love*." Despite my apparent openness to the idea that Henry Blumenthal was the one guy on earth I might be able to make room for in my life, the words *in love* still made me feel roughly the same way I felt when a former client, who was on the board of directors of the Bronx Zoo, made me meet with him to discuss his living will and testament in the Birds of Prey house.

"Okay, sure. I'll give you that," Erica acknowledged.

"Thank you."

"But you are falling. You may still be in the early stages, hanging onto the edge of the cliff, but—sweet, darling sister, whom I love and adore with every fiber of my being—the fall is imminent. Which leads me to . . . the clock is ticking."

"Oh, my gosh, Erica! Look, I haven't even officially been on a date with the guy yet. Besides, just because I may be open to a relationship doesn't mean I've changed my mind about not wanting kids."

She laughed so hard I once again had to pull the phone away from my ear. Finally, she composed herself enough to say, "I just meant you'd better hurry and get into Bloomingdale's if you want to have time to pick out a dress that's going to knock his socks off."

Oh. Cool.

I hated that I was resorting to getting all "dolled up" in order to impress a man. But at the very same time that I was beating myself down with judgmental disappointment, my heart was racing in giddy anticipation. I could already imagine the expression on his face. The one I was going for. If I did this right, he would look at me like I had looked at the view of Central Park from the window of our suite.

Nice, McKenna. Next time be sure to try and get people to compare you to the Grand Canyon too. For good measure.

I said goodbye to Erica and promised to call her after the fund-raiser and then skirted my way through the throngs of people and temptations from Magnolia Bakery until I found the evening-gown department—admittedly, not a department I had spent much time in through the years. In fact, I wasn't typically a Bloomingdale's girl at all. The Big Brown Bag had never provided me with much temptation, and with my schedule the past few years, I did most of my shopping online through one of those personal-shopper subscription services. It was great. I provided my measurements, my preferred colors, and my preferred style—a little something I liked to call "Yes, I'm a girl. What of it?"—and I got new clothes delivered to my apartment every few weeks. My old suits got dropped off at Goodwill on a regular basis, and I always got to go to work looking like I put a lot of effort into my appearance.

"Can I help you?" A woman who appeared to be sixtyish—though her beautiful white hair was accompanied by the skin and body of a twenty-five-year-old—approached me as I wandered aimlessly.

"Um . . . I hope so. I have no idea what I'm doing, but I have about"—I glanced down at my watch—"two and a half hours to completely reinvent myself. Not that I'm trying to change who I am. I'm not. I just want to reinvent my *style* a little bit. And I wouldn't even be bothering with that except I think this guy likes me as I already am. So I don't *have* to change. I just . . ." I couldn't help it. I couldn't stop rambling. I was thinking about Henry, and all my insides were turning to goo, and I felt like one of those wooly mammoth recreations I'd seen in pictures of the La Brea Tar Pits. My wooly mammoth mate and my wooly mammoth baby were looking on helplessly, and all I could do was throw my trunk up in the air and trumpet as loud as I could as I gave in to the power of the goo. "We've known each other since we were kids, but I really want him to look at me with new eyes tonight, if that makes sense."

The salesclerk—Marlene, her name tag informed me—smiled and nodded. "You've come to the right place." She gestured behind her to a showroom of every style and color of evening gown and cocktail dress. And then she added with a wink, "Finding that extra little boost toward falling in love happens to be my specialty."

Chapter 17

After I'd spent roughly the gross domestic product of some little nation I wouldn't have been cruel enough to assign even to Henry in Model UN—like Tuvalu—I thanked Marlene, swung by the shoe department, made a quick detour to the makeup counter, and hurried to the Bloomingdale's salon. I didn't have an appointment, of course, but Marlene had told me to ask for Angie and tell her Marlene had sent me—and that it was "a love emergency." I did as I was instructed and was quickly laying down my American Express card for a wash, trim, blowout, and a quick tutorial on a few elegant updo options.

Apparently, I now spent money on my apartment, clothes for work, food, Gerald, and trying to make Henry Blumenthal forget how to speak when I walked in a room.

I hailed a cab on Lexington Avenue and climbed in with my Big Brown Bag, Medium Brown Bag, and Little Brown Bag, and asked the driver to drop me off at the Plaza. And then I realized that for all the benefits of sharing a luxurious suite with Henry, attempting to get ready in secrecy could be a bit of a challenge. It seemed ridiculous to have to sort through my options, knowing we could cut through Central Park on Sixty-Sixth and be at my apartment on Seventy-Second in about fifteen minutes, but there was currently a clerk from work named Annemarie living there. I could probably offer to knock a hundred dollars off the rent for the month and she'd happily let me use my bathroom, but it sure did seem like a waste to not get ready surrounded by the twenty-four-karat gold-plated bathroom fixtures of the Plaza.

> Hey there. Getting ready to head back to the Plaza to start getting ready. I won't be in your way, will I? I know you said you have meetings.

Nice. It was just ever so slightly possible that I was actually going to be really good at this whole romance thing. I saw his texting-in-progress bubble pop up seconds later, and I stared at my phone in impatient anticipation.

> Not at all. Just finished getting ready and heading out now. I have to be there early to meet with the PBS people. Sorry I won't be able to escort you in tonight.
> Btw . . . Is it weird that I miss you already?

I clutched my phone to my chest and sighed and then started typing.

> Not weird. Sort of wonderful, actually. See you in a couple hours.

I stood in front of the gold-plated mirror and stared at myself. At least I thought it was me. I didn't really recognize the curves I was flaunting, courtesy of my new champagne-colored Hervé Léger gown. The bandage pattern hugged me in all the right places, and the scoop neckline differed radically from my usual professionalism-first, comfort-is-a-close-second style. (Or, as Erica so eloquently observed when I FaceTimed with her once I was fully dressed, "I didn't know you had boobs!")

I opted for the simplest of the hairstyles Angie had made accessible for me and pinned my hair up in the back and sported sleek bangs in the front. My new peep-toe heels with the ankle strap completed the look and added just the right amount of pizazz between the hem of my dress and the floor. Of course, the slit running to just above my knee added a nice little touch of pizazz all its own.

I decided to splurge one last time for the day on an Uber Black luxury ride, even though the Paley Center was only about a mile away, just in case Henry happened to be standing outside when I pulled up. I ordered the ride on the app and then threw my phone, ID, credit card, room key, lipstick, and tissues into the clutch Marlene had encouraged me to buy. I pulled my new wrap around my shoulders and then, satisfied I had everything I needed, stepped into the hallway.

Just a few minutes later, I pulled up in front of the Fifty-Second Street entrance of the Paley Center for Media in a Bentley Flying Spur—*totally* worth it, whether Henry was watching or not—and stepped out onto an actual red carpet. No . . . I wouldn't have felt nearly as cool and confident in that moment if I'd arrived in a 2011 Ford Focus Hatchback. I made my way in and followed the signs to the Steven Spielberg Gallery, gave the man at the door my name—which he cross-checked on his clipboard—and then entered the room full of Hank Blume's most elite New York City supporters.

It didn't take long to spot him. The tuxes were pretty much all the same, but the ways the men were carrying themselves were not. I knew Henry would rather not be wearing a tux. I just instinctively knew he would rather be in a comfortable pair of jeans and a pullover. He would rather be out in nature observing and learning than stuck in a stuffy room where everyone wanted a piece of him. But that didn't change the fact that while everyone else seemed to be striking a pose—when cameras were pointed at them and when they weren't—Henry was being himself.

Another thing that was the same among most of the men: their hair. Even the twentysomethings in the room were apparently compelled to mold their hair into a shellacked impersonation of Darrin from *Bewitched*. But not Henry. His blond locks were as natural and free as ever, as if they could not be tamed, no matter the occasion.

He was midconversation with two middle-aged men who kept slapping him on the back. Henry kept laughing at whatever they were saying, but I could detect him subtly searching for escape. When he saw me, he found it.

His eyes widened as his gaze connected with mine. I told myself to remain calm as his focus began moving downward, taking in every inch of me before working his way back up, even more slowly. My hands were resting at my side and I begged them not to twitch. I also hoped they would have enough decorum not to grow so sweaty that little pools formed on either side of me. For the most part, everything behaved pretty well—though I would have to have a very serious conversation with my heart later. If it kept beating like that, the whole room was going to hear.

It was just about the time his eyes locked with mine again—just about the time I got to take in the sight of the delicious grin on his face—when Darrin-from-*Bewitched* number one said something apparently hilarious, and Darrin-from-*Bewitched* number two (I guess that would make him Dick Sargent) slapped Henry on the back again. But of course Henry wasn't paying any attention to them up until that moment. Also, if I had to make an educated guess, I don't think Henry was actually breathing properly up until that moment. The slap on his back seemed to intersect with a sharp intake of breath, and the night's guest of honor was suddenly caught in the middle of a coughing fit.

I covered my mouth and laughed as people rushed around him to bring him water and pat him on the back and do all sorts of things that I'm sure they thought were helpful. But as soon as Henry regained his composure, he stepped away from them and toward me.

And I was gratified to realize that his hard-fought composure had been lost again.

"Wow," he breathed after standing in front of me in silence for ten seconds or so.

"That's supposed to be my line."

He chuckled. "I know. And I really did try to think of another one. For the life of me, I couldn't."

"You look pretty fantastic yourself. How's it going so far?"

He took another step forward, and I felt a rush of adrenaline every time his vision wandered. Bless his heart . . . He really was *trying* to stay focused on my eyes. I appreciated the effort every bit as much as I appreciated how badly he was failing.

"Pretty good, I think. I mean, mind-numbingly dull, but good. There's lots of money rolling in, so— I'm sorry," he said with a start, interrupting himself. "I just have to say you really do look . . . I mean . . ." He ran his hand through his hair and spent a moment chewing on his bottom lip. "Here's the thing." His eyes darted around the room, and then he grabbed my elbow and ushered me with an urgency I didn't understand to a shadowed space in a corner. "I'm hesitant to rave too much," he said once we were out of the flow of traffic.

I smiled at him in amused confusion. "Why is that?"

"I guess because I have reels and reels of film of you in my head, and it all takes my breath away."

Yes, I'd stepped out of a Bentley and onto a red carpet in a designer gown, but manufactured confidence could only take me so far. Admittedly, the feelings I had acknowledged to Erica that I was developing for Henry—and the certainty I felt that I wasn't developing them alone—took me a bit further. But *this.* I wasn't equipped to handle this. I folded my arms across my abdomen for the first time all night. I felt exposed, and that was thrilling and terrifying.

"I really can't imagine it *all*—"

"Homecoming. Junior year." A familiar grin overtook his face, and his eyes began to twinkle. He was accepting my challenge. "You were sitting on the curb in your gown—which, if I recall correctly, had been Erica's, and you thought it made you look like a Spice Girl, which, trust me, was not the negative thing you seemed to think it was—and you had your head tilted back so Jared could throw corn nuts into your open mouth."

Laughter exploded from me. "Oh, yeah . . . That was an alluring moment."

The grin stayed in place but he took a step toward me. "First day of senior year, I nearly ran over you in the parking lot."

I gasped. "I'd forgotten about that!"

"You were so mad. You walked over to my window and shook your fist at me like . . . I don't know . . ." He shook his head and chuckled. "All it made me think of at the time—and still, honestly, when I think about it—was Sophia from *The Golden Girls.*"

"You nearly killed me!"

"Oh, relax, Sophia." He winked and I melted. "I did come awfully close to hitting you, and I'm sorry about that. But I was in a line of cars trying to get out of the parking lot after school, and I couldn't have been moving faster than ten feet a minute. I daresay you would have survived."

"Well, yeah. But that's not the point." I had no battle in me. Only total surrender.

"You're right. It's not. The point is that you refused to even look at me for weeks after that, and that meant I got to stare at you with unabashed delight across every room we were in together, and you were none the wiser." He took another step, and for whatever reason I no longer needed my arms to shield me. They fell lifeless against my hips. "When you showed up with Jared at the Armory . . . I really thought all the reels had been archived. I was so proud of myself for how in control I was, and for putting all those ancient feelings behind me, until you blabbered on about not knowing James Earl Jones was the voice of Darth Vader and Mufasa. And that was it. I was back there, with my massive crush on you and my reels of film on endless loop. So I guess maybe I'm afraid that if I really allow myself to acknowledge that the sight of you straight-up knocked the air out of my lungs tonight, I might have to acknowledge that I don't have any control over this thing at all. It's not you at a certain age that I'm crazy about or you when you're all dressed up or wearing sweats or you when you're chewing me out in the school parking lot or you when you're being more brilliant and working harder than everyone else. It's just . . . *you*, McKenna."

I took a deep breath. The first breath of *any* magnitude that I'd taken in several minutes or so, it felt like. When it released, it took with it years of certainty. A lifetime, really. Years of focus and a single track.

"I've never . . ." The words got stuck on the way out, and self-consciousness threatened to overtake me once more. I closed my eyes and kept them closed as I cleared my throat and tried again. "I've never felt like this, Henry. I don't have a clue what I'm doing, and that scares me to death."

He grabbed the sides of my face in his hands and pulled my lips to his with a sense of desperation. "Hey," he whispered against me as he pulled away slightly. I opened my eyes and was met with his, looking intently at me. "I'm pretty sure that's what makes it worth doing."

I threw my arms around his neck then and held him, and he

countered by wrapping his arms around my waist and pulling me closer.

"I know you need to go talk to people," I said into his ear, though I desperately hoped he'd turn down my considerate and understanding offer and instead stand there in the corner, holding me for the rest of the evening.

He sighed, I think as sorry to get back to reality as I was. "I do." He pulled away from me, and I prepared to watch him walk away, but he put out his hand and said, "Have you ever met Ron Howard?"

I looked down at his hand and took it. "Ron Howard the director or Ron Howard who runs that one funeral home in Durham?"

He smirked. "That's Ron Howards. Also a really nice guy. But what do you say we go over there, and I introduce you to Opie?"

Chapter 18

For nearly thirty minutes he introduced me around and talked about Marilla. Each time he built up her story as if it already had a violin soundtrack behind it and narration by Sally Field—what we *didn't* know every bit as appealing as what we did—and then by the time he introduced me as a branch on Marilla's family tree, they were pulling out the checkbooks. It was easy to understand why he'd wanted me to accompany him to New York.

Getting me to realize I was falling in love with him was the bonus he may or may not have been hoping for.

I was getting pretty good at playing my part too. In fact, we made a good team. And with my newfound tolerance of romance, I didn't even have a difficult time embellishing my beliefs about why Marilla never stepped foot on American soil.

I was fairly certain we'd spent at least a minute or two speaking with every person in the room when one more middle-aged man in a tux interjected himself into a conversation and thrust his hand out for Henry to shake. "Hank. It's great to meet you. Ty Monroe. Wallis, Monroe and Burkhead."

My eyes flew to his face to confirm the fact that required no confirmation. Yep, it was him, alright. He fit right in with the roomful of self-important, see-and-be-seen social elites, though the hair implants had never allowed him to pull off the shellacked style without drawing attention to what he clearly hoped everyone believed was real. Instead, he resembled Taylor's Shaving Fun Ken doll after Mom cut the chewing gum out of his hair.

I realized too late, back in the present moment, that I should have been focusing my attention elsewhere during those seconds while Mr. Monroe rattled off his credentials and the way the firm had supported the arts through the years and basically just tried to impress Henry as everyone had tried to all evening. Possibly, I should have been searching for a reason to excuse myself so I could hide under the nearest table. Even more helpfully, I probably should have been looking at Henry. Because Henry was certainly looking at me . . . attempting to interpret every single thought racing through my mind.

"Ty, I'm sure you know Ms. Keaton."

I gulped down enough air to fill my lungs and then hoped that all of my involuntary bodily functions would take it from there. I didn't know how I was going to get through the exchange to come—whatever it ended up looking like—but I was definitely going to have to shift into autopilot on some things so I could focus all my energy onto the things that might not come so naturally.

I put my hand out for him to shake. "It's nice to see you again, Mr. Monroe."

He unabashedly surveyed me from head to toe. I quickly discovered I didn't like it *nearly* as much as when Henry had done the same. By the time his eyes made it back to mine, they were wider, and his lips had contorted into a Cheshire cat grin—and I felt like I needed a shower to clean off the icky Ty Monroe slime.

He took a step toward me, blocking Henry out as he did. "Well, now, my memory's not what it used to be, but I'm quite certain I'd remember if we'd met."

I've worked for you for thirteen years.

I do the majority of the work—and get none of the pay or recognition— for your most high-profile clients.

Less than three weeks ago, you took everything I've worked for my entire life and treated it with all the importance of those "top bachelors in New York" designations you buy for yourself each year.

Of course, the problem was that any one of those facts would most likely jar his memory and reveal exactly who I was. And Henry would be there for the unveiling.

"Um . . ."

"Brockovich? Is that you?"

The friendly countenance of Jeremiah Burkhead came up behind me, and the relief I momentarily felt at the distraction quickly faded in anticipation of the reminder Mr. Monroe was no doubt preparing to receive.

Ty, you know McKenna. She's the junior partner who embezzled all the money you were preparing to spend on that cruise with Tom Brady and Gisele Bündchen.

Thankfully, he said no such thing.

"Hey, Ty . . . I saw Anderson Cooper at coat check. If you want to talk to him, you might want to grab him before Anita does."

Mr. Monroe cursed under his breath. "Of course Wollensky's here." He composed himself, and the smile returned to his face as he faced me. "It was lovely to meet you, Ms. . . ." In a fleeting moment of panic, he looked to Jeremiah for assistance.

"Brockovich," he assisted with a sly grin in my direction.

"Yes, Ms. Brockovich." He took my hand and kissed my knuckles and then hurried off in pursuit of Anderson Cooper.

Most of the tension dissipated from the air as Jeremiah stuffed his hands into his pockets and took a step toward me. Those brown eyes were still deep and warm, though I'd sort of moved on from my brown-eyes phase. They still looked kind, though, and that comforted me. He'd always been the one who broke away from the uptight,

high-class lawyer stereotype that the other name partners gleefully
endorsed. I'd always believed he cared about the work, cared about
our clients, and overall was just a decent human being. The humanity
he had shown me in the boardroom that day had probably been the
only thing to keep me from shattering into a million pieces.

On the outside, anyway.

"You look phenomenal. I never would have recognized you." He
grimaced and closed his eyes tightly, then opened one of them back
up to peer at me cautiously. "I'm sorry. I didn't mean . . ."

"No, I get it. This is a little different from the style I go with when
sorting through briefs over Swiss-and-tomato sandwiches."

"On pumpernickel. Don't you dare forget the most important
component of the McKenna."

I did a double take and then laughed. "I hope that means they've
gone ahead and made it official."

"I won't stop campaigning until—"

"'Brockovich'?" Henry asked.

I looked at him to explain the inside joke—*multiple* inside
jokes, actually—and flinched at the sight of his crossed arms and
the burning-red tops of his ears. Uh-oh. I had forgotten that Henry
Blumenthal was more intuitive than most men. More intuitive than
most people of any gender, actually. And, unless I was mistaken, I
was guessing it had taken him about a second and a half to surmise
that Jeremiah Burkhead was the guy from work I had once thought I
was going to marry and from whom I had fled to Durham to escape.

I swallowed hard and begged my involuntary functions to maintain the status quo and for the voluntary ones to start kicking into
gear. Henry was looking to me for an explanation but also working
hard to believe he had nothing to worry about, I was pretty sure. I
smiled at him in a way I hoped was comforting.

"Mr. Burkhead and I worked together on a big class-action suit a
while ago. He took me under his wing, I guess." I didn't know if it was

worse to give Henry too many details or not enough. "You know . . . like he was the Albert Finney character and I was—"

"Erin Brockovich. Yeah. I get it."

Henry's tone was cold and indifferent for the first time since we, along with Jared, had ducked out of the soiree. At least at the time I had interpreted it as cold and indifferent. I knew now, of course, that how he treated me had been an attempt to cover up the fact that he actually felt the opposite of cold and indifferent. There was little room for doubt that his current behavior represented the same attempts at cover-up—and maybe a little bit of self-protection.

Jeremiah's eyes darted back and forth between Henry and me, and then he put out his hand. "I'm Jeremiah Burkhead. I'm a huge fan, Mr. Blume. All the way back to *New York*. I've lived here for twenty-five years, but you really brought out my affection for this city."

Henry shook his hand, but his eyes remained on me. "I get that a lot."

"Hey, can I talk to you in private for a moment?" I asked him and then offered a polite and apologetic nod at Jeremiah. I began to walk back toward our private corner from before, certain he would follow by my side, but I'd only taken two steps when I heard Henry's voice, still behind me.

"Actually, there are some people I need to say hello to. Why don't I give the two of you a moment to catch up?"

I turned back and shook my head, but he was already gone. I was left standing alone with Jeremiah, who looked understandably confused by what had just occurred.

"So, um . . ." My eyes darted around but couldn't locate Henry. "How are you? How's"—*oh, crap*—"your daughter?"

"She's great. Louisa's always great, if you ask me." He smiled, and I couldn't help but smile back—especially since I was stifling a giggle. *It's always the last von Trapp you think of.*

It wasn't his fault. I was sure of that. Whatever the debacle happening behind the scenes, and no matter how totally screwed up a lackadaisical independent audit or inexcusably bad bookkeeping had made things—and regardless of how heartless Mr. Wallis and Mr. Monroe had been in their desire to dispose of me—it wasn't Jeremiah's fault. I still knew that I wouldn't be half the attorney I was without his influence on my life and career, and he'd never been anything but kind to me.

"I'm glad to hear it," I replied. "And how are things at—"

"How do you know Hank Blume?"

I was taken aback by his abruptness at interrupting me, but it didn't take me long to realize he had stepped into a potentially awkward situation with deftness and wisdom. *What were you thinking, McKenna? You can't ask him how things are going at W, M and B while you're the subject of an ongoing investigation. He really shouldn't be talking to you at all.*

"Oh, um . . . we went to school together."

"College or—"

"No, high school. And junior high, but I didn't really get to know him until—"

"Look, McKenna." He grabbed me by the elbow and guided me toward the corner directly across from the giant poster of the cast of *Scandal*. That wasn't the corner Henry and I had stood in. We'd been across from the cast of *Friday Night Lights*. "I know this is an impossibly awkward situation, but thanks for being so reasonable about everything."

I hadn't realized how tightly wound every muscle in my body had been as we attempted to make small talk, but a small acknowledgment of the elephant in the room actually helped my shoulders relax from up around my ears.

All the same, it *was* impossibly awkward, and I couldn't stop myself from looking around the room to make sure no one could overhear. "I don't blame you," I stated with as much matter-of-fact precision as I could. *Stay cool. Stay collected. Don't allow talking about this for the first time with someone who was there to witness your life's low point cause your mascara to run.*

"I appreciate that." He placed his hand on my shoulder and went to the effort to lower himself to my height so he could look directly in my eyes as he said, "I do. And for the record, I know—probably better than any of the rest of them—what a great attorney you are. You just made a bad judgment call. That's all. I know it's not going to be easy, but you'll bounce back from this—"

"Hang on." I shuffled my feet away from him, and his hand fell to his side. "You think I did it? You actually think I embezzled three hundred thousand dollars?"

Silly me. Having been so worried about smearing my makeup just seconds earlier, and now there I was feeling like I might projectile vomit all over every flat surface at the Paley Center.

He held his hands palms up in front of him. "It doesn't really matter what I *think*, does it? The investigation concluded that—"

"Wait. Wait, wait, wait." I clutched my abdomen with one arm and grabbed on to the wall to stabilize myself with the other. "The investigation *concluded*? It's . . ." I couldn't feel my face. "It's *over*?"

It was somewhat difficult to piece together reality underneath the pink neon tribute to the cast of *Pretty Little Liars*, but it appeared as if all the color left his face and his eyes grew dark. "You hadn't heard?"

What kind of a question was that? Did I have the countenance of a woman who was in the know?

It felt as if someone's hands were wrapped around my throat—not choking me so much as applying pressure at various points to see how I responded. *Does that hurt? How about now? Can you breathe if I do this?*

"I don't understand. I didn't do it. I didn't do *anything*—" My toes and fingers began to tingle, and I began wringing my hands together in an attempt to bring feeling back to them. "What do I do now? What are my options? What sort of recourse—"

"McKenna, listen to me." He stepped back in closer and spoke softly. His hands kept reaching out, but then he would pull them back before he actually touched me. "I'm going to do all I can to advocate for you."

"Okay." I leaned back completely against the wall. It was the only way I was going to stay upright. "Okay. So you think there's still a chance—"

"No, you need to hear what I'm saying." He stepped closer until he was only inches from me, and he grabbed both of my hands in his. "The investigation is complete. It was conclusive. There's nothing I can do about that. But I'm going to urge the board not to press charges. I can't guarantee you won't be disbarred, but I'm going to do all I can to keep jail time out of the equation, okay? You have my word on that."

I wanted to stand up for myself. I wanted to fight for justice—it was my *job* to fight for justice. But right there, in that moment, I didn't feel like Erin Brockovich. And I certainly didn't feel like McKenna Keaton.

I nodded and pleaded with my legs to support me for just a little longer. "Thank you."

"Hey, look." He cleared his throat, looked around the room, and then took a step back from me. "We really shouldn't be talking about this. I'm sorry I said anything. I thought you knew. I'm sorry, McKenna. Truly."

I think he walked away then, though I didn't see him go. I didn't see Henry walk up to me. I didn't see *anything*, actually. The neon and the music and the chatter and the posters of the cast of *Nip/Tuck* all combined to create a sensation akin to what I'd always imagined it would be like to have my life pass before my eyes. Except there was nothing there. Everything I'd centered my entire life around was gone, and the images that were supposed to be there, representing a lifetime, were frames with nothing in them.

"Are you okay?" Henry asked with urgency. His palm was on my cheek and then my forehead. "Come on, let's get you some air." He wrapped an arm around my waist and supported me through the throngs of rich people, across the lobby, and out the door onto Fifty-Second Street.

The temperature outside was easily thirty-five degrees cooler than it was inside the crowded Steven Spielberg Gallery—where my wrap remained in coat check—and the drop jarred me back to reality. "I'm okay," I lied feebly.

"I think your definition of 'okay' is different from mine. Come here." He wrapped his arms around me and held me close, and I rested my forehead on his shoulder, burying my face in his tux jacket. "What happened? What did he say to you?"

"It's nothing." Even I couldn't make out the muffled words I was speaking into his lapel, and I was the one saying them. I pulled my face away, but his arms didn't relent. "Sorry. I hope I didn't make a scene."

He kissed the top of my head. "Do you think I care if you made a scene or not? Tell me what happened, McKenna."

I opened my mouth and prepared to say the words.

I lost my job.

I lost my career.

I lost everything I've worked for my entire life.

There are people who believe I did something I would never—could never—do.

But I couldn't tell him any of that, could I? When I'd asked him to trust me, I'd expected a very different eventual conversation. I'd been ready to tell him about a misunderstanding. An embarrassing speed bump. I hadn't exactly thought out how I would tell him that I had come to a crossroads, and I was either going to have to choose to accept the false accusation and be known forevermore as a thief, or gear up for the biggest battle of my life. A battle I could probably never win.

And either way, his reputation wasn't going to be done any favors by being associated with me.

"We just, um . . . We had some unresolved issues to discuss."

He released me from the confined comfort of his embrace but kept his hands on me, gently rubbing up and down my bare arms, where goose bumps were beginning to appear. "Well, if that was a conversation about making sure you have the right witness lined up for a trial or something, you guys take your work too seriously."

In my chest I felt like I chuckled, but it didn't make its way out of my mouth, or even to my face. I also meant to speak. Again, nothing quite made it out, and he continued.

"Can I safely assume he's the guy from work you were talking about at lunch? The reason you had to take a leave of absence? The, um . . ." He rubbed my arms one last time just as I shivered, and then he took off his tuxedo jacket and wrapped it around me. The black wool was lucky enough to have absorbed much of Henry's warmth, and I tightened it around me, desperate to experience the same sensation. "The guy you were engaged to?"

I wanted to clarify that I had never been engaged to Jeremiah Burkhead. Yes, I understood how the words I'd said could have confused him, but there was a very big difference between being engaged to someone and thinking you might marry them someday. For a period of about two years in the nineties, Erica had been completely convinced she was going to marry Freddie Prinze Jr., but Jared somehow managed to steal her away before she and Freddie could register at Tiffany's. Words mattered.

But I couldn't tell him the full story—that I was probably going to be featured in the next annual issue of *NYU Law* magazine with a picture of me holding my Vanderbilt medal for outstanding contributions to the NYU School of Law through community service behind illus-trated jail bars and a heading that said, "What Went Wrong?" And if I couldn't tell him that story, but I corrected his version of what he knew, what was I apart from a woman who, up until she started fall-ing for Henry Blumenthal, didn't have a romantic bone in her body and had chosen her prospective ideal mate based on his LinkedIn profile more than the consideration of any human emotions?

Actually, what I was—or at least what I would be perceived as—was a woman who had just had a total breakdown in a room full of socialites over a man she'd decided would be her future husband, though he knew her only as an underling. And after witnessing what Henry had no doubt just witnessed, how could he avoid drawing his own dramatic conclusions as to why I was taking a leave of absence?

I was basically Glenn Close in *Fatal Attraction*, and I would be boiling rabbits before the night was through.

"Like I said, we just had some unresolved issues—"

"But you can't tell me what those issues are?"

"It's not worth telling, Henry."

He scoffed and folded his arms across his chest. "Look, McKenna, I want to go with you on this. I really do. But I'm going to need a little more to go on than that."

Between the heat of his jacket, the fire being shot at me from his eyes, and the white-hot rage that was suddenly turned up all the way and bringing my blood to a rolling boil—perfect rabbit temperature—I was plenty warm all of a sudden.

"You've known me for about a minute, Henry. What right do you think you have to insist you get to know everything about my life?"

"Excuse me? I've known you for about a minute?" His fingers went to his collar and untied his bow tie and unbuttoned the top but-ton of his collar in a move so deft and swift it was almost indiscernible. Henry wasn't one to let discomfort and confinement stand in his way for long. "I've known you for a lifetime, and I don't exactly think I'm asking to read your diary here, McKenna. One of my donors, at *my* fundraiser, just made the strongest person I've ever known crumble at his words. And sure, maybe there were unresolved things, or whatever weak, escapist explanation you just threw at me, but nothing about anything I just saw gives me great comfort that it's all taken care of now and you and I can pick up like nothing ever happened."

"Well, if you can't trust me—"

"I'm not the one displaying a lack of trust here!"

A valet-parking attendant approached us. "Mr. Blume, if you'd like, you're welcome to step into the booth back there for a little more privacy—"

"We're fine!" we both shouted in unison, and then Henry apologized to the kid while I stepped aside. Not into the booth, which I could tell just from sight would smell like Cheetos and AXE cologne, but a little bit out of the way of the documentary fans stepping in and out of luxury cars.

Henry looked around once he was done with his apology and then hurried over to my position by the wall once he spotted me. "This has nothing to do with trust, McKenna. At least I really don't want it to. I'm not worried about your past relationships or anything like that. But if you and I are going to make this work, you have to let me in a little bit here."

See, this was exactly why I'd never wanted the distraction of love. It wasn't that I was a selfish person, I don't think. (Allow me to again point you to my Vanderbilt medal—minus the metal bars.) But how are you supposed to fight for what's best in your life if it isn't necessarily best for the person you care about? You have to make a choice, right? And why would you choose weakness over strength? Letting someone in was one thing, but if the outcome was going to be the same whether you let them in or not, what was the point of making them lose respect for you in the process?

"Jeremiah and I had some unresolved things to sort through.

That's all, Henry. Yes, I got a little emotional—last I checked, emotions are permissible—but it's over now." I stood up straighter, pulled off his jacket, and said a fond farewell to all sorts of definitions of warmth as I handed it back to him. "That's the end of it."

He took his jacket from me and folded it over his arm as he took in a deep breath and let it out. "And that's what you're sticking with?"

I shrugged. "That's all there is."

Those teal eyes bore into me. Pleaded with me, it seemed. But what other options were there? I stared back, unflinching, until he finally shook his head and scoffed. Then he looked down at his feet for a moment, ran his hand through his hair, and then met my unwavering gaze long enough to say, "Alright. Well, take care, McKenna." And then he got to go back inside, taking all the warmth with him.

Chapter 19

I couldn't face going back into that suite. I called the Plaza while I waited for my Uber—an uncomplicated, unassuming Honda Civic—and by the time I pulled up, a concierge was standing by the curb with my bag. I was soon back to JFK, changing my clothes, and changing my flight information—paying the fees with money I would probably soon be wishing I had saved for extravagances like milk and deodorant. Just like I was wishing I had suffered through the luggage wheels rolling over my toes on the AirTrain rather than have an Uber drive me to Queens on toll roads. If wishes and dreams were peaches and cream, we'd all have a merry Christmas.

Or whatever.

At 2:07 a.m. I landed at Raleigh-Durham, and thirty-six minutes later I was dropped off at my parents' house. It wasn't until I was walking up to the front door that I had the next in a very long line of too-little-too-late thoughts.

I should have gone to Erica's.

There was not going to be any way to get into Mom and Dad's

house without waking them. I didn't have a key. Not that I wanted to wake Erica or Jared, either, but there would be fewer questions at the sight of me on their porch in the middle of the night when I was supposed to be in New York.

I took a deep breath and allowed my finger to hover over the doorbell for a moment. For the first time ever, I was deeply regretful that I had never been a rebellious teen who snuck out of the house. I was nearly forty years old. Shouldn't I have *some* experience climbing up a trellis and in through a window by this point in my life? But just as I was acknowledging that would *never* be me and I was preparing to face the inevitable concerned questioning of my parents, I spotted Taylor's car in the driveway.

Not good. But in this case, better.

"Hello?" She answered her phone groggily on the second ring.

"Hey, Tay. I'm at the door. Can you let me in without waking up Mom and Dad?"

"McKenna?"

"Yes." My utter exhaustion kept me from adding the "obviously" I probably would have thrown in there any other time.

I was so tired. A day that had begun right there at my parents' house was finally on the verge of ending, nearly twenty hours later, but it felt like so much more than a stupidly long day. In twenty hours my entire world had shifted on its axis. Repeatedly. When I looked back on my life and picked out the best and worst moments, those twenty hours were going to be featured prominently in multiple highlight reels, and I knew I would feel the pain of that when I awoke. Just like I would feel the pain of leaving a brand-new, very expensive wrap from Bloomingdale's at the Paley Center. But that was tomorrow's pain. I just needed today's to end.

The foyer light switched on, the dead bolt clicked, and then Taylor was standing in front of me in her adorable cloud-covered pajamas and her hair in a bun on top of her head.

"Are you okay?" she asked as soon as she saw me, but then before I could answer, she must have realized I was not. "Come on, get in here." Taking my bag from me, she carried it over to the foot of the stairs while I came in the rest of the way and shut the door behind me. She rushed back over to assist and handled the locks while I stood there and attempted to get my bearings for a minute.

"Thanks," I muttered.

"Of course."

She stood in front of me, her face alert and concerned, but she was silent. And maybe it was the silence that broke me. The unexpected discernment and restraint from my little sister. The understanding that it wasn't the time to nag or ask questions or assume that she knew what was happening. Whatever it was, the only words that came out of her mouth were, "Oh, Kenna," and then I was accepting her offer of open, loving arms and crying big, ugly tears into her shoulder. It was the sort of messy, out-of-control weeping I'd always thought was unrealistic when it happened in movies, but if the day had taught me anything, it was that the lines between fantasy and reality, dreams and nightmares, and joy and despair were all so much more confusing than I had ever imagined.

❀

I woke up once in the night with a start, like when you dream you're falling. I couldn't help but wonder if I was going to be a step or two away from that feeling all the time now.

Taylor was cuddled up beside me in the daybed, her head on my shoulder and her arm across my hip. It was uncomfortable and constrictive, but it also felt warm and safe, and I was careful not to wake her—even if that meant I wasn't able to get back to sleep.

At least I seemed to be all cried out. That was a relief. My tear ducts were probably already contemplating going on strike. The last waking hour had given them more of a workout than they'd had in decades. They'd surely demand at least twenty more years to rest up before they'd show up for work like that again.

What am I going to do?

Moonlight reflected off of the mirror, and tree branches created shadows all along the opposite wall, and I tried to focus on those calming scenes. We were less than one week into spring, and already I could hear crickets chirping outside, and the light breeze rustling through the trees should have been more relaxing than listening to Matthew McConaughey read me a bedtime story on my sleep app. But I couldn't stop asking myself that question. What in the world was I going to do?

I would have to move out of my apartment, of course. I would have to leave New York. For good. It had taken me years to start making enough money to live the way I did—without a roommate, in a simple one-bedroom on the Upper West Side—and there was no way I could stick around while I figured out how to make it all happen again.

Maybe Zabar's would hire me. I was in there at least three times a week for asiago-cheese bagels and, when work was particularly stressful, black-and-white cookies nearly as often. Perhaps I could convince them I was trustworthy enough to be hired on as the cheesemonger's apprentice, despite being disbarred and disgraced.

Don't get ahead of yourself, McKenna. You still have the truth on your side.

Yeah . . . but neither Wallis, Monroe, nor Burkhead seemed too concerned about that nagging little detail. I'd always believed the truth was absolute, so how had the investigation conclusively determined a separate reality? I'd have to get to the bottom of it—and then I'd have to figure out how to deal with whatever I discovered.

The weight of all those concerns made me feel as if I were falling, but it was when I thought of Henry that I felt like I had already fallen and was reduced to a crumpled heap on the pavement.

I'd made it as long as I had without him, and I wasn't fooling myself that I couldn't go on if he wasn't there. I could. I would. But it felt like I'd been born and raised in the Arctic Circle or something. I'd spent time in an igloo and was an expert at ice fishing. And then I got whisked away for one glorious, sunny day in Fort Lauderdale. Now that I was back home, would I adjust again? Or was the cold forever ruined for me because I knew how it felt to be warm? Hopefully, someday Fort Lauderdale would be nothing more than a memory of an extraordinary day. I wouldn't feel the sand beneath my toes, and I wouldn't smell the salty ocean air, and it wouldn't make me feel colder in comparison every time I thought about the sun on my skin. Eventually, my senses would recover from the shock and remember that they were more than just able to handle the frigidity. They were made for it.

Taylor emitted a little snore as she rolled over on her other side, facing away from me. Great relief spread throughout my torso as I was able to stretch it out now that her arm was gone, but her bony little butt jabbing into my hips provided a new discomfort. And still, I scooted a bit closer to absorb her warmth.

❀

I managed to stay pretty much tucked away for a couple days, getting caught up on sleep and getting really good at *pretending* to sleep whenever someone opened my door and asked if I was coming down for a meal. I did a lot of thinking and, covertly, a little more crying. Taylor was a pretty good confidante. Not that I told her much of anything. But after I woke up that first morning, she said, "Things didn't work out with Henry?" I confirmed that they didn't, and she'd been protecting my privacy and sneaking food into my room ever since.

But on day three I heard more than the usual commotion downstairs, and a different sister was the one to poke her head through the door and offer up fruit and yogurt. My back was to the door, so I could keep pretending to sleep, but when she said, "Hey . . . Are you awake?" I rolled over to face her. I'd been dreading the moment when she got there, because I knew it would all come spilling out. She was the only one who knew everything about work and everything about Henry, and in her presence I would have to quit lying to myself that none of it mattered. But I think my heart actually sighed in relief at the sound of her voice.

I looked at her for a minute as she softly closed the door behind her and set the tray of food and coffee on the ironing board, which I had adopted as my bedside table, and then I sat up on the edge of the bed. She sat beside me and wrapped her arms around me, and before I knew it, I was crying again. This time was different, at least. Tears fell slowly and gently.

A few minutes later I was sitting against the pillows of the daybed spooning yogurt into my mouth, and Erica was curled up at the foot with her chin propped up on her fists, asking the obvious question.

"So, what are you going to do?"

"I don't know. It depends on what we're looking at here. I mean, it's one thing if this is all a result of someone's gross incompetence. But if we're talking about something more sinister—"

"Like what? You think you were framed?"

I shrugged. "I think I have to consider that possibility. Either way, I'll have to fight it. But W, M and B is one of the biggest, most powerful firms in the country. I can't imagine finding an attorney who would be willing to go up against them on something like this."

"Why do you need to find an attorney? Can't you do it?"

A half smile slipped onto my lips. "I appreciate the vote of confidence. I really do." And, truthfully, there were moments when the fire was lit in my gut and I knew I would give just about anything for the opportunity to stand up against Ralph Wallis or Ty Monroe in court. "But it would be kind of like letting a doctor perform surgery on the chief of staff of a hospital in the middle of a malpractice suit when their medical license is on the line. While everyone's waiting to find out if you're a murderer, they don't let you hold the scalpel."

She shifted up into a sitting position just as there was a light tap on the door. Taylor opened the door a crack and popped her head in. "Oh, sorry . . . I was just going to see if you were hungry. Looks like you're good. I'll leave you two to chat."

Erica smiled at her. "Thanks. I'll be out in a few."

Taylor smiled back at both of us and then inched backward and began pulling the door closed again, but I stopped her—surprising all three of us, I think.

"Hey, Tay? Do you want to come in?"

"Um . . . sure. If you don't mind."

She stepped in and shut the door behind her and then looked around to figure out the best place to sit. She walked toward the beanbag chair, but I scooted over and patted the mattress next to me. Taylor looked at Erica with wide eyes, and Erica smiled in response. I understood the bewilderment. Like I said, I'd had lots of time to think during the past three days of pretending to sleep. And maybe I was built for a different, arctic sort of life rather than Florida living, but that didn't mean I couldn't build a fire once in a while.

Taylor sat next to me and wrapped her arms around her knees. "You look better today," she said to me. "Your color, I mean. You have more color in your cheeks."

Taylor only knew as much as I had confirmed: that things hadn't worked out with Henry. And still she hadn't asked me a single question since. I didn't wonder how much Erica had told her, because I knew Erica would never betray my confidence. As well as my sisters got along with each other, I knew Erica's first allegiance was to me, as mine was to her.

For the very first time in my life, I found myself worrying about how that made Taylor feel.

"So here's the thing, Tay," I began, my eyes darting around the room and my voice cracking.

Apart from *Up Close & Personal*, there was really only one other movie I'd been obsessed with when I was younger: *Legends of the Fall*. I was in love with Tristan—as we were *all* in love with Tristan—and I'd watched it over and over and over. Even though I knew that Samuel was going to die. I knew that Tristan and Susannah would never live happily ever after. Without fail, I knew going in that my heart was going to break when Brad Pitt sat at Samuel's grave and wept over not being able to save his brother. And yet, like a complete fool, I put myself through that agony time and time again.

I don't know how to explain the way I was feeling in that moment, sitting there on that bed with my sisters, except to say it was like I had just popped my worn VHS copy of *Legends of the Fall* into the VCR, had used the time dedicated to the trailers of *A River Runs Through It* and Winona Ryder's *Little Women* to adjust the tracking and turn out the lights, and as that epic soundtrack by James Horner began, I was bracing myself for the glorious pain.

"I'm pretty sure I'm in love with Henry. I don't know, really. I've never . . . Yeah . . . I'm in love with him." I focused my eyes back onto their faces and saw that they were both staring at me with eyebrows raised and tears glistening, and it was the first time I realized they had the same beautiful almond-shaped eyes. "I'm so mad at myself for letting that happen." I swiped the back of my hand across my suddenly wet cheeks. "I mean, this is love, right? Is that what this is? I hate it. I seriously hate it, you guys."

Taylor wrapped her arms around me and pulled me closer to her.

Erica laughed humorlessly before saying, "It's the worst, isn't it?" She rubbed my feet through the blanket and sniffed.

"Why do people do it?" I asked. I knew it was a ridiculous

question, but I legitimately needed an answer. Though I sensed the answer was probably as incomprehensible as the reason why I was always filled with hope that maybe *this* time Tristan would find love and happiness and contentment and no one would ever be able to take it away from him.

Taylor rested her head up against mine, let out a deep breath, and said, "As if we have any choice."

Chapter 20

That evening I received a phone call from Carrie Keats in Accounting. "Hey, Carrie, hang on a second," I answered and then hopped up from my beanbag chair and closed the door. I'd started leaving the door open. That was progress, even if I wasn't quite ready to return to the dining room and be social. "Okay, sorry about that," I told her as I sat down on the edge of the daybed.

"Hi, McKenna. Are you where you can talk for a few minutes?" Her voice was soft and kind, but also somewhat shaky.

"Sure." My temples began throbbing. "Feel free to make it quick. I'm sure this can't be any more fun for you than it is for me."

After a couple seconds of silence, she asked, "Make *what* quick?"

"Aren't you calling to officially let me know the results of the investigation?"

"Oh, goodness, no. I hope I'm too far down on the totem pole for that sort of thing."

I released a gust of air and placed my hand on my trembling knee to try to still it. I just needed this part to be over with so I could figure out what came next. "I wish they'd do it already. It's just cruel at this point."

"Okay, listen, I'm going to tell you something. Something I

overheard. But, first of all, I don't actually know what I'm talking about here. And second of all, you know that if anyone found out I told you anything—"

"I won't say anything, Carrie. You have my word."

I had no idea what she was about to tell me, but my pulse drumming in my ear and my instincts churning in my gut offered their familiar guarantee that this was going to be a confidence worth keeping. There's a very good reason that more than 90 percent of all cases in the United States are resolved with a plea bargain. It's usually worth doing whatever you have to do to unlock that little bit of information you couldn't get your hands on otherwise.

She took a deep breath and let it out. Then again. And I waited. She could take all the time she needed. The adrenaline coursing through my veins juxtaposed against the sudden perfect stillness of my knee assured me the situation was completely under control.

"Okay, so earlier today, Mrs. Lewisham came into the Accounting department and told Mr. Rosado that the boss had done it again." She paused, probably expecting me to ask which boss had done what, but I knew better than that. Carrie wasn't on trial, of course, but the rules of examination remained the same. Witnesses who wanted to talk would almost always reveal more if you let them decide for themselves how much to share.

"Take your time, Carrie. I really appreciate this."

She took one more deep breath, but rather than release it, she used it as fuel. "She said he—I'm not sure which he; she didn't say—had written a check out of the wrong account, and we needed to issue another one. No big deal. Except then Mr. Rosado said, 'I can't attribute it to 3776 since the account's not active,' and Mrs. Lewisham said, 'I guess 5289 will be fine this time.'"

Admittedly, if those were all the plea-bargaining chips my coworker had, I'd see her in court. But I knew she wasn't done yet. "Then what happened, Carrie?"

"Well, as soon as Mrs. Lewisham left, Mr. Rosado muttered something, and I really can't be sure . . . but I swear it sounded like he said, 'I guess it's poor Owen's turn now.'"

Owen? The only Owen I knew was Owen Long. He was another junior partner at the firm. Owen hadn't been there as long as I had, but he was probably only two or three years behind me. Nice guy, if somewhat featureless. Not that I knew him well. All I really knew about him was that he was single, flossed his teeth at his desk, had once asked me out in 2018 (for my response, see note about flossing), and was a walking database of knowledge on overturned case histories.

"'Poor Owen'?"

Carrie sighed. "Owen Long's expense account number is 5289."

"Okay . . ."

"Again, I don't know *anything*, McKenna, but . . . I do know that 3776 is yours."

❁

The next morning I received a phone call from the Human Resources department of Wallis, Monroe and Burkhead, wishing to set up an in-person meeting with me. The following Monday I was back in New York, being officially told that the audit had proved I'd misappropriated $301,427.82 of the firm's money. I hadn't embezzled, apparently, so much as played a little fast and loose with expense accounts. I demanded to see the reports and was told they would absolutely present those to me—as soon as some of the data was no longer tied up in litigation with other misappropriating employees.

I was so grateful for Carrie's heads-up, and I was able to listen to every word from the HR lady with clear and wary ears. Yes, I was listening intently, but I also had to work hard to keep my mind from wandering. How many high-powered celebrity clients could Ty

Monroe wine and dine with $301,427.82? How many diamonds could Ralph Wallis buy his mistress?

But I couldn't betray the confidence. Carrie would undoubtedly be fired—and possibly worse—if I did. So everything depended on my access to the reports. Then, hopefully, I would be able to defend myself based on the facts—or, as I suspected, the fabricated facts—before me. It was possible that the reports really were tied up in litigation, and it didn't even raise that many red flags when I was told I would have to wait another three to six months to receive my copies. (Seriously. The law is slow.)

As frustrating as it all was, I was surprised to discover I was actually somewhat grateful to be forced to wait just a little bit longer. After all, what it really came down to, in regard to next steps, was the total and complete reevaluation of everything I'd ever wanted in my entire life.

Yes, I was innocent. Yes, there definitely seemed to be a complex embezzlement or laundering scheme in motion at W, M and B. But it was difficult to center my hopes and dreams around single-handedly fighting disbarment for as long as it took, with only some affordable lawyer from the Durham Yellow Pages who kept his office in a strip mall by my side. I refused to sign anything that could be taken as an admission of guilt, but I also walked out of W, M and B for the last time having agreed to not practice law in the state of New York—the only state in which I had taken the bar exam—as I awaited further contact and all those embargoed reports. So, what options did I have in the meantime?

I tied up loose ends in New York over the next two weeks and then moved to Durham, officially. I stayed with my parents for another two weeks after that, lined up a seasonal job as an adjunct law professor at North Carolina Central University, and then found a little apartment on West Chapel Hill, just six miles from my parents' house. By adding just one word to my title—*Visiting* Professor of Corporate Litigation—and remaining vague in my answers to questions about W, M and B's remote-office policy (and turning the attention whenever possible to how happy I was to have more time with them), I was able to satisfy my family's curiosity.

Look, I didn't love having to be anything other than completely truthful. I hated it, in fact. But even the American Bar Association acknowledges that a certain amount of deceit to help identify wrong-doing is sometimes a relevant and accepted practice. I was most assuredly in the process of attempting to identify wrongdoing. I feared I would never be able to accomplish that if my parents, my little sister, or, worst of all, Henry, were looking at me like a broken shell of the strong, independent woman they'd once known me to be. I just wasn't sure I could win if they believed I had failed. So I'd carry on a bit longer. At least I'd bought myself some time through the end of summer.

And then, seemingly in the blink of an eye, it was time for Taylor and Jackson to get married.

We worked all week preparing for multiple parties, all of which were to take place at the Keaton home. I still wasn't in much of a partying mood—you know, what with the recent complete annihilation of my personal and professional life over the course of five minutes and all—and at first I didn't do much to hide the fact. But it was shortly after Taylor sweetly offered to postpone everything that I realized I needed to throw myself completely into an unfamiliar role. That of supportive, smiling sister who loves nothing more in the world than to polish silverware and stuff mushrooms.

"Kenna, I'm going to postpone the wedding," she'd said. "Right now you just need me to act like love is stupid, and I'm fine with that. Fie on love!"

My future brother-in-law was also super supportive in his own way. "Well, actually, my parents are already halfway here from Atlanta, and my brother and sister-in-law are flying in from Tokyo . . . It may be a little late to catch them. But maybe we can tone down the number of hearts on the centerpieces or something?"

From that moment on I'd had no choice but to put the comprehensive unraveling of my heart on the back burner and focus instead on the start of my sister's commitment to a lifetime of love.

I have to admit, I did a pretty good job of faking it. And before long, I wasn't really faking it. Not entirely, anyway. I got to know Jackson better as he and I were sent on countless missions into town to pick up food and pick up and send back flowers that were intended for the Heaton funeral rather than the Keaton wedding. (Considering neither Jackson nor I had noticed the arrangement had a sash draped over it that read "Loving Grandmother," we may not have been the best people for the job in the first place.) When my niece and nephews got restless, I got to cement my role as Awesome Aunt McKenna by swinging through the drive-through at Chick-fil-A and buying them large frozen lemonades. (Which served the dual "awesome aunt" purposes of ruining their dinner and sending them into sugar shock.) And I got to think, for the most part, about things that had nothing to do with disgrace and disbarment and that big Henry Blumenthal-shaped hole in my heart.

So by Thursday night before the wedding, once all the prep work was done for the big day, and Taylor and Jackson were off having dinner with Mr. and Mrs. Boyd, and my parents had taken April, Cooper, and Charlie to Silver Spoon for catfish and hushpuppies (which their eventually guilt-ridden awesome aunt hoped they were able to eat), and Erica, Jared, and I were eating the ugly throwaways from the hors d'oeuvres that had been prepared throughout the day, and Jared and I were sharing a bottle of wine, I was actually open to having a conversation about life's possibilities. And that's when Jared said this:

"You know . . . You probably won't actually die if you're not married by forty."

"Jared!" Erica exclaimed, but she still laughed with complete abandon.

He continued, undeterred. "But if you want to be safe, you've still got plenty of time. When's your birthday? November? I have complete confidence in your being able to meet a guy, fall in love, and get married in a year and a half."

I couldn't tell if he was serious or not. I really couldn't. And based on the way Erica's laughing eyes transformed into daggers aimed at her husband, I didn't think she was too sure either.

"She's not looking for a husband, Jared. It's not like all she's ever wanted was to get married and Henry was her last-ditch effort." Erica glanced at me to make sure I was still okay before she proceeded. "This was something real, and she's not ready to cast out her net and—"

"Well, hang on a minute." I leaned across the coffee table with my wine glass in my outstretched hand, and Jared refilled me. "Let's think about this for a minute. Is it really so crazy to think about nailing this down so I don't die like all of our other spinster ancestors?"

"This is what I'm saying!" Jared exclaimed, and he and I laughed uproariously.

Erica was not amused. "You're not a spinster. You're a beautiful, successful, powerful woman who has never been swayed for even a moment away from her drive toward what she wants in life."

I gulped down some more wine and nodded as the burn overtook my throat and chest. "Thank you for that. But I'm not successful anymore. I'm not powerful. And as far as never being swayed . . . Well, I felt pretty swayed by Mr. Blumenthal."

Erica leaned in and rested her elbows on her knees. "Again, that's its own thing. Henry was—"

"What? 'The one'?" I asked, using her words from our phone call outside of Bloomingdale's. Her cheeks turned pink. She knew she was trapped. "If he was the one, what do I do now, Erica? Are you saying I should just accept that he was my one chance—"

"'Fancy, don't let me down,'" Jared interjected and then giggled at his Reba McEntire quote with an amount of pride that really should have been reserved for accomplishments like presenting the first waffle cone at the 1904 World's Fair. Call me presumptuous, but it didn't seem the good Doctor Pierson was accustomed to drinking wine.

"—and since it didn't work out with him, that's that?" I disregarded him, even as the corners of my mouth twitched in amusement.

She shook her head. "I'm not saying anything." Erica *completely* disregarded her husband. No twitching involved. "I'm just trying to defend you and what you've always said. If you want to find someone, of course I believe you can find someone. I didn't know you cared about that."

Hmm. She had made an interesting point. When had we switched sides of this argument?

"I don't know if I do." I stood up from the chair and began pacing around the living room. "But you have to admit that's super depressing. That is so much more depressing than the idea of there never having been 'one' at all, you know?"

Erica stood up and went around to the back of the couch and leaned up against it while I paced back and forth. "I've been avoiding the obvious suggestion, but why don't you talk to Henry?"

"And say what?"

Jared turned around and sat up on his knees on the couch, facing me. "I looove you, Henry." Then he made a whole bunch of kissy-face noises.

Erica shushed him and rolled her eyes in my direction. "You'll have to excuse him. It's past his bedtime, and he has the pure, untouched liver of a Buddhist monk." In response, he flirtatiously pinched her bottom, and she yelped, jumped up, and walked over to me—leaving him to laugh at his additional World's Fair achievements. ("Look! I created the hot dog!")

I nodded my head in his direction and lowered my tone. "I know Jared's an idiot, but you really did get a good one there. Let's take him as an example. Jared's one of the guys I went to school with, and now he's settled down, happy marriage, kids, mortgage, orthodontia practice . . . the whole nine yards. Do you even think there are all that many good, available men left at my age?"

"Again, I feel like I'm saying all the obvious things, but *Henry's* available."

"Is he?" I threw my hands up in the air. "It's been nearly two months. I have no idea what he's up to, nor is there any reason why I should. We were . . . a fling. That's what we were. And I'm not used to flings, Erica. So of course it felt like more than it was. When you don't eat sugar for your entire life, a few bites of kettle corn are going to hit your body like Pixy Stix and a two-liter of Mountain Dew."

"Henry was in Virginia last weekend. Saw it on Facebook."

It was most assuredly Jared's voice saying the words, but where they were coming from caused a bit of confusion. Erica and I stretched our necks around to the couch and saw only Jared's brown Oxford-clad feet popping up over the back of it. After one quick glance at each other, we walked around to the other side together and found him with all the blood rushing to his head as he dangled back between the couch and the coffee table.

"And you had children with this man," I muttered to her.

She chuckled and covered her mouth. "Heaven help me, I still think he's the hottest thing on two legs."

"Which is probably where he should be before he passes out."

She got on one side of him, and I got on the other, and we helped him stand up, and then we all plopped down on the couch together.

"I think I really hurt him, Erica," I said softly after a few moments. "All he was asking me to do was trust him enough to tell him the truth. And in return, all I did was ask him to trust me as I lied to his face."

"And you think he knows you lied?"

"I do. I don't know what he believes, but he wasn't buying what I was selling." I sighed. "For someone I claimed had known me for about a minute, he knows me pretty well, I'm afraid. And my choices now, if I want to talk to him, are to either tell him the truth—in which case I have to take a chance that he'll believe I'm innocent—or to keep letting him think I had to take a leave of absence and eventually give up my career because I was so crazy obsessed over my boss that I couldn't even function when he rejected me. I can't win here."

"You know what? You probably won't die if you don't get married before you turn forty," Jared stated with authority as he chewed on a malformed cream-cheese pinwheel.

Erica and I leaned back on the couch to steal an amused eye roll at each other behind his head, and then we sat back up and smiled at him.

"Yeah, you said that already, honey."

I reached out and poked a flat meatball with a toothpick and stuffed it in my mouth. "Maybe I should see who's out there."

"*Really?*" Erica asked, turning to face me. "I mean, whatever you want to do, McKenna. Obviously. But I'm just . . . well, shocked, I guess."

I shrugged. "The fact is, I liked the feeling. You know? The feeling of having someone's arms around me. Of laughing with someone. Of getting to know someone. Of . . ." I reached for another meatball and sighed. "Of not thinking about work all the time."

"But you *love* thinking about work!" Jared mused as he turned to me with a truly concerned expression on his face.

I couldn't quite agree with my sister's "hottest thing on two legs" assessment, but regardless of his level of inebriation, Jared Pierson was quite possibly the sweetest man on planet Earth.

I patted him on the back, feeling the need to comfort him. "I know. I always have. But . . . I might not *have* work anymore. And the thought of having *nothing* is just a little much."

Erica cleared her throat and reached behind Jared to put her hand on my shoulder. I looked at her and offered a sad half smile and a shrug as we looked at each other, a lifetime of things said and unsaid passing between us.

Jared spoke up quietly. "It would be nice to have a date for the wedding."

I laughed. "It *would* be nice to have a date for the wedding. But it's . . ." I looked at my watch. "Nine o'clock on Thursday. The wedding is on Saturday. Do we really think anyone is sitting around in Durham, still single at forty, relatively sane and pleasant, looking for a date this weekend?"

Jared shrugged and then lifted his arms and wrapped one around Erica's shoulders and one around mine. "Don't take this the wrong way, but *you* are. What's to say you're the only one?"

There was no denying it felt like a very low moment, but I couldn't escape the feeling that the moment was also interlaced with hope. Maybe one of those guys would be "the one." The *actual* one. Maybe, someday, when we were old and gray and surrounded by our grandchildren, we would look back and laugh at the ridiculous path that had led us to each other. An entire lifetime focused on a career that ultimately amounted to nothing; a depressing pattern in a family tree that perhaps made me just a little more aware of my mortality and the brevity of life; a man who had made me believe in the possibility of love and the benefits of companionship—and who smelled like teakwood and kissed with skillful abandon, and whose eyes I'd thought it might not be so awful to get lost in forever.

Though I probably wouldn't mention that part to my grandkids.

An hour later I retired to my room, shut the door, collapsed into my beanbag chair, and spent a solid three minutes staring at my phone.

I'd waited too long. In two months we hadn't talked or texted or discussed research or even sent each other a social-media friend request. I'd waited too long, and at the same time, if I put it off for another two months, I still wouldn't know what to say.

I clicked on his name in my contacts list, butterflies bouncing off the walls in my stomach and a few of them somehow escaping into my lungs. At the sound of the first ring, I thought to look at the time. It was too late to call. And it was definitely too late to hang up.

"This is Henry. I never remember to check my messages, so if you actually want to talk to me, maybe try a text. Otherwise, feel free to speak into the black hole that is my voice mail. See ya."

I shook my head and chuckled as the tone indicated it was time for me to speak.

"Hey, Henry. It's McKenna. I, um . . . Yeah, to be honest, I'm a little relieved to know you don't check your voice mail. Maybe by the time you listen to this, I'll have a clue what it is that I actually need to say to you. For now, I guess I just want to say that I'm sorry. For . . . for lots of things. I used to see a therapist—well, several therapists, all told—for anxiety issues. Of course, you knew me in high school, so I doubt that comes as a huge surprise. You know me *now*, so I doubt that comes as a huge surprise," I muttered and then cleared my throat. "Anyway, my first therapist used to tell me that being human was not a weakness, and the truth is I still struggle with that. No matter how true it is. I guess . . . I guess what I really want to say, though, is that you made me feel human in a way I don't think I ever had before. And . . . well . . . I didn't hate it. Thanks for that."

I flicked away the tears rolling down my cheeks and felt the torrent of emotion building up in my throat, and though I knew there was so much more to say, I had no choice but to hang up before the black hole of Henry's voice mail recorded the evidence of just how human I could be.

Chapter 21

I have to admit, there have been times through the years when I really haven't been so sure, but now I think I can confidently say Taylor really does love us."

Erica and I were twirling in front of a mirror in the bedroom we had shared in Mom and Dad's house, admiring the absolutely breathtaking bridesmaids dresses our little sister had chosen for us. We'd had them on before, of course, but until now they hadn't been accompanied by styled hair, perfect makeup, and ankle-strap heels that made it look like our legs went on for days.

Erica scoffed. "She loves *you*, anyway. I can barely get this thing zipped up."

Ah. Well, *I'd* been twirling. It seemed Erica had actually been flitting about trying to squeeze herself in and zip herself up. The pattern is surprisingly similar.

"Here, let me help." I stood behind her and found the zipper amongst the delicate chiffon and gave it a slight tug. Hmm. I gave it a less slight tug. "Suck in." She did as she was told, and I was able to finish the job. Okay, so she'd put on a few pounds. Between family life and the end of the school year, and one sister's move back home and the other's planning of a wedding, she hadn't exactly had time to make it to the gym every day. She still looked gorgeous in the symmetrical A-line in . . . What was the color called again? Vermicelli? Vermin? Something like that. Regardless, it reminded me of a pretty shade of rust at sunset, and I loved it. "Look at you, hot mama." I let out a catcall whistle as I stood behind her and looked at her reflection in the mirror. "Jared won't be able to keep his hands off of you."

She emitted a groan and a dry laugh simultaneously as her hands went to her abdomen. "Yeah, that's the problem."

It took a second to register, and then my eyes shot open wide. "Hang on, are you—"

"Did you know they call it a *geriatric pregnancy*? *Geriatric*! I looked up the definition of the word, and it's literally 'an old person who is receiving special care.' Why don't they just call it a 'death's doorstep pregnancy'?"

I moved between her and the mirror as my hands covered my mouth and my eyes grew even wider. "Erica!" My hands instinctively reached out and touched her tiny little baby bump. "Are you serious?"

"Yep. Serious as being referred to as a geriatric at forty years old." But suddenly her face didn't look as serious. All her features softened, and a smile began to spread. "I must be out of my mind."

"Oh, my gosh. You should be sitting." I ushered her over to the daybed from her adolescence and forced her to sit as she laughed. "You can't stand up in those heels all day!"

"I'm fine, McKenna. These are the ones Taylor picked out."

"I know, but—does she know?" She shook her head. "Then tell her. She'll understand. This dress would still look great with some cute ballet flats or . . . I don't know. Do you want me to get you some Crocs or something? Would that be more comfortable?"

She laughed again. "I'm fine. Really. And I *do not* want to tell Taylor yet. I don't want to tell anyone. Do you understand? We're going to let Taylor have her day. Sometime after she and Jackson get back from their honeymoon . . . We'll tell everybody then."

I nodded my understanding and agreement to her terms. "So who knows?"

"Just you and Jared."

"Oh, the kids are going to be thrilled!" The smile fell from her face like her marrionettist had forgotten they were responsible for her strings. "Aren't they?"

She seemed to force herself out of a trance she had momentarily fallen into and cleared her throat as the smile returned. "Definitely. It's just . . ."

"What?"

"Well . . . I had a miscarriage last year."

"You *what*? When? Why didn't you tell me?" I shook my head and brushed away the question with my hand. It was selfish and didn't matter. And yet . . . "Seriously, Erica? How did I not know that?"

She shrugged. "You didn't know because I didn't tell you. You had a lot going on at work—you were working on that big class action, and you were on track for partner, and . . ." Her shoulders, bare apart from spaghetti straps, rose and fell again.

"And what?"

"Just don't worry about it. It's not like there was anything you could have done."

"Well, no, but . . ." My eyes began to sting. Actually, everything in me began to sting. "Erica, why didn't you tell me?"

She took a deep breath and then squared her shoulders to face me. "The fact is, we lost the baby very early. I didn't know I was pregnant until I wasn't. And, well . . . I thought you might think it wasn't a big deal." She reached out her hand and placed it on mine, feeling the need to comfort me even when it should have been the other way around. "I couldn't bear the thought of you acting like it wasn't a big deal. Because to Jared and me, it was a very big deal."

"Is that really what you think of me?"

"Now, you listen here. You're my little sister, and I'm your biggest fan. You're my absolute best friend in the entire world." I opened my mouth and attempted to say, "And you're mine," but no sound came out. Nevertheless, she smiled and said, "I know." She squeezed my hand tightly. "Sometimes I think you just spend so much time convincing yourself that no one could ever understand you that you occasionally lose sight of trying to understand other people. With that, I just couldn't risk it."

I bit my bottom lip to keep it from trembling. "I'm sorry."

"And I'm sorry I didn't tell you. But I'm really glad you know about this." She took a deep breath and stood up and brushed her hands over her waist. "The thing is, even if the term *geriatric pregnancy* is a crime against women, there's a reason they call it that. It's risky. So I guess I'm just hesitant to spread the word too much until I absolutely have to."

I used the tips of my pinky fingers to dab at the moisture beneath my eyes before our mother's makeup masterpiece was ruined. "Well, don't take this the wrong way, but you were about a centimeter away from having to walk down the aisle in sweats and a T-shirt. I don't know how long you'll be able to keep this secret."

"I know. But today's all about Taylor." She chuckled and copied my pinky dab. "Just keep the safety pins handy."

The new Mr. and Mrs. Boyd could not have picked a more beautiful spot for their wedding than my parents' wooded backyard. They'd kept it intimate and classy—a true family-and-friends affair for forty or so. That was Jackson's choice. Taylor had initially wanted a big church wedding to which all of Durham would have undoubtedly been invited, but Jackson had pushed for intimacy. He wanted a day they would treasure and remember rather than a stress-filled photo opportunity. He'd also proposed in private and had already won her over to the side of never shooting pink or blue chalk out of a cannon but rather finding out the sex of their future babies when they either did or didn't see male genitalia on an ultrasound. As he said, "Like the pilgrims did it."

He was a funny one. As it turned out, I'd sort of hit the brother-in-law jackpot.

The reception afterward was a bit less intimate but no less comfortable and personal. We stayed right there at Mom and Dad's house. Dad fired up the grill, a friend of Jackson's played DJ, and the party began. The entire neighborhood had willingly offered up their driveways and street parking—anything for Scott and Annie—and then all the neighbors moseyed over to congratulate the happy couple at various times throughout the day.

I had been prepared to kick into mother-hen mode with Erica, but I needn't have worried. Jared had it covered. He hardly allowed her to lift a finger—not that it was all that different from when she wasn't pregnant.

Cooper and Charlie made instant friends with Jackson's "super cool" nephews from Atlanta. April was given the uber important job of documenting the day with casual photographs—a role she took very seriously, if her continual cries of, "Daddy! Stop making goofy faces in every picture!" were any indication. And my parents relished their roles as host and hostess. Taylor and Jackson laughed with guests, ate with the gleeful abandon that only young people with thriving metabolic systems can feel, and just generally glowed with love and joy.

Everyone was happy. Everyone was taken care of. And apart from occasionally refilling the punch bowls, that left very little for me to do except try to carry on a conversation with Jimmy Clark Jr.

After my Thursday-night musings about how it might be nice to have a date for the wedding, Jared had mentioned seeing our old classmate—and my old high-school boyfriend—at Food Lion a few weeks prior. With my brother-in-law's insistence that he seemed really nice, wasn't married, and went by James now, I tracked down Jimmy Clark Jr.'s phone number. No, he hadn't quite managed to maintain his fidelity through the homecoming DJ's playing of "Pony" by Ginuwine, but it had been twenty years. Surely he had matured.

"You look hot," he "complimented" as he approached me at the grill where I had been left to man the burger station while my dad ran in for more cheese slices. Dad quickly returned to the grill, placed his hand on my back, reclaimed the tongs, and relieved me of my duties.

"Um . . . thanks." I smiled at Jackson's brother Mason as Jimmy and I walked away from the burger line. "You look nice too."

And the truth was, he did.

"I meant you look hot . . . like, because it's hot out." He smiled. "I'm not so crude as to just go up to my date and say she's hot. Manners maketh the man!"

Well, *that* was embarrassing. Not quite as embarrassing as standing there for a few more seconds, waiting for him to say something like, "You do look lovely though" or "Although, I have to say . . . that dress . . ." or "But now that you mention it . . ." Nope. There was nothing else.

"So, James . . . Have you kept up with anyone from high school?" We picked up a couple of cups of punch—I made a mental note to swing back by and fill it up in ten minutes or so—and made our way to a couple of chairs on the periphery of Mom and Dad's property.

"Oh, sure. Do you know, um . . . What's her name? Michelle? Oh, man. I can't remember her last name. Do you remember her?"

"I . . . I'm not sure."

"You know. Michelle."

"I guess I'm not the best at remembering—"

"*Michelle!*"

I promise you, the man was looking at me like I was one of those people on *Wheel of Fortune* who buys an *A* rather than take a chance on solving GRE_T W_LL OF CHIN_.

"I don't know who Michelle is!" I shouted.

He looked taken aback by my outburst and spent a moment pouting before saying, "Well, anyway, I go out with her sometimes. Everybody else cool moved away or moved to the 'burbs and settled down or whatever. I kind of thought there would be more of my friends here."

I tilted my head in confusion and a growing sense of wonderment. "At my little sister's wedding?"

"Sure. I know everybody in Bull City." Ugh. I'd never known anyone my age who was *from* Durham who'd actually referred to it as Bull City. "But I don't know anybody here. Except Peterson."

"Peterson?"

He pointed to Jared, who was standing behind Erica's chair, rubbing her shoulders as they laughed together, a smile the size of the GRE_T W_LL OF CHIN_ on his face. "Not sure why he's here. We don't know any of the same people."

If not for the fact that I'd actually allowed myself to get my hopes up when Jimmy Clark Jr. showed up at my doorstep looking handsome in his classy suit, driving an Audi, and offering a single long-stemmed rose, I would have been enjoying it all much more than I was.

"Well, you know he's my brother-in-law." Nothing. "As in, he's married to my sister." Total blankness. "And his name's Pierson. Jared Pierson."

"If your sister's already married to Peterson, whose wedding did you say this is?"

Alrighty then. I put my hand out for him. "James, would you like to dance?" I was at least going to get some dancing out of the deal before I sent him on his merry way.

He smirked as he took my hand. "Sure."

There was a rented wood-parquet floor in the middle of the backyard, and Taylor and Jackson were currently in the center of it, swaying to Lady Gaga and Bradley Cooper (from one of the few movies more depressing than *Legends of the Fall*, though it didn't have the pull over me that Tristan did). Other couples danced all around them, but when Jimmy and I took our places, we were the only couple Taylor was watching. She raised her eyebrows and smiled, then subtly pointed Jackson to look our way. I just rolled my eyes in their direction and shook my head. *Don't get your hopes up about this love match, kids.*

Now, he wasn't a bad dancer, truth be told. His style was a little more *In Living Color* Fly Girl than Fred Astaire or Gene Kelly, but he picked up his feet, never stepped on my toes, and competently led me with a firm-but-gentle hand appropriately placed on my lower back. All in all, I was pleasantly surprised.

The conversation was another thing.

"Where did you learn to dance?" I asked him as Gaga faded and Ed Sheeran took over.

"I've always liked to dance. Since high school." He pulled back from me slightly and stared at me as if seeing me for the first time. "Hey, didn't you and I go to a dance together? You've danced with me before. I was good then, too, huh?"

I chuckled. "Well, you and I did indeed go to a dance together, but I've never danced with you. You were sort of busy all night."

To see all the pride welling up in him, you'd have thought I'd just told him, "America owes you a debt of gratitude, son."

"You know what?" I intercepted whatever he was about to say as his mouth opened. "I'm not a great dancer, so I kind of need to focus on what I'm doing. Is it okay if we don't talk?"

He seemed all too happy to comply, but unfortunately not until after he said, "Whatever will help."

With my eyes and his mouth both closed for the next few

moments, I actually started having a lovely time. It was so gratifying to listen to the laughter and upbeat conversation all around me, and I was able to rest my head on his shoulder and just get lost in the music and the happiness and the glorious seventy-six-degree, low-humidity day. Everything had come together to create an absolutely perfect day for my baby sister, and for as long as Jimmy Clark Jr. was willing to silently lead me around the dance floor, I was content letting everything that did not exist within the confines of my parents' property slip away for a little while.

"Do you mind if I cut in?"

My contentment was instantly shattered, replaced by a thrill running up and down my spine at the sound of his voice. I couldn't stop my fingernails from digging into Jimmy's shoulders at the sight of one of the men I'd spent homecoming with all those years ago while my date danced with every girl at Jordan High. Probably including the mononymous Michelle.

"Henry? What are you doing here?"

Chapter 22

As usual, Henry looked **fantastically out of** place and as if he owned the joint, simultaneously. He was wearing olive-green slim-fit chinos and a white linen button-up with the sleeves rolled up above his elbows and the top unbuttoned to a little below his collarbone. He was a bit wrinkled but perfectly put together, and I wanted nothing more than for Jimmy Clark Jr. to hand me over to him at once.

"Who are you?" he asked instead as he continued to twirl me and tightened his grip on my waist.

I didn't feel threatened. I'd lived as a single woman in New York for most of my adult life, and apparently there is only one entry in the Christmas gift catalog next to "What to get the single Manhattanite female in your life." Self-defense classes. Well, two entries. Sometimes we receive bottles of wine. All we do is go around drinking and defending ourselves.

So, yeah, even if we weren't in a public space and even if Henry wasn't standing *right there*, I could take on a bully if I needed to. All I was really worried about was making sure Henry knew that Jimmy Clark Jr. was no longer my dance partner of choice.

"It's okay, James. He can cut in."

"You know this guy?"

"I do. So do you. You remember Henry Blumenthal, don't you?" I'd wasted enough time, and I wasn't entirely sure Henry wasn't going to bolt if I didn't get over there soon. Jimmy and I were on the complete other side of the dance floor now, and Henry's eyes were darting around and his feet were easing back. Yep . . . I was about to lose him. "I'm going to go dance with him. Sorry to be rude, but you're free to go anytime you like. Or, you know, stay and help yourself to a burger." I extracted myself from his arms and scurried across the parquet in my heels.

"Hey!" I called out to Henry from the edge of the dance floor just as he backed up onto the grass and turned on his heel to go.

He stopped and turned back around. "Hey. Sorry to—"

"No, you didn't."

"I wasn't trying to make it a whole thing." He stepped back onto the dance floor, and I moved back step for step with him, trusting he wouldn't allow me to bump into anyone. "It just seemed like the debonair way to make my presence known."

Out of the corner of my eye, I saw Erica talking to Jimmy Clark Jr. and Jared patting him on the back as they escorted him across the yard toward the street. My heart did not weep.

"It was very debonair. I'm sorry that my date was a Neanderthal who apparently never watched an episode of *Melrose Place*."

"*Melrose Place*?"

I shrugged. "Or *The Love Boat*, maybe? I don't know. I just feel like I've never actually seen anyone cut in except on television."

He smiled. "Maybe I should go back and do some research. I'm not sure I did it right. You know, since you and I still aren't dancing."

I stood up straight and opened up my arms into a slow-dance position and made myself available to him. His smile turned into a soft smirk as he looked down at his feet, took a step forward, looked back up at me, placed his right hand on my waist, and scooted my body up against his. His left hand took my right, and I gulped in as much air as I could swallow without choking on it. I knew that I was preparing to re-enter that rare air space in which breathing and thinking and a steady pulse were all things that required a lot of focus.

"For the record, I had no intention of crashing a wedding today," he said once we'd found our rhythm. "I was going to drop some things off for your dad, but when I saw all the cars I put it together. I would have just driven away, but your mom was out front talking to a neighbor." He shrugged. "She insisted I stay."

"I'm glad."

"I'm a tad underdressed."

"Are you kidding? This is a millennial wedding, my friend. My sister's friends have passed through here in everything from shorts and muscle shirts to white tie and tails."

Henry pulled his head back to look at my face. "Seriously?"

I nodded. "Oh, yes. And a top hat. Not kidding. So I'd say you are the mean, median, *and* mode in this little wedding experiment."

With a snicker he replied, "Mrs. Towie would be so proud—you spouting off mathematical terms like that."

"Wow. Mrs. Towie. That's a name I haven't heard in a while. Do you think she's still alive?"

"Are you kidding? I'm pretty sure she was 142 years old when she was teaching us calculus."

With no warning, he released his hand from my waist and propelled me out in a spin, guided by his left hand grasping my right over my head, and then dipped me gracefully and pulled me back to him—and our bodies were somehow closer together than they had been before.

We swayed in silence for a while, and then he said, "I should have called. I'm sorry."

"*I* should have called," I argued.

"You did."

My eyebrow lifted. "It appears I fell for the false security offered by the black hole of your voice mail."

"Yeah, well, certain missed calls warrant more rapid retrieval of messages than others." His cheeks puffed up, then he exhaled. "I was glad you called. I'm . . . I'm really glad you called, McKenna."

"I don't think I even said anything. Not really."

"Oh, I don't know about that."

I turned my face away from him as much as I could without looking like a barn owl, and then I stretched my face in an attempt to rein in the threatening tears. I still felt unsteady, so I bit down on the inside of my cheek. But then I was thrown off balance in a much more pleasant way.

"Can we talk about this dress for a minute though?" His dance stature morphed as he lowered his left hand to my waist and his arms wrapped around me. I lifted my arms and looped them around his neck, and then our faces were so close I couldn't avoid the memory of how he tasted.

"Do you like it?" Coy was not typically a comfortable go-to for me, but I suddenly understood its benefits in a way I never had before.

"You're stunning." He swallowed hard, and I watched in fascination as his Adam's apple bounced up and down, and then a jagged breath slipped through his teeth and the bottom lip he was chewing. "You've always been stunning."

I didn't know what was happening. I didn't know where we stood. I didn't know if anyone was watching. I didn't know if we were friends or more or *nothing*, in the middle of our final farewell. But I knew one thing for sure.

I was madly in love with Henry Blumenthal, and a life without him in it would never be quite as good as I knew a life with him could be.

"Thank you for noticing," I whispered, and then I felt stupid and wished I could suck the words back in. "Wow, that did not come out the way I meant it to. I didn't mean, 'Thank you for noticing that I'm stunning.' Although, yes . . . thank you for that." I sighed and buried my head into his shoulder as all the blood in my body moved north to my face. "Not that I'm saying, 'Yes, I'm stunning, and it's about time someone noticed.' I just meant that Jimmy Clark Jr. didn't notice anything except how sweaty I was."

"*That's* who that was! I knew I recognized him."

I lifted my head. "Oh. Yeah. I just . . ." He wasn't asking for an explanation, and I didn't feel as if I owed him an explanation. It was funny how those two facts were combining to make me feel as if I wanted to give him one. "I just wanted a date for the wedding. Nothing like being such a catch that your cheating ex-boyfriend from high school is your best option." At what point did feeling comfortable with someone become a detriment to humiliation?

His feet stopped, and mine stopped between them. "I would have been your date."

"How could I have asked?"

Our eyes locked, and he appeared to be grappling for an answer. I guess nothing came to him because he just tightened his arms around my waist, and we began mingling with the other dancing couples again.

Maybe I could tell him about W, M and B. Maybe he would trust me. Maybe he wouldn't doubt me for a second. Maybe, in his eyes, even in the truth, I wouldn't be a failure. And . . . then what? Would he forgive me for lying to him? For not trusting him in the first place?

Maybe.

Warmth overtook his eyes as he raised his fingers to my face and tucked a deviant wave behind my ear. "Do you know what I've always found so attractive about you?"

The soft, lyrical stylings of Ed Sheeran faded, and a deep, booming, pulsating-through-my-body-like-I'd-been-defibrillated techno beat took over. Was it techno? No, that wasn't quite right. That's what we'd called it in my day, but now it was GED or EMT or something like that. Taylor had shown me her playlist for the reception, and for every two or three nice, danceable songs by the Ed Sheerans and Lady Gagas of the world, there was one assault on my ears by people like SAINt JHN and R3HAB and RØRY, and other names that made me feel like I was playing a word puzzle game that I didn't quite understand.

"This is awful!" Henry called out to me over the suddenly much louder music, and his hands dropped from my waist. "I don't know how to dance to this."

I couldn't blame him for that. It was supposed to be dance music, right? Wasn't that actually the point? How could anyone find a beat?

Not that any of Taylor and Jackson's contemporaries were having any difficulty. For them, it appeared the party had finally gotten started, and we were surrounded by twentysomethings having a wee of a time. A discernible rhythm was not a requisite for their dancing, apparently.

"Did we just turn eighty years old?" I yelled back to him. "I've never felt more like a senior citizen in my life."

He pointed away from the dance floor with his thumb. "You wanna?"

"Sure." I nodded, though the truth was I didn't want to step away. I didn't want to stop dancing with him. I was afraid that the spell was about to be broken. Although, let's face it: the spell had already had the life beaten out of it by the auditory equivalent of fifteen million strobe lights.

But just as I was accepting that the magic had come to an end, a dramatic record-scratch sound blared over the rented speakers, and the dulcet tones of Savage Garden brought peace and calm to the chaos. Our young, sweaty friends groaned—but then quickly seemed to remember they were at their friends' wedding, not some trendy nightclub with Jay-Z and Beyonce or whichever celebrities people wanted to go clubbing with these days—and most of them started swaying to what they undoubtedly viewed as super-lame pop music. I glanced over at the DJ's table, curious to see if the position had been overtaken by the ghost of Casey Kasem, and saw Taylor standing there smiling at me with Jackson behind her, his arms wrapped around his new bride. Erica and Jared were there, too, bent over the laptop, pointing out to the DJ what I could only presume they viewed as acceptable song choices for the moment Henry and I were sharing.

And just like that, a new spell had been cast.

Henry didn't ask me if I wanted to continue dancing. He just took my hand and pulled me to him and said, "Have I mentioned how great you look in this dress?"

"You have, actually. Not that I'd be entirely opposed to starting the whole conversation over again, from the top." *In fact, could we just start the past few months again, from the top? How about the past twenty-five years?* "Although I think you were just beginning to tell me what you always liked about me."

"Ah. That's right." He repeated the twirl move from before, but this time he pulled me back to him with a guided, protective force that made me laugh as the wind got knocked out of me a little bit against his body. He grinned at my laughter and once again tucked renegade curls behind my ear. His fingers lingered in my hair this time, and I couldn't resist slipping my arms up around his neck and weaving my fingers through the shaggy blond strands at the nape of his neck. "But I wasn't saying what I liked about you. I was beginning to tell you what I always found so attractive about you."

"And they're not the same?"

He paused, and his eyes wandered to my lips as he thought about that. "Yes and no." His eyes returned to mine, leaving me to lick my lips—which had suddenly gone very dry—in semiprivacy. "You see, what I always found so attractive about you was that you've always known who you are, McKenna. You've always known what you wanted. While the rest of us were either trying to live up to everyone else's expectations for us or trying to avoid expectations altogether, you already had your own plan. Your own expectations. I might not have had the words for it then—and I certainly wouldn't have had the courage to express them—but even as a teenager, I thought that was the sexiest thing I'd ever seen."

This is our song.

Even as the thought flitted through my brain, I was amazed by how I felt it rather than thought it. Every muscle and nerve ending and blood cell in my body understood that they needed to remember everything that was happening. Every word that was being said. Every time the corners of his eyes crinkled. Every point of contact between his body and mine. And whenever I thought about any of those things, for the rest of my life, they would be accompanied by the soundtrack of an overplayed, undeniably schmaltzy Savage Garden song from the late nineties. And every time I heard that song for the rest of my life—every single time—my muscles and nerve endings and blood cells would take me back to this moment. This perfect moment in Henry Blumenthal's arms.

"You weren't a normal teenager any more than I was, were you?"

The corners of his eyes crinkled, and my blood cells took note. "No, I suppose I wasn't." Those dazzling eyes—which, reflecting the sunlight as they currently were, made me feel like I would never be able to see the ocean's depths, no matter how hard I looked— were fixed on me for several seconds, and then, just as what seemed to be a sad smile started to appear, he sighed and pulled me closer against him. His face was beside me instead of in front of me, so I didn't have time to confirm the suspicion of sadness. But his next words took care of that for me. "So, when are you going back to New York?"

I scrunched my eyes together as tightly as I could and rested my cheek on his shoulder. *Welcome back, reality.* A gentle tear slipped onto his white linen as I opened my eyes and said, "I'm not sure, actually."

My arms had been around his neck, but I slipped them down around his waist and held on for dear life. His arms were resting on my shoulders, and we weren't so much dancing as just holding each other in the middle of a crowd of couples. I begged time to stand still, but I had no hope that it would give in to my plea. The song was about to end, but it was worse than that. I either had to tell him everything or tell him nothing. If I told him everything, I would be taking my chances that he would choose me in spite of the lies. In spite of the questions about my moral character. Would he always wonder if I could be trusted? Would there always be just a little bit of question as to whether or not I'd been worth it? Ty and Jeremiah had been at the fundraiser, so was it a safe assumption that W, M and B was a corporate sponsor? How much money was that? If he chose me, he'd lose it, surely. Was that the cost of the truth?

Besides, he'd always been attracted to the girl who knew what she wanted. The girl who'd always known who she was. Right now, I was further away from that girl than I'd ever been. When he realized that, would the feelings begin to fade? Would the attraction downgrade to a sentimental fondness?

On the other hand, to tell him nothing would be to allow him to keep believing that, maybe, what I'd wanted more than anything— more than my career, more than my reputation, more than New York, more than *him*—was a romance with Jeremiah Burkhead. How could he possibly ever love a version of me that had so easily proven everything he thought he knew about me—everything that attracted him to me—to be an illusion?

"Your dad said you're teaching at NCCU?"

My head shot up. I should have expected him to know at least that much. "Um, yeah. Just . . . well, it's just a short-term contract for now. Through summer classes and some online courses."

"So you officially left W, M and B?"

I cleared my throat. "Yeah." That truth conflicted with a lie most of my family still believed. It was all growing more complicated with each question he asked.

Think faster! Think faster! My brain really needed to figure out its decision. The risky truth or the potential-extinguishing silence?

"But you'll be going back to New York?"

"Where will you—"

"I'm heading there myself for a few days, actually. I'm leaving tonight. I've got some meetings lined up with the curator at the National Immigration Museum."

"At Ellis Island?"

He nodded. "I'm taking a crew with me, and we're going to start getting some B-roll."

Savage Garden faded into "Iris" by the Goo Goo Dolls—a song that I was certain still met all of the Piersons' requirements, even if *City of Angels*, the movie it was from, was perhaps more depressing than *A Star Is Born* and *Legends of the Fall* combined. But the magic was once again gone. And this time the music couldn't shoulder the blame for us. He stopped dancing and pulled away, and every nerve ending seemed to suffer from instant freezer burn. "Anyway, that's boring."

"It's not!" I insisted. "I'm fascinated by all of this. In fact, I guess we should talk about what my role will be, moving forward. With the film. I mean, if you still want me to have a role. If not, I understand. Do you need me to go with you?" Did he *need* me? I chuckled self-consciously. It was all unraveling so quickly, and all I wanted was to rewind the clock. "I guess you've done some pretty good work, but truthfully I'm not sure how you've made it this long without me." *Stop talking, McKenna. Just stop talking.*

He swallowed hard, no humor visible on his face, then reached out and brushed his knuckles against my cheek. "The truth is I'd love nothing more than for you to go with me. But, you know, with us . . ."

"Yeah."

"I just don't know that it's a good idea."

"No, definitely. I get it."

He took another step away, then sighed and said, "I should probably get going."

"Okay."

He led me as we excused our way through the dancers. Jackson and Taylor were swaying in each other's arms on the edge of the parquet, and as Henry walked past he shook the groom's hand and hugged the bride and congratulated them both. Taylor looked over his shoulder at me, and I shrugged and smiled in a way that I hoped said, "Ah, well, thanks for trying." It must have said exactly that, because tears instantly welled up in her beautiful, compassionate eyes.

Henry offered a wave to Jared and Erica, who had returned to their seats near the grill, as we crossed the lawn. They waved back while demonstrating the same sad understanding that Taylor had. We walked in silence until he stopped in front of a Prius at the end of the driveway.

"Is this you?" I asked.

He shook his head. "I'm parked down the street." But he was clearly ready to say goodbye right where we were.

"I'm really glad my mom made you crash the wedding."

He ran his fingers through his hair. And then he sighed and stuffed his hands into his pockets. "Look, McKenna, I travel a lot. I have a favorite butler or concierge at about fifteen different hotels around the world. I could tell you my favorite place to eat in all fifty states. Half the time I don't know if I'm coming or going, and I continually live out of a suitcase. But Durham is home base."

"It is?"

"Sure. I've had an apartment here since I graduated college. I mean . . . I'm only here probably fifty days a year, but Durham is *home* for me. But I know it's not for you." He took a deep breath and released it slowly. "New York City is the love of your life. And I think it needs you as much as you need it."

Was that it? Was *that* the reason, in his mind, that he and I couldn't have a future? I could work with that. New York wasn't an option, and a girl could do a lot worse than fifty days a year with Henry Blumenthal. "I'm here now." My voice rose about an octave, and I felt my lip begin to tremble. I felt *everything* begin to tremble. "My family's here. And . . . I mean, we don't always get everything we want, Henry." *Sometimes we don't get anything.* "Durham's not the absolute *worst* place to—"

"McKenna!" I flinched in response to the frustrated growl that released from his throat, immediately following the emphatic use of my name. "Don't turn your back on everything you've ever wanted and everything you've worked toward just because you're wondering if maybe everyone else has been right and you've been wrong about what your life is supposed to look like. Don't do that. You know what you want, and you know who you are. And you're the only one who needs to." He pulled his hands out of his pockets and rubbed his face, then glanced at his watch. "I've got a plane to catch."

I tried to focus on regulating my breathing enough to get through this torture without making him think any less of me than he already did. "Okay."

He reached out and rubbed my upper arms and then pulled me into a gentle embrace. He sighed against my hair and muttered, "Hang in there, okay? You'll be back home soon. I'm sure of it."

I'll never be home ever again. "Thanks for cutting in."

He released me and smiled. "For the second time in my life, Jimmy Clark Jr.'s loss was my gain."

Chapter 23

Are you sure you don't need me** to do anything else?" Jared asked Mom and Dad as he walked in the back door after taking the last of at least nine million bags of garbage and fourteen billion loads of recyclables to the end of the driveway for pickup.

"You're sweet," my mom replied as she collapsed onto the couch next to Erica—where she was sitting, sorting unnecessarily through cards and wedding gifts, as Jared had instructed her, to keep her from getting roped by the pregnancy-unaware into more strenuous cleanup work. "But everything else will wait until morning. If you don't get the kids home and to bed soon, they're going to be worthless for their day at the trampoline park with Sodie tomorrow."

Erica and I each glanced at my nephews and niece—all of whom were currently making up slumbering additions to various pieces of furniture around the room—and then smiled at each other. "Really, Mom, Dad doesn't have to take them tomorrow. I can't imagine how exhausted you both must be."

"What's that?" Dad asked as he rounded the corner from the kitchen and joined us in the living room. "You'd better not be putting the kibosh on my plans. I need to jump around on trampolines for a while to keep myself from feeling as ancient as I know the fact that I just married off my baby makes me."

"Fair enough." Erica looked behind her at Jared. "You ready?"

"Whenever you are."

"I don't know how we're going to get all of these snoring lumps into the car."

He walked over to Cooper, who was asleep on the floor with April's feet propped up on his back from the chair above him, as if he were her ottoman. Jared gently nudged his rib cage with the side of his foot. "Hey, Coop. Time to go, buddy." Cooper groggily obliged, and April awoke with a start when her feet dropped to the ground when he moved.

"That one's a lost cause," Erica said, referring to Charlie, who had yet to demonstrate signs of life from the loveseat as his dad shook him gently and said his name.

With a sigh, Jared picked him up and threw him over his shoulder in a fireman's carry. "Good night, Keatons!" he called out as he ushered the two zombies through the front door.

Erica, who had long ago changed out of her constrictive dress and heels and into baggy shorts, a loose T-shirt of Jared's, and flip-flops, leaned over and kissed Mom on the cheek and then stood from the couch. I got up and headed to the door and waited for her there while she told Dad goodbye. When she got to me, I opened up my arms and whispered in her ear, "Just think. You'll be adding a car seat to the mix pretty soon."

She chuckled and hugged me. "Nope. You forget, this time I have what I never had before. A built-in babysitter in the form of my oldest child. I only travel alone from here on out." She pulled away and looked behind her to make sure no one was within hearing distance, but Dad had just sat down next to Mom and was wrapping his arms around her as she leaned against him. They weren't paying any attention to us whatsoever. "Are you doing okay?"

I shrugged. "I don't know what choice I have."

"I'm sorry. I really thought Savage Garden would do the trick. Almost like it would serve as a prom dance the two of you never got to share."

"It sort of did." I squeezed her hands. "And I appreciate it. But we couldn't live there forever. The present was bound to catch up with us eventually."

I closed the door behind her after promising to call her the next day to arrange lunch, and then I sat in the armchair across from my canoodling parents.

"Thanks for all your help today, McKenna," Dad said through a yawn. "I'm pretty sure it was exactly the day your sister wanted."

I nodded and smiled. "I'm pretty sure it was. She looked gorgeous, didn't she?"

Dad kissed the top of Mom's head. "All of my girls did." He shifted, and my mom raised herself up. "I couldn't have been prouder of all of you." He kissed her again and stood up. "Good night. I love you both."

He began walking toward the stairs, but I stopped him. "Hey, Dad? Henry said he brought something for you. Did he find something on Marilla?"

"He didn't tell you?"

"Tell me what?"

He picked up a manila envelope from the entryway table and reached out to me. I walked over and took it from him. "Not everyone's ancestor warrants an official letter from the deputy archivist of the United States, so that's not for nothin'."

I looked up at him in surprise as I pulled the pages from their envelope. "No, it's really not."

"Well, good night."

"Good night, Daddy." I settled onto the opposite end of the couch from my mom just as she stood.

"I'm going too. Are you staying here tonight?"

"Thought I might, if that's okay."

"Of course. I'll see you in the morning."

"Night, Mom."

I was still in my dress, though the shoes had long ago been abandoned, and as soon as I was alone, I hiked it up to midthigh and lay back on the couch. I ran my finger over the letterhead of the National Archives and then fluffed up the pillow under my neck before I began reading.

Dear Henry,

Maybe one of these days you'll send me an easy one. Knowing you, I won't be holding my breath. Miss Keaton remains a bit of an enigma. The work you and Mr. Keaton had already done made it relatively easy to track her down, but it took a while to dig up anything of substance. We cross-referenced the manifests, but the only names that overlapped apart from hers were members of the crew. We chased those leads to see if there was perhaps a romantic connection to a crew member, as you had suggested, but that came up empty.

I was about to call it, but then we were able to unearth microfiche fragments of letters—none of which were in great condition and none of which were ever delivered to their intended recipients. They were somehow saved from the *Calinsia*—the ship she was on. There was a letter to a family member (we can't tell who it's addressed to, but the level of familiarity makes us suspect a sister) in which Marilla expressed her "fidelity to see this through, though none understand my need to do so."

I've included copies of the letters, though, again, there are few discernible words of high impact apart from an excerpt in a letter from her final voyage that I think you'll find interesting. We have no idea who this one is to, but toward the end she wrote, "Though

I long to see you, I carry not the dream of the new land as you do. Fear not for me. It is for the born days of a new generation that I toil. It is for them that I dream."

Henry, call me crazy, but I think Marilla Keaton was a sort of vigilante midwife onboard the *Calinsia*. She never would have been hired to serve in any sort of official capacity, of course, since the lives of passengers just wouldn't have mattered that much to shipping companies. The Steerage Act required them to report the dead, but as you know there were no penalties for lives lost. What did lead to steep penalties, however, was exceeding the authorized number of people aboard. I can't imagine a scenario in which a shipping company would willingly hire on a spinster to take up valuable occupancy, all to save lives that, to them, just wouldn't have mattered in the least.

I'm going out on a limb here, but I believe she repeatedly bought passage at her own personal expense to help ensure a future generation of Americans made it to shore. I suppose we'll never know for sure, but here's what I do know: sometimes as many as thirty women gave birth in steerage on a single early nineteenth-century journey across the Atlantic, and the infant mortality rate on similar vessels across a ten-year period averaged 28 percent. There was not a single report of infant death on any of Marilla's five voyages.

Hope this helps. Give me a call next time you're in DC, and we'll have lunch.

> Sincerely,
> Sid Griegson
> Deputy Archivist of the United States

"Wow," I breathed. In that moment, I wasn't thinking of Marilla as my spinster ancestor—I was seeing her as the star of a Hank Blume film. I knew Henry well enough, and I certainly knew his work well enough to know he would see beyond the facts on the page. The storyteller would merge with the historian, and he would present her story in spellbinding fashion.

She had not dreamed of America, but she had dreamed of what America stood for.

Tears welled up in my eyes as the true romance of her story resonated, and pride swelled in my heart as I began to imagine how much more beautiful her life would appear in Henry's skilled hands.

I put Mr. Griegson's letter behind the other two pages and tried to make out what I could from the nearly impossible to read microfiche. I stared at the pages for the longest time until I faded off to sleep, my mind full of questions and pride and sadness and a commitment to always mail my letters.

"Should we wake her up so she can go to her room?" I heard my dad whisper.

"No, she seems to be sleeping pretty soundly," my mom whispered back. "She must have been here all night. A little longer won't hurt anything."

In my sleepiness I must have agreed with her, because the next thing I knew my eyes were fluttering open, my dress was down as far as my knees, thank goodness, and the sun was definitely in a different position in the sky than it had seemed to be through my eyelids while my parents whispered.

I stretched my arms over my head and sat up—though a night on the couch didn't make that the easiest thing for my achy joints—then bent over and picked up the dropped Marilla documents. I carefully folded them and returned them to their envelope, which I set on the coffee table, stood up, and adjusted my dress as best I could.

"Good morning, sleepyhead," Mom greeted me with a sunny

smile as I stumbled into the kitchen. "You look like you had a wild night."

I scoffed. "I don't think I budged. I didn't realize how tired I was."

"Well, if it makes you feel any better, I bet Taylor and Jackson got a lot less sleep than we all did."

I nearly spilled the coffee I was pouring. "Eww, Mom! *No*, that doesn't make me feel better!"

She looked at me with a look of confusion on her face and then began giggling like a schoolgirl. "No! I just meant because they waited at the airport all night and then their red-eye to Bora Bora was delayed until this afternoon because of a storm near Tahiti! *Someone* has a dirty mind."

"Yes. And it's usually you." I sat down across from her at the table and began sipping the hot coffee and watched her as she took a sip of her own and turned a page of her book. "Has Dad already gone to pick up the kids?"

She rolled her eyes upward. "Yes. You should have heard him and Charlie talking about it yesterday. I'm not sure who was more excited."

I was midsip when I heard the unmistakable sound of a phone vibrating, but I couldn't tell where it was coming from. "Do you hear that?"

Tilting her head, she listened for a moment, then pointed to the counter when recognition dawned. "I plugged your phone in this morning. It was on the coffee table."

I saw it across the kitchen, lighting up. "Oh! Thanks." I hurried over and picked it up, and my breath caught in my throat when I saw the name that popped up. I cleared my throat and swiped to answer it, then hastily disconnected it from the charger and scurried into my dad's study.

"Hello?"

"Good morning, Brockovich. How are you?"

What in the world could he want? I steadied myself against the drafting table and put all of my effort into making sure my voice sounded like I'd been up for hours, preparing my wrongful termination suit against W, M and B.

"I'm well, thank you, Mr. Burkhead. And how are you?"

"I'm doing great. It's not often I get to call with news this good, so this is a day I'll be sure to jot down in my diary."

I should have brought my coffee with me. Not because I needed the caffeine anymore. No, I was jarringly, irreversibly awake and alert. But it would have been nice to have something in my hand to help keep it from shaking.

"Good news, huh? Well, I'm anxious to hear it."

"We owe you an apology, McKenna. It looks like our auditors made a huge mistake. I'm . . . Well, we're *all* just mortified, of course. You know, these things happen. But you never expect them to happen to someone who has been such a valuable member of the team for such a long time."

I leaned against the edge of the table and attempted to swallow down the bitter taste in my mouth. But it just wasn't going away. It wasn't sitting right. There was no way on earth that months of hell were going to be resolved with a breezy phone call. And the hotter my face grew, the more the bitterness overtook my senses. "A mistake?"

Breezy vanished in the blink of an eye. "Yes, a mistake. Look, I don't know what your friend has told you, but it was all a simple mistake. I'm making it right, so if I were you, I'd do the smart thing, Keaton."

My head was spinning. It was *him*? He was the boss who had done it again? And how in the world had he found out that Carrie had called me? Clearly this was no auditing error we were talking about—as I'd been fully aware of for a while—but I'd watched the man defend others for countless hours, and until that moment I'd never once heard him sound defensive.

Regardless of how he knew about Carrie, I knew I had to keep protecting her. But I also needed answers. And as any good attorney knows, it's significantly easier to get answers when your witness isn't feeling their breeziest.

"I'm sorry, Mr. Burkhead, but you're going to have to explain to me how deliberate misappropriation of a check supposedly written from the wrong account can be classified as a 'mistake.'"

The line was silent for a moment, then he chuckled in a slightly unhinged fashion. "So he *does* know more than he let on. I knew it."

He? Had Jeremiah Burkhead gone completely off the deep end?

"I knew it. It couldn't have been the first time a donor's check bounced, and I don't care how much money you're contributing to his films, that's not the sort of thing he would usually call about himself, I'm sure. It pays to have friends in high places, I suppose."

Hang on . . . *Henry?* Was *Henry* my friend he was talking about?

He sighed. "Okay, tell me what it's going to take to get you back." My gut told me to let him keep talking, and I knew that under normal circumstances his gut would tell him to shut up. These were not normal circumstances. "You'll get retro pay, of course. A raise. And you're back on senior-partner track like none of this ever happened, obviously." He paused for me to speak, and I kept waiting. "McKenna, I need you back. I'm a better attorney when you're around. I think . . ." He took a deep breath, and then the next series of words released like a geyser—fast, forceful, and dangerous if you didn't keep your distance. "You know me, Brockovich. You know I'm better than this. I'll make sure it's all taken care of on this end. I'll own up to the mistakes and make sure no one holds you responsible for anything, and then you and I can turn W, M and B into something even better."

"You mean like Wallis, Monroe, Burkhead and Keaton?" I closed my eyes and allowed myself one brief moment to mourn the loss of the dream. It was right there. I didn't fully understand the magnitude of the mess he had made, but I knew that if I wanted to put all of that aside and just reach out, I could grab everything I'd ever wanted. More than what I wanted, what I deserved. What I'd worked my entire life for. My hopes and dreams and aspirations and sacrifices . . . It had all led to this moment.

"Done. I'll make it happen."

My one moment passed. Instead of grabbing the brass ring, I reached out and took a tissue from the box on my dad's drafting table and dabbed away the tears that had fallen. And instead of envisioning how good it would feel to tell everyone what I had accomplished and how proud of me they would be, I saw Henry's face in my mind and heard his voice, challenging and believing in the best version of the girl he never stopped impressing.

You know what you want, and you know who you are. And you're the only one who needs to.

"I had this mentor who once told me, 'Take twenty-four hours for personal decisions, forty-eight hours for career decisions, and seventy-two hours for legal decisions.'"

He chuckled softly and said, "Of course. Take your time. That was some of my better wisdom, after all."

"But the thing is, Mr. Burkhead, I don't need to take forty-eight hours. I don't need to take forty-eight seconds. I'm not going to waste one more minute of my life working for the likes of you. What's more, I'm not going to let you get away with this. You don't get to ruin people's lives and then go about your business."

"Really?" He laughed so loud I had to pull the phone away from my ear. "Forgive me, but you're prepared to go up against W, M and B, knowing the resources we have?" Was that pity in his voice or just outright scorn? Either way, if I wasn't mistaken, it was laced with just enough fear to bolster my confidence. "You know I think highly of you. But don't even think about casting yourself as David in this little scenario. If you come at us with your stones and your slingshot, I'm not going to have any choice but to stomp you so far into the ground that you won't be able to get a job playing a lawyer in a community theater production of *12 Angry Men*. You know how good I am at what I do."

"Yes, I do. The problem—at least for you—is that you know how good *I* am at what I do. Going up against me *and* the truth?" I clicked my tongue against my teeth. "You've picked the wrong side of this one."

I pushed the End Call button and dropped my phone as if it were the griddle side of my plugged-in George Foreman grill that I cooked all my meals on throughout the entirety of law school. Loose, discombobulated pieces of jigsaw puzzles floated around in my brain, finding their neighbors one by one and clicking into place. Details were zooming past my eyes as if the *Millennium Falcon* had just shifted into warp speed, so I shuffled through my dad's things until I found an unused steno pad and a pen to jot down facts and suspicions.

I didn't know what was coming, but I was going to be ready.

Chapter 24

I finally made my way back into the kitchen, pages of scrawled thoughts in my hands, and my mom looked up in concern and curiosity as I walked in. "Is everything okay?" My eyes began to sting and feel heavy, and she jumped up from her chair and had me in her arms before a single tear could fall. "Baby girl. It's okay. Tell me everything."

And I did. I walked her through every moment of the past several months, correcting the version of the story that I had allowed and guided them all to believe from the moment I showed up at the front door, melting in my winter coat.

"Why didn't you tell us?" she asked once I had gotten her all caught up—all the way through Henry maybe somehow scaring Jeremiah Burkhead into giving me my job back.

I blew my nose on a napkin she had handed me before she grabbed the entire box of tissues from the counter and set it on the table in front of me. "I don't know. It was embarrassing."

"McKenna Rae, don't you tell me that you thought we would believe that embezzling thing for even a moment."

"No, it wasn't that." I sniffed. "It wasn't entirely that. It was just that . . ." I reached out with shaking hands for my mug and swallowed down a huge gulp of room-temperature coffee. As soon as I put it back on the table, Mom grabbed it, took it over to the sink, dumped it out, and brought me back a fresh, hot cup. "I failed. You know?"

"No, I don't know."

"Look, Mom, I know you believe in me, and I appreciate that. I do. I know you're on my side, no matter what. But my entire life, no one's understood me. No one's . . ." I exhaled, took another drink, then closed my eyes and gathered my thoughts. "No one's ever thought I chose the right life. No matter what I've accomplished, the questions I always get are 'When are you going to settle down?' 'When are you going to start a family?' Mom, I've never felt like I needed to fall in love. I've never wanted kids."

She reached out and put her hand on mine. "But then you *did* fall in love. Right? And who knows? Maybe one of these days you'll change your mind about wanting kids—"

I pulled my hands away and jumped up. "See? Do you see what you just did?" I balled my hands into fists and closed my eyes. "I don't want to change my mind. Maybe I will. I don't know. But you and everyone else act like I'll never quite be complete until that happens. I have goals and dreams, and I've never wanted to walk away from them like you did—"

"Is that what you think?"

I felt nauseous as I realized what I had said. "I'm sorry. I didn't mean to—"

"Why don't you sit back down?"

"Mom, I really am sorry—"

"McKenna, sit."

It was a tone of voice I hadn't heard in more than two decades, but muscle memory caused me to sit down without another word or thought of argument.

"I knew you never quite forgave me for getting pregnant. I wish I knew how to explain to you how it feels to know your daughter believes you ruined her life." I opened my mouth to argue, but she held up her hand and silenced me. "New York was always special to you in a way it wasn't to the rest of us, and I knew then like I know now that it broke your heart to leave." She grabbed a tissue and dabbed at her eyes, but her voice was strong and unwavering. "And it broke my heart that I broke your heart. But you listen to me, and you listen good. I never walked away from my dreams. If that's what you think happened, then it's no wonder you chased yours so hard. And I'm proud of you for that. But McKenna . . . *You* were my dream. Your father was. Erica. Taylor. April and Cooper and Charlie. Jared and Jackson. You and I may have different dreams, but don't you think for one moment, young lady, that mine matters any less than yours. And don't you dare treat me like I didn't work just as hard for mine as you've worked for yours. Do you understand me?"

"Sometimes I think you just spend so much time convincing yourself that no one could ever understand you that you occasionally lose sight of trying to understand other people."

Erica's voice in my head caused the tears to flow freely as I got down on my knees in front of my mom and wrapped my arms around her waist. I laid my head in her lap, and she ran her fingers through my hair and shushed me lovingly.

"For the record," I whimpered a couple minutes later, "I never blamed you for ruining my life. I blamed Taylor."

We both laughed through our tears, even as I made a mental list of all the people I'd lost sight of trying to understand.

"So, what now?" Mom asked me several minutes later once tears had been dried, therapeutic laughs had been shared, and a second pot of coffee had been brewed.

I shrugged. "I don't know. I need to talk to Henry, of course. I don't really understand what his role in any of this was, but it's time I at least make sure he knows I'm not Glenn Close." She looked at me questioningly, so I added, *"Fatal Attraction.* The thought that he knows even a little bit about the type of person Jeremiah apparently is . . . and that he believes I could have been hung up on someone like that . . ."

"Well, believe it or not, I was actually asking what came next for your career, but that doesn't seem to be what you're most concerned about." She lifted her mug to her lips and smiled.

I folded my arms on the table and dropped my head onto them. "I don't know what to do, Mom."

"I don't think you give yourself enough credit." She began stroking my hair again. "You've always looked at following your brain and following your heart as going two separate directions. But isn't it possible that they can both lead you to the same thing?"

My head flew up so quickly my mom startled. "I have to go to New York."

"That's my girl."

After packing with one hand and reserving plane tickets on my phone with the other, I took the quickest shower of my life. Forty-five minutes later Mom was dropping me off at Raleigh-Durham. I got checked in and rushed to my gate with ten minutes to spare before boarding began.

"Kenna? Hey, Kenna!"

I turned around at the sound of Taylor's voice, shouting at me from the other side of a Smarte Carte kiosk. I just barely had time to plant my feet before she barreled into me and wrapped me in a bear hug.

"What are you doing here?"

Trusting the guidance of my brain and my heart. "Taylor, I'm so sorry."

Her face fell. "Oh no. What's happened?"

I shook my head and rubbed my hands up and down her arms as

her big, expressive eyes grew misty. "No, no, no. Sorry. Everything's fine. Nothing's happened. I just . . ." I glanced back at my gate. Eight minutes to go. "When does your flight leave?"

"In about an hour. We were supposed to fly through LA, but now they're rerouting us to San Francisco—"

"Hey, I'm sorry. I really don't want to be rude, and I *am* interested. But my flight boards in seven minutes, and—"

"*Your* flight?" The anime eyes filled to the brim again as she looked at the departure board at my gate and then back to me. "You're going back to New York? When were you going to tell me if I hadn't seen you? Were you even going to say goodbye?"

My brain wanted to fuss at her for jumping to conclusions. For asking the wrong questions. But they weren't the wrong questions at all, were they? I'd spent her entire lifetime not giving her any assurance at all that I wouldn't do exactly that sort of thing to her.

"I lied to you." I looked down at my shuffling feet and adjusted my backpack straps. "I didn't come home for your engagement party. I should have, but I didn't. I came home because I had to. I, um . . ." I raised my eyes back to her face and found her staring at me with concern. "It turns out my boss was stealing money from the company—at least I think that's what was happening—and he framed me for it."

She gasped and covered her mouth with her hands. "Oh, Kenna."

"I lost . . . Well, I thought I lost everything. And then I told you I was going to marry him. The boss. And of course that just made it all so much worse."

"Jeremiah was the one who framed you?"

I nodded. "I'm pretty sure. I still have some stuff to sort out. But . . . yeah."

She stood there in silence, processing it all. She should have been yelling at me. For lying to her, for neglecting her, for so many things. And yet I instinctively knew that if I waited there long enough for her to figure out what she wanted to say, her words would be kind and loving and forgiving, and I just couldn't allow her to let me off the hook so easily.

"Oh, Tay, I'm so sorry." The dam protecting the world from the tears I'd stored up for years proved fallible once again, and I had to choke out the words through my sobs. "I was the worst sister in the world to you. And all you ever did in return was love me so much more than I deserve. The truth is I resented you from the moment I found out Mom was pregnant with you. In my mind, it was your fault we had to leave New York. I . . ." I sniffed and took a wet, messy breath. "I blamed you for ruining my life, and I never got past that. I blamed you for everything that went wrong after that. I never had a panic attack in my life until we moved back here, so *that* was even your fault. And there were times when I knew I was hurting you. When I knew you just wanted me to confide in you like I confided in Erica. But I never knew how to do that, Tay. When my world was shattering, I always felt like everyone was craning their necks to check me out like the car accident on the side of the road. And I know that wasn't intentional. Just . . . No one knew what to do. But Erica was like my first responder, you know? When everything was at its worst, she rushed in. So those were the two roles you both got stuck in. The one who caused the wreck and the one who swept in to fix it. And that wasn't fair to either of you. You didn't cause the wreck. Life did. Or circumstances or chemical imbalances or bad attitudes. I don't know. All of it. But it wasn't you."

She threw her arms around me, and we sobbed together until we heard the boarding announcement for my flight.

Taylor pulled back abruptly, beaming, her mascara having stood the test even as her face was covered in enough moisture to relieve the drought of a small Western town. "You're going to New York to find Henry, aren't you?"

I laughed and sniffed and wrapped my arms around her again. Doggone it if I didn't *love* that she had asked the wrong question.

Chapter 25

I was in the air for less than an hour and a half, and in that time I second-guessed what I was doing more times than the lady I was sitting next to told me she'd never been on a plane before. And trust me. That was many, *many* times. The only decision I was certain of by the time we taxied up to the gate at JFK was that I would not be taking the AirTrain. I had worn open-toed sandals, and I was not in the mood to let luggage wheels crush my exposed appendages.

I ordered a Lyft and hopped in, hoping that my instinct to head to the Plaza was the right one. I didn't sleep on this drive as I had in Antonia's vehicle. I had far too much to think through. I wanted to just show up. I wanted to take him off guard and see the look on his face and, again, I hoped my instincts were right—but I couldn't be entirely sure it would be a pleasant surprise.

Did you get to New York okay?

I waited for his reply to my text, wondering if I perhaps should have sent that question to him *before* I got on a plane. If he responded, "Plans changed. I'm in Indianapolis," I would have to believe once and for all that this romance stuff was not for me.

I did. Thanks for checking. You doing okay?

I released a little noise that sounded a bit like a cat mewing. My driver looked at me in the rearview mirror but quickly darted his eyes away once he had confirmed I was not giving birth to kittens.

"Sorry," I muttered. But I couldn't help it. Just knowing that we were both there. Knowing that I was going to see him soon. Knowing that he still liked me enough not to have blocked my phone number. In an instant, I knew that where Henry was concerned, this romance stuff *was* for me.

I'm good. Can we talk later? What's your day look like?

I held my phone so tightly my knuckles turned white. That felt like the right thing to say when I typed it. It was the perfect way to find out where he might be throughout the day. But what if he said he wasn't ready to talk to me yet? Worse, what if he said, "Can I just call you quickly now? I have a date later"? I had not thought this through at all.

I'm shooting at Battery Park all day. Sort of noisy. Call you tonight?

He was the man of my dreams. That's all there was to it. Not only was he kind and generous to me, despite the fact that I had given him every reason to believe I'd had a total meltdown after an affair with my boss, but he still called the park at the southern tip of Manhattan Battery Park. They'd renamed it The Battery a few years ago, but I didn't know any dyed-in-the-wool New Yorkers who had been able to make the change in how they referred to it.

Perfect. Thanks.

"Excuse me?" I glanced down at the Lyft app on my phone for my driver's name. "Oscar? I need to go to Battery Park instead of the Plaza Hotel."

"Then change it on the app."

"I know, but you're going to want to take the Thirty-Fifth Street exit toward downtown instead of the Thirty-Seventh toward cross-town, and that's coming up pretty quick—"

"You'd better hurry, then."

You will not be getting five stars from me, Oscar.

I typed as quickly as I could and breathed a three-star-at-best sigh of relief when we drove out of the Midtown Tunnel and onto the Thirty-Fifth Street exit. I used the remainder of the trip down FDR Drive to mentally practice what my opening line might be.

"Is now a good time to talk?"

"If you don't kiss me right now, I'm going to throw your camera into the Hudson."

"You couldn't have been shooting at Shake Shack or something? I'm starving."

"I'm sorry about everything, and you're the most wonderful man in the world, and I'm as crazy about you as you probably thought I was about Jeremiah, except I somehow know this is much healthier than whatever you thought to be the case there, because I'm actually not that sort of crazy."

Yeah, it was going to be a game-time decision. Each option had its merits.

"Here we are," Oscar said to me as he came to a rolling stop. "Battery Park."

I looked out the window. "No, this is a Starbucks."

"See all that green over there? It's a park. Head toward the Statue of Liberty, and you'll find what you're looking for."

He had dropped me off easily three blocks early, but somehow I'd even been able to find the romance in Oscar's instructions and promise.

"Thank you very much," I said with a smile as I grabbed my backpack and climbed out. I crossed State Street and approached The Battery proper, and about the time I got to the Seaglass Carousel, I had to stop and catch my breath. Not because of the amount of walking. Are you kidding? I walked more than those four blocks to get from the Fifth Avenue entrance to the law collection at the New York Public Library. No. My breath was stolen by my city.

I stood on the sidewalk and took advantage of a temporary reprieve from heavy foot traffic to slowly take in the 360 degrees of history, life, and beauty all around me. I was surrounded by some of Manhattan's most iconic, most historic views. The Brooklyn Bridge. Ellis Island. Lady Liberty.

None of which would yet have been there to greet Marilla if she'd ever stepped foot on this new land.

But Castle Clinton would have been, and I knew instinctively that the red-tinted stone building along the water's edge—a muted salute to New York's history, surrounded by progress and setbacks that had long ago attempted to leave it behind—was the ideal filming location for an upcoming Hank Blume masterpiece.

I hoisted my backpack farther up on my shoulder and jogged the rest of the way to the National Monument, then joined the line to walk into the fort. Families, couples, and individuals were circling all around inside, reading the inscriptions, surveying the artifacts, and listening to park rangers sharing tales from the Castle's storied history. But there was no film crew in sight.

Pushing my way through the tourists, I headed out the way I had come in and walked past the Bosque Fountain, where children were shouting and squealing in delight each time the water underfoot shot up, as high as fifteen feet into the air. And then I spotted two men holding camera gear, a woman with a headset, and another woman with a clipboard. I hurried over to where they stood, near the sculpture *The Immigrants*. They appeared to be talking about potential shots and looking through cameras in preparation rather than actually filming.

"Excuse me? Are you with In Blume Productions?"

The woman with the clipboard looked up at me. "Who are you?"

"McKenna Keaton. I'm a friend of Henry's."

She looked me over and sized me up for a moment, presumably to make sure I wasn't a stalker or fangirl or something. (Did Henry have stalkers and fangirls? I would have to investigate that further.) Then, seemingly convinced I presented no threat, she pointed me toward the Harbor.

I turned and squinted through the sunlight bouncing off the glimmering jets from the fountain and made out a tousled blond head standing along a railing on the other side. "Thank you," I said over my shoulder and began circumventing the laughing children.

"Maybe you can get him to hurry up!" she called after me. "Tell him we're losing the light."

I was about fifteen yards away from him when I felt my phone begin to vibrate in the pocket of my blue jeans. There was no thought of answering it, of course.

That is, there was no thought of answering it until Henry turned his body and leaned his left hip against the railing in front of him, and I was able to see that he was holding his phone up to his right ear. I reached into my pocket as quickly as I could, and when I saw his name, my eyes filled with warm tears. The water those kids were splashing in couldn't possibly represent as much joy as the water running down my cheeks, knowing that for whatever reason, he was standing there, staring out at the Statue of Liberty, thinking of me.

"Hello?" I stopped progressing and leaned up against a tree to watch him.

"Hey. What are you up to?"

"Oh, not much." I couldn't wipe the stupid grin off of my face. "I thought you weren't going to be able to talk until later."

"Is this a bad time?"

"Not at all."

He ran his left hand through his hair and then faced outward toward the waterways. "I guess curiosity got the better of me. As far as what you want to talk about, I mean."

I glanced back at his, from the looks of it, increasingly impatient film crew, who were now not only irritated with their boss but, if the death glares I was receiving were any indication, their boss's self-declared friend who was doing nothing to hurry him along.

"Well, I know you're busy. I don't want to keep you from anything."

He looked over his left shoulder in the crew's direction but didn't linger. He turned back to Lady Liberty, rested his elbows on the railing, and settled in.

"There's not really much happening right now. So what's up?"

I attempted to stifle the giggles, and the combination of the giggles and the tears made my voice sound sort of warbly. "My dad showed me what you gave him. About Marilla, I mean."

"Oh. Yeah." He stood up straight and switched the phone to his left ear, and his right hand began flexing around the top of the railing. "It's not quite as romantic as an ill-fated affair with the captain of the ship, but I think her reality is pretty great."

I took a few steps in his direction, fully aware I wasn't going to be able to go much longer without needing to see his face. "So do I."

That right hand gripped the railing more tightly. "You do? What happened to believing there would never be a justification good enough for her not to disembark?"

I paused on the pathway as four children, wet from the fountain, scurried across, and then I resumed my slow, methodical approach. "I think for her, staying on the ship was probably the bravest thing she possibly could have done. She knew what she wanted to do with her life, and she never swayed from that. I think that's remarkable."

His flexing hand froze, and he switched ears again. "Sounds like someone else I know."

"Maybe. But you know what?" I cleared my throat and attempted to swallow down the emotion. "I think it can be just as brave and just as remarkable to reevaluate your life and acknowledge that you've outgrown your dream." *Call it like it is, McKenna.* "To start pursuing a new dream."

I was five feet away from him and couldn't bring myself to take another step. I was close enough to hear him without the assistance of the phone—even as his voice competed with the people all around and the ripples and the crashes of the waves.

He watched the Staten Island Ferry pass in front of Liberty Island and swiped at his eyes. "What are you saying?"

"Henry . . ." I said with all the strength my voice could rally as I pulled the phone away from my ear.

He kept the phone up to his ear as he turned around, no doubt thinking his name had been spoken by a waiting crew member. When he saw me, understandable confusion floated across his expression. His brow furrowed, and then he looked briefly down at the ground before raising his eyes to look at me again. He lowered his phone and stuffed it into his pocket while his lips moved nearly imperceptibly, although no sound was emitted.

"Henry, I'm ready to get off the boat."

A chortle escaped from him in three strained releases of air and emotion, and then he looked up to the sky and rubbed his eyes roughly with the palms of his hands. Then, when I was about a millisecond away from wondering if I had driven him to madness—not of the desirous, loving sort I felt for him but the run-and-jump-in-the-Hudson sort—he looked back at me with eyes so full of love and emotion and anticipation that I knew if I ran to him, his arms would be open for me. And that's exactly what I would have done, if he hadn't already taken the two large steps necessary to cup the sides of my jaw in his hands and pull my face to his.

A whimper escaped in the last moment before my lips' ability to do anything but respond to the urgency of his was taken away from them. My fingernails dug gently into his lower back in an attempt to hang on for dear life as his passion carried me away. His hands made their way to my hair, and he combed his fingers through before wrapping one arm around my shoulders while his knees bent and his other arm wrapped around my waist and pulled me up onto my tiptoes when he straightened his legs to his full height.

"Ahem." The sound came from the side of us. Or was it the sound of my heartbeat pulsating against my temple? Maybe it was my lungs, desperately fighting for air but losing in their battle against my other internal organs, which were adamantly defending their needs as more pressing. "Excuse me, Henry. Sorry to interrupt."

Okay, that *definitely* didn't come from inside of me. There wasn't a single cell in my body that would have dared commit an act so traitorous.

My eyes fluttered groggily, and his warm, crinkling, Mediterranean Sea eyes were there in front of me, so close and so open to me that I could almost see every thought and fantasy and dream of me behind them.

"What is it, Robin?" he asked, his lips brushing against mine. And it was that—someone else's name being spoken against my mouth— that caused me to awaken from the Henry sleep state I'd have gladly stayed in forever.

I cleared my throat and diverted my eyes from his as I pulled away. His arms released me, but as soon as I began to take a step away to allow him to work and allow myself to cool off, he grabbed my hand and held it. I looked down at our interlaced fingers and the way his thumb was tracing circles on my skin while Robin talked about lighting and operating hours and . . . yada yada yada. None of that mattered. I mean, it did. It mattered a great deal. But Henry was taking care of that. All I needed to do was stand there and bask in the fact that he was working hard and loving me at the exact same time.

"I love you so much it's stupid!" I blurted out.

His thumb stopped moving on my hand as I sheepishly raised my eyes and looked at Robin. She wasn't really the one I wanted to be looking at right then, but if I looked at Henry, I knew I might melt into a pool of affection and contentment that I wasn't prepared for. At least when I looked at Robin, the worst thing I had to fear was death by embarrassment.

"Sorry," I muttered to her. "I didn't mean to interrupt."

A smirk overtook her ruby-red lips. "You know what? I think we have enough day shots for now. Some night shots might be nice. I'll give you two a minute while I go get the guys set up."

Then she was gone, and Henry was still holding my hand, and I had no choice but to look at him.

"McKenna—"

"Hang on," I interjected.

I was looking into those eyes again, and there wasn't a single doubt in my mind that he was about to tell me he loved me too. I'd always been a woman who liked to stay a few steps ahead, so in the time it took him to utter my name, I had realized how it was all about to play out. He was going to say something mind-blowing and perfect, I was going to jump into his arms again, and then the next thing I knew, Robin would be saying something like, "You know what? I think we have enough summer shots for now. Some winter shots might be nice."

"We have to talk about some things first."

The corner of his mouth rose. "You mean *before* I tell you how in love with you I am?"

I know a great place to buy coats on Sixteenth Street. Tell Robin and the guys they're on me.

"Yes." I sighed. "But *please* hold that thought. Okay?"

He tilted his head to meet my eyes and then gestured toward a bench behind him. "Want to sit?"

I nodded and we walked to the bench, hand in hand. He sat down and turned toward me, with his knee propped up on the seat, and I realized everything in me felt on the verge of spontaneous combustion. At least I was aware. I'd always assumed spontaneous combustion was, well, spontaneous.

I pulled my hand out of his. "Actually, you sit. I'll stand."

I saw something in him shift. His posture became less relaxed, and his foot dropped down, and he put his arm on the back of the bench—I think in an attempt to look like he wasn't worried. But I'd made him worry. I'd made him question whether or not what he thought was happening between us was actually happening at all.

"What is it?"

"I lied to you. I didn't have to take a leave of absence because I went crazy over my boss. I never even dated him. It's true there was a time when I thought I might marry him someday, but sort of in the same way you might think you're going to build an addition on your house someday. It just seemed like a logical next step I'd take when the time came."

He exhaled and leaned forward, resting his elbows on his legs. He tilted his head up to look at me. "Okay . . . So why *did* you take a leave of absence?"

My fear of not being able to carry on a conversation without attacking his lips was surpassed by a fear of my knees not being able to support me, so I sat down.

"You know . . . the embezzling. But I think you know all about that already."

His eyes flew open, and he sat up straight. "Is this the face of a guy who knows all about the embezzling?"

"I didn't actually embezzle anything, Henry! No. Sorry! I was set up. I'm pretty sure it was Jeremiah. And he said you had been digging around—"

"Hang on. The checks?" I nodded, and he jumped up from the bench and began pacing. "He wrote a huge check from W, M and B the night of the fundraiser, and it bounced a couple days later. My office was going to call to deal with it, but I told them I'd take care of it. I . . . Well, I'm not super proud to admit it, but I wanted a chance to scope the guy out a little. I didn't know exactly what was going on between the two of you at the Paley Center, but I didn't believe your story. Not for a minute." He stopped pacing and looked at me. "Sorry for not trusting you."

I scoffed. "Are you kidding? Considering I was lying to your face, I'd say you made the right call."

He sat down beside me again. "Still. Sorry. But I wasn't digging around. I didn't even get the chance to talk to him. It was an assistant—"

"Mrs. Lewisham?"

"Yeah. All I did was tell her about the check; she said it was an accounting error, we had another check within a week, and W, M and B became a platinum sponsor."

We sat in silence for several seconds, each of us seemingly mesmerized by the sight of the ferry returning to port.

"I should have told you. I was just . . . humiliated. You know? I didn't know what it would mean. For you, for me . . . for us. Three hundred thousand dollars, Henry. That's how much they accused me of taking. Like you said, I always knew what I wanted, and I fought for it. But for a while there, I didn't know if I had any fight left. I didn't even know what I was supposed to be fighting for or fighting against. I sniffed. "I just didn't know what you'd say to any of it."

He turned his body toward me on the bench and propped his arm up on the back again. With his elbow still resting there, he reached his hand out and began manipulating my unruly waves in his fingers. "I think I would have said how sorry I was. The whole thing . . ." He sighed. "It sucks, McKenna. And no, there was no way it was ever going to be easy to get things back on track. But if there is anyone who was always going to find a way, it had to be you." A smile overtook his lips. "If nothing else, I think I probably would have asked if I could please stay by your side and have a front-row seat for whatever came next."

I threw my arms around his neck and pressed my lips against his, and he pulled me against his chest. He dipped me beneath him, and I leaned back, across his legs, supported by his strong embrace. When we finally came up for air, he said, "Am I allowed to tell you I love you now?"

"I don't know. Robin and the guys are probably getting pretty impatient."

His hair surrounded his face as he looked down at me and grinned. He kissed me once more—slowly and deliberately, like every single shared breath was the creation of a memory we'd come back to time and again—and then said, "They haven't been waiting nearly as long as I have. They can wait a little longer."

Epilogue

Is he here yet?" Cooper asked me for the eighty-thousandth time in the span of an hour.

I stopped my pacing in front of the door. "I'm excited to see him too." *You have no idea.* "But you have to stop asking me that, pal. How about I make you a deal? When he gets here, I'll make sure no one apart from me knows before you do."

"But that's not fair, Aunt McKenna. Why do you get to see him first?"

Oh, I don't know. Maybe because I'm madly in love with him and I haven't seen him in nearly a month, and if his arms aren't around me and his lips aren't on mine within about five minutes, I'm throwing on my coat and maybe some shoes, if I think of it, and heading out in this freak November Durham snowstorm and hunting him down.

As true as all that was, I decided to go with, "Because I'm taller, and I can see through the window in the door."

He stomped his way toward the kitchen and grumbled, "Not fair."

"Is he here yet?" a voice called out from the landing at the top of the staircase, and I turned around with my hands on my hips.

"You're as bad as your son!"

"Sorry." Jared made his way down the stairs. "I just miss him so much."

"I know you do." I patted him on the shoulder before he sulked away.

Henry had been in the United Kingdom for six weeks. Nothing quite so glamorous as hobnobbing with the Duke and Duchess of Cambridge this go-round. Rather, he'd been capturing footage and conducting interviews in England and Ireland—the last scheduled shoots for *She Dreams of America*. I had accompanied him for the first two weeks of the trip, and then I'd had to return to New York for discovery and depositions for Jeremiah's trial as well as the pretrial hearing, which had been that morning.

Henry had been out of the country for all of that. He'd also missed my thirty-ninth birthday, Charlie's fifth birthday, Thanksgiving, and Erica officially growing to the size of a beautiful, glowing version of Violet Beauregarde after she ignored Willy Wonka's instructions and turned into a blueberry.

Carrying twins will do that to you.

"Nothing yet, huh?" Taylor asked as she joined me by the door.

"Nope." I lowered myself down from my tiptoes and turned away from the window with a sigh. "How pathetic am I?"

"It's called being in love." She smirked at me. "Still hate it?"

I returned the smirk as heat rose to my cheeks. "Not entirely."

"He's here!" I suddenly heard Cooper and Jared exclaim simultaneously.

My eyes grew wide, and I looked through the window again, but I didn't see anything. "No, he's not!" I called out. "Don't do that to me. It's just cruel!" But then I felt Taylor's hand touch my shoulder gently, and I turned around.

"I came in through the garage so I didn't track snow," Henry said from the doorway to the kitchen. We stared at each other with goofy smiles on our faces much longer than should have been comfortable, but as much as I wanted to run into his arms, I couldn't stop drinking in the sight of him.

His hair was a little longer and as thick and unruly as ever. He had a new scratch across his cheek that would probably become a new scar, courtesy of a run-in with a Galway ram three weeks prior. He carried with him the exhaustion befitting a man who had spent a month and a half working eighteen or twenty hours a day to make sure the project lived up to his standards, but also the joy and exuberance that accompanied loving every single moment of it.

"Uncle Henry, I got a new bike." His ever-faithful shadow, seven-year-old Cooper Pierson, was standing beside him. "Dad said I can't ride it today, because of the snow, but maybe when the snow melts you can come over to my house and see it."

Uncle Henry.

All three of the Pierson kids had begun calling Henry that shortly after we returned—together—from my impetuous trip to New York. At first it had weirded me out beyond belief, but Henry never seemed to mind. We never made any sort of announcement to the family, and I was pretty sure neither one of us had ever used the terms *boyfriend* and *girlfriend*. From Battery Park on through the six months since, we just *were*. It felt new and exciting, but in some ways it also felt like we had always *been*.

His second shadow, thirty-nine-year-old Jared Pierson, appeared on the other side of him. "You will not believe the speaker system I got installed in my car last week. Since we had to turn my office into a nursery for the twins, Erica said I could take drives whenever I need time alone. Of course, you're welcome to—"

"Hey, fellas?" Henry placed a hand on each of their shoulders but never took his eyes off me. "I'm going to go say hello to McKenna now. We'll talk more later."

"Henry? Is that you?" Dad came rushing out of his study. "I thought I heard your voice."

"I'm on it," Taylor muttered to me under her breath, and then she cleared her throat and cut our dad off at the pass. "Daddy, we're going to let Kenna and Henry have a minute. But Jackson was hoping you could show him that new information you found about our ancestor who was on the *Mayflower*. Weren't you, Jackson?"

"There is nothing I want more." Jackson sighed as he stood from the couch.

"Happy to," Dad replied. "But it's not the *Mayflower*. It's the *Susan Constant*. Beardsley Keaton III was one of seventy-one men aboard when it arrived in Jamestown . . ."

His voice faded away just as Henry finally reached me. And still, I think that goofy grin remained locked on my face.

"I missed you," Henry whispered.

"I missed you more. But not as much as everyone else, apparently."

He was still chuckling when his lips captured mine, but neither of us were laughing for long.

We finally pulled apart at the sound of Erica's voice. "I have to pee."

Jared groaned as he hurried over to assist. "Alright, who let her sit on the couch? Sweetheart, you know the couch just swallows you." Henry winked at me and, hand in hand, we walked over to the couch to assist. "Everyone keeps forgetting the rule. You don't help her down unless you stick around to help her up."

An hour later all eleven of us crammed around Mom and Dad's massive dining-room table for a belated Thanksgiving celebration. Between Henry being in the UK, me traveling back and forth to New York, and Erica being forced to stay in bed a lot of the time, it felt like a minor miracle to have us all together again. As soon as the turkey had been carved and all the sides had been passed around, Henry stood from his chair and cleared his throat. At the exact same moment, I clinked the side of my glass with my knife to get everyone's attention. We looked at each other in surprise.

"Oh, sorry," he said. "Were you going to say something?"

I tilted my head toward him and spoke through my teeth. "I have news. About the trial. Were *you* going to say something?"

He shook his head and sat back down next to me. "You go ahead."

"I don't mind if—"

"I insist." He squeezed my knee and smiled.

"Okay." I smiled back and looked down the table to make sure I had everyone's attention. All eyes were on me.

"Did you say you have news about the trial?" my mom asked. "Good news, I hope."

Pretrial had been scheduled for 9:00 a.m. in Manhattan, and I was back in Durham by 2:00 p.m. That meant there was a pretty good chance the news was either very good or very bad.

"Jeremiah took the plea." I had intended to build up to it more than that, rather than just blurting it out, but I was too excited.

Only Henry responded with enthusiasm in kind, because only Henry really understood the emotional relief I was feeling. "I knew it!" He pumped his fist in the air and then wrapped his arms around me. "I'm so proud of you," he whispered in my ear as he hugged me.

It had been a long few months in regard to work matters. The next day, after The Battery, while Henry worked, I had gone back to the thirty-second floor of the Seagram Building. With self-confidence and courage I wasn't sure I would have possessed twenty-four hours earlier, I marched past Mrs. Lewisham and into Ralph Wallis's office and told him everything. Apparently, I hadn't been the first to express concerns about Jeremiah, but everyone else had either still feared him or had been swayed by the brass ring they had been offered. Within hours, company accounts had been frozen, a thorough investigation was initiated, and Jeremiah was put on leave. And because I had been able to do what no one else had—implicate Mrs. Lewisham and Mr. Rosado as accessories—there was no one to tie up the loose ends.

Mr. Wallis tried to get me back at W, M and B—soon to once more be Wallis and Monroe, of course—but that felt like a backward move. Even if, as I suspected, the name would soon change yet again and add a Keaton to the mix. Instead, I consented to being hired on as an independent attorney to represent the firm. Now that I had my first high-profile victory under my belt, I intended to use the momentum to start my own firm. The next step was passing the bar in North Carolina, since it seemed like I would be splitting my time between here and New York. There was still a disbarment hearing to prepare for, but as of that morning when Jeremiah pleaded guilty to three counts of larceny by embezzlement, one count of grand larceny by extortion, and six counts of second-degree falsifying business records, it was essentially over.

"Is he going to jail?" April asked.

I shook my head. "No. That's how we got him to admit he was guilty. But he will owe a lot of money, and he won't be an attorney anymore. And all of the innocent people he hurt will be able to move on with their lives. That's what matters most."

"Well, while we're celebrating . . ." Taylor's voice grabbed everyone's attention just as Henry stood from his chair once again. "Oh, sorry, Henry! I forgot. You were going to say something."

He scooted his chair up underneath him once again and sat back down. "No . . . um, I was just going to toast McKenna."

Taylor's eyes grew wide. "Quite right! You should do that. Never mind. What I was going to say can wait. This is Kenna's moment." She smiled at me, and I could tell the happiness was genuine, but her eyes were glistening.

Jackson's hand grabbed hers on the table and squeezed, and then they both got very absorbed in swirling their forks around in their mashed potatoes.

"Taylor." I waited until she was looking at me from across the table, and then I looked into her eyes with a glistening gaze of my own. "Thank you. But there's no such thing as too much good news. Please share yours."

Her grin expanded, and then, after a quick glance at Jackson, she exclaimed, "We're pregnant!"

Even Erica managed to heave herself out of her chair and hurry around to embrace them. There were tears and laughs and questions and squeals enough to fill up the family's joy meter for a very long time.

"Okay, now," my mom called out after a couple minutes. She wiped tears away with her cloth napkin. "Dinner's getting cold."

The table grew increasingly loud as we ate and celebrated, and when Henry stood up one more time, no one even noticed at first. Well, I did. I noticed everything he did. But it took him clinking his glass as I had a few minutes prior to get everyone else's attention. I couldn't imagine what he could possibly be preparing to say, but I did know that it was a perfect day and nothing could ruin it.

"I have to say, Keatons—and Piersons and Boyds—I love being part of this family. I never had this. This big, boisterous, loving group of people who cheers each other's victories and shares in the heartache. Thank you for welcoming me in." He looked down at me and brushed his finger across my jawline. "McKenna Keaton, you're the best thing in my life. And I'm not sure if I'll ever be able to make you understand just how much—"

"Um, Henry?" Erica interrupted quietly.

I shook my head at him in dismay, feeling the need to apologize on behalf of us all. I shot an exasperated glare at her. What was she doing? If she thought it was funny for him to be interrupted again, she was wrong. It wasn't funny. It wasn't funny at all.

"Are you guys seriously not going to let me get through this?" Henry's frustrated tone as he collapsed back into his chair made me wonder if he was wishing he could take back all the nice things he had said about my family.

"I really am *so* sorry to interrupt," she insisted. "But, well . . . My water just broke."

Everyone kicked into gear immediately. Jared tossed ten-year-old April his keys and shouted, "Warm up the car!" My niece just stared at the keys in her hand with a terrified expression on her face.

Jackson wrapped his arm around her and kissed the top of her head and then took the keys from her hand. "I've got it."

Henry rushed over to Erica, and he and Jared each grabbed an elbow and helped her up while my dad pulled Cooper and Charlie aside, out of the way.

"Tay?" Erica reached her hand out, and our little sister ran to her. "Can you go to our house and get my bag? It's in our bedroom closet."

Taylor nodded that she would and kissed Erica on the cheek, and then she hurried off, meeting Jackson at the door as he came back in. Ten seconds later their car was pulling out of the driveway.

Erica was the calmest of anyone, of course. "Mom, can you and Daddy take care of the kids? Maybe bring them to the hospital for a little while, and then bring them here and put them to bed if things go on too long?"

"Of course, sweetie." Mom's mascara-stained napkin was getting quite the workout tonight. She started walking Erica to the door as Jared and Henry lagged behind.

Henry wrapped his arm around Jared's shoulders and said with a smile, "Everything's going to be fine."

"But she's only thirty-six weeks—"

"And how many times did the doctor tell you guys the goal was to get her to thirty-five? She's healthy, the babies are healthy . . . and you're the father of five, my friend. *Five!* What were you thinking?"

Jared laughed and pulled Henry in for a quick hug. "You'll be there, right?"

Tears sprang to my eyes in response to seeing them spring to Henry's. He swallowed hard and cleared his throat. "Of course."

Jared pounded his fist on Henry's arm twice and then caught up with Erica, who was almost to the door. I had been so caught up in watching everyone that I hadn't said a word to either one of them, so I ran over to catch Erica before I missed her.

"We'll see you there," Dad said, kissing her on the cheek and ushering the kids out the door. Mom squeezed Erica's hand and then followed Dad out.

"Hey." Tears flooded my cheeks as I reached her. I'd missed the births of kids one, two, and three—and I was overwhelmed with gratitude that I'd be there for four and five. "I love you."

She opened her arms, and I gently sidled up as close to her as I could. "I love you too."

"I'm going to make sure the oven's off and everything, and then we'll get there as soon as we can."

"If you think of anything you need us to pick up or do or anything, let me know," Henry added.

Erica smiled and looked at Henry. "Just finish what you started. I'll do all I can to make sure these little guys don't make their appearance until their aunt McKenna and uncle Henry get there."

I shut the door behind them and watched through the window as Jared helped Erica maneuver into the car. And then I turned around to find Henry five feet in front of me, down on one knee.

"You have to marry me, McKenna. You just have to. I had all these words prepared to try and make it romantic and special, but what it comes down to is . . . you just *have* to say yes. This is my family. *You're* my family. And I want this—I want *you*—for the rest of my life."

He reached into his pocket and pulled out a ring box, then

opened the box and pulled out the most stunning ring I'd ever seen. "In New York six months ago, while you were off being the strong, amazing woman I love, telling Ralph Wallis exactly what he needed to do to save his firm, I was frustrating my crew beyond belief because all I could think about was you." He stood up and walked to me slowly. "I ended up wandering to this art-deco antiques store in the Bowery. I saw this, and it reminded me of the Chrysler Building, so I bought it. Right then and there. Less than twenty-four hours after I told you I love you. Because everything had changed.

"I slept eight solid hours that night. I hadn't done that in twenty-five years. Probably because I didn't want to stop dreaming of the moment I would ask you. The moment you would say yes." That new scar intersected with a dimple as he smiled. "I didn't want to stop dreaming of the way I wouldn't be able to stop talking about how much I love you, and the moment you would finally say yes and kiss me, just to shut me up."

There are all sorts of dreams. And sometimes they come true.

Acknowledgments

Before I dive in too deep, I need to address the 2020-size elephant in the room. *The Do-Over* is my pandemic book. It's the one I brainstormed and attempted to unleash creativity for as I sat in the same spot in my house, day in and day out. It's the one I was trying to find inspiration to write while simultaneously thinking, *What's the point? Bookstores will never open again.* It's the one that was neglected while I chose to instead spend my time binge-watching '90s sitcoms that made me, for just a little while, forget what was happening in the world and pretend we could all still get away with wearing hats and vests like Blossom.

But it's also the one that allowed me to funnel so many of my doubts and uncertainties into a character whose life had been turned upside down, but who came out on the other side having discovered the blessings unearthed by the turmoil. I'll be eternally grateful to McKenna for that. And, truth be told, I'll be eternally grateful to 2020. Oh, it was horrible. No denying that. But it also allowed me to discover the freedom of never wearing shoes, the joy of Zoom chats with family and friends, the power and potential of online church campuses, and the pleasure of bingeing all six seasons of *The Nanny*. There were blessings unearthed by the turmoil.

So many of those blessings were delivered through or came in the form of the following people, each of whom contributed to the writing of this book in an immeasurable way:

You know . . . you can think you like your family, but you don't really know for sure until you're forced to shelter in place with them for months at a time. As it turns out, Kelly, Ethan, and Noah . . . I actually really like you guys. A lot. As weird as it may sound, some of the most treasured memories of my entire life were made while we were all in quarantine. I love you guys with my whole heart.

And in the midst of lockdown, Turnitis was born. The Turners in Colorado and the Whitises in Kentucky now get together on Zoom every single week. My dad, mom, and sister are the -itis half, and they're the blessings that have been there since the very beginning. But Turnitis has unearthed all sorts of wackiness, and I love every minute of it.

Laura Wheeler, you had me at Hufflepuff. By the time we got to *WandaVision*, it was a done deal. And then, just for good measure, we had Henry. Your insight and perspective challenged me to help H and McK become who they needed to be. More than anything, I'm so grateful for the unwavering support you've offered again and again during a time of unprecedented distraction and stress. You'll never know what that's meant to me.

Jocelyn Bailey, *The Do-Over* began with you—as did my welcome into the Thomas Nelson family. Thank you, my friend. Although we only worked on one complete book together, your impact will continue to be present in everything I write.

Kelsey Bowen, you know that's true of you as well. Golly . . . I've sure been blessed in the editor department.

And that most certainly includes you, Leslie Peterson. You somehow find a way to make me look like I know what I'm doing. Thank you for that.

Amanda Bostic, Becky Monds, Nekasha Pratt, Kerri Potts,

Margaret Kercher, Jodi Hughes, and the rest of the HCCP family . . .
I'm in awe of you all. Thank you for your hard work, passion, kind-
ness, and brilliance.

And now I'd like to invite you into the scariest part of the
acknowledgments. The section in which I try really hard not to forget anyone, and during which I issue a blanket apology to everyone
I will still, inevitably, forget. I'm overwhelmed by the fact that there
are always so many people to thank. There are too many people who
feel alone in this world, and I genuinely wish they could experience
the amazing network of people in my life who make each day better.
To quote Ted Lasso, the wisest fictional character since Charlotte
from *Charlotte's Web* . . . "I feel like [I] fell out of the lucky tree, hit
every branch on the way down, ended up in a pool full of cash and
Sour Patch Kids."

Thanks to David, LeeAnn, Secily, Tod, Jenny, Anne, Tonya, and
all the people who are my day-to-day teammates or providers of hugs
or providers of laughs or providers of support or providers of stability
or providers of healthy competition or providers of inspiration. (And
sometimes all of the above.)

A special shout-out and much love to my friends (aka the sisters
who actually read my books . . .) Chris Jager and Cherie Zondervan.
Many thanks to Angie, Lisa, and Maria (aka the Steady On gals) for
being prime examples in my life of just how much God cares about
the details. I'm so glad he saw fit to bring us together. And so much
love to my sweet, genius Her Novel Collective author partners. You
all inspire me each and every day.

Caitlyn Santi and Sharon Vega-Cardona . . . when I look back at
the turmoil of the pandemic, the two of you will always rise to the
top among the blessings!

And then, of course, I have to thank the artistic/pop culture influ-
ences that played an immeasurable role in the writing of this book.
My friend Kerry Winfrey described her hero in *Very Sincerely Yours*

as "Hot Mr. Rogers." So I may be stealing from her somewhat when I tell you I always thought of Henry Blumenthal as "Sexy Ken Burns," but it can't be helped. Thanks, Ken Burns. (And Kerry Winfrey.)

Each of my books has a soundtrack in my head, and *The Do-Over*'s exists in a playlist I call "McKenna's New York." Harry Nilsson, Jim Croce, Joni Mitchell, Carly Simon, Billy Joel, John Lennon, and more Simon & Garfunkel than any woman my age should ever listen to. (Okay, let's face it . . . that could be said about the entire playlist. And really all of my musical tastes in general.) In truth, this story shaped itself into my love letter to New York, as seen through McKenna's eyes, and I'm so grateful to the artists whose legacy of fascination with NYC stood in the gaps when McKenna and I were too raw.

Thanks to random Eddie Bauer catalog dude who hung out on the corkboard in my office for months, completely cementing Henry's style in my mind.

Thanks to *Legally Blonde*, *Legal Eagles*, and *The Pelican Brief*, which came together to make me feel as if I knew everything I needed to know about lawyering.

Thanks to Sutton Foster and Sean Astin who, from day one, starred as Erica and Jared Pierson in my mind. I had the benefit of seeing their interactions play out in my imagination as I wrote, and seriously, y'all . . . those two need a sitcom together. (You're welcome, world.)

Robert Redford. That is all.

And finally—but also first, foremost, and forevermore—thank you to my Savior and friend, Jesus Christ. Your love for me is everything, while my love for you and others is so lacking. I want to be more like you, Jesus. Help me to love more and to love better. Help me to love like you.

Discussion Questions

1. McKenna walks into the boardroom of Wallis, Monroe and Burkhead expecting a promotion, but is confronted with accusation instead. Have you ever been certain you understood what you were walking into, only to be taken by surprise?

2. McKenna has a difficult time reconciling her childhood memories of Henry with the adult reality before her. Why do you think the chaos in her career made her more susceptible to being thrown off balance by Henry's reappearance? Talk about the unprecedented vulnerability McKenna was feeling, and what role that played in her relationships.

3. McKenna's heart seems to beat in time with the rhythm of New York City. Is there a city or location that means a lot to you?

4. Misguided and unfair though it may be, the resentment McKenna feels toward Taylor shapes and propels her

throughout her life. Have your negative feelings about a person or situation ever spurred you toward positive action?

5. Are there any unusual patterns in your family tree? Any family mysteries? Any notable family names, such as Beardsley?

6. Henry quotes Madeleine L'Engle when he says, "One of the problems of being a storyteller is the cultivated ability to extrapolate; in every situation all the what ifs come to me." Be a storyteller and consider the following possibilities:
    a. What if McKenna had never spoken with Carrie Keats from Accounting?
    b. What if Ty Monroe and Jeremiah Burkhead had not been at Henry's fundraiser?
    c. What if Henry had not cut in while McKenna was dancing with Jimmy Clark Jr.?

7. There are all sorts of dreams, and sometimes they come true. Trace that thread of connection through the eyes of three Keaton women—Marilla, Annie, and McKenna—and their very different dreams.

8. Ultimately, McKenna tells Henry she's ready to get off the boat. What exactly did she mean by that, and why was it so meaningful to Henry?

About the Author

Bethany Turner has been writing since the second grade, when she won her first writing award for explaining why, if she could have lunch with any person throughout history, she would choose John Stamos. She stands by this decision. Bethany now writes pop culture–infused rom-coms for a new generation of readers who crave fiction that tackles the thorny issues of life with humor and insight. She lives in Southwest Colorado with her husband, whom she met in the nineties in a chat room called Disco Inferno. As sketchy as it sounds, it worked out pretty well in this case, and they are now the proud parents of two teenagers. Connect with Bethany at seebethanywrite.com or across social media @seebethanywrite, where she clings to the eternal dream that John Stamos will someday send her a friend request. You can also text her at +1 (970) 387-7811.

seebethanywrite.com
Instagram: @seebethanywrite
Twitter: @seebethanywrite
Facebook: @seebethanywrite